THE ESSENTIAL J.R.R. TOLKIEN SOURCEBOOK

A Fan's Guide to Middle-earth and Beyond

George Beahm

George Beahm

Illustrated by Colleen Doran

New Page Books
A division of The Career Press, Inc.
Franklin Lakes, NJ

THE ESSENTIAL J.R.R. TOLKIEN SOURCEBOOK
EDITED BY CLAYTON W. LEADBETTER
TYPESET BY EILEEN DOW MUNSON

Cover illustration and design: Jean William Naumann
Printed in the U.S.A. by Book-mart Press
Art by Colleen Doran © 2003 by Colleen Doran
Art by Donato Giancola © 2003 by Donato Giancola
Art by Steve Hickman © 2003 by Steve Hickman
Art by Tim Kirk © 2003 by Tim Kirk
Art by Michael Kaluta © 2003 by Michael Kaluta
Art by David Wenzel © 2003 by David Wenzel
Photographs of Sideshow-Weta collectibles © 2003 by Sideshow-Weta
Photographs of swords by United Cutlery © 2003 by United Cutlery

To order this title, please call toll-free 1-800-CAREER-1 (NJ and Canada: 201-848-0310) to order using VISA or MasterCard, or for further information on books from Career Press.

The Career Press, Inc., 3 Tice Road, PO Box 687,
Franklin Lakes, NJ 07417
www.careerpress.com
www.newpagebooks.com

Library of Congress Cataloging-in-Publication Data

Beahm, George W.
  The essential J.R.R. Tolkien sourcebook : a fan's guide to Middle-earth and beyond / by George Beahm.
    p. cm.
  ISBN 1-56414-702-9 (pbk.)
  1. Tolkien, J. R. R. (John Ronald Reuel), 1892-1973—Handbooks, manuals, etc. 2. Tolkien, J. R. R. (John Ronald Reuel), 1892-1973—Film and video adaptations—Handbooks, manuals, etc. 3. Tolkien, J. R. R. (John Ronald Reuel), 1892-1973—Collectibles—Handbooks, manuals, etc. 4. Middle Earth (Imaginary place)—Handbooks, manuals, etc. 5. Fantasy fiction, English—Handbooks, manuals, etc. 6. Fantasy films—Handbooks, manuals, etc. I. Title.

PR6039.O32Z566 2004
828'.91209--dc22

                                    2003044293

Say "friend" and enter:

This book is for

Colleen Doran.

Acknowledgments

To **Douglas A. Anderson**, for bibliographic assistance and answering all my e-mails about Tolkien; to **Stephen Spignesi**, who stopped working on his own books to help me with mine; to **Ned Brooks**, who scanned images, answered Tolkien-related questions, and provided contacts; to the artists who pushed away their drawing boards to help out with interviews and art—**Tim Kirk**, **Donato Giancola**, **Steve Hickman**, **Michael Kaluta**, and **Dave Wenzel**. Thanks, too, are due to Michael Whelan, who gave time for an interview, despite his crushing workload in finishing up his current assignment.

I owe a special thanks to the fellowship of publishing professionals at New Page Books, who, despite an impossibly unforgiving deadline, rose to the challenge and, as a team pulling in the same direction, took my raw manuscript and produced a beautiful book. Handsomely typeset and elegantly designed, this book shows their care and craft for book publishing: **Ron Fry**, publisher, who believed in this book; **Clayton Leadbetter**, editor, who worked tirelessly to make this book as good as it could possibly be; **Eileen Munson**, whose design work as formatter showcases the words and art to their best effect; **Gina Marie Cheselka**, who ably assisted in the preliminary editorial work; **Stacey A. Farkas**, editorial director, who shepherded this book through production from start to finish; and finally, **Mike Pye**, whose work and ideas also helped improved it. This book bears the watermarks of their professionalism on every page.

And, finally, to **Colleen Doran**, who was an integral part of this book from its beginning: Despite a professional workload that kept her at the drawing board for seven days a week, she squeezed in time to produce nearly two dozen original pieces of art done especially for this book. In addition, she provided an interview; turned over her entire Tolkien collection for me to have on hand as I worked on this book, which proved to be invaluable; assisted me in the photography of her many Tolkien collectibles; promoted this book online and through her contacts at *TheOneRing.net*; and was my sounding board on this project, as we discussed Tolkien and all things in Middle-earth. Thank you, Colleen.

"In that realm a man may, perhaps count himself fortunate to have wandered, but its very richness and strangeness tie the tongue of a traveller who would report them. And while he is there it is a dangerous for him to ask too many questions, lest the gates should be shut and the keys be lost."

—J.R.R. Tolkien, *On Fairy Stories*

Contents

Foreword   The Day of His Death Was a Dark, Cold Day 13
By Stephen Spignesi

Introduction   17

Chapter 1   Books by Tolkien 21

The Hobbit, or There and Back Again   21

The Lord of the Rings   24

The Silmarillion   31

The History of Middle-earth   34

Other books by J.R.R. Tolkien   35

Chapter 2   Books About Tolkien 41

Chapter 3   Visual Adaptations of *The Lord of the Rings*: 59
The Film and Related Book Tie-In Products

DVDs   59

Books   66

The Official *Lord of the Rings* Fan Club   70

Chapter 4   Sound Advice: Audio Adaptations 71

Audio Adaptations   73

Musical Adaptations   75

Chapter 5   Printed Products 81

Stationery Goods   81

Posters   84

Lithographs and Photographs   87

Art Prints, Giclée Prints, and Original Art   87

Calendars   90

Chapter 6   The One Ring Replicas 93

Chapter 7   Licensed Movie-Related Collectibles 99

    Decorative Items   99

    Clothing and Apparel   100

    Jewelry   101

    Standups   102

    Action Figures and Dolls   103

    Board Games and Puzzles   106

    Computer Software   106

    Sideshow/Weta   107

    Swords by United Cutlery   120

    Stamps   125

    Coins   126

    Miscellaneous Collectibles   127

Chapter 8   Gaming and Miniatures 131

Chapter 9   The Noble Collection 145

Chapter 10   Smaug's Stash: Tolkien Treasures 151

Chapter 11   Visions of Middle-earth: Tolkien Art 167

    Tolkien Artists: A Selective Overview   168

Interviews and Art by Select J.R.R. Tolkien Artists   175
   Tim Kirk's Works   175
   Colleen Doran: Drawn to Please   180
   Steve Hickman: The Art of Imagination   184
   Donato Giancola's Classical Art   188
   Michael Whelan: The Master   194
   Michael Kaluta: Flights of the Fantastic   199

Chapter 12   The Literary Landscape of Tolkien's World 203

Chapter 13   Tolkien Websites: The Road Goes Ever On............................ 213

Chapter 14   The Essential J.R.R. Tolkien: My Personal Picks 225

Final Word   The Importance of Story... 231

Appendix A   Glass Onion Graphics 235

Appendix B   *The Lord of the Rings* Motion Picture Trilogy: 237
             The Exhibition

Appendix C   Tall Towers, Brave Kings, Wise Wizards, and 239
             Precious Rings: A Celebration of Fantasy Art

Appendix D   Flights of Imagination.. 241

Appendix E   Ted Nasmith, His Tolkien Art, and the Chalk Farm Gallery. 243

Appendix F   Tolkien, Licensing, and Copyrights...and Wrongs.................. 247

About the Author and Illustrator 257

I love W.H. Auden's poetry.

The title of this essay is a line from Auden's poem, "In Memory of W.B. Yeats," one of my all-time favorites, although the line could easily be read to describe that day, in September 1973, when the world lost J.R.R. Tolkien.

Auden's ode to Yeats is powerful, sad, and compelling, and its opening line— "He disappeared in the dead of winter"—I have long considered to be a truly evocative rendering of someone's death.

Likewise, I am an enormous J.R.R. Tolkien fan, and that admiration is something similarly felt by great W.H. Auden. In a 1954 *New York Times* book review titled "The Hero Is a Hobbit," Auden wrote, "No fiction I have read in the last five years has given me more joy than *The Fellowship of the Ring*."

Indeed.

During the days when I was thinking about Tolkien, this essay, and the tome by my good friend George Beahm that you now hold in your hands, I received an e-mail from an old friend. Nancy and I grew up together and she was my date for my junior prom. She was writing to wish me a happy birthday and to order a copy of the limited edition of my novel. In her note, she reminisced a little and told me how much fun she had had at the prom. Coincidentally, while I was cleaning my office a week earlier, I had come across my high school diploma. I opened the leather binder and there was our prom picture. Nancy was radiant with blonde hair and a blue gown—in fact, she looked like Arwen, or even Galadriel—and because Catholic high schools of the time did not allow facial hair (perhaps they still don't?), I was clean-shaven. (I grew my beard the following summer and have not looked back.)

"But Steve, what does that prom story have to do with Tolkien?" I hear you asking.

Fair question, and I have a good (and relevant) answer: The theme for my junior prom was Lothlórien.

The Lord of the Rings fans know of Lothlórien as the fabled golden woods, "Lórien of the Blossom," the land on the banks of the River Celebrant, to the east of the Misty Mountains and southeast of Khazad-dûm. Lorien was probably founded sometime long before the First Age, perhaps around the time of the Great Journey, and it serves as a sanctuary of sorts (albeit briefly) for Frodo and company in the trilogy.

When I was in high school in the 1970s, *The Lord of the Rings* was huge. Everyone had read it, usually more than once, and everyone had a sense that we were living witnesses to a seminal moment in the history of English literature. If I recall correctly, the trilogy was actually *assigned* to my freshman English class. This was extraordinary! A three-volume fantasy epic being taught in high school! Today, the literary merit and importance of *The Lord of the Rings* is universally recognized; back then, science fiction and fantasy were not usually found in high school curricula, especially *Catholic* high school curricula.

The Lord of the Rings tells the story of the great conflict at the end of the Third Age between Sauron the Dark Lord and an alliance of men and elves. A humble hobbit named Frodo Baggins was summoned by fate to return the One Ring to the fire in which it was made and the trilogy tells of his sacred quest.

The Elvish inscription found on the One Ring ("One Ring to rule them all..."), on the base of the plastic ring enclosure containing the One Ring.

The recent, glorious, three-part movie version of the trilogy (and Peter Jackson's *The Lord of the Rings* is, without question, simply one long movie broken up into three parts) has renewed interest in Professor Tolkien and his works. The movies have also introduced Frodo, Gandalf, Saruman, Elrond, Gollum, Boromir, and all the other denizens of Middle-earth to a new, younger audience, while rekindling the interest in the story for those of us who read the books when they were first released.

This book by George Beahm speaks to the worldwide interest in hobbits, elves, dwarves, men, orcs, and all the other people, places, and things of Middle-earth and its environs. Here you will find a cornucopia of resources certain to provide you with any and all information you may want or need about J.R.R. Tolkien and *The Lord of the Rings*.

For instance, I will probably never forgive my friend George for regaling me in his book with details about the Allen & Unwin "Bible paper" edition of the complete *The Lord of the Rings*. This magnificent volume, which George correctly describes as a work of art, retails for £100 ($161 American) and is a little rich for me—especially considering that it would be the fifth or sixth copy of the trilogy I would be adding to my library.

George's book also includes details on everything from jewelry to letter openers, action figures to signed letters, and candy to Websites, while providing accurate and authoritative information on precisely what makes a collectible "collectible," how to value autographs and limited editions, and what to buy when you are on a budget.

In a recent poll conducted by the Modern Library, *The Lord of the Rings* was the Library's readers' fourth favorite novel of all time. Fantasy aficionados have long rated the epic as the greatest fantasy novel ever written. In a wonderfully synergistic development, *The Lord of the Rings* movies are receiving similar praise and admiration.

George's book will serve well all who cherish Professor Tolkien's tale—all of us who use "Gandalf" as their screen name and all who use "Gimli" or "Bombadil" as their password.

George Beahm has applied the same care and attention to detail to this book about Tolkien and his work as he did to his earlier works about Stephen King, Michael Jordan, Tim Kirk, Anne Rice, and Vaughn Bode. George understands that admirers of a writer, artist, or sports figure are enriched by learning more about them and their work.

Thus, I say with certainty, as if I had seen this truth myself in one of the seven Palantíri brought to Middle-earth by Elendil, we Hobbits are all enriched by this fine book, and I am grateful to George for inviting me to be a part of it.

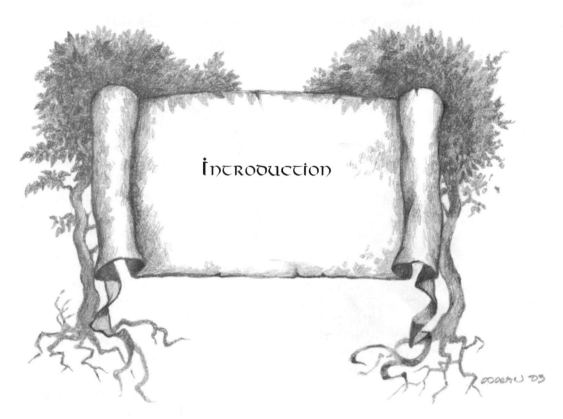

Introduction

The product of 13 years of part-time work, *The Lord of the Rings* was typed using two fingers by J.R.R. Tolkien, not once, but twice. Originally published by Allen & Unwin in 1954–55 in three volumes, *The Lord of the Rings* was deemed, because of its length, such a risky proposition that Tolkien received no book advance; he was an equal partner in a profit-sharing plan...*if* the book made money, which seemed doubtful to the publisher. Tolkien admitted his new book was rather unlike his previous book, *The Hobbit*. This new book, written not for children but for adults, would have to find a new audience.

"My work has escaped from my control," Tolkien wrote in a letter (February 1950) to Allen & Unwin, "and I have produced a monster: an immensely long, complex, rather bitter, and rather terrifying romance, quite unfit for children (if fit for anybody); and it is not really a sequel to *The Hobbit*, but to *The Silmarillion*."

Tolkien's understandable fears proved unfounded: Not only was *The Lord of the Rings* a best-selling classic, but in 2001 it was adapted as a live-action film by New Line Cinema, directed by New Zealand film director Peter Jackson—a make-or-break risk for the studio, which invested approximately $300 million.

Executives at New Line Cinema were justifiably concerned, but when *The Fellowship of the Ring* was released in December 2001, it became apparent to all—critics, Tolkien fans, the Hollywood community, and most important, the moviegoers—that this was *exactly* what the public had been waiting for: timely and timeless, the battle for Middle-earth, symbolic of the eternal struggle between the forces of darkness and the forces of light, struck a resonant chord with its tale of Everyman in the guise of an uncommonly brave Hobbit, who assumed a terrible burden and changed the fate of the world.

It was, simply, a tale for our troubled times.

Grossing more than $1 billion worldwide, the film adaptation of *The Fellowship of the Ring* had a salutary effect in the bookstore. Their interest piqued by the film, moviegoers rushed into bookstores to find out more about the book and its creator, only to discover that one could spend a lifetime wandering through Middle-earth, because finding one's way would be no easy task. With its half century of publishing history, *The Lord of the Rings* is available in editions to suit every budget and every taste—from inexpensive mass market paperbacks to magnificently illustrated hardback editions.

From Sideshow/Weta, a sculpture of the dreaded Balrog.

No wonder newcomers to Middle-earth feel overwhelmed: the wealth of material by and about Tolkien, in every conceivable form, staggers the imagination.

As to the genesis of this book: Soon after *The Fellowship of the Ring* debuted in theaters nationwide, I was in a Barnes & Noble bookstore in Newport News, Virginia, where I saw what had to be a commonplace scene. Faced with multiple editions of *The Lord of the Rings*, a young girl and her parents tried in vain to determine what edition to buy. I overheard her say that she wanted to write a school paper on Tolkien and wanted a biography and a critical study.

Understandably confused by a wall of books by and about Tolkien, she had no idea where to begin looking—a problem facing millions of new readers, who won't know enough about Tolkien to know what to buy.

I knew that no Tolkien sourcebook was available, but one was urgently needed. Ideally, such a book would be hundreds of pages long, with hundreds of color photos, covering everything from 1954 to present day—a virtual encyclopedia of everything that had ever appeared in print.

A life-size sculpture, from Sideshow/Weta, of Gandalf the White on his steed, Shadowfax, on display at the 2003 Book Expo in Los Angeles. (Photo courtesy of Colleen Doran.)

I, too, would welcome such a useful resource, but the immediate need is a general book to orient the new reader and to update seasoned readers with current information.

On December 17, 2003, the third installment, *The Return of the King*, will premiere in theaters nationwide and bring to a satisfying conclusion the magnificent—a word I do not use lightly—movie adaptation of *The Lord of the Rings*. The subsequent year will see the release of its DVD (in a regular and extended version), and possibly the release of all three films in a final, extended DVD edition. But the Tolkien celebration won't end there, because 2005 will mark the 50th anniversary of the publication of *The Fellowship of the Ring*, and Tolkien's publishers will take full advantage of that fact to promote *LotR* in bookstores worldwide, as will The Tolkien Society in England, which will hold its biggest conference ever, scheduled one week after the World Science Fiction convention to be held in England that year—celebrations of special magnificence!

If you are a newcomer to Middle-earth, I say: Speak, friend, and enter! As you will soon discover, there is much to explore and many wonders to see, but only if you know where to look.

Not all who wander are lost, but it's too easy to lose your way in Middle-earth without a roadmap, so I hope this book will set you on what will surely be a long and enjoyable journey through the enchanting realm imagined and chronicled by J.R.R. Tolkien.

Note: To minimize repetition, where applicable, *The Lord of the Rings* is abbreviated to *LotR*.

The Hobbit, or There and Back Again

The Hobbit, or There and Back Again, the prelude to *The Lord of the Rings*, was originally published by Allen & Unwin on September 21, 1937. According to Tolkien scholar Douglas A. Anderson, its first printing was small—only 1,500 copies. Published in hardback with 10 black-and-white illustrations and two maps furnished by the author himself, *The Hobbit* garnered positive reviews and, as its publisher, Stanley Unwin, predicted, led to a public demand for more stories about hobbits.

As a novel, *The Hobbit* holds its own as an engaging story well worth reading, but when read before tackling *The Lord of the Rings*, *The Hobbit* establishes a framework for the larger work to follow and whets the appetite for more information about hobbits, Middle-earth, and those who dwell therein: wizards, elves, dwarves, trolls, and the minions of evil.

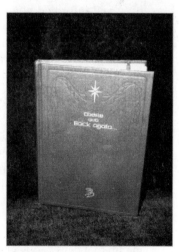

A journal bearing the title "There and Back Again," from the title of The Hobbit.

The Hobbit Recommended Editions

From Houghton Mifflin, the U.S. publisher of the Tolkien canon, there are several editions of *The Hobbit* in print, depending on your literary taste and budget:

✦ **The Collector's Edition** ($35). For gift giving, the clear choice is the hardback "Collector's Edition" of *The Hobbit*. With its full-page color illustrations, two-color typography, and green leatherette binding with matching slipcase, this edition is eye-catching and very attractive. Any Tolkien fan would be delighted to get a copy of this as a gift.

✦ **The Most Informative Edition** ($28). Especially useful for students or readers who want to know more about the book, its history, and a thorough explication of its text, the hardback of *The Annotated Hobbit* (Revised and Expanded Edition, 2002) is the book of choice. With annotations by Tolkien expert Douglas A. Anderson, who also provides

---

The Publishing Story Behind *The Hobbit*

"In a hole in the ground there lived a hobbit."

And so begins the book that brought an Oxford professor from the relative obscurity of academe to a larger world.

Early reviews were positive, heralding great expectations from a new storyteller who showed great promise.

From *The New Statesman & Nation*:

"His wholly original story of adventure among goblins, elves and dragons...gives...the impression of a well-informed glimpse into the life of a wide other-world; a world wholly real, and with a quite matter-of-fact, supernatural natural history of its own."

Echoing *The New Statesman*, *The Observer* commented:

"Professor Tolkien's finely written saga of dwarves and elves, fearsome goblins and trolls, in a spacious country of far-off and long ago...a full-length tale of traditional magic being...an exciting epic of travel, magical adventure... working up to a devastating climax."

The Times (of London) called it "a solidly delightful book" and "a fascinating excursion into the early English scene."

The best, and most accurate, assessment of *The Hobbit* came from Tolkien's friend C.S. Lewis, who rightly concluded, in the *Times Literary Supplement* (Oct. 2, 1937), that "Its place is with *Alice, Flatland, Phantastes, The Wind in the Willows....* [The] prediction is dangerous: but *The Hobbit* may well prove a classic."

C.S. Lewis was right. *The Hobbit* not only proved to be a classic, a book beloved by generations of readers, but a bestseller as well—a book that continues to sell at a brisk pace, in more than 40 languages worldwide. As Douglas A. Anderson affirmed in his introduction to *The Annotated Hobbit*, "There is no doubt that *The Hobbit* is a worldwide classic, for all ages, and all times."

The U.S. edition of The Annotated Hobbit, *edited by Douglas A. Anderson.*

a lengthy and informative introduction to the book, *The Annotated Hobbit* offers the full text of the novel itself and also extensive appendices, including "The Quest of Erebor," which recounts how Gandalf came to enlist Bilbo Baggins in the adventure with the dwarves; "On Runes," with a dictionary; a bibliography with extensive notes about the various editions of *The Hobbit*; and a useful map of Wilderland.

→ **The Best Illustrated Editions** ($17.95–$35). Intended for gift giving, two illustrated editions are available: a $35 hardback with color plates by British artist Alan Lee—renown for his Tolkien art, and a set designer for Peter Jackson's film adaptation of *The Lord of the Rings*—and a $29.95 hardback or $17.95 trade paperback, with 48 color paintings by an American artist best known for his work on children's books, Michael Hague.

The U.S. edition of The Hobbit, *illustrated by British artist Alan Lee.*

Other editions include:

→ *The Hobbit: Young Reader's Edition* ($10), which has cover art of the great dragon Smaug by the author, and includes a teaser chapter from *The Lord of the Rings*.

→ *The Hobbit* ($16 hardback), with cover art by the author.

→ *The Hobbit* ($12 trade paperback), with cover art by Alan Lee.

→ *The Hobbit* ($18 hardback, $10 paperback), with cover art by Peter Sis. This edition sports black-and-white illustrations by the author and, textually, is as close as possible to Tolkien's original work, according to Douglas A. Anderson, who wrote a note on the text.

Though *The Hobbit* is an entertaining story—a well-told tale, albeit with a juvenile flavor because of Tolkien's habit of addressing the reader directly—its story elements lay the groundwork for what would follow: *The Lord of the Rings*.

In *The Hobbit* we learn how the One Ring came to Bilbo Baggins, who in turn would give it to his nephew, Frodo. We also learn about Gollum, who plays a pivotal role in the long tale that follows, and we meet the wizard Gandalf, who assumes an even more significant role as the war for Middle-earth clouds the horizon.

A packaged edition of The Hobbit, *published by HarperCollins UK, containing the book, postcards, a map, and a CD of J.R.R. Tolkien reading excerpts from the book.*

New readers who want more information about how Bilbo Baggins came to find himself in an adventure of a lifetime may be surprised to learn that Tolkien wrote a narrative that was originally intended for publication in the appendices of *The Lord of the Rings*. However, the piece in question, "The Quest of Erebor," was omitted from it but subsequently published in a posthumous collection, *Unfinished Tales*. (It is also available as Appendix A of *The Annotated Hobbit*.) It is "Gandalf's account of how he came to arrange the expedition to Erebor and send Bilbo with the Dwarves," wrote Tolkien.

J.R.R. Tolkien on *The Hobbit*

In the book trade, catalogs are issued to promote forthcoming releases. The catalog copy is usually written by the marketing department, but in Allen & Unwin's 1937 *Summer Announcements*, Tolkien's own copy appeared:

> "If you care for journeys there and back, out of the comfortable Western world, over the edge of the Wild, and home again, and can take an interest in a humble hero (blessed with a little wisdom and a little courage and considerable good luck), here is the record of such a journey and such a traveler. The period is the ancient time between the age of Faerie and the dominion of men, when the famous forest of Mirkwood was still standing, and the mountains were full of danger. In following the path of this humble adventurer, you will learn by the way (as he did)—if you do not already know all about these things—much about trolls, goblins, dwarves, and elves, and get some glimpses into the history and politics of a neglected but important period.

> "For Mr. Bilbo Baggins visited notable persons; conversed with the dragon, Smaug the Magnificent; and was present, rather unwillingly, at the Battle of Five Armies. This is all the more remarkable, since he was a hobbit. Hobbits have hitherto been passed over in history and legend, perhaps because they as a rule preferred comfort to excitement. But this account, based on his personal memoirs, of the one exciting year in the otherwise quiet life of Mr. Baggins will give you a fair idea of this estimable people, now (it is said) becoming rather rare. They do not like noise."

The Lord of the Rings

Though the film adaptation of *The Lord of the Rings* is a laudable achievement—indeed, the three films, taken as a whole, stand not only as a cinematic achievement par excellence but as a testament to the wizardry of special effects—the book itself is even more impressive. An estimated half million words in length, the story itself is buttressed by an appendix of 128 pages that provides the back story, which is more appropriate to a work of nonfiction than fiction.

The story behind its publication is a tale in itself. When *The Hobbit* was originally published, publisher Stanley Unwin wrote Tolkien, "A large public will be clamouring next year to hear more from you about Hobbits!"

The problem, however, was that Tolkien wasn't planning a sequel about hobbits. He was planning to publish *The Silmarillion*, which predated *The Hobbit*.

Tolkien submitted *The Silmarillion* to his publisher, along with other works, and, in due course, his publisher reiterated the obvious need for another hobbit tale. As he explained to Tolkien in a letter:

> What we badly need is another book with which to follow up our success with *The Hobbit* and alas! neither of these manuscripts (the poem and *The Silmarillion* itself) quite fits the bill. I still hope that you will be inspired to write another book about the Hobbit.

Tolkien's reply, in part, stated that he would "give this thought and attention..." and, in fact, did so. Soon after the letter was written, Tolkien began the first chapter of *The Lord of the Rings*, "A Long-expected Party."

Starting the novel was one thing, but finishing it, quite another. Begun in December 1937, the book was completed in February 1950—13 years later. To Tolkien, who recognized that he was more a starter than finisher in literary matters, the singular achievement of *finishing* it stood out in his mind.

In offering Allen & Unwin *LotR*, he, in fact, gave his publisher more than what was expected—a deeper, richer, and, admittedly, darker work of fiction that, unlike its predecessor, was clearly not intended for children.

Given the continued popularity of *The Hobbit*, one would think that the road to publication for *The Lord of the Rings* would have been smooth, but it was not. Stung by the rejection of *The Silmarillion*, and courted by another publisher who, in fact, had his sight set on acquiring the profitable *Hobbit*, Tolkien actively downplayed the book and its commercial possibilities to Allen & Unwin and issued an ultimatum, as well.

Stanley Unwin, forced to make a decision about *The Lord of the Rings* based on an incomplete manuscript, was put in an untenable position. Tolkien's ultimatum to him—requiring either a prompt yes or no—was met with a polite but firm rejection, which cleared the road for its publication by another publisher.

In what has to be, in retrospect, one of the worst book publishing decisions of all time, Milton Waldman of Collins—after several inquiries from Tolkien—finally declined to publish the book, citing its length and publication costs. Collins imprudently passed on what turned out to be one of the most enduring and profitable fantasy franchises of all time.

Three years after Stanley Unwin rejected Tolkien's ultimatum, the book remained unpublished. Tolkien, realizing his mistake, wrote to Unwin in June 1952 and began fence-mending, clearing the way for its publication.

By November of that year, Allen & Unwin accepted *The Lord of the Rings*, which was subsequently published in three volumes—the first and second, *The Fellowship of the Ring* and *The Two Towers*, in 1954, and *The Return of the King* in 1955.

Because of its division—one book published in three separate volumes—*The Lord of the Rings* is often mistakenly termed a trilogy, when, in fact, it is not. The book is clearly one story, not three, and its division was merely a publishing convenience dictated by economic concerns.

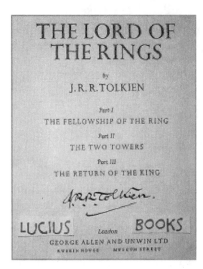

The title page of The Lord of the Rings, *signed by Tolkien, offered for sale by Lucius Books, of England. (Photo courtesy of Lucius Books.)*

The book-buying public that had clamored for more stories about hobbits embraced *The Lord of the Rings* with enthusiasm. The central story is about a hobbit named Frodo Baggins (the favorite nephew of Bilbo Baggins), who inherits the ring and assumes the considerable burden of taking the ring back to Mordor to destroy it—an epic quest that defined the Third Age of Middle-earth.

Predictably, *The Lord of the Rings* has spawned numerous imitations, but even after half a century, *The Lord of the Rings* stands alone. The literary works it inspired are pale imitations, lacking its historic, geographic, and, perhaps most distinctive of all, linguistic underpinnings that give Middle-earth its solidity, its sense of reality.

I am in general agreement with Tom Shipley, who, in his excellent critical overview, *J.R.R. Tolkien: Author of the Century*, concluded: "No one, perhaps, is ever again going to emulate Tolkien in sheer quantity of effort, in building the maps and the languages and the histories and the mythologies of one invented world, as no one is ever again going to have his philological resources to draw on."

As for Tolkien himself, his impetus in writing *The Lord of the Rings* wasn't fame or fortune, though both, in hindsight, were inevitable byproducts of having written the most influential fantasy novel of the 20th century. As stated in the foreword to the second edition of *The Lord of the Rings*, he wrote it "for my own satisfaction." He added that he had "...little hope that other people would be interested in this work, especially since it was primarily linguistic in inspiration and was begun in order to provide the necessary background of 'history' for Elvish tongues."

Ironically, though Tolkien had submitted *The Silmarillion* for publication years before he submitted *The Lord of the Rings*, the former work remained unpublished—due, mostly, to his endless niggling of details—until 1977, when his son and literary executor, Christopher Tolkien, took on the formidable task of editing the book into publishable form.

Christopher Tolkien would go on to edit several more books of his father's, works of scholarship that involved carefully sifting through literally thousands of pages of manuscript and typescript to make whole the complete history of Middle-earth.

Of Titles and *The Lord of the Rings*

The narrative bridge between *The Hobbit* and *The Lord of the Rings* can be found in the prologue to *LotR*, which is a detailed explication of hobbits, pipe-weed, the geography of the Shire, and "Of the Finding of the Ring."

Clearly, hobbits have a large and important role to play in the War of the Ring—especially Frodo Baggins, who is appointed the Ring Bearer at the Council of Elrond, where he chooses to accept the burden of taking the ring to its eventual destruction. The fellowship consists of nine, representing all the races in Middle-earth: one wizard, two men, one elf, one dwarf, and four hobbits—a number mirroring the forces against them, symbolized by the nine Ringwraiths, once powerful kings of men, who, corrupted by the rings of power, became shadows of themselves and fell under the dominion of Sauron.

"*The Lord of the Rings* is a good over-all title," Tolkien concluded, in a letter to Raywin Unwin (August 8, 1953), but the matter of individual titles for each volume was a matter of concern, because *LotR* is properly six books plus lengthy appendices.

In a March 1953 letter, Tolkien suggested:

- Volume #1: *The Ring Sets Out* [book 1] and *The Ring Goes South* [book 2].

- Volume #2: *The Treason of Isengard* [book 3] and *The Ring Goes East* [book 4].

- Volume #3: *The War of the Ring* [book 5] and *The End of the Third Age* [book 6].

In that same letter, he suggested alternative, simplified titles:

- Volume #1: *The Shadow Grows*.

- Volume #2: *The Ring in the Shadow*.

- Volume #3: *The War of the Ring* or *The Return of the King*.

 In an August 1953 letter, Tolkien suggested another set of titles, with the statement that "I am not wedded to any of the suggested sub-titles; and wish they could be avoided. For it is really impossible to devise ones that correspond to the contents; since the division into two 'books' per volume is purely a matter of convenience with regard to length, and has no relation to the rhythm or ordering of the narrative...."

In the end, Tolkien suggested—in a subsequent letter in August to his publisher—the titles that were in fact used:

- Volume #1: *The Fellowship of the Ring*.

- Volume #2: *The Two Towers*.

- Volume #3: *The Return of the King* (alternate title, *The War of the Ring*).

It can be rightly said that what J.R.R. Tolkien had begun—to construct a fantasy world with such detail that it has the solidity of our own—his son had finished. The history of Middle-earth is now thoroughly chronicled, properly recorded, and it's a monumental testament to the imaginative genius of its creator, J.R.R. Tolkien, and the dedication of his son Christopher.

The first volume was published in 1954. A trade hardback priced at 21 shillings (the equivalent of $4 U.S., not adjusted for inflation), it had a first printing of 3,500 copies.

As with any book, *The Fellowship of the Ring* had its detractors, but in the main the critics praised it. Predictably, the most favorable review came from fellow Inkling C.S. Lewis, who wrote: "Such a book has of course its predestined readers, even now more numerous and more critical than is always realised. To them a reviewer need say little, except that here are beauties which pierce like swords or burn like cold iron; here is a book that will break your heart."

The Fellowship of the Ring was followed by *The Two Towers*, published later that year, with *The Return of the King* following in 1955. Now that it could be judged in its entirety, was it "juvenile trash" (the opinion of Edmund Wilson, writing in *The Nation*) or was it a work of wonder as W.H. Auden suggested in the *New York Times*: "...no fiction I have read in the last five years has given me more joy"?

Tom Shippey, author of *J.R.R. Tolkien: Author of the Century*, argues convincingly that Tolkien's most famous and celebrated book is indisputably a literary work of substance:

> ...*The Lord of the Rings* has established itself as a lasting classic, without the help and against the active hostility of the professionals of taste; and has furthermore largely created the expectations and established the conventions of a new and flourishing genre. It and its author deserve more than the routine and reflexive dismissals (or denials) which they have received. *The Lord of the Rings*, and *The Hobbit*, have said something important, and meant something important, to a high proportion of their many millions of readers.

Critics notwithstanding, *The Hobbit* has sold more than 40 million copies since its publication, and the various volumes of *The Lord of the Rings* have sold 50 million copies in more than 35 languages worldwide. Clearly, Tolkien achieved his laudable goal of writing, as he explained in the foreword to the second edition of *LotR*—a "really long story that would hold the attention of readers, amuse them, delight them, and at times maybe excite them or deeply move them."

Clay Harper, the caretaker of the Tolkien publishing program at Houghton Mifflin, explained in an online interview on his publisher's Website that:

> More than 45 million copies of Tolkien's work have been sold in the United States since 1938. After each point in its long history when the audience has expanded dramatically, the work has never

seemed to fade in popularity. Now Tolkien's work has been passed down through several generations, from parent to child as well as from friend to friend, and each generation finds in his stories an inspiring set of values and ideals that fits its own life and times.

A steady backlist seller, *The Lord of the Rings* was discovered by a new audience in December 2001, when New Line Cinema released the first of three live-action movies directed back-to-back by New Zealand film director Peter Jackson.

According to Clay Harper of Houghton Mifflin, in 2001, an astonishing 11 million copies of Tolkien's books sold in the United States alone, due to the anticipation of the December 2001 release of *The Fellowship of the Ring.* J.R.R. Tolkien, finally, had been discovered by moviegoers who, until then, had probably never heard of him.

Trade paperback movie tie-in editions of The Fellowship of the Ring *and* The Two Towers, *published in the United States.*

Though Tolkien detested allegory and roundly denied that *LotR* was allegorical in intent, the fact remains that a strong case can be made for allegory and its contemporary relevance. In Tolkien's fantasy tale, the free world bands together to fight the forces of darkness from its strongholds, the two towers of Orthanc and Barad-dûr—a comparison eerily apt in a world reshaped by the events of September 11, 2001, dominated by the collapse of two prominent towers in downtown Manhattan.

Allegorical or not, *LotR* speaks to us at a time of moral ambiguity, a time of confusion and indecision, and a time when, more than ever, we need heroes that will rise to the occasion and do battle against the orcs, the Sarumans, and Saurons of the world.

The Lord of the Rings Recommended Editions

In print continuously since its original publication, *The Lord of the Rings* is currently available in various editions—as a single volume and as a trilogy—to suit every budget and taste:

The front cover of the special edition of The Lord of the Rings, *with stamping in various colors. This was for the early printings of the one-volume edition printed on India paper (that is, Bible paper—so thin that this one-volume trilogy is only 1 inch thick).*

❖ **The Most Elegant Edition** (£100). Printed by Allen & Unwin in one volume with a matching slipcase, the "India paper" edition—so named because of the thin paper stock typically used to print bibles—is visually distinctive: the book itself is approximately 1-inch thick, which surprises most people at first glance. (Typically, the book, when printed on normal paper stock, is thick as a brick, with a 2-inch spine.) This is not so much a book to read as one to treasure; the book is simply a work of art.

❖ **The Most Imaginatively Packaged** ($75). A one-volume edition packaged in a gift box, with an appropriately themed pair of bookends featuring Bilbo Baggins inside his hobbit hole at Bag End and Gandalf rapping on its door with his staff. Perfect for gift-giving.

One of two pieces comprising the set called "No admittance except on party business," from the first chapter of The Fellowship of the Ring. *Gandalf raps on the door of Bilbo's hobbit hole with his wizard's staff. Manufactured by Sideshow/Weta, this is no longer available from them. Both pieces are now packaged with a one-volume edition of* The Lord of the Rings *and sold by Houghton Mifflin as a gift set.*

The second piece of the "No admittances except on party business" bookend set by Sideshow/Weta. Bilbo Baggins, in his hobbit hole, answers Gandalf's rapping at the door.

❖ **The Best Illustrated Edition** ($80). Printed on semi-glossy paper to enhance the art by Alan Lee, this three-volume set with matching slipcase is available separately at $27 per volume.

❖ **The Best Single-Volume, Illustrated Edition** ($70). The "commemorative edition" to celebrate Tolkien's centenary, this one-volume edition is illustrated with 50 full-color illustrations by Alan Lee.

→ **The Collector's Edition** ($75). A one-volume edition bound in red leatherette with matching slipcase, the text is printed in two colors. (This complements the collector's edition of *The Hobbit*, bound in green leatherette.)

→ **The Standard Edition** ($65). The three volumes in this set come with a matching slipcase and feature color jacket art by Alan Lee. They are available separately at $22 apiece.

→ **The Cleverest Packaging** ($70). The millennium-edition, boxed set of seven books, with laminated hard covers in a matching slipcase. The six books comprising *The Lord of the Rings* spell "T-O-L-K-I-E-N" across its collective spine. My concern, though, is with the glue binding, which will not hold up after repeated readings.

The one-volume gift edition of The Lord of the Rings *published in the United States. It has red leatherette binding with stamping on the exterior boards and comes with a matching slipcase.*

The Silmarillion

Published posthumously in 1977, *The Silmarillion* was, as Tom Shipley (*J.R.R. Tolkien: Author of the Century*) put it, "the work of his heart." Originally submitted at the request of Stanley Unwin, who had hoped for a book to follow *The Hobbit*, *The Silmarillion* was not a narrative tale but, instead, a book of pseudo-history. As such, it wasn't what Unwin had hoped for, so he rejected it. In a letter dated December 15, 1937, Unwin wrote: "*The Silmarillion* contains plenty of wonderful material; in fact it is a mine to be explored in writing further books like *The Hobbit* rather than a book in itself."

Tolkien initially bristled at the constructive criticism but soon came to realize that a sustained narrative was, in fact, what was needed and therefore requested by Unwin, who spoke for Tolkien's readership that preferred stories to pseudo-history. Soon thereafter, Tolkien began writing "A Long-expected Party," which would be the first chapter of *The Lord of the Rings: The Fellowship of the Ring*.

In the seemingly interminable wait between the original submission in 1937 (and subsequent rejection) and eventual publication of *The Silmarillion* in 1977, Tolkien fans speculated as to the book and its contents.

Fans got a glimpse when Clyde S. Kilby published *Tolkien and the Silmarillion* in 1976, but the following year fans got the full monty. Edited by Christopher Tolkien, *The Silmarillion* was finally published, rendering Kilby's speculations moot.

In his foreword to the book, Christopher Tolkien wrote:

> *The Silmarillion*, now published four years after the death of its author, is an account of the Elder Days, or the First Age of the World.

In *The Lord of the Rings* were narrated the great events at the end of the Third Age; but the tales of *The Silmarillion* are legends deriving from a much deeper past, when Morgoth, the first Dark Lord, dwelt in Middle-earth, and the High Elves made war upon him for the recovery of the Silmarils.

The Silmarillion Recommended Editions

➤ **The Illustrated Edition** ($35). A companion book to the illustrated editions of *The Hobbit* and *The Lord of the Rings*, this edition is illustrated by British artist Ted Nasmith. (**Note:** In 2004, a new edition will be published, with 20 new paintings. Like the three-volume illustrated edition of *The Lord of the Rings*, with art by Alan Lee, the new edition of *The Silmarillion* will be printed using one paper stock instead of text stock and glossy stock for art, which allows placement of art as appropriate.)

➤ **The Second Edition** ($28 hardback, $14 trade paperback). This includes a 1951 letter written by J.R.R. Tolkien.

When *The Silmarillion* was rejected by Tolkien's publisher, he fired back a letter the next day, bristling that "My chief joy comes from learning that *The Silmarillion* is not rejected with scorn....But I shall certainly now hope one day to be able, or be able to afford, to publish *The Silmarillion!*"

The Silmarillion would not be completed in his lifetime. A perfectionist and a literary niggler, Tolkien's biblical accounting of the First Age of Middle-earth, with its obvious Christian parallels, was clearly not a narrative on the order of *The Hobbit* or *The Lord of the Rings*; it was, in fact, for those devoted readers who religiously read every word of the 128-page appendices in *LotR*.

In 1976, Clyde S. Kilby published *Tolkien & The Silmarillion*, an accounting of a summer spent with Tolkien, with the hope that he could assist in editing *The Silmarillion* for publishing as soon as possible. Wild rumors about the book had circulated for

> ### The Delaying of *The Silmarillion*
>
> "The three jewels shining with the light of the Two Trees, made by Fëanor in the years following the unchaining of Melkor. The Silmarilli were the greatest works of craft ever produced by the Children of Ilúvatar, and, like the Two Trees, their creation could not be duplicated. The shell of the jewels were composed of silima, but at their heart was the ever radiant light of the Trees, and the Silmarilli shone by themselves. They were hallowed by Varda so that any impure hand touching them would be burned and withered."
>
>
>
> —Robert Foster,
> *The Complete Guide to Middle-earth*

years previous, but Kilby's sympathetic portrait of Tolkien was the first reliable accounting of the book that fans felt might never be published, for whatever reasons.

As Kilby found out, Tolkien was distracted by matters both large and small, matters compounded by his popularity and fame. A man who paid attention to the smallest detail, no matter how trivial, Tolkien never grasped the big picture: that the completion of *The Silmarillion* was, at that point in his life, more important than any other literary effort.

Everything, it seemed, distracted Tolkien from this paramount task. As Kilby recounts in his book, W.H. Auden had contracted to write a "brochure" on Tolkien, who felt its mere publication was a distraction of the first order. An exasperated Tolkien wrote, "I wish at any rate that any book could wait until I produce *The Silmarillion*. I am constantly interrupted in this; but nothing interferes more than the present pother about 'me' and my history."

Another interruption—the publication of an unauthorized edition by Ace Books of *The Lord of the Rings*—likewise commanded, and held, his attention to the point that it, too, prevented him from focusing his long overdue attention on the completion of *The Silmarillion*. As Kilby pointed out, "I failed to understand why he could not see instantly that the Ace edition need not usurp even one day of his time. It was purely a legal matter and only needed to be handed over to his lawyer."

Kilby's visit was in 1966 and when he left to return home to the United States, it became clear that the days were growing longer, but *The Silmarillion* was no closer to completion, despite Tolkien's best efforts.

On September 2, 1973, J.R.R. Tolkien passed away, leaving *The Silmarillion* unfinished, to the great dismay of his fans. The story of the jewels of power, it seemed, would be lost forever. "At Tolkien's death his story of the First Age of Middle-earth was incomplete—how incomplete nobody will ever know," wrote Kilby.

The only person who knew was Tolkien's son Christopher, who assumed the literary challenge of sifting through mountains of unpublished papers to bring *The Silmarillion* together in a cohesive whole. Published in 1977 in trade hardback, a staggering 1 million copies sold by year's end.

In his foreword to *The Silmarillion*, Christopher Tolkien wrote that "...throughout my father's long life he never abandoned it, nor ceased even in his last years to work on it.... On my father's death it fell to me to try to bring the work into publishable form." He noted, too, that beyond *The Silmarillion*, "There is indeed a wealth of unpublished writing by my father concerning the Three Ages, narrative, linguistic, historical, and philosophical, and I hope that it will prove possible to publish some of this at a later date."

That material would eventually see publication as the 12 volumes of *The History of Middle-earth*, which Christopher Tolkien edited.

As for *The Silmarillion*, it was to be grander than its author had imagined. In it are "Quenta Silmarillion" (The History of the Silmarils), "Ainulindalë" (The Music of the Ainur), "Valaquenta" (Account of the Valar), Akallabêth (The Downfall of Númenor), and a long piece titled "Of the Rings of Power and the Third Age."

Ideally, one would want to read *The Silmarillion* first, because it's set in the First Age of Middle-earth, then read *The Hobbit*, which sets the stage for the Third Age and is then chronicled in *The Lord of the Rings*, an accounting of the War of the Ring. (Optionally, *Unfinished Tales* and the 12-volume *History of Middle-earth* would fall, chronologically, after *The Silmarillion*.)

The History of Middle-earth

Of J.R.R Tolkien's children, only Christopher Tolkien followed in his father's academic and literary footsteps. Currently living in France, Christopher—the literary executor of the Tolkien estate—rarely travels to England, and then only on critical business.

Two U.S. hardback volumes from The History of Middle-earth.

He has devoted most of his time in bringing to light the pseudo-history of Middle-earth with the posthumous publications of *The Silmarillion, Unfinished Tales,* and most notably, the 12-volume *History of Middle-earth,* a work of scholarship that could only have been undertaken by "an accredited student of hobbit-lore" (as J.R.R. Tolkien termed his son, in a letter drafted April 1956 to Joanna de Bortadano).

Of the 12 volumes, the middle four—volumes 6 through 9—comprise a subset of special significance: The History of *The Lord of the Rings.*

Taken as a whole, the 12 books are a remarkable testimony to the creativity of J.R.R. Tolkien and the industry and painstaking scholarship of his son Christopher.

To answer the most obvious question: For most readers, interested in narrative but not exposition, these books will likely be more than they'd want or need to know; however, for readers who appreciate the philological and historical impetus that created *The Lord of the Rings*, this series is a gold mine of information, spanning all the Ages of Middle-earth.

In the United States, the preferred editions are the hardbacks; in the United Kingdom, two editions are especially noteworthy: the deluxe editions (fine paper, gilt edges, slipcased), which collects all 12 volumes in three handsome hardbacks: Volume 1–5, 6–9, and 10–12 (£100 each).

An attractive, affordable alternative is a trade hardback edition of three volumes in matching cloth, with slipcase (£150).

The History of Middle-earth consists of:

1. *The Book of Lost Tales.*

2. *The Book of Lost Tales 2.*

3. *The Lays of Beleriand.*

4. *The Shaping of Middle-earth.*

5. *The Lost Road.*

6. *The Return of the Shadow.*

7. *The Treason of Isengard.*

8. *The War of the Ring.*

9. *Sauron Defeated: The End of the Third Age.*

10. *Morgoth's Ring.*

11. *The War of the Jewels.*

12. *The Peoples of Middle-earth.*

In addition, HarperCollins UK has issued an index to the 12 books, *The History of Middle-earth Index* (£9.99), edited by Christopher Tolkien, with his introductory notes for each volume. (There is no equivalent U.S. edition currently available, alas.)

Other Books by J.R.R. Tolkien

Most Tolkien fans will limit their exposure to Middle-earth to hobbit stories— *The Hobbit* and *The Lord of the Rings*; however, if one has more than a casual interest in his work, there are other books by him that are worth your attention. (Note: Unless otherwise noted, the books listed are U.S. editions and in print.)

⇝ ***Bilbo's Last Song*** (Knopf, $12.95, hardback). The text is an original poem, written by Bilbo Baggins, just before he takes a ship from Middle-earth to the Undying Lands. An elegiac piece, it is illustrated by Pauline Baynes with charming watercolors—Baynes is an English artist whose long association with Tolkien goes back to *Smith of Wootton Major* (Ballantine Books).

It was written for and subsequently given as a gift to Joy Hill, an employee at Allen & Unwin who, at Tolkien's request, took on the daunting task of handling the crush of correspondence that his fame brought late in his life.

⇝ ***Farmer Giles of Ham*** (Houghton Mifflin, $17, hardback). Edited by Christina Scull and Wayne G. Hammond, illustrated by Pauline Baynes. According to Tolkien biographer Humphrey Carpenter (*J.R.R. Tolkien: A Biography*), this book was originally published in 1949, with illustrations by Baynes, about whose work Tolkien wrote: "They are more than illustrations, they are a collateral theme."

This is an expanded edition with the full text of the original book, a map, the original story outline, the original illustrations by Baynes, and notes toward an unpublished sequel, about which Carpenter wrote:

> At one time Tolkien considered a sequel to it, and he sketched the plot in some detail; it was to concern Giles's son George Worming and a page-boy named Suet, as well as re-introducing Chrysophylax the dragon, and it was to be set in the same countryside as its predecessor.

The U.S. hardback expanded edition of Farmer Giles of Ham.

Farmer Giles of Ham was initially not the success its author and publisher had hoped: of its first printing of 5,000, an unimpressive 2,000 had sold, prompting Tolkien to complain that insufficient advertising dollars was the culprit—misplaced criticism, because Tolkien himself had earlier noted that the book didn't have commercial appeal. In a letter to C.A. Firth at Allen & Unwin (August 31, 1938), he wrote: "I see that it is *not* long enough to stand alone probably—at least not as a commercial proposition (if indeed it [could] ever be such a thing)."

The story itself is novella length and is an appealing tale of a farmer who fights off a giant and is rewarded by the king with a sword, Tailbiter, which carries its own score to settle—a sword that formerly belonged to a dragonslayer. Not surprisingly, when a dragon shows up, the king calls on Farmer Giles to deal with this new intruder, as well.

➤ *Finn and Hengest*, by J.R.R. Tolkien, edited by Alan Bliss (HarperCollins UK, £7.99, trade paperback). Two Old English poems about fifth-century heroes Finn and Hengest, told in *Beowulf* and *The Fights at Finnesburg*. Obscure poems with a history of controversial interpretation, they are the subject of Tolkien's clarifying lectures, published in this book.

➤ *Letters from Father Christmas*. Though purportedly written by Father Christmas, these illustrated series of letters written to the Tolkien children— John, Michael, Christopher, and Priscilla—were in fact from their father, who wrote annual installments every Christmas beginning in 1920.

Of course, in time, the children grew up and realized that the real author *was* their father, but until then his children enjoyed these humorous tales from the North Pole, especially the antics of an accident-prone Polar Bear who always managed to get in the way.

A revised gift edition (Houghton Mifflin, $20) is available as a traditionally printed book; however, given the nature of this literary work, its spirit is best captured in the gift book edition (Hougton Mifflin, $19.95), which has 10 envelopes with pullout letters and pictures. A mini-book edition (Houghton Mifflin, $5.95), designed as a stocking stuffer, is also available.

➤ ***The Hobbit: An Illustrated Edition of the Fantasy Classic*** (Ballantine Books, $15, trade paperback). An abridged graphic novel adaptation with art by David Wenzel (cover art by Donato Giancola). The only graphic adaptation (that is, comic book art) of any of Tolkien's fiction, Wenzel's only regret was that his deadlines didn't permit the luxury of devoting the time he felt necessary to render the art to the degree he desired.

➤ ***The Monster and the Critics*** (HarperCollins, $22.95, trade paperback). A collection of seven nonfiction pieces spanning three decades: "On Fairy Stories" (his well-known essay explicating his notion of subcreation), "English and Welsh" (a critical essay), "Sir Gawain and the Green Knight" (a translation by Tolkien), a valedictory address given at Oxford, and two essays on *Beowulf*— "Beowulf: The Monsters and the Critics" and "Translating Beowulf."

➤ ***Mr. Bliss*** (Allen & Unwin, out of print hardback). After the success of *The Hobbit*, Tolkien's publishers, anxious to capitalize on its success, asked him for more work for possible publication, and one of those submitted was this charming children's story, *Mr. Bliss*. His publisher read it and wanted to publish it, but Tolkien had profusely illustrated it in color, so they asked him to redraw and simplify the rendering, to keep costs down. Tolkien, distracted by other matters—personal, professional, and academic—never followed through, with the result that the work remained unpublished until 1983, 46 years after it was submitted and accepted.

An amusing tale of Mr. Bliss and his comical car misadventures, the inspiration for the story was Tolkien's purchase of his first car in 1932.

➤ ***Poems from The Hobbit*** (Houghton Mifflin, $5.95). In page count (56) and in size (a miniature book), this small gem collects all eight poems from the book and Gollum's riddles, as well. The real bonus is the inclusion of Tolkien's own art, with 30 drawings and paintings.

➤ ***Roverandom***, edited by Christina Scull and Wayne G. Hammond (Houghton Mifflin, $12). A children's story written to console J.R.R. Tolkien's then 4-year-old son Michael, after he lost his favorite toy dog at the beach, this short novel (25,000 words) is illustrated by the author, as well.

➤ ***Sir Gawain and the Green Knight/Pearl/Sir Orfeo***, translated by J.R.R. Tolkien (Del Rey, $6.99, paperback). With an introduction by Christopher Tolkien, this is a collection of three medieval poems: "Sir Gawain and the Green Knight," "Pearl," and "Sir Orfeo."

➤ ***The Tolkien Reader*** (Ballantine Books, $6.99, paperback). An anthology collecting some of his miscellany, this shows the many sides of Tolkien: the scholar (a play titled *The Homecoming of Beorhtnoth, Beorhtheml's Son*), the intensely autobiographical and allegorical ("Leaf by Niggle"), the essayist (a seminal piece on fairy tales), the humorist and children's writer (*Farmer Giles of Ham*), and poet (*The Adventures of Tom Bombadil*).

One wishes that it also included *Smith of Wootton Major*, but even as is, it's a good cross-section of Tolkien's varied literary interests and his wide-ranging imagination.

➤ *Unfinished Tales of Númenor and Middle-earth*, edited by Christopher Tolkien (Houghton Mifflin, $26 hardback, $14 trade paperback). In his introduction to the book, Christopher Tolkien made an important distinction between *The Silmarillion* and this book: "That *The Silmarillion* should remain unknown was for me out of the question, despite its disordered state, and despite my father's known if very largely unfulfilled intentions for its transformation...." This book, observed Christopher Tolkien, was another matter entirely:

> The narratives in this book are indeed on an altogether different footing: taken together they constitute no whole, and the book is no more than a collection of writings, disparate in form, intent, finish, and date of composition (and in my own treatment of them), concerned with Númenor and Middle-earth.

J.R.R. Tolkien acknowledged that he considered the pseudo-history of Middle-earth supplementary reading. In the appendices to *The Lord of the Rings*, he writes: "Those who enjoy the book as a 'heroic romance' only, and find 'unexplained vistas' part of the literary effect, will neglect the Appendices, very properly."

For those to whom the appendices matter very much, *Unfinished Tales* is a worthy addition, including narratives from the First, Second, and Third Ages of Middle-earth.

The book has a fold-out map of "The West of Middle-earth at the End of the Third Age," drawn by Christopher Tolkien.

Literary Piracy: Ace Books Plunders Middle-earth!

"This paperback edition and no other has been published with my consent and cooperation. Those who approve of courtesy (at least) to living authors will purchase it and no other."

—J.R.R. Tolkien, from the back cover of the Ballantine paperback editions of *The Lord of the Rings*.

The Lord of the Rings: The Illegitimate Edition

A war was fought not *in* but *over* Middle-earth in 1965. Under the legal pretext that *The Lord of the Rings* was not protected by copyright in the United States, Ace Books—after being rebuffed in its attempt to legitimately publish the book in mass market paperback—made plans to publish an illegitimate edition. As Humphrey Carpenter so devastatingly put it, in his biography of Tolkien, "Early in that year it was learned than an American publisher who appeared not to suffer from an excess of scruples was planning to issue an unauthorized paperback edition of *The Lord of the Rings*, almost certainly without paying royalties to Tolkien."

The legal consideration revolved around the matter of imported sheets of the British edition, rebound for the U.S. edition: the number of sheets rebound exceeded the limitation for copyright protection. This consideration was for the benefit of U.S. printers—the idea being that by keeping the number low for importing and rebinding sheets, it would force book publishers to use U.S. book printers, thus keeping them in business; no one, however, imagined that the loophole would be used as an excuse to publish a pirated edition!

Tolkien, hard at work on revisions for *Smith of Wootton Major*, now found himself with a major, unforeseen distraction on his hands. To prevent Ace Books from stealing sales, Ballantine Books was forced to issue a new edition with revisions to secure copyright protection.

Tolkien, understandably upset at Ace Books, began writing notes to all his correspondents to pass the word on that Ace Books, in Orc fashion, was ripping him off.

An orc archer from the mines of Moria. This sculpture is from the Sideshow/ Weta collection.

Ballantine's editions cost more, and Ace Books benefited from the cost advantage. Readers who didn't suffer from an excess of scruples bought the cheaper edition, with the result that Ace Books sold 100,000 copies.

Middle-earth had been literarily plundered, but what Ace couldn't anticipate was the loyalist backlash from a united Tolkien fandom, aided by the vocal support of the Science Fiction Writers of America (SFWA), many of whose authors published at Ace Books. Together, the collective strength of Tolkien fans made it clear that Ace may have won a battle, but it would lose the war. In the United States, Middle-earth was Ballantine's territory, not Ace's. Booksellers, pressured from ardent Tolkien fans, stopped carrying the book, and Ace Books could see the writing on the wall.

As the Ballantine editions' sales rose and the Ace editions' sales fell, as the objections of Tolkien fans and professional writers in SFWA reached a fever pitch, Ace wisely threw in the towel and agreed not to reprint once its existing stock had been depleted. In a misguided gesture of good faith, Ace had hoped to salvage a little goodwill out of fandom by stating that they would donate royalties to SFWA, to help new writers. But when Tolkien got wind of that, he rightly asserted his unassailable position: He—not a writer's group—could use the money, and as the author who had been violated, didn't he deserve compensation? He did, and Ace finally relented, with the result that royalties of 4 percent were paid to Tolkien. It was not much, but the money was distinctively felt, as Tolkien explained in a February 1966 letter to W.H. Auden: "The half of this which I shall retain after taxation will be welcome, but not yet great riches."

Tolkien, having retired on a modest pension from Oxford in 1959, was like any other author—he could always use the money, even though it was half the normal royalties paid.

The Ace edition, however, did have one salutary effect: Its low cover price of 75¢ made it affordable to college students, who couldn't even afford the more expensive Ballantine edition at 95¢, much less the $6 hardback editions.

With this distasteful and distracting matter behind him permanently, Tolkien turned his attention back to *Smith of Wootton Major*, which was subsequently published in 1967.

CHAPTER 2

BOOKS ABOUT
J.R.R. TOLKIEN

Not surprisingly, there are more books *about* Tolkien and his work than there are books *by* Tolkien. Though most of the books about Tolkien are academic in nature—the kind of books the Tolkien Estate favors, because Tolkien himself was a professor and firmly entrenched in the academic world—the most accessible books, and the best-selling books of their kind about Tolkien and his works, appeal to its popular culture.

Every year sees a new bumper crop of books about Tolkien, on every conceivable aspect of his life and work, and with more on the way. As Tolkien expert Douglas A. Anderson correctly observed, "The real heyday [for books about Tolkien], both popular and scholarly-wise, is coming."

Reading a book about Tolkien is not necessary to appreciate the fiction. In my opinion, considering that Tolkien straddled both universes—popular culture and the critical community—specialized books addressing his varied interests may enhance the reading of the principal texts.

Clearly, this is one area in which the new reader will easily find himself hopelessly lost in a sea of books. To paraphrase Samuel Taylor Coleridge's *Rime of the Ancient Mariner*: water, water everywhere, but with what to slake one's thirst?

To assist the new reader, I have provided capsule reviews of the books about Tolkien, with an emphasis on "in print" titles. With few exceptions, out-of-print or self-published books are not addressed.

When I began looking at the sheer volume of books about Tolkien, it was clear that a secondary bibliography composed of books, magazine articles, and pieces in critical journals would be very useful, but such a work would entail years of research, approaching the complexity of the forthcoming Tolkien reference books, *The J.R.R.*

Tolkien Companion and Guide (Houghton Mifflin), which is a two-book set totaling 1,600 pages! (There is, after all, over a half decade of criticism to chronicle—
critical extracts and photographs, as appropriate.)

The Atlas of Middle-earth, by Karen Wynn Fonstad (Houghton Mifflin, $24, trade
paperback, revised edition). In an October 1953 letter to Allen & Unwin regarding *The Lord of the Rings*, Tolkien worried about "The maps. I am stumped. Indeed in a panic. They are essential; and urgent; but I just
cannot get them done.... I feel that the maps ought to be
done properly.... Even at a little cost there should be pic-
turesque maps, providing more than a mere index to what
is said in the text."

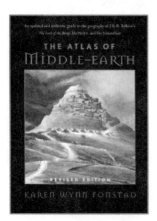

The front cover of The
Atlas of Middle-earth.

The maps, of course, were eventually completed, with
the assistance of his son Christopher, but the geography
of Middle-earth still remained largely uncharted in map
form, until the publication of Karen Wynn Fonstad's
The Atlas of Middle-earth in 1981, which was revised and
updated in 1991 to include the publications of his posthumously published books.

A cartographer by trade, Fonstad provides hundreds
of two-color maps and diagrams that give us an appreciation for the richness and detail of the geography of
Middle-earth.

Fonstad comments on the book's genesis, after reading *The Hobbit* and *LotR*:

> ...I immediately developed an explorer's need to map and classify
> this (to me) newfound world. The complexity of history, diversity
> of landscapes, and proliferation of places were so overwhelming
> that I longed to clarify them with pen and ink for my own satisfaction.
> I wished for one gigantic indexed map, showing every place-name
> and all the pathways.

One could not ask for anything more: maps of the First Age and the Third Age,
regional maps, maps from *The Hobbit* and *The Lord of the Rings*, thematic maps
(such as climate, vegetation, languages), and a complete index for cross-reference.

A Tolkien Bestiary: A Bestiary of the Beasts, Monsters, Races, Deities and Flora, by
David Day, edited by Nancy Davis (Grammercy, $24.99, trade paperback). In his

preface to the book, Day explains what a "bestiary" is: "A bestiary is a book about beasts. In the Middle Ages, when the bestiary was most popular, it was the equivalent of an encyclopedia of natural history, revealing fabulous beasts and monsters to the curious." This book, as he explains, is a rather broad interpretation of that word, because it discusses more than just the beasts of Middle-earth—Day provides individual listings of the people of Middle-earth, as well. The book is illustrated by 11 artists, whose work is of varying quality: color and black-and-white, pencilwork and pen-and-ink, illustrative and very stylized. The artists are, curiously, not credited, though the art itself is referenced by subject matter and page number. As for the text, it is written for the layman and does not have page references to the principal texts—an omission (to my mind) that mars an otherwise accessible book.

Note: Though Day states that "It is a comprehensive encyclopedia that describes, illustrates and historically delineates all his creations," the reader is advised that Day is referring to general creations by race, not specific individuals, therefore, you'll find no listing for Aragon, Bilbo Baggins, Frodo Baggins, and so on.

After the King: Stories in Honor of J.R.R. Tolkien, edited by Martin Greenberg (Tor Books, $16.95). Greenberg, who is the most prolific anthologist in the fantasy/ science fiction field, has done for Tolkien in this book what he's done for the field's other best-known writers, such as Isaac Asimov, Ray Bradbury, and H.P. Lovecraft: He's assembled an original anthology of fiction to honor the writer. As expected, the stories run the gamut, but overall, it's a strong collection and a worthy addition to any fantasy library. The contributors include: Poul and Karen Anderson, Peter S. Beagle, Gregory Benford, John Brunner, Stephen R. Donaldson, Karen Haber, Barry Malzberg, Dennis L.M. McKiernan, Andrew Nortong, Robert Silverberg, Judith Tarr, Charles de Lint, Emma Bull, Elizabeth Ann Scarborough, Harry Turtledove, Jane Yolen, Mike Resnick, and Terry Pratchett.

Bored of the Rings: A Parody of J.R.R. Tolkien's Lord of the Rings, by Henry Beard, Douglas Kenney, and the Harvard Lampoon Staff (New American Library, $12, trade paperback). This book will separate Tolkien fans into two groups: those who have a sense of humor...and those who desperately *need* one. Short in length (as parodies ought to be), but long on laughs and irreverence, *Bored of the Rings* dates itself with its many references to drugs—a dead giveaway that it was originally published in the 1960s. The only book of its kind, this send-up bears a cautionary note: "This paperback edition, and no other, has been published solely for the purpose of making a few fast bucks. Those who approve of courtesy to a certain author will not touch this gobbler with a ten-foot battle lance." At least the folks at the Harvard Lampoon, unlike some other authors, are honest—it's about the moolah.

Celebrating Middle-earth: The Lord of the Rings as a Defense of Western Civilization, by John G. West, Jr. (Inkling Books, $10.95, trade paperback). An anthology of papers given at a conference at Seattle Pacific University in November 2001. The papers were written by John West, Peter Kreeft, Janet Leslie Blumberg, Joseph Pearce, Kerry L. Dearborn, and Phillip Goggans.

The Complete Guide to Middle-earth: From The Hobbit to The Silmarillion, by Robert Foster (Ballantine Books, $13.95, trade paperback). Originally published by Jack Chalker's Mirage Press in 1971 under the title *A Guide to Middle-earth*, this is the text of the revised and expanded edition published in March 1978. I imagine Foster is already hard at work to update it because of the posthumous publication of *The History of Middle-earth*, but even as is, it's the best concordance in print on the people, places, and things to Tolkien's fictional universe. What makes it especially useful is that entries are indexed by book and page number, so you can consult the original reference. It is an indispensable addition to any Tolkien collection and the perfect book for new readers who want to understand the many references found in the fiction. Wrote Foster in an introduction to the revised edition "This *Guide* is intended to be supplementary to the works of Professor Tolkien and no more; its value is that it can clarify deep-hidden historical facts and draw together scraps of information whose relation is easily overlooked...."

Defending Middle-earth: Tolkien, Myth and Modernity, by Patrick Curry (Harper-Collins UK, £7.99, trade paperback). Curry vigorously defends *LotR* from its detractors who dismiss it as fantasy, by exploring his thesis that it is significant because of its contemporary relevance as a cautionary tale that addressed ecological concerns: the wanton destructiveness, needless intrusion, and presumptive arrogance of modern man.

Finding God in The Lord of the Rings, by Kurt D. Bruner and Jim Ware (Tyndale House Pub, $12.99, hardback). Bruner, an executive with the conservative Christian group Focus on the Family, and Ware, a graduate of Fuller Theological Seminary, join forces to find God in *The Lord of the Rings*. The purpose of the book, they state, is "to help fans of *The Lord of the Rings* discover how the rich fabric of Tolkien's fantasy world enhances a Christian understanding of our real world." The authors accomplish this by picking specific scenes and themes from *LotR* and finding parallels in the Bible—linkages that any careful reader could discern for himself. Written for the layman and lacking the depth that a scholar would bring to this subject, this book doesn't appear as much to be about *The Lord of the Rings* as it is a means for the authors to proselytize.

Frodo's Quest: Living the Myth in The Lord of the Rings, by Robert S. Ellwood (Quest Books, $18.95, trade paperback). An Emeritus Professor of Religion (University of Southern California), Ellwood is well qualified to discuss Frodo's journey (and burden) as a spiritual quest. Readers who enjoy Joseph Campbell's extensive examination of the nature of myth will find much of interest in this thorough, well-written book.

The Hobbit: A Journey Into Maturity, by William H. Green (Twayne Publishers, $31, hardback). A critical analysis intended for students and scholars.

The Hobbit, 3D: a Three-dimensional Picture Book, by J.R.R. Tolkien, illustrated by John Howe (Picture Lions, £14, juvenile title). A color pop-up book with scenes from the novel, including Mirkwood spiders, Smaug the Dragon ("the Chiefest and Greatest of Calamities") and the Battle of Five Armies.

Hobbits, Elves, and Wizards: Exploring the Wonders and Worlds of J.R.R. Tolkien's The Lord of the Rings, by Michael Stanton (Palgrave Macmillan, $12.95, trade paperback). An English professor at the University of Vermont, Stanton has taught *LotR* for over a quarter century. His book is targeted to the general reader or for students at the high school or college level. A contextual book, it offers a summary of the trilogy, background information about Middle-earth, and a thorough discussion—organized by race—of its varied inhabitants: the hobbits, elves, wizards, orcs, and so on.

The Inklings Handbook: A Comprehensive Guide to the Lives, Thought and Writings of C.S. Lewis, J.R.R. Tolkien, Charles Williams, Owen Barfield and Their Friends (Chalice Press, $32.99, hardback). For readers who have no inkling of the linkage among these men—an Oxford group known as "The Inklings"—this book is a good overview of this fraternal order of learned men who enjoyed camaraderie and conversation and gave readings of works in progress. Tolkien read parts of "Leaf by Niggle," *The Hobbit*, and *The Lord of the Rings* to fellow members.

The Inklings: C.S. Lewis, J.R.R. Tolkien, Charles Williams, and Their Friends, by Humphrey Carpenter (HarperCollins UK, £8.99, trade paperback). The best look at the Inklings by Carpenter, who edited Tolkien's letters for publication and wrote the only authorized biography. For this book, Carpenter had access to unpublished diaries and letters that lend this book a depth the other books on the Inklings lack.

The J.R.R. Tolkien Handbook: A Concise Guide to His Life, Writings, and World of Middle-earth, by Colin Duriez (Baker Book House, $12.99, trade paperback). A reader-friendly, introductory overview to the man and his work on *LotR*. Especially useful to new fans who might be intimidated by the more expansive overviews, this is an accessible text for practically everyone.

J.R.R. Tolkien: Myth, Morality, and Religion, by Richard L. Purtill and Joseph Pearce (Ignatius Press, $13.95). Originally published in 1984, this is a reprint edition, with the addition of a new preface by Pearce, who has published several books on Tolkien. A fascinating examination of morality and Roman Catholicism in Tolkien's fiction.

J.R.R. Tolkien's Lord of the Rings (Modern Critical Interpretations), edited by Harold Bloom ($37.95, hardback, Chelsea House Pub). At first glance, it seems odd that Bloom would be the editor for this book, because he admits that he didn't enjoy them; but at second glance, it does allow him a certain perspective that, at a time when the bookshelves are groaning with adulatory tomes, is timely. Especially useful for students looking to explore Tolkien's trilogy, these pieces, though dated, are worth your time.

J.R.R. Tolkien's The Hobbit and The Lord of the Rings (Barrons Book Notes), by Anne M. Pienciak (Barrons Educational Series, $3.95, paperback). Plot synopses, discussions of the story elements (characters, setting, theme, style, point of view, form, and structure), and supplementary material useful for students wanting to write research papers on Tolkien's two major works.

J.R.R. Tolkien and His Literary Resonances: Views of Middle-earth, by George Clark and Daniel Timmons (Greenwood Publishing Group, $62.95, hardback). An excellent book examining Tolkien in a very broad literary context, its contributors are well-known scholars who discuss his literary sources and put his work in juxtaposition to other writers. Though too expensive for individual purchase, it properly belongs in schools and public libraries where students and scholars can access it.

J.R.R. Tolkien: A Biography, by Leslie Ellen Jones (Greenwood Publishing Group, $49.95, hardback). A well-written and researched biography, though its high cost will keep it out of reach from the general reader—it's priced for library collections. Readers who want a more affordable edition may want to check out the authorized Humphrey Carpenter's *J.R.R. Tolkien: A Biography*, which is available in trade paperback for $14 from Houghton Mifflin.

J.R.R. Tolkien: The Man Who Created THE LORD OF THE RINGS, by Michael Coren (Scholastic, $4.99, trade paperback). A biography for young readers, written by Coren, who covers Tolkien's life in seven chapters. This is a straightforward accounting; readers who want more detail are advised to seek out Humphrey Carpenter's biography.

J.R.R. Tolkien: Architect of Middle-earth, by Daniel Grotta (Running Press, $18.95, trade hardback). A biography of Tolkien profusely illustrated by the Brothers Hildebrandt.

J.R.R. Tolkien: Master of Fantasy, by David R. Collins (Bt Bound, $16.10, hardback). A biography for young readers, this book is unbalanced in approach. Its readers will likely be more interested in the events of Tolkien's life as storyteller, thus, they will likely skip over the early years and go directly to the latter years. Visually, the book has some interesting photos, but some seem like filler, and, unfortunately, the art by William Heagy is—to my eye—crudely drawn and ugly.

J.R.R. Tolkien, by Charles Moseley (Northcote House Pub Ltd, $22.50, paperback). A well-written and illuminating overview of Tolkien's life and work, Moseley's critical discussion explores his fiction as the product of a world-builder, an imaginative sub-creation steeped not only in myth, but firmly grounded on a critical base.

J.R.R. Tolkien, by Michael White (Alpha books, $14.95, trade paperback). A straightforward biography that relies heavily on Carpenter's previously published biography and collection of Tolkien's edited letters. **Note:** A useful list of Websites is provided.

J.R.R. Tolkien, by Andrew Blake (Headway, $9.95, trade paperback). One in a series providing a concise introduction to major cultural figures, this book discusses Tolkien's life and worth in a critical framework, with review material at the end of each chapter to reinforce the principal text. A useful study for older students.

J.R.R. Tolkien: A Biography, by Humphrey Carpenter (Houghton Mifflin, $14, trade paperback). Originally published in hardback in 1977, this revised edition is *the* biography of choice. All other biographies on Tolkien owe much to Carpenter's, which is consulted as the leading secondary source of information. Unlike Carpenter, however, the biographers that followed have not had the exclusive access that he enjoyed, such as Tolkien's family, friends, and papers—all possible because this is an authorized biography. As a result, Carpenter's book has a depth that no other biography can match. Wisely, Carpenter has decided to leave the explication of Tolkien's text to scholars; Carpenter has, instead, written a straightforward biography that covers Tolkien's life and work with thoroughness. And because Tolkien himself never wrote—or intended to write—an autobiography, the task was left to others. One might wish that his son Christopher Tolkien assay such a task. He is, after all, in the ideal position to do so, but has shown no sign of doing so. For that reason, I'm grateful that someone such as Carpenter took on the task, because his biography is neither hagiography or interpretive biography, with an emphasis on literary dissection. It is, instead, a very readable general biography for all of Tolkien's readers, complete with appendices that include the Tolkien family tree, a chronology of events (personal and professional) in his life, a chronological listing of Tolkien's publications, an acknowledgement of sources, and a very detailed index. Indispensable reading and the gold standard against which all other biographies will inevitably be compared, this is the best such book in print.

J.R.R. Tolkien: Artist and Illustrator, by Wayne G. Hammond and Christina Scull (Houghton Mifflin, $25, trade paperback). Because *Pictures by Tolkien* is long out of print and commanding premium prices on the secondary book market, the publication of this book, with its illuminating text, is a welcome addition to any Tolkien collection.

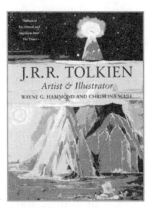

The front cover to J.R.R. Tolkien: Artist and Illustrator, *by Wayne G. Hammond and Christina Scull.*

Tolkien considered himself a writer first and downplayed his skills as a designer and artist, but as this book amply shows, his artistic efforts were commendable. His illustrations, charming in their own right, show that he clearly had an artistic vision of Middle-earth that buttressed his narratives. Rare indeed is the writer who can also illustrate his own fiction!

In 1937, when the subject of a U.S. edition of *The Hobbit* had arisen, Tolkien downplayed his own artistic efforts on the book. As for the illustrations:

> I am divided between knowledge of my own inability and fear of what American artists (doubtless of admirable skill) might produce. In any case I agree that all the illustrations ought to be by the same hand: four professional pictures would make my own amateurish productions look rather silly.

Tolkien sold himself short—his illustrations for *The Hobbit* are simply delightful. In fact, of the nine editions in print in the United States, only two feature the art of others—Alan Lee and Michael Hague.

This art book, with more than 200 reproductions, most in color, shows the artistic side of Tolkien: calligrapher, cartographer, book jacket designer, illustrator, and inveterate doodler—proof positive that he could not only write about Middle-earth, but capture it visually with delightful art that fans have loved over the years.

The text by Hammond and Scull is excellent and well-informed, as you'd expect.

The J.R.R. Tolkien Companion and Guide, by Christina Scull and Wayne G. Hammond (Houghton Mifflin, $70, boxed set). At this writing these books have not yet been published, but they promise to be invaluable and works of painstaking scholarship, like Scull and Hammond's other books about Tolkien. From the publisher's catalog copy:

> Designed to be the essential reference works for all readers and students, these volumes present the most thorough analysis possible of Tolkien's work within the important context of his life. *The Reader's Guide* includes brief but comprehensive alphabetical entries on a wide range of topics, including a who's who of important persons, a guide to places and institutions, details concerning Tolkien's source material, information about the political and social upheavals through which the author lived, the importance of his social circle, his service as an infantryman in World War I—even information on the critical reaction to his work and the "Tolkien cult." *The Chronology* details the parallel evolutions of Tolkien's work and his academic and personal life in minute detail. Spanning the entirety of his long life including nearly 60 years of active labor on his Middle-earth creations, and drawing on such contemporary sources as school records, war service files, biographies, correspondence, the letters of his close friend C.S. Lewis, and the diaries of W.H. Lewis, this book will be an invaluable resource for those who wish to gain a complete understanding of Tolkien's status as a giant of 20th-century literature.

Trade paperbacks of two of Tom Shippey's books.

J.R.R. Tolkien: Author of the Century, by Tom Shippey (Houghton Mifflin, $26 trade hardback, $14 trade paperback). An accessible, critical text by a writer who is sympathetic—in every sense of the word—to Tolkien, Shippey is a former Oxford professor who taught from the same syllabus used by Tolkien; furthermore, Shippey held the same Chair that Tolkien held at Leeds University—the Chair of English Language and Medieval Literature.

Shippey's thesis is that fantasy is the dominant literary mode of the 20th century; furthermore, by popular and critical acclaim, Tolkien's masterwork, *The Lord of the Rings*, is the fantasy book of the century and, therefore, Tolkien is the "most influential author of the century."

J.R.R. Tolkien: A Descriptive Bibliography, by Wayne G. Hammond with the assistance of Douglas A. Anderson (St. Paul's Bibliographies, hardback). Though out of print and in need of updating (it was published in 1993), this book focuses only on Tolkien's work, and provides a wealth of information unavailable anywhere else: books and periodicals are covered, with an emphasis on first appearances (described physically), with an essay on each major edition—*The Hobbit*'s entry, for instance, runs 15 pages. This is a detailed, exhaustive, and indispensable resource for book collectors.

JRR Tolkien's Sanctifying Myth: Understanding Middle-Earth, by Bradley J. Birzer and Joseph Pearce (Intercollegiate Studies Institute, $24.95, hardback). A well-written, well-researched study of Tolkien's spirituality; specifically, the influence of Roman Catholicism on the man and his work.

The Languages of Middle-earth, by Ruth S. Noel (Houghton Mifflin, $16, paperback). Unlike other authors, whose names, places, and, especially, languages are the products of sheer imagination with no linguistic underpinnings, Tolkien was a philologist—he loved words and their meanings, and was fluent in several languages and dialects. For instance, when a reader at Allen & Unwin, after reading *The Silmarillion*, criticized it for its "eye-splitting Celtic names," Tolkien responded, in a December 1937 letter, that "personally I believe (and here I believe I am a good judge) they are good, and a large part of the effect."

Tolkien knew whereof he spoke!

Noel's book—the first book of its kind, published in 1974—provides a useful introduction to Tolkien's imagined languages, but the serious student interested in linguistics might first want to examine the numerous language-related Websites that benefit from more recent scholarship.

Note: I feel that this book is overpriced, at $16 for a small paperback of 207 pages. For that kind of money, one would expect a hardback, not a mass-market paperback.

Lord of the Rings: The Mythology of Power, by Jane Chance (University Press of Kentucky, $19.95). An examination of the book in light of its mythology of power and its relevance to the 20th century.

Note: Tolkien had an active distaste of allegory, as he stated in the foreword to the second edition of *LotR*: "But I cordially dislike allegory in all its manifestations, and always have done so since I grew old and wary enough to detect its presence." It is not likely, then, that he would have favored the allegorical approach to this book.

The Magical Worlds of The Lord of the Rings: The Amazing Myths, Legends, and Facts Behind the Masterpiece, by David Colbert (Berkley Pub Group, $13, trade paperback). This book is very reader-friendly. It's a good introduction to the story behind the story, as it were, of Middle-earth, intended for young readers, new readers, and the general reader. Colbert is the author of a similar book, *The Magical Worlds of Harry Potter: A Treasury of Myths, Legends, and Fascinating Facts* (Broadway Books).

The Magical World of J.R.R. Tolkien, by Gareth Knight (Sun Chalice Books, £9.99, trade paperback). Knight bills himself as "one of the world's foremost authorities on ritual magic, the Western Mystery Tradition, and Qabalistic symbolism. He trained in Dion Fortune's Society of the Inner Light, and has spent a lifetime rediscovering and teaching the principles of magic as a spiritual discipline and method of self-realization." This is one of four books in a series called The Magical Worlds in which he examines the lives of the Inklings to show a linkage between their creative imaginations and the wisdom they glean thereby, and the power of magic as a manifestation of the human soul.

The Maps of Tolkien's Middle-earth, by Brian Sibley (Houghton Mifflin, $25, boxed set). A slipcased collection of four full-color, large-format maps illustrated by John Howe. Includes a 64-page hardback book "describing in detail the importance and evolution of geography within Tolkien's epic fiction."

Meditations on Middle Earth: New Writing on the Worlds of J.R.R. Tolkien, edited by Karen Haber (Griffin, $13.95, trade paperback). This is an original anthology of essays about Tolkien's fiction as seen (mostly) from the perspective of fantasy writers. An eclectic collection with essays of varying quality, the high points include pieces by Terry Windling, Douglas A. Anderson, and Ursula K. LeGuin, who has previously explicated Tolkien's use of rhythm and language in a previously published chapbook, *From Elfland to Poughkeepsie* (Pendragon Press). Other contributors include all the usual suspects: Harry Turtledove, Raymond Feist, Terry Pratchett, George R.R. Martin, and the late Poul Anderson.

Well-known Tolkien artist John Howe provides illustrations drawn in pencil, but these are minor efforts—rough sketches at best—and hardly representative of what, artwise, he is capable of.

Myth and Magic: The Art of John Howe (HarperCollins, $35, hardback). The conceptual artist for the Tolkien movies has assembled 250 of his sketches and paintings for this collection, drawing on *The Hobbit*, *The Lord of the Rings*, *The Silmarillion*, and *The History of Middle-earth*.

Myth & Middle-earth: Exploring the Medieval Legends Behind J.R.R. Tolkien's Lord of the Rings, by Leslie Jones (Open Road Pub, $14.95, trade paperback). In a 1951 letter to Milton Waldman—a 10,000 word explication on *The Lord of the Rings* and *The Silmarillion*—Tolkien wrote about the roots to *LotR* and said he desired to write an English myth, because other great countries had their respective myths:

"There was Greek, and Celtic, and Roman, Germanic, Scandinavian and Finnish (which greatly affected me); but nothing English...." Tolkien, of course, accomplished what he set out to do: to give England its own distinctive myth...This book acknowledges the obvious historical influences—Norse and Germanic—and also Celtic. A useful examination of myths from various countries that, in part, influenced or inspired Tolkien.

Myth Maker: J.R.R. Tolkien, by Anne E. Neimark, illustrated by Brad Weiman (Harcourt, $17, hardback). A biography for young readers, a straightforward accounting of his life, times, and literary works.

Myth Maker: J.R.R. Tolkien, by Anne Neimark (Bt Bound, $12.65, hardback). A biography for young readers, a straightforward accounting of Tolkien's life and work.

One Ring to Bind Them All: Tolkien's Mythology, by Anne C. Petty (University of Alabama Press, $18.95, trade paperback). This is an expanded edition, with a new introduction and an updated bibliography. A well-regarded, classic book examining the mythology of *The Hobbit* and *The Lord of the Rings*.

The People's Guide to J.R.R. Tolkien: Essays and Reflection on Middle-earth from TheOneRing.net, edited by Erica Challis (Cold Spring Press, $16.95, trade paperback, distributed by Simon & Schuster). In 1999, a Website (*www.TheOneRing.net*) was set up to provide news on the highly anticipated movie trilogy. In short order, it grew to encompass news, reviews, photo galleries, and so on, totaling more than 800 Web pages. It has become *the* premiere fan Website, and on it one can find much talk about the goings on in Hobbiton and beyond.

This book is a print version of the Website, with articles about Tolkien in general, with an emphasis on film coverage of the Jackson trilogy.

Its principal audience is the hard-core fan; new readers will likely be somewhat disoriented. Written by, and for, Tolkien fans—and I emphasize the word "fans" in its best sense: ardent admirers or devotees—this book is just as it is advertised. It is an informal, spirited discussion of all things in Middle-earth from frequent travelers who know and love the territory well.

A Question of Time: J.R.R. Tolkien's Road to Faerie, by Verlyn Flieger (Kent State University Press, $18, trade paperback). From the editor of *The Tolkien Legendarium: Essays on the History of Middle-earth* and *Splintered Light: Logos and Language in Tolkien's World*, *A Question of Time* investigates the importance of time and dream in his works. Granted access by the Tolkien estate and the Bodeleian Library in Oxford to unpublished material, Flieger sheds new light on Tolkien as a modern writer. "As a traveler between worlds, he was also a traveler in time, shuttling restlessly between the grubby, smoke-stained present of his own century and the faerian past of his imagination. It is this very oscillation that, paradoxically, makes him a modern writer...."

Readings on J.R.R. Tolkien, edited by Katie de Koster (Greenhaven Press, $34.95, hardback). An abridged collection of previously published essays, its audience is the advanced reader with some familiarity with Tolkien's principal works.

The Road to Middle-earth, by Tom Shippey (Houghton Mifflin, $13, trade paperback). In his preface to this third (revised and expanded edition) edition, Shippey writes:

> After Tolkien's death I felt increasingly that he would not have been happy with many of the things people said about his writings, and that someone with a similar background to his own ought to try to provide—as Tolkien and E.V. Gordon wrote in the "Preface" to their 1925 edition of *Sir Gawain and the Green Knight*—"a sufficient apparatus for reading [these remarkable works] with an appreciation as far as possible of the sort which its author may be supposed to have desired."

Shippey writes insightfully and authoritatively about Tolkien's sources of inspiration—literary and, especially, philological. Personally and professionally sympathetic to Tolkien, Shippey, in his afterword, writes: "This book's main purpose has been to provide the material for a more thorough and appreciative reading of Tolkien."

In that purpose, Shippey has succeeded admirably. Readers and students who want to read a critical study before venturing further will find this book accessible, informative, and illuminating, shedding considerable light on Tolkien's literary inspirations.

Splintered Light: Logos and Language in Tolkien's World, by Verlyn Fieger (Kent State University Press, $19, trade paperback). In his foreword to the second edition of *LotR*, Tolkien writes, "...[*The Lord of the Rings*] was primarily linguistic in inspiration and was begun in order to provide the necessary background of 'history' for Elvish tongues."

By the time Tolkien completed his history of Middle-earth, he emerged as a world-builder, a storyteller whose work displaced the fictional requirement of "the willing suspension of disbelief" (as Coleridge put it), by instilling a firm belief in Middle-earth because of its own reality.

This book is an excellent explication of Tolkien's languages as an outgrowth of the myths of Middle-earth, and essential reading for anyone who wants to fully appreciate Tolkien's background as a philologist that informs all of his fiction.

Tales before Tolkien: The Roots of Modern Fantasy, edited by Douglas A. Anderson (Del Rey, $27.95 hardback, $14.95 trade paperback). At this writing, this book has not yet been published, but Anderson provided me with a table of contents and his introduction, which allows this brief entry.

In his introduction, Anderson writes: "To better appreciate Tolkien's achievement one needs to better understand Tolkien's own roots, and the roots of modern fantasy." Anderson's thesis is that Tolkien's "greatness" was in his ability to synthesize diverse influences—literary and historical—to bring a new depth to fantasy literature.

The stories selected for this anthology are arranged chronologically and show the diversity of imaginative literature that inspired Tolkien.

Anderson rightly points out that the general reader with no familiarity of fantasy erroneously assumes that the field began, and ended, with Tolkien. This is not true, of course, because the beginnings of fantasy literature go back to the Anglo-Saxon poem, *Beowulf*, about which Tolkien had written extensively and authoritatively.

Among the contributors are George MacDonald, Andrew Lang, William Morris, H. Rider Haggard, L. Frank Baum, Lord Dunsany, William Hope Hodgson, Arthur Machen, and James Branch Cabell—a veritable "who's who" of literary practitioners who celebrated the literature of the fantastic.

The Journeys of Frodo, by Barbara Strachey (HarperCollins, $22.95, trade paperback). An atlas of 51 maps that shows the journey of Frodo from Hobbiton to Mount Doom in Mordor. A very useful guide for readers who want a roadmap, as it were, of his epic quest.

The Letters of J.R.R. Tolkien, edited by Humphrey Carpenter, with the assistance of Christopher Tolkien (Houghton Mifflin, $24.95 trade hardback, $15 trade paperback). A supplementary book to Carpenter's *J.R.R. Tolkien: A Biography*, this collection of letters is required reading. A prolific letter-writer, Tolkien's correspondence ranged from short one-page letters to a 10,000-word letter to a prospective publisher who asked for more information about *The Lord of the Rings* and *The Silmarillion*. Collecting family correspondence—most of them to his son Christopher—and business correspondence, this book gives us Tolkien in his own words.

The first letter in the book is to his fiancée, Edith Bratt. It is presumed to have been written in October 1914. The last letter was written to their daughter, Priscilla Tolkien, in August 1973.

Tolkien came from a generation when he felt that gentlemen acknowledge correspondence, and so he spent a disproportionate amount of time answering fan mail, which often dealt with technical questions about *LotR* that he delighted in answering. Certainly one wishes he would have spent the time in preparing promised books—*The Silmarillion*, regrettably, was published posthumously—and writing new fiction.

Given that Tolkien was a voluminous correspondent, there remains a score of letters that have never surfaced, from 1918 to 1937. Carpenter is not alone in his desire that these eventually come to light, because a revised edition, especially with letters from those missing years, would be welcomed by all.

Read Carpenter's biography to get an overall view of Tolkien's life and work, and then read this collection of letters to fully understand and appreciate Tolkien's many facets. **Note:** This edition has an expanded index.

Tolkien and The Lord of the Rings: A Guide to Middle-earth, by Colin Duriez (Hidden Spring, $17, trade paperback). A good overview, with a look at the man, his life, and his work; a look at *LotR*; an A-to-Z listing of people, places, things, and events; and a literary look at the principal fiction. New readers will find this to be a good place to start when exploring Middle-earth.

Tolkien Magnet Postcards, by the Brothers Hildebrandt (Running Press, $12.95, paperback). Though packaged as a book, it's actually a collection of magnetic postcards (4 x 6.5 inches), with art by the Brothers Hildebrandt, who published three consecutive Tolkien calendars for the U.S. market. These postcards are designed to be pulled out of the book and mailed.

The Tolkien Companion: The Indispensable Guide to the Wondrous Legends, History, Languages, and Peoples of Middle Earth [sic], by J.E.A. Tyler (Gramercy, trade hardback). Originally published in 1975, this reprint edition, published in 2000, obviously needs updating. It is a concordance to the people, places, and things in Middle-earth. Unlike Robert Foster's *The Complete Guide to Middle-earth* (Ballantine Books), this book lacks what I consider to be essential to this kind of book: page references to the source material. Also, this book is more interpretive than Foster's, whose matter-of-fact, objective approach may prove more useful, especially for students, scholars, and researchers.

Tolkien: Man and Myth: A Literary Life, by Joseph Pearce (Ignatius Press, $14.95, trade paperback). Readers looking for a biography will be mildly disappointed, because although this appears at first glance to be a biography, it is not. It is, however, a carefully written examination of the philosophies that informed Tolkien's worldview and the extent to which his religious views affected his fiction, notably *LotR*.

Tolkien: A Celebration: Collected Writings on a Literary Legacy (Ignatius Press, $12.95, trade paperback). A good collection of general essays on Tolkien's work, including George Sayer and Walter Hooper, both of whom knew him personally. As the publisher put it, "The works are examined theologically, philosophically, culturally, ecologically, mystically, and historically, as the various contributors seek to understand the profundity of Tolkien's achievement."

Tolkien and the Great War, by John Garth (Houghton Mifflin, $25, hardback). A general biography that examines World War I and its impact on Tolkien's fiction. Garth's thesis is that *The Lord of the Rings* is an outgrowth of his experiences during the war.

In a foreword to the second edition of *LotR*, Tolkien addressed the matter of WWI and its significance and impact on his novel, because many people felt it must have been allegorical:

It is neither allegorical nor topical.... The crucial chapter, 'The Shadow of the Past,' is one of the oldest parts of the tale. It was written long before the foreshadow of 1939 had yet become a threat of inevitable disaster.... Its sources are things long before in mind, or in some cases already written, and little or nothing in it was modified by the war that began in 1939 or its sequels.

Tolkien concluded this line of discussion by firmly stating that "The real war does not resemble the legendary war in its process or its conclusion."

Garth's thesis is intriguing, but Tolkien himself, although admitting that "an author cannot of course remain wholly unaffected by his experience," concludes in the end that it's fruitless to try to determine where the real world ends and the fantasy world begins in regard to fiction.

Tolkien's Ordinary Virtues: Exploring the Spiritual Themes of The Lord of the Rings, by Mark Eddy Smith (Intervarsity Press, $11, trade paperback). Smith is neither critic nor theologian, and his book is neither fish nor fowl; that is to say, the book falls short of the mark. A simplistic interpretation of *LotR*, this book lacks the depth that others with more specialized training would bring to the task. Written in a very conversational prose, this book is frothy fare.

Tolkien's Legendarium: Essays on The History of Middle-earth, edited by Verlyn Flieger and Carl F. Hostetter (Greenwood Publishing Group, $62.95, hardback). Though priced for libraries, this volume of Tolkien criticism is worth adding to your book collection. There are many familiar names in this collection, including Christina Scull and Wayne G. Hammond (the team that wrote *The J.R.R. Tolkien Companion and Guide* and *J.R.R. Tolkien: Artist and Illustrator*); Verlyn Flieger (author of *A Question of Time* and *Splintered Light*); Douglas A. Anderson, who contributed a bibliography of Christopher Tolkien's work; and others. There is also an essay of special interest by the late Rayner Unwin, who contributed "Early Days of Elder Days."

A Tolkien Treasury: Stories, Poems and Illustrations Celebrating the Author and His World, edited by Alida Becker (Courage Books, $14.98, trade hardback). A good introduction to Tolkien, this companion-style book is divided into two sections. The first, "Tolkien and Middle-earth," is of more general interest, with a biography, reviews of *LotR* (the early reviews by W.H. Auden and Edmund Wilson), a chronology of *The Hobbit* and *LotR*, and essays on Tolkien. An eight-page color insert of *The Lord of the Rings* paintings by Tim Kirk follows, reprinting plates from his calendar. The book's second section, "Frodo Lives: A Look at Tolkien Fandom" draws all its material from Tolkien fanzines, with poems, a parody, songs, haiku portraits, recipes, articles, and fannish pieces (that is, personal essays).

A miniature edition is also available ($4.95, Running Press). It is designed as a gift book and features poetry excerpts and art, notably Tim Kirk's.

Book Publishing: A Gentleman's Profession

Before his death on November 23, 2000, Rayner Unwin—son of Stanley Unwin of the publishing firm Allen & Unwin—reflected on how the book publishing industry had changed: It used to be a gentleman's profession when the editorial department had the final say, but now the sales and marketing department share that duty.

After determining the costs to publish *The Lord of the Rings* in three volumes, Rayner cabled his father that he believed it was a work of genius but would lose £1,000. His father replied that if he really felt it was a work of genius, he was free to lose the £1,000. In other words, the book was perceived not as a potential profit-maker, but a prestige book, the kind that enhances the reputation of the firm but not the bottom line.

Tolkien, who did not received an advance for the book, agreed to a profit-sharing plan in which he would get nothing until the book made its costs back; afterward, he and the publisher would share equally in the profits...if any.

Those terms turned out to be more profitable for Tolkien than the standard royalty arrangement (usually 10 percent of the retail cover price).

"In those happy days no second opinion was needed. If I said it was good enough to be published, it *was* [published]," said Rayner Unwin, in an interview that appeared on the extended DVD of *The Fellowship of the Ring*—the last interview he ever gave.

Time and circumstances change, though, and despite having the crown jewels of *The Hobbit* and *The Lord of the Rings*—the silmarilli of Tolkien's literary efforts—the firm's unfocused book line handicapped profitability.

In 1990, HarperCollins bought Unwin Hyman, formed after Allen & Undwin joined with Bell & Hyman in 1985. Taking draconian measures to fatten profits by trimming the book line and personnel, HarperCollins now was responsible for marketing, selling, and promoting Tolkien and his books.

It was the end of an era and a bittersweet end to Tolkien's original publisher, a highly regarded book firm that had weathered many previous storms.

Since then, HarperCollins has not only published Tolkien's books profitably, but has done so wisely and well.

Note: For those who want to know more about Stanley Unwin and Rayner Unwin, two books are worth your attention: *The Truth About Publishing,* by Stanley Unwin, and *George Allen: a Remembrancer*, by Rayner Unwin, which has a lengthy section detailing his decades-long involvement with Tolkien.

When all is said and done, credit must be given to Allen & Unwin for taking the considerable risk in publishing what seemed to the firm and to the author as a dubious proposition—a long romance tale with questionable financial prospects. To its credit, Allen & Unwin took that risk when no other publisher would and, by doing so, has earned its place in publishing history.

Tolkien's Art: A Mythology for England, by Jane Chance (University Press of Kentucky, $19.95, trade paperback). Chance is an English professor at Rice University. Originally published in 1980, this updated edition examines the sources and influences on Tolkien's work.

Tolkien's Middle-earth and Monsters Postcard Book, illustrated by John Howe, Ted Nasmith, Roger Garland, and Alan Lee (HarperCollins UK, £7.99, paperbound). Comprised of 40 postcards, which are designed to be extracted from the book, it features art by the best-known Tolkien illustrators.

Treasures from the Misty Mountains: A Collector's Guide to Tolkien, by James H. Gillam (Collector's Guide Pub, $30.95, trade paperback). The only book of its kind, with 500 color photos of Tolkien material (by and about him), the book is actually an illustrated bibliography. Published in 2001, just before the first movie (*The Fellowship of the Ring*) was released, it covers as much movie tie-in product and memorabilia as possible, but necessarily falls short because the preponderance of tie-in products that followed. Ideally, one would want more information—especially on out-of-print material—and more text. The book would ideally be published as a searchable CD-ROM, but this book is a very good place to start if you're looking to build a Tolkien collection and want to see what the actual items look like.

Visualizing Middle-earth, by Michael Martinez (XLibris Corporation, $21.99, self-published paperback). Technological advances have given self-published authors a viable alternative to remaining unpublished: Books can be printed in small runs or on demand—printing a single copy on demand (that is, when it sells). The upside is that it promises to bring to print some books that, otherwise, would never see print. The downside is that the reader must do his own research, because reviews from sources such as *Publishers Weekly*, *Booklist*, and *Library Journal* are unlikely—they don't review self-published books. That said, this book is a very informal book that the general reader would find interesting, as can be seen by the chapters: "Can Middle-earth survive the commercialization of Tolkien?" (My answer: yes.) "Love, Middle-earth Style," and "Would Sandra Bullock be a good Mrs. Isildur?" Hardcore fans will probably not care for this book's light touch or tone, but most people will find it accessible and modest, as is its author.

Women Among the Inklings: Gender, C.S. Lewis, J.R.R. Tolkien, and Charles Williams, by Candice Fredrick and Sam McBride (Greenwood Publishing Group, $62.95, hardback). Priced for libraries, this book has a very narrow focus—the male camaraderie that was at the heart of the Inklings and their attitudes toward women. For a broader look, consult *The Inklings Handbook*.

World of the Rings: The Unauthorized Guide to the Work of J.R.R. Tolkien, by Iain Lowson, Peter MacKenzie, and Keith Marshall (Reynolds & Hearn, $12, trade paperback). This book is principally concerned with the movie adaptations to a degree the average reader will find tediously excessive. Those seeking the story behind the movie are best advised to read Brian Sibley's authorized look at the visual adaptations, *The Lord of the Rings: The Making of the Movie Trilogy* (Houghton Mifflin).

CHAPTER 3

VISUAL ADAPTATIONS OF
The Lord of the Rings:
The Film and Related
Tie-In Book Products

The film industry is currently in a technological transition. The videotape is on its way to extinction, eventually to be replaced by the DVD format, with its vastly superior sound and picture quality and its enhanced storage capacity for more data. There will come a day when VHS tapes are no longer available—indeed, DVD rentals now exceed VHS rentals—and for that we can be grateful; VHS tapes are in every way inferior to the DVD format. For this reason, I do not recommend the VHS editions and will not discuss them here, because interested readers with DVD players will prefer compatible editions.

DVDs

The Fellowship of the Ring

Full-Screen ($29.95). This is the version released in the theaters, severely cropped to fit the conventional television screen. Typically, the left and right edges are simply chopped off to ensure the movie "fits" the television screen.

The second disc gives you a glimpse of the making of the movie—a behind-the-scenes look at the making of the film, numerous vignettes (short pieces, up to five minutes) exploring the culture and geography of Middle-earth, a preview of *The Two Towers*, the original TV and movie ads, the lovely Enya music video ("May It Be"), a preview of the video game version (in other words, an advertisement), and a preview of the Special Extended DVD Edition (another advertisement).

Director Peter Jackson states in an interview on the supplementary disc that he's not fond of the term "Director's Cut" because it implies that what was released in the theater was not what the director had intended. In his case, however, Jackson states that the film, as released on the big screen, was *exactly* what he intended, but he's glad to have the opportunity to issue an extended DVD set, so he can incorporate additional footage and supplementary material.

I do not recommend the full-screen format, because it sacrifices footage for format.

Wide-Screen ($29.95). This is the version released in the theaters with a picture proportion that, on a conventional television set, will mirror that which is seen on the movie screen. Termed letterboxing, this format will yield black bars on the top and bottom of the picture, which some people find distracting. (Solution: Buy a wide-screen television, if you're a real movie buff).

This is the preferred edition. It is priced right, and it has the theatrical release with additional footage (30 minutes) incorporated into the film itself and the aforementioned disc of supplementary material.

The expanded DVD set of The Fellowship of the Ring.

For fans who want the additional scenes and some of the supplementary bonus material on the second disc, this is a recommended buy.

Platinum Series Special Extended DVD Edition ($39.99). This is the extended wide-screen version with two additional DVDs, "The Appendices," which includes documentaries and art galleries, for an in-depth, behind-the-scenes look at how the movie was made.

This is *the* edition of choice—the best buy: all the features you'd want at a reasonable price.

Platinum Series Special Extended DVD Edition Collector's Gift Set ($79.92). This is for hard-core, serious collectors only: a pair of small bookends, a new version of the documentary on the film produced by National Geographic, trading cards, a selection of special editions of the fan club magazine—all encased in a collector's box designed by Tolkien illustrator Alan Lee.

Don't buy this for yourself—save your money and get the $39.99 edition—but consider buying if you want to give a Tolkien fan a gift to remember.

One of the two pieces sculpted by Weta Workshop for inclusion in the Collector's Gift Set of The Fellowship of the Ring.

In an interview on the extended DVD, Peter Jackson said that he's a big fan of the extended DVD precisely because it does what can't be done on the movie screen—restore footage and provide back matter that greatly enhance one's appreciation of the film. In the case of *The Fellowship of the Ring*, the "plain vanilla" edition is anything but. The first disc is the theatrical release with integrated additional footage, and the second disc is jam-packed with the kind of features moviegoers love.

The attention to detail shown in the movie release is also evident in the DVD release. Peter Jackson had the foresight to realize that documenting every facet of the making of *The Fellowship of the Ring* was critical for its DVD release. Therefore, on the supplemental disc, there's an extended behind-the-scenes look at how the movie was made (short features irritatingly termed "featurettes"), with segments on "Finding Hobbiton," "Hobbiton Comes Alive," "Believing the World of Bree," and more, all of which give the viewer a sense of the geography and people of Middle-earth as well as the actors and their perceptions—especially to new fans who haven't read the book and are likely to be confused by the large cast of characters.

I also enjoyed the Enya music video "May It Be" and all the original theatrical trailers and television spots. I didn't even mind the not-so-blatant advertising for other products, such as the preview of *The Two Towers*, the preview of the *Two Towers* video game, and Elijah Wood (who plays Frodo Baggins) thumping the drum for the extended DVD edition. There's plenty of room for such supplemental material, so what's the harm? It's there if you want to see it.

Retailing for $29.95, the two-disc DVD set of *The Fellowship of the Ring* sells as low as $22 from online merchants.

As good as the full-screen and wide-screen editions are, the *real* winner, by a wide margin, is the Platinum Series Special Extended Edition. Retailing for $39.99, the online price is approximately $27.99—a bargain in anyone's book, especially in this

The Art of the DVD

In their eagerness to capitalize on sales, studios have rushed to reissue their movies in DVD format. Until recently, however, the reissues have largely been afterthoughts, with content reflecting their lack of planning—neither adding nor subtracting, the DVD is a facsimile of the VHS edition from years ago. And let's face it, it's a waste of the medium, because a DVD can hold so much more content than a VHS tape, with the added benefit that content on a DVD is more accessible, whereas a VHS tape must be fast-forwarded or rewound—a real aggravation when seeking a specific scene.

Had Peter Jackson released *The Fellowship of the Ring* on DVD as shown exactly on the movie screen, few people could complain; the movie was magnificent and a high point in film history. Indeed, taken as a whole, the movies—buttressed by their excellent DVD releases and (mostly) excellent tie-in products—have raised the bar for future filmmakers who want to give good value to consumers.

case, because this edition offers better packaging, more supplemental printed material, and—best of all—*two* additional DVDs of material not available on the full-screen or wide-screen editions.

A lot of thinking and imagination went into developing these packages, which show an astonishing attention to detail. Even before I read Sibley's book on the making of the movie trilogy, I could tell that Peter Jackson was a perfectionist, the kind of person who goes to extraordinary lengths to get the tiniest details right. He is most assuredly a precise and exacting man, and it certainly shows in how he envisioned the extended DVD package.

First, the packaging: The box itself shows the Doors of Durin, the dwarf-doors that can only be opened when the right words are spoken. Inside the box, five panels unfold to reveal a printed booklet and four DVDs—the extended movie in two DVDs and two DVDs comprising the appendices ("Part One: From Book to Vision" and "Part Two: From Vision to Reality").

The booklet's case is illustrated, appropriately, with a watercolor by film conceptualizer Alan Lee, who depicts a pivotal scene when the fellowship has opened Durin's Door and are dwarfed by the cavernous Mines of Moria, with steps, columns, and archways receding in the background; a light from Gandalf's staff provides scant illumination of the vast hall, most of which is covered in shadow.

The case also has a map showing the route of the Fellowship, starting from the Shire, winding its way through the mountains where the Mines of Moria are located, and ending northwest of Mordor at Amon Hen, near the Falls of Rauros.

As for the contents, the booklet accompanying the DVD set tells us that "with no constraints on the film's running time, director Peter Jackson extended the movie by more than 30 minutes—with more character development, more humor, more story, more of J.R.R. Tolkien's world." It is, then, an *expanded* version of the movie, with the new scenes seamlessly integrated into the whole, and new music scored to ensure continuity.

It is, in short, the preferred version of the movie.

In the note explaining the two-disc appendices, we are told that:

> Making the motion picture trilogy of *The Lord of the Rings* is certainly a once-in-a-lifetime opportunity, and Peter Jackson wanted to make sure he captured it *all* for posterity.... Everyone—cast, crew, Weta Workshop and Digital—contributed their time, resources, treasures, and memories to this DVD.

The booklet provides a guide to scenes, with notations on the extended scenes—handy if you want to go directly to them, instead of viewing the movie from start to finish. To visually explain the appendices, a four-panel "tree," with leaves branching out, explains the interrelationship of the additional material. For instance, early storyboards branch out to "The Prologue," "Orc Pursuit Into Lothlórien," and "Sarn Gebir Rapids Chase."

Just as the movie *flows*, the tree-like flow chart shows how the contents of the appendices have been grouped thematically, so areas of interest are colocated and instantly accessible. Complete with still frames and video clips, the appendices—mirroring Tolkien's own appendices in *The Lord of the Rings*—comprise the back story. It's there if you want it, but it's not necessary to enjoy the movie itself. Middle-earth, after all, is fictional world-building on a grand scale, and the newcomer will find a detailed road map to be most useful.

The only thing that these DVDs do not provide is the requisite screen with which to properly view it. Clearly, some movies are made for the big screen—the large canvas is needed to show it off to the best advantage—and, in my opinion, nothing less than the best will do. (A flat plasma-screen television of at least 42 inches will set you back $4,500, though a projection television is a reasonable alternative, with a screen as large as 70 inches, currently available for $3,000 or less.)

For most of us, however, the best we can hope for—or afford—is a Sony Trinitron or Sony Wega. Both are excellent choices, especially the sets in wide-screen proportion.

Then sit back and let the movie take you away to Tolkien's imaginative universe, as envisioned by Peter Jackson, who has carefully and lovingly brought the book to the screen—and, by doing so, has introduced millions of people to the wondrous world of Middle-earth.

Easter Eggs in Middle-earth

Software programmers invented the "Easter egg," a hidden, special feature in the software—usually a message, picture, or credits—that can be seen only when certain keys are pressed. In other words, you have to know exactly where to look and how to access it.

In the extended DVD of *The Fellowship of the Ring*, there are two Easter eggs, if you know where to look. Usually, Easter eggs are well-kept secrets known only to insiders, but the Internet has changed that: an Internet search will turn up numerous references to the aforementioned Easter eggs, so my sharing them with you is not a sin.

Easter egg #1: On disc one, click down to the scene of the "Council of Elrond" and then highlight it. Click down and an image of the One Ring will appear. Click on it and Peter Jackson introduces a hilarious MTV spoof, of which I shall say nothing—you will understand why words fail me after you view it—except to say that I wish someone would do a short film parody, because this small sampling had me in tears.

Easter egg #2: On disc two, the trailer to *The Two Towers*. To access it, go to the menu selection and click down to the far right hand side of the screen where scene 48 is located. Then click down on the remote control and a hidden symbol, two towers, will pop up. Click on it to play the trailer.

The Two Towers

Full-Screen ($29.95). Visually edited to fit a conventional television screen, this two-disc set includes the theatrical trailers, two documentaries on the making of the film, short vignettes on the culture and creatures of Middle-earth, the music video of "Gollum's Song" by Emiliana Torrini, a short film by Sean Astin, a short behind-the-scenes preview of *The Return of the King*, a preview of the video game based on the movie, and—if you have a compatible computer—links to an online Website with exclusive content.

Again, my recommendation is to forgo the full-screen version in favor of the widescreen (letterboxed) edition.

Wide-Screen ($29.95). This is a good value. The letterbox format allows you to see the movie exactly as it was shown at the theater, with the bonus disc of supplementary material.

The Platinum Series Extended Edition: Wide-Screen ($39.99). This is the best value. It is not only in wide-screen format, with additional footage (40 additional minutes incorporated in the original film), but includes two discs that comprise the appendices with a wealth of material that is available nowhere else.

The Platinum Series Extended Edition: Collector's Gift Set ($79.92). This edition adds the collectibles that are available nowhere else: a polystone statue of Gollum, with a printed companion piece from concept sketch to digital character, and a DVD highlighting the Weta Workshop.

This is a good buy, my precious! We wants it!

From Book to the Silver Screen

As early as 1958, Tolkien and his publisher were approached by Hollywood with an offer to bring *The Lord of the Rings* to the big screen. Seeking—as he and his publisher put it—a large amount of cash or kudos, they were open to any overtures.

The first came from Morton Grady Zimmerman, who proposed an animated feature and presented a story line to Tolkien, who found it incomprehensible. In an April 1958 letter to Rayner Unwin, Tolkien wrote: "I should say Zimmerman, the constructor of this [storyline], is quite incapable of excerpting or adapting the 'spoken words' of the book. He is hasty, insensitive, and impertinent.... He does not *read* books."

Peter Jackson's Quest for the Ring

"The Lord of the Rings remains one of the greatest books ever written. All I am offering is an interpretation, but hopefully one that will take the fantasy film to an entirely new level of adventurousness and believability."

—Peter Jackson

It was Tolkien's first encounter with the Hollywood film industry, and not unlike the experience of most writers who discover, often too late, that the movie and book industry sometimes make strange bedfellows.

Thankfully, the proposed animated feature was never made, which, in retrospect, is probably a good thing. From Hollywood's point of view, *The Lord of the Rings* presents several problems in terms of adaptation, which is why no reasonably faithful version *could* be made until recently. Here are the principal reasons why:

1. **Length and Cost**: The average screenplay is approximately 120 pages of script—one page per screen minute. The half-million words that comprise *The Lord of the Rings*, however, is a complex novel that cannot be compressed to 120 pages without sacrificing its story.

   In order to adequately translate the book to film, it would require an unprecedented commitment on the part of a studio, because it would mean taking a considerable risk. Such a costly endeavor, in time and money, is enough to scare most studios away.

   In this instance, the risk extended to three films made simultaneously, to keep costs down and maintain continuity, which translated to almost $300 million, making *The Lord of the Rings* the most expensive movie ever made.

   Playing high-stakes poker on this scale is enough to make any studio executive blanch. On the upside is the prospect that the film could potentially be a billion-dollar franchise (or more), but the prospect of its downside was daunting—the studio could not only lose a fortune on the first movie, but go on to compound it with two more possible financial flops, which would almost certainly force the sale of the studio itself to another company.

2. **Director Commitment**: The average film takes one year out of a director's life, but this project would require a three-year commitment, which is more than most directors can afford. In addition, it would take a director who could—to quote from *The Hobbit*—"smell elves": someone who not only loved the book but wanted to do it justice and ensure fidelity, to capture the essence of Middle-earth on film.

3. **Special Effects**: From a technical point of view, this presented the largest challenge. Since *Star Wars* debuted in 1975, special effects have become increasingly sophisticated. In fact, as filmmakers are fond of saying, anything that can be imagined can be brought to life on the big screen through special effects.

   For a fantasy film, *The Lord of the Rings* presents formidable challenges. It is an imaginative work translating to hundreds of potential scenes that would have to be brought to life—painstaking, difficult work, at best.

   In short, the special effects wizards would have to perform their best magic to convince people that Middle-earth does indeed exist.

Although the opening weekend is critical, the second weekend is more telling; if attendance drops significantly, the movie will likely be a financial bust. Marketing initially brings the movie to the public's attention, but good reviews and, especially, strong word of mouth combine to pack the theaters with not only new customers but repeat viewers, as well, for (hopefully) a long engagement.

As director Peter Jackson put it (*Time* magazine, December 2, 2002), "The pressures on us before the first film came out were, obviously, fairly extreme. We never talked about that much. Nonetheless, it was there with you every single day."

Thankfully, "The gamble paid off," wrote *Time* magazine's Jess Cagle. "*Fellowship* turned out to be the second highest grossing film of 2001 and firmly established Jackson as the next George Lucas. The movie went on to gross $860 million worldwide and was honored with 13 Oscar nominations, including Best Picture."

Books

Movie Tie-In Editions

The official line of movie tie-in books is worth your attention. Published by Houghton Mifflin—the U.S. book publishing company that has in print nearly 100 different editions of books by and about Tolkien—the tie-in books are oversized, in full color, and available both in hardback and trade paperback.

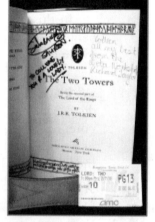

As with the DVDs, the movie tie-in books were planned as an integral part of the movie package: When moviegoers went into bookstores, they'd find these familiar books on the shelves.

A warmly inscribed copy of The Two Towers, *from the collection of Colleen Doran, bearing the signatures of Sala Baker (the actor who played Sauron) and Richard Taylor (Weta workshop creative director).*

Overview

The Lord of the Rings Official Movie Guide (Houghton Mifflin, $24.95 hardback, $14.95 trade paperback). This is the first book in this series, which accurately bills itself as:

> ...a celebration of the films...a lavishly illustrated behind-the-scenes guide which includes full-color photos of the cast, locations, sets, monsters and costumes, together with exclusive interviews with Peter Jackson and all the principal cast. It also features an entertaining overview of the conception, design and filming of the trilogy over the last five years...."

The movie tie-in edition of The Lord of the Rings Official Movie Guide.

The Lord of the Rings: The Making of the Movie Trilogy, by Brian Sibley (Houghton Mifflin, $17.95, trade paperback). To be read after *The Official Movie Guide*, this is a close-up, in-depth look at the making of all the movies, with more than 300 color photos, extensive interviews with the cast and crew, and a behind-the-scenes look at every aspect of the production of these movies.

The Fellowship of the Ring

The Lord of the Rings: The Fellowship of the Ring Photo Guide, edited by Alison Sage (Houghton Mifflin, $9.95, trade paperback). Intended for children (ages 8 and up), this chronological, photo-illustrated overview of the movie emphasizes images over text: designed to be an introduction to the movie.

The movie tie-in edition of The Lord of the Rings: The Making of the Movie Trilogy.

The Lord of the Rings: The Fellowship of the Ring Insider's Guide, by Brian Sibley (Houghton Mifflin, $6.95, trade paperback). Intended for children (ages 8 and up), this is an overview.

The Lord of the Rings: The Fellowship of the Ring Visual Companion (Houghton Mifflin, $19.95, trade hardback). Especially useful to new readers, this oversized encyclopedia provides a photo-illustrated guide to the characters, places, landscapes, events, and key artifacts of the movie, with explanatory text. This 72-page book includes historical information (an overview of the Rings of Power and of the Last Alliance of Elves and Men), and the characters and places: Hobbits, Bag End, Bilbo Baggins, Frodo Baggins, Samwise Gamgee, Meriadoc Brandybuck, Peregrin Took, Men, Bree, Aragorn, Boromir, Elves, Elrond, Arwen, Legolas, Lothlórien, the Lady Galadriel, Dwarves, Gimli, Moria, the Istari, Gandalf the Grey, Saruman the White, the Dark Powers, Orcs, Uruk-Hai, and the Nazgûl.

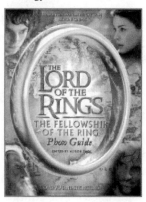

The movie tie-in edition of The Fellowship of the Ring Photo Guide, *for children.*

The Lord of the Rings: The Art of The Fellowship of the Ring, by Gary Russell (Houghton Mifflin, $35, trade hardback). This is a "must have" book. With more than 500 black-and-white and color images, from rough conceptual pencil sketches to finished paintings, this is an in-depth look at the concepts, storyboards, and images rendered by Alan Lee, John Howe, and others who conceptualized the look of the movie. The art is supplemented with interviews

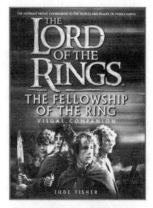

The movie tie-in edition of The Fellowship of the Ring Visual Companion.

The movie tie-in edition of The Lord of the Rings: The Art of The Fellowship of the Ring.

conducted with Peter Jackson, Richard Taylor (head of Weta), and many of the 200 artists at Weta.

In the introduction to the book, Russell writes:

> Although this is a celebration of the frequently unseen, often ignored aspects of film-making (from concept to execution) rather than a traditional behind-the-scenes publication—there are other books designed to do that—it is worth spending some time on introductions before "looking at the pictures.

The result is a fascinating book for anyone who wants to know how a movie is conceived—how it is originally envisioned by conceptual artists, who then work with other artists to give shape and form to the final product.

The Two Towers

The Lord of the Rings: The Two Towers Photo Guide (Houghton Mifflin, $8.95, trade paperback). For children ages 8 and up, this emphasizes photos with simplified, explanatory text. (A page of stickers of the main characters is bound into the back of the book.)

The Lord of the Rings: The Two Towers—Creatures (Houghton Mifflin, $8.95, trade paperback). For children (ages 8 and up), a pictorial overview of creatures—fair and foul—seen in *The Two Towers*. Attached to the inside back cover is a fold-out poster of Gandalf confronting the Balrog on the Bridge at Khazad-dûm.

The Lord of the Rings: The Two Towers Visual Companion, by Jude Fisher (Houghton Mifflin, $18.95, hardback). Like her previous book, this is a photo-illustrated

The movie tie-in edition of The Two Towers Photo Guide, *for children.*

The movie tie-in edition of The Two Towers: Creatures.

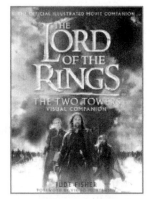

The movie tie-in edition of The Two Towers Visual Companion.

guide (more than 100) to the characters, places, and landscapes of this movie. Included is a four-page, fold-out battle plan of the attack on Helm's Deep.

The Lord of the Rings: The Art of the Two Towers, by Gary Russel (Houghton Mifflin, $35, hardback). Like his previous art book on *The Fellowship of the Ring*, this book is a "must buy." With more than 600 conceptual sketches—pencils, watercolors, photographs of models, and finished pieces—this book shows how the text of Tolkien's novel was visually developed into designs that were finalized for the movie itself.

The movie tie-in edition of The Lord of the Rings: The Art of the Two

The Return of the King

The Lord of the Rings: The Return of the King Photo Guide, edited by David Brawn (Houghton Mifflin, $8.95, trade paperback). Written for children (ages 8 and up), with a "Family Tree" pullout, this is understandably heavy on photos and light on text.

The Lord of the Rings: Gollum, edited by Brian Sibley, with Andy Serkis (Houghton Mifflin, $9.95, trade paperback). Written for children (ages 8 and up), this book thoroughly looks at the CGI-created character Gollum, as interpreted by Andy Serkis.

The Lord of the Rings: The Return of the King Visual Companion, by Jude Fisher (Houghton Mifflin, $18.95, trade hardback). Like its predecessors, this principally showcases the people and geography of Middle-earth.

The Lord of the Rings: The Art of The Return of the King, by Gary Russell ($35, hardback, Houghton Mifflin). Like its two sister books, this is a "must buy." Jampacked with hundreds of conceptual designs—pencil renderings, watercolors, and finished paintings—it shows how the book was visually interpreted from its basic text to finished film.

The Lord of the Rings: Weapons and Warfare, by Chris Smith, with John Howe (Houghton Mifflin, $29.95, trade hardback; $18.95, trade paperback). One of the most challenging and time-consuming aspects of making this movie trilogy was manufacturing the diverse weapons used in combat, from close-in fighting to force-on-force engagements. This book catalogs and discusses the various weapons wielded by friend and foe alike.

According to Weta director Richard Taylor, "We designed and made 48,000 pieces of armor and had four people working 10 hours a day just producing chain mail. We also produced 2,000 weapons, including swords, spears, pikes and maces, longbows, crossbows, daggers, knives and axes."

The Official *Lord of the Rings* Fan Club

Fan clubs are obviously for the hard-core fans. In this case, it's for the die-hard Tolkien fans who also happen to love the movie and simply can't get enough, despite the mountain of merchandised products available—the *LotR* geeks, in other words.

Two issues of The Lord of the Rings Fan Club Magazine, *published by Decipher.*

The annual membership is $29.95, which buys you a subscription (six issues, bi-monthly) of *The Lord of the Rings Official Fan Club Magazine*, a 10-percent discount on merchandise, 10-day advance notification on new products, and access to its online community.

The key benefit is the magazine, which is professionally produced. It is a letter-size publication of approximately 80 pages, with the usual material you'd expect to find in a fan club-oriented magazine: a mail column (too cutely titled "Mailbaggins"), a news column, profiles on those involved in the making of the film, interviews with actors, a behind-the-scenes look at the craftsmen and artists who produced goods for the movies, and so on.

For those who are newcomers, back issues are also available, though at collector's prices—$45 for the first issue and $30 for all other issues thereafter.

Chapter 4

Sound Advice:
Audio Adaptations

In a letter to Rayner Unwin (*The Letters of J.R.R. Tolkien*, August 29, 1952), Tolkien wrote:

> I have recently made some tape-recordings of parts of the Hobbit and The Lord (notably the Gollum-passages and some pieces of "Elvish") and was much surprised to discover their effectiveness as recitations, and (if I may say so) my own effectiveness as a narrator, I do a very pretty Gollum and Treebeard.

According to Humphrey Carpenter, in *J.R.R. Tolkien: A Biography*, Tolkien was staying with a friend of C.S. Lewis, George Sayer, who owned a tape recorder. Initially suspicious of the newfangled device, Tolkien "pretended to regard Sayer's machine with great suspicion, pronouncing the Lord's Prayer in Gothic into the microphone to cast out any devils that might be lurking within." Tolkien, however, warmed up to the machine and later bought one himself, "and began to amuse himself by making further tapes of his work."

The Sayer recording was eventually issued by Caedmon Records on an LP, then reissued on cassette and CD, under the title *The J.R.R. Tolkien Audio Collection*.

Though not all of Tolkien's works have been adapted for audio, the principal works are available as straight readings and dramatizations, on cassette and CD.

Purists will undoubtedly prefer an unabridged reading to an abridged dramatization, but give the latter a try, preferably before you buy. The dramatizations are not necessarily better or worse than an unabridged reading, but clearly *different*. It's an audio adaptation as contrasted to a movie, which is an audiovisual adaptation.

An encyclopedic listing of every edition, U.S. and U.K., of every audio adaptation ever produced is beyond the scope of this book; I've limited my list to U.S. editions that are still in production, unless there's a notable U.K. edition for which there is no U.S. equivalent.

ISBN numbers are provided for each edition, to distinguish it from all others. When ordering these products from your bookseller, the title and ISBN are especially useful in identifying the specific edition.

J.R.R. Tolkien and the Art of the Spoken Word

The act of storytelling is steeped in the oral tradition—a tradition Tolkien celebrated. Not surprisingly, Tolkien, though not a professional reader, was an effective reader of his own work. An exacting writer, he reads carefully, precisely, relishing the sounds of the individual words.

The CD paper jacket for an insert of The Hobbit *from the British gift pack edition. On this CD, Tolkien reads excerpts from the book.*

To hear Tolkien's own voice, especially his delightful and spirited interpretation of Gollum, is to hear the character come alive in a unique way—well worth the price of admission by itself. It makes one wish that Tolkien had recorded more of his work, and in a professional studio, instead of these informal recordings made on monophonic equipment.

Publishers Weekly, reviewing *The J.R.R. Tolkien Audio Collection*, said that "The charming voice of Tolkien, bringing Middle English accenting to the craggy characters of the Middle-earth, is irresistible." I concur. The master's voice reads selections from *The Hobbit, The Fellowship of the Ring, The Two Towers, The Return of the King*, and *The Adventures of Tom Bombadil*.

In addition, Christopher Tolkien reads from *The Silmarillion*: "Of Beren and Lúthien," "Of the Darkening of Valinor," and "Of the Flight of the Noldar."

Though Christopher Tolkien, with his precise British accent, gives a good reading, my preference is for his father's, whose readings are more spirited and passionate, and in which fictional characters take on their own, distinctive voices, lending a depth that a "straight" reading cannot match. J.R.R. Tolkien, it seems, had a touch of dramatic actor in him, which his son lacks.

Whether one prefers the father or the son, or the material from *The Lord of the Rings* or *The Silmarillion*, one fact remains clear: The sole recording of its kind, this audio collection is most definitely a "must hear."

Audio Adaptations

Farmer Giles of Ham and Other Stories (Houghton Mifflin, $15, ISBN 0618114807). An abridged reading by Derek Jacobi on two cassettes.

The Fellowship of the Ring (Recorded Books, $49.99, ISBN 0788789813). An unabridged recording by Rob Inglis on 16 CDs, running time is 20 hours.

The Hobbit (Recorded Books, $39, ISBN 0788789821). An unabridged recording by Rob Inglis on 10 CDs, running time is 11.25 hours.

The Hobbit (Bantam Books-Audio, $25.95, ISBN 0553471074). A dramatization by the BBC.

The Hobbit (Houghton Mifflin, $25, ISBN 0618087850). An abridged recording by Martin Shaw on four cassettes.

The Hobbit (Bantam Books-Audio, $39.95, ISBN 0553455621). A dramatization by the BBC. Five CDs.

The Hobbit (Bantam Books-Audio, $25.95, ISBN 0807288837). A dramatization by the BBC. Cassettes.

The Hobbit (Bantam Books-Audio, $39.95, ISBN 0807288845). BBC Radio dramatization. Four CDs.

J.R.R. Tolkien Audio Collection (Harper Audio, $25, ISBN 155994675X). An abridged recording of selections read by J.R.R. Tolkien from *The Hobbit, The Lord of the Rings,* and *The Adventures of Tom Bombadil.* Portions of *The Silmarillion* are read by his son, Christopher Tolkien. Running time: 4.5 hours. (This was originally issued by Caedmon as an LP record.)

J.R.R. Tolkien Audio Collection (HarperAudio, $25, ISBN 0694525707). CD.

J.R.R. Tolkien reads an excerpt from The Hobbit. One CD, a component of *The Hobbit* Gift Pack (HarperCollins UK, £19.99, ISBN 0007105096). The pack consists of a hardback edition (regrettably printed on pulp paper), eight color postcards, a foldout map by John Howe, and a CD recording of Tolkien reading the encounter between Bilbo Baggins and Gollum.

J.R.R. Tolkien Reads The Hobbit and The Fellowship of the Ring (Caedmon Audio, $12, ISBN 0694522236). Excerpted readings by J.R.R. Tolkien on two cassettes.

Letters From Father Christmas (Houghton Mifflin, $15, ISBN 0618087842). Unabridged reading by Derek Jacobi. Two cassettes.

The Lord of the Rings performed by J.R.R. Tolkien (Caedmon Audio, $24, ISBN 0898452236). Excerpted readings by J.R.R. Tolkien on cassette.

The Lord of the Rings (Bantam Books-Audio, $69.95, ISBN 0553456539). A dramatization by the BBC on 13 CDs. Boxed set.

The Lord of the Rings (Bantam Books-Audio, $59.95, ISBN 0553472283). A boxed set. A dramatization by the BBC.

The Lord of the Rings (Soundelux Audio Publications, $49.95, ISBN 0881422703). A dramatization by Mind's Eye on 12 cassettes, running time is 12 hours.

The Lord of the Rings (Soundelux Audio Publications, $59.95, ISBN 1559351209). A dramatization by Mind's Eye on nine CDs.

The Lord of the Rings (Recorded Books, $129.99, ISBN 1402516274). An unabridged reading by Rob Inglis on 30 CDs, running time approximately 48 hours.

Pearl and Sir Orfeo (HarperCollins Audiobooks, $14.95, ISBN 0001053744). Two poems as translated by J.R.R. Tolkien, read by Terry Jones, on two cassettes.

The Return of the King (Recorded Books, $49.99, ISBN 0788789848). An unabridged recording read by Rob Inglis on 16 CDs, running time is 15 hours.

Roverandom (HarperCollins AudioBooks, $15, ISBN 0001055356). An abridged reading by Derek Jacobi. Two cassettes.

The Silmarillion (Bantam Books-Audio, $64.95, ISBN 0553456067). An unabridged reading by Martin Shaw on 13 CDs.

The Silmarillion (Bantam Books-Audio, $59.95, ISBN 0553525409). An unabridged reading by Martin Shaw on 12 audio cassettes.

Sir Gawain and the Green Knight (Trafalgar Square, $14.95, ISBN 0001053736). Read by Terry Jones. Two cassettes, unabridged.

Tales from the Perilous Realm (BBC Radio Collection, $16.95, ISBN 0563401427). A dramatization by Brian Sibley. Two cassettes.

Tales from Tolkien (BBC Radio Collection, £15.99, ISBN 0563401427). Performed by Michael Hordern, Brian Blessed, and Nigel Planer. Dramatizations of four Tolkien works: *Farmer Giles of Ham*, *Smith of Wootton Major*, *The Adventures of Tom Bombadil*, and "Leaf by Niggle."

The Two Towers (Recorded Books, $49.99, ISBN 078878983X). An unabridged recording read by Rob Inglis on 14 CDs, running time is 16.75 hours.

Musical Adaptations

I would draw some of the great tales in fullness, and leave many only placed in the scheme, and sketched. The cycles should be linked to a majestic whole, and yet leave scope for other minds and hands, wielding paint and music and drama....

—J.R.R. Tolkien, in a letter to Milton Waldman in late 1951.

More than any other fantasy work, *The Lord of the Rings*—filled with romantic imagery, poetry, songs, and verse—has inspired musicians to interpret the book. Though most of these are by fans who share music files online or self-publish in minuscule printings, the commercially produced CDs, licensed through Tolkien Enterprises or approved by the Tolkien Estate, add a new, aural dimension to the enjoyment of Tolkien's works.

With those thoughts in mind, here's some sound advice: If you are seriously interested in sampling some of the music, begin your search at *www.tolkien-music.com*, which has an alphabetical listing and links to 872 artists who have set Tolkien's fiction to music. In addition, the site has a page of links that provide further information and discussions about Tolkien-inspired music.

Given the sheer numbers of recordings, most home-brewed, I'll restrict my discussion to commercially produced recordings available directly from the publisher or from *www.amazon.com*.

For most Tolkien fans who have seen and enjoyed the movies, the logical place to begin is the official soundtracks, which are, in a word, breathtaking. Composed and conducted by Howard Shore, and performed by the New Zealand Symphony Orchestra, the music—as it must—complements but does not overwhelm the on-screen visuals.

"Opera. That's how I'm thinking of it—as if I were composing an opera," Howard Shore told Brian Sibley in *The Lord of the Rings: The Making of the Movie Trilogy*. Shore's musical interpretation is a seamless fit to the film itself. For instance, for *The Fellowship of the Ring*, "Concerning Hobbits" is lighthearted and playful, which contrasts sharply with the darker tones that inevitably follow as Sam Gamgee and Frodo Baggins leave all that's familiar and comfortable behind, to set out on a perilous journey. Another cut, "The Bridge of Khazad-dûm," is dark and ominous, and uses drumbeats as a musical motif to underscore the war-drums as the Fellowship is pursued through the Mines of Moria, where Gandalf the Grey falls in battle with the dreaded Balrog.

Peter Jackson told Howard Shore, in *The Lord of the Rings: The Making of the Movie Trilogy*, that he was largely on his own with only the most general directions. "I really don't have any director-type notes. It's up to you to wrestle with the performance of it." He then turns to Brian Sibley and says, "I'm tone deaf and really don't know a thing about the creation of music. So I limit my input to saying things like 'Could that be a little bit quieter?' or 'Maybe that could be a bit more exciting,' and, amazingly, Howard always seems to find a way to make it happen.'"

Though the selections are mostly symphonic, there are vocals—haunting, evocative, memorable. For *The Fellowship of the Ring*, Enya contributes "Aniron: Theme for Aragon and Arwen" and, even more elegiac, "May It Be," which is one of the finest pieces she's ever recorded.

"May It Be" was nominated in the category of "Best Achievement in Music in Connection with Motion Pictures (Original Song)" for the 74th Annual Academy Awards, at which Enya performed the song. Unfortunately, she did not win. On the other hand, Howard Shore was justifiably recognized for his fine work in scoring *The Fellowship of the Ring*, and won an Oscar for "Best Original Score."

The soundtracks include:

➔ *The Fellowship of the Ring* (regular edition, $19.98).

➔ *The Fellowship of the Ring* (limited edition; no longer in production). The extra money buys better packaging, but you can't judge this "book" by its cover: There are no bonus tracks on this CD, though there are enhanced features that promote Enya's musical presence. In short, save your money—buy the regular edition.

➔ *The Lord of the Rings: The Fellowship of the Ring Song Book* ($14.95). Sheet music for the film score with piano, vocals, and chords. Includes photographs from the film.

➔ *The Two Towers* (regular edition, $19.98).

➔ *The Two Towers* (limited edition, no longer in production). Better packaging, but this time there is a bonus track: "Farewell to Lórien" by Hilary Summers, an orchestral piece with vocal backups—very ethereal.

➔ *The Two Towers* (Internet limited edition, $29.98). The limited edition of *The Two Towers*, with additional material: five character cards (used as cover illustrations for the regular edition); printable maps of Middle-earth, Rohan, and Gondor; a Two Towers "print and color set"; the Two Towers movie trailer; a Two Towers image gallery; lyrics and poems; score music video and "Making of the Score" video; and screensavers and buddy icons.

➔ *The Lord of the Rings: The Two Towers Song Book* ($14.95). Sheet music for the film score with piano, vocals, and chords. Includes photographs from the film.

The Tolkien Ensemble

www.tolkienemsemble.com

Formed in 1995, this group of six Danish performers has set an ambitious goal of creating the musical interpretation of all the poems and songs found in *The Lord of the Rings*.

To date, three CDs have been published, issued in four editions: *An Evening in Rivendell* (1997), *A Night in Rivendell* (2000), *24 Songs from The Lord of the Rings* (2001), and *At Dawn in Rivendell* (2002).

1. *An Evening in Rivendell with The Tolkien Emsemble: Selected Songs from The Lord of the Rings by J.R.R. Tolkien*, by Caspar Reiff and Peter Hall (Classico, $15.98, one CD).

2. *A Night in Rivendell with the Tolkien Emsemble: Selected Songs from The Lord of the Rings by J.R.R. Tolkien*, by Caspar Reiff and Peter Hall (Classico, $15.98, one CD).

3. *J.R.R. Tolkien: 24 Songs from The Lord of the Rings*, by The Tolkien Ensemble. This is a gift set comprised of *An Evening in Rivendell* and *A Night in Rivendell* (Classico, $24.98, two CDs).

4. *At Dawn in Rivendell*: *The Lord of the Rings, Songs and Poems by J.R.R. Tolkien*, by The Tolkien Ensemble and Christopher Lee, music by Caspar Reiff and Peter Hall (Universal, $16.98, one CD). **Note:** To hear Lee read "One ring to rule them all..." in his deep, impressive baritone voice is worth the purchase price.

Metrognome Studios

www.metrognomestudios.com

Metrognome Studios was formed by Kevin Pearce and James Prior. Inspired by the works of J.R.R. Tolkien, these composers, in addition to managing their studio, spent six years creating *One Ring*.

One Ring (Metrognome Studios, $12.99, one CD). This small press recording, licensed from Tolkien Enterprises and published in a limited edition run of only 1,000 copies, is a labor of love. As the musicians who recorded this CD explained (quoted from *http://www.metrognome.demon.co.uk/compose.htm*):

> *The Lord of the Rings*. What a magnificent story. Probably the single most influential fantasy story of all time. Tolkien knew how to infuse the magic of imagination, to create a rich and emotive tale that would last for years because of its simple depth and beauty. As musicians, we wanted to be able to express some of that wonder, and be able to recreate the world of Tolkien in sound and melodies.

Available only by Web order directly from the musicians, James Prior and Kevin Pearce, this hour-long CD provides two bonus tracks, accessible only by a linked Website (that information is provided when you purchase the CD).

Broceliande

www.broceliande.org

As quoted from the group's Website (*www.broceliande.org*):

> Broceliande plays Celtic music from the British Isles and the Medieval and Renaissance music of the European courts, castles, and countryside. Featuring stellar vocal and instrumental harmonies, their entrancing sound is built on the interweaving of up to 4-part vocals with the lyrical music of the Celtic harp, octave mandolin, cello, guitar, flutes, whistles, percussion, harmonica, and melodian.
>
> Their repertoire includes original arrangements of traditional and Early music and ranges in feel from driving, danceable Celtic beats to haunting, atmospherically lovely harp-based ballads. Their lyrics, including some in Medieval French and Portuguese, speak of love and longing, quests and revels, magic and transformation, in an evocative style in the same vein as Loreena McKennitt, Clannad, and Alan Stivell.

Broceliande's limited edition *The Starlit Jewel* is currently out of print, but according to its publisher, a second printing may be forthcoming in 2004. Licensed from the Tolkien Estate, this is an unusual offering; rather than simply interpreting the text musically, it sets poetry to music, some of which is by the late Marion Zimmer Bradley, a well-known fantasy writer in her own right.

As expected from a musical group that plays principally at Renaissance fairs, the music has a minstrel-like quality that seems appropriate to the book.

In a review by The Mythopoeic Society (a nonprofit organization devoted to promoting fantasy and mythic literature), *The Starlit Jewel* is a gem of an album—Paula DiSante writes:

> There are bracing thrills and breath-catching beauties to be found here, thanks to the multifarious miracles of Davis's ardent interpretation. In its new incarnation, *The Starlit Jewel* continues to delight and astound. This dazzling re-release was well worth the wait. It should find an honored place in many a Tolkien-lover's CD collection.

Madacy 2 Label Group #3193

Composed by Johan De Meij and performed by the London Symphony Orchestra, *The Lord of the Rings: Symphony No. 1* ($18.98) is comprised of six tracks: "Gandalf," "Lothlórien," "Gollum," "Journey in the Dark," "Hobbits," and "The Sorcerer's Apprentice."

David Arkenstone

store.yahoo.com/neopacifica

Music Inspired by Middle-earth (New Pacifica, $19.98), by David Arkenstone. Tracks include: "Hobbits from the Shire," "Road to Rivendell," "Quest," "Moria," "Lothlórien," "Galadriel's Mirror," "Riders of Rohan," "Palantir," "Arwen and Aragorn," "To Isengard," "In the Land of Shadow," "Field of Cormallen," and "Grey Havens."

The publisher states:

> Perhaps it is natural for composers to exhibit the desire to musically illustrate other artistic works that have moved them in a powerful, lasting manner. Yet, it can be tricky to present an interpretation of a major artistic work that is beloved by so many, and has been intimately personalized by their own imagination. That being said, it was quite simply a joy for us to musically portray our impressions of the incredible world created by Master Tolkien. The inspirations for this recording have been developing for many years, and this wonderful book has been a major source of joy in our lives.

As expected, there are other musical interpretations that strike me as being out of sync with the work itself: pop rock, rock, and New Age are wildly interpretive. My recommendation: sample some of the orchestrally inspired and folk-song inspired works, because both are consistent with the "feel" of Middle-earth.

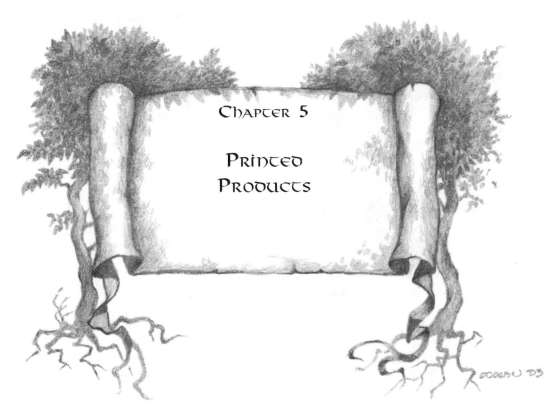

CHAPTER 5

PRINTED PRODUCTS

Stationery Goods

Address Book

Dark green cover with *"The Lord of the Rings* address book" on the front, with an image of a tree (Cedco Publishing, $7.95). Measures 3.5 x 4.5 inches, 96 pages.

Bookmark Set

***The Fellowship of the Ring* Bookmark Set** (Antioch, $19.95). Seven bookmarks, each with a tassel; the Frodo bookmark has a replica of the One Ring attached to its tassel. The seven include: Frodo, Legolas, Gimli, Gandalf the Grey, Strider, Lurtz, and Saruman.

***The Two Towers* Bookmark Set** (Antioch, $20.95). Seven bookmarks, each with a small character-related metal symbol attached to its tassel. Included are Frodo and Sam, Merry and Pippin, Legolas and Gimli, Gandalf the White, King Théoden, Éowyn, and Aragorn.

A selection of bookmarkers: Frodo Baggins, Legolas Greenleaf, Strider (Aragorn), and Boromir.

Bookmarker of Aragorn with emblem tassel.

Journals

Deluxe Journal (Cedco Publishing, $15.95). Brown faux-leather cover, foil stamping, and loop enclosure. The cover bears the words, "The Lord of the Rings" on the front, and an image of a tree. Measures approximately 6 x 8 inches.

Arwen Journal (Cedco Publishing, $7.95). Blue cover with a die-cut window displaying a scene from the movie: Arwen wielding her sword as she takes a stand against the Nine Riders. Measures approximately 4 x 6 inches.

Frodo Journal (Cedco Publishing, $7.95). Green cover with a cut-out window displaying a scene from the movie: Frodo holding Sting. Measures approximately 4 x 6 inches, 240 pages.

The Lord of the Rings **Crow of Saruman Icon Journal** (Cedco Pubishing, $12.95). Blank-page journal measuring approximately 6 x 8 inches, 240 pages. Faux-leather cover with foil stamping on the cover: a crown design and the legend, "The Lord of the Rings."

The Lord of the Rings **Icon Journal Set** (Cedco Publishing, $33.95). A set of three blank journals (each 240 pages), with faux-leather covers: the Tree of Gondor, the symbol (crow) of Saruman, and the One Ring. The journals are also available separately for $12.95 each.

The One Ring Icon Journal (Cedco Publishing, $12.95). Blank journal with 240 pages, bound in red faux-leather. The front cover shows the One Ring inscription and the legend, "The Lord of the Rings."

The One Ring Tree of Gondor Icon Journal (Cedco Publishing, $12.95). Blank journal with 240 pages, bound in black faux-leather. The front cover shows the Tree of Gondor and the legend, "The Lord of the Rings."

The Fellowship of the Ring **Brown Journal** (Cedco Publishing, $15.95). Bound in brown faux-leather, this 240-page journal bears the legend "The Lord of the Rings: The Fellowship of the Ring," with a tree symbol.

There and Back Again: **A Journal** (Cedco Publishing, $15.95). Bearing the same name as the subtitle of *The Hobbit*, this deluxe journal features a red faux-leather cover, foil stamping, and a loop enclosure. Measures approximately 6 x 8 inches.

The Lord of the Rings **Small Journal** (Cedco Publishing, $12.95). The black cover displays silver stamping of the crow of Saruman icon and the words, "The Lord of the Rings."

Letter Openers

Miniature Collectible Sting Sword Letter Opener (The Noble Collection, $44.95). A replica of Sting (Frodo's sword) measuring 4.75 inches, set in a base made of cold-cast porcelain.

Miniature Collectible Witch-king Sword Letter Opener (The Noble Collection, $44.95). A replica of the sword wielded by the Lord of the Nazgûl, the sword measures 8 inches, set in a base made of cold-cast porcelain.

Mousepads

***The Fellowship of the Ring* Mousepads** (New Line Cinema, $16.95). A set of two: One shows the One Ring surrounded by a cast of characters; the second shows Gandalf, surrounded by the other members of the Fellowship, with a backdrop of Middle-earth.

***The Two Towers* Mousepads** ($16.95). A set of two: One shows Gollum/Sméagol; the second shows Aragorn, Legolas, and Gimli.

Postcard Books

Hobbit Postcards book (HarperCollins, $10.95). A set of 20 oversized postcards, with art by Alan Lee, Roger Garland, and John Howe.

***LotR* Postcards Book** (HarperCollins, $10.95). A set of 20 oversized postcards, with art by John Howe and Alan Lee.

School

Datebook (Cedco Publishing, $12.95). Personal organizer. Brown cover with "The Lord of the Rings" on the front, and a map of Middle-earth.

Locker Calendar (Cedco Publishing, $9.99). Published annually, the locker calendars measure 7 x 10 inches (when hung up, 7 x 20 inches), and are designed to hang inside a student's wall locker at school. The calendar starts with August and ends with December of the subsequent year.

Student Planner (Cedco Publishing, $10.99). Published annually, the student planner features month-at-a-glance and weekly planners, as well. The calendar starts in August and ends in August of the subsequent year.

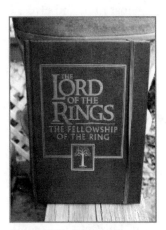

Lord of the Rings: The Fellowship of the Ring *datebook.*

Posters

Note: Full-size posters measure 27 x 40 inches, mini-posters measure 16 x 20, and door posters are approximately 5 feet tall.

The Two Towers: **Frodo and Sam** ($15.95). Measures 27 x 40 inches. Sam in the foreground; Frodo in the background. The poster records a pivotal scene from the movie, in which they discuss their motivation to continue in the face of insurmountable odds and increasing danger. Sam says, "Those were the stories that meant something, even if you were too small to understand why, but I think, Mr. Frodo, I do understand. Folks in those stories had lots of chances of turning back, only they didn't. They kept going, because they were holding onto something."

Return of the King: **Teaser Poster featuring Aragorn** ($15.95). Measures 27 x 40 inches. A portrait close-up of Aragorn holding his sword, Anduril, in front of him.

The Fellowship of the Ring: **Gandalf and Frodo in the Mines of Moria** ($19.95). Measures 27 x 40 inches. Printed on Elite Gloss paper stock—a higher quality than conventional glossy stock used for movie posters—this poster had its origins as a newspaper print ad; however, after Ian McKellen posted this on his Website, fans asked for a copy. The result is a slightly revised version, emphasizing the text—a dialogue between Gandalf and Frodo, who talk about fate, personal responsibility, and decisions made—and those yet to be made.

The Two Towers: **Final Movie Poster** ($15.95). Measures 27 x 40 inches. A double-sided poster showing the two towers—Isengard and Orthanc, flanking the heroic main characters.

The Two Towers: **Saruman** ($15.95). Measures 27 x 40 inches. A double-sided poster showing Saruman overlooking his newly formed army set to march off to battle against men and elves. On the top, the words, "A NEW POWER IS RISING."

The Fellowship of the Ring: **Pillars of Argonath** ($15.95). Measures 27 x 40 inches. Shows three small watercraft plying the misty waters, headed through the Pillars of Argonath—statues of Isildur and Anarion.

The Fellowship of the Ring: **Final Movie Poster** ($15.95). Measures 27 x 40 inches. Shows Frodo as the nucleus, surrounded by other main characters; beneath them, the Ringwraiths.

The Hobbit Poster Collection (HarperCollins UK, $22.95). This poster book is an oversized trade paperback, 11.5 x 18 inches. The art is by Alan Lee and features six paintings illustrating *The Hobbit*.

The Lord of the Rings Poster Collection (HarperCollins UK, $22.95). This poster book is an oversized trade paperback, 11.5 x 18 inches. The art is by Alan Lee and features six paintings illustrating *The Lord of the Rings*.

The Two Towers: **Gollum Poster** ($8.99). Measures 25 x 35 inches. Close-up of Gollum saying, "It came to me. My own. My precious."

The Two Towers: **Legolas, with bow and arrow** ($4.99). Measures 16 x 20 inches. Legolas with drawn bow, taking aim.

The Two Towers: **Aragorn Teaser Poster** ($8.99). Measures 25 x 35 inches. Shows Aragorn with drawn sword held upright in front of him, flanked by Arwen and Éowyn.

The One Ring Door Poster ($12.99). Measures 23 x 62 inches. Features the text of the complete poem, "One ring to rule them all...." A simple, striking design depicts the gold ring with the inscribed Elvish text, and its English translation above.

Heroes of *The Two Towers* Poster ($8.99). Measures 25 x 35 inches. Shows Faramir, Éowyn, Éomer, Théoden, and the companions from the movie.

The Two Towers: **Eye of Sauron Poster** ($8.99). Measures 25 x 35 inches. The lidless Eye against the backdrop of Orthanc, with the One Ring inscription on its periphery.

The Two Towers: **Door Poster** ($12.99). Shows the two towers: Orthanc and Barad-dûr.

The Two Towers: **Legolas Door Poster** ($12.99). Shows Legolas, with bow drawn, taking aim.

The Rohirrim and the Three Hunters Door Poster ($12.99). Shows Aragorn, Gimli, and Legolas, with the lidless Eye of Sauron in the background and the Riders of the Rohirrim in the foreground.

My Personal Picks

1. *The Fellowship of the Ring* **Teaser "A" Poster** (25 x 25 inches, $8.99). This is a classic image: Frodo Baggins, played by Elijah Wood, holds the One Ring in his hand. The expression on his face—a mixture of disbelief at its significance and wonder at its power, so great that it throws an entire world into war—sums up the trilogy perfectly. The One Ring is a burden, and destiny chose him to carry it to Mordor for its destruction. (The variant poster, 'B,' shows the same scene, but Frodo is looking down at the ring.)

2. **The One Ring** in two editions: a door poster (21 x 62 inches, $12.99) and a smaller poster (25 x 36 inches, $9.99). Pictured is a bold, simple, and elegant design, featuring the One Ring juxtaposed against a black background.

3. **Classic Map of Middle-earth Foiled Dufex Poster** (25 x 35 inches, $24.99). Printed on silver foil-lined board using UV transparent inks, this poster is then enhanced by hand with engravings to give it a unique visual effect.

4. **Bodeleian Library Hobbit Exhibition Posters**. Using Tolkien's own art for *The Hobbit*, these three utterly charming and delightful illustrations were re-printed as library exhibition posters, including the wraparound cover to *The Hobbit*. Available from The Tolkien Society (*www.tolkiensociety.com*) and from the Bodeleian Library at Oxford University.

5. **Gandalf and Frodo Mines of Moria Poster** (27 x 40 inches, $19.95). From *The Fellowship of the Ring*, this poster shows a contemplative moment that is shared between Gandalf and Frodo as they sit in the Mines of Moria: Frodo laments that he has been given the Ring and wishes none of this had ever happened, and with his wizard's wisdom Gandalf replies, "So do all who live to see such times, but that is not for them to decide. All we have to decide is what to do with the time that is given to us."

Poster Sources

Literally hundreds of posters—unofficial and official, non-film related and film-related, and book-related—have been published. As expected, the bulk of what's currently available are film tie-ins, ranging in size from mini-posters (16 x 20 inches) to door-size (5 feet tall!), in full color and printed on glossy stock, with retail prices of $20–$30.

A detailed, encyclopedic listing of every poster is beyond the scope of this book; however, the Websites listed have online catalogs, in color, with supplementary information on size and, where applicable, source material.

There is no single source that provides all the posters, but here's where to check out the current selection:

➔ The official *Lord of the Rings* Web store (*www.lordoftherings.net/ index_flat_shop.html*), located on the official Website for the movie.

➔ The Official Lord of the Rings Fan Club (*www.lotrfanclub.com*). Members pay an annual fee and get, among other benefits, a 10-percent discount on merchandise; everyone else can register and pay full retail. Although the fan club Web store does duplicate the inventory of the movie Web store, it also offers some posters that are not available anywhere else.

➔ Lordoftheringshop.com (*www.lordoftheringsshop.com*). Not affiliated with the film. There are numerous Web stores that offer Tolkien merchandise, but this one is fairly comprehensive in its selection of inventory, which is listed alphabetically and thematically for quick reference. Its poster selection is extensive and organized by movie for easy access.

➔ AllPosters.com (*www.allposters.com*). Not affiliated with the film. A Web store with a wide selection of Tolkien posters. (Type in "lord of the rings" in the search engine).

➔ The Tolkien Society (*www.tolkiensociety.org*). A nonprofit organization in England, its poster selection includes four color images from *The Hobbit* with Tolkien's own illustrations, published to promote Tolkien exhibits at the Bodeleian Library in England.

→ TolkienTown.Com (*www.tolkientown.com*). Billing itself "The World's Largest Tolkien Store," it has an impressive line of posters, including some that are out of print.

→ The Tolkien Shop (*www.tolkienshop.com*) offers an excellent selection of out-of-print posters. This retail store, located in the Netherlands, is run by a longtime fantasy fan, Rene van Rossenberg, who is a learned lore-master and a Tolkien expert of the first rank.

Lithographs and Photographs

Lurtz (actor Lawrence Makoare) Photograph (Decipher, $35). An edition of 140 produced for the *LotR* Fan Club, this 8 x 10-inch glossy photo was signed by Makoare at the San Diego Comicon 2002, and comes with a certificate of authenticity.

Witch-king Lithograph (Decipher, $20). A limited edition lithograph of 3,000 copies, this is a scene from *The Fellowship of the Ring*, when the Witch-king confronts Frodo at Weathertop. Measures 12 x 16 inches, printed on archival paper. (Available only through the *LotR* Fan Club.)

Sauron Lithograph (Decipher, $20). A limited edition of 3,000 copies, this is a scene from *The Fellowship of the Ring* in which the One Ring glows on the finger of Sauron as he prepares for battle. Measures 12 x 16 inches, printed on archival paper. (Available only through the *LotR* Fan Club.)

Cave Troll Lithograph (Decipher, $20). A limited edition of 1,500 copies, this is a scene from *The Fellowship of the Ring*, when the Fellowship is attacked in the Mines of Moria by a company of orcs and a cave troll. Measures 12 x 16 inches, printed on archival paper. (Available only through the *LotR* Fan Club.)

The Fellowship of the Ring Lithograph (Decipher, $18). No limitation number stated. A scene of the forming of the Fellowship at the Council of Elrond.

Balrog Lithograph (Decipher, $20). A limited edition of 1,500 copies, this is a scene from *The Fellowship of the Ring*, when the Balrog and Gandalf face off at Khazad-dûm.

Gimli (actor John Rhys-Davies) Photograph (Decipher, $35). A numbered edition of 200 produced for the *LotR* Fan Club, this 8 x 10-inch glossy photo is signed by Davies and comes with a certificate of authenticity bearing the number of the photo.

Art Prints, Giclée Prints, and Original Art

Though there has been a wealth of Tolkien art published in every conceivable format, art prints—typically sold through galleries or directly from the artists—are the exception, not the rule, because these are normally published by the artists, who retain copyright to the original art and, thus, reproduction rights.

The economics of printing museum-quality prints has traditionally been out of reach to all but the most successful artists, because the economy of scale doesn't favor small runs—a 30 x 40 print, in full color, in a run of 1,000, could cost $5,000 or more, depending on where the artist goes to get the printing done.

Typically, an artist will sell 5–10 percent of the print run to recover printing costs, but it means carrying the majority of the prints in inventory until they sell, which could be many years.

An increasingly popular alternative is the Giclée (that is, inkjet) print, which offers several advantages: First, it is possible to achieve a fidelity to the art that cannot be achieved by conventional printing methods such as offset lithography; second, it allows the image, after color corrections or whatever other manipulations the artist makes, to be stored indefinitely and printed on an "as needed" basis, or printed on demand, in other words; and, third, it allows prints to be made on a variety of papers, including canvas, to suit the buyer.

The quality of Giclée printing has risen and the costs for the high-end machines (notably the Epson printers) has dropped dramatically, with the result that Tolkien artists may well start printing their art themselves, instead of being forced to rely on commercial printers.

Because there is no requirement to carry an inventory with this printing method, orders will likely be printed as they are received, which eliminates the requirement of long-term inventory storage.

In terms of papers, the print-buying public has responded enthusiastically to Giclée prints produced on canvas stock, because these look more like originals, do not require matting, and do not require glass; in fact, they look like oil paintings, which allows the artist to make minor touch-ups or highlights as needed to lend a personal touch that lithographic prints lack.

To give you an idea as to size and pricing, the Brothers Hildebrandt offer most of their Tolkien paintings as signed and numbered Giclée prints. The cover for their 1977 Tolkien calendar featuring Gandalf is available as a 16 x 20 inch Giclée print, in an edition of 50 copies, for $200; larger sizes are correspondingly more expensive: 20 x 32 inches, $325, and 32 x 44 inches, $650.

Traditionally, museum-quality prints are produced in a numbered and signed edition, and, once that edition has sold out, no further reproductions in any size are available—good for investors, but not good for collectors who want the image but don't want to pay collector's prices. For these collectors, the "open edition" (no limitation as to how many are printed) offers a cost-effective alternative.

Because most artists prefer to spend time painting as opposed to handling print orders, most are represented by galleries that act as middlemen, which is the case with the Brothers Hildebrandt (*www.spiderwebart.com*) and Ted Nasmith (*www.chalkfarmgallery.com*).

Giclée technology ideally lends itself to self-publishing, so artists' Websites are the place to go to see if any prints are available.

As more Tolkien-related museum-quality art prints appear on the market, here's a quick overview of what you need to know when buying prints.

✦ **Open edition**: This term means that the print run is open-ended—there is no limitation to the number of prints being made. In terms of collectibility, this means that the print will not rise rapidly in value, because the artist can, and will, always print more.

✦ **Limited edition**: Usually hand-numbered and signed by the artist, the Certificate of Authenticity specifies the exact number of prints sold. Because of the limitation, once the print is sold out, prices will rise as per market demand.

✦ **A remarque**: an original sketch, usually in pencil, in the border of a print. (The remarques for Michael Whelan's "Gunslinger" print added $100 to the cost of the print itself.)

✦ **Artist Proof**: Usually marked "AP" or "A/P" and sometimes numbered, these are traditionally the first few copies run off for evaluation purposes only, to fine-tune the press for the regular print run.

✦ Most limited edition prints are accompanied by a limitation notice to show the specifics of the print itself. If buying a print on the secondary market, ask if a COA (certificate of authenticity) is available.

A Few Words on Original Art

Original art is, and will always be, unique. One-of-a-kind, original art is literally irreplaceable. For fans wanting to buy original Tolkien art, there are several options:

✦ Go to major conventions such as the World Science Fiction Convention or the San Diego Comicon. That is where you will likely see fan and pro artists selling art directly, at a dealer's table or in an art show.

✦ Contact galleries that deal with fantasy artwork. Galleries are in the business of representing artists and, if they don't work with the artist of your choice, can usually locate him and negotiate a price based on fair market value for an existing work of art. In addition, the gallery can act as a broker for a commissioned piece. (This is usually, though not always, more expensive than buying directly from the artist, because galleries traditionally charge a 50-percent sales commission.)

✦ Bid at an auction house; all the big-name auction houses now sell on eBay, offering a range of originals priced from the low to high end.

✦ The direct approach: Contact the artist directly, through his publisher or through his Website. The advantage is that this method allows the buyer to establish a relationship with the artist, which can lead to early notification of new originals or prints for sale, or notification when time is available for new commissions.

A Few Words on Art Commissions

Want a specific scene from your favorite book? Some artists accept commissions, which they do between their regular assignments.

The ground rules for commissions:

- ✤ **Down payment**: Artists usually want a deposit after accepting the job. Typically, the deposit is 50 percent, with the balance due before delivery of the artwork.

- ✤ **Time**: Pro artists juggle several assignments, so commissions are done in their spare time. For this reason, most commissions take from six to 12 months to complete. *Don't* commission an artist unless you are patient and willing to wait.

- ✤ **Copyright**: The artist retains copyright (the right to make copies). All you have bought is the physical ownership of the art itself. You own *no* reproduction rights.

- ✤ **Direction**: If an artist takes a commission, he's usually willing to illustrate a specific scene, with the caveat that he usually doesn't need to know every tiny detail—he's an artist and can visually imagine a scene *and* put it on paper. For instance, telling an artist that you want a scene of the Fellowship walking through the woods during the day is sufficient art direction—he doesn't need you to tell him what color clothes Legolas should be wearing! (Even Tolkien left the details to the reader's imagination.)

- ✤ **Medium**: Costs go up as the medium dictates. From inexpensive to expensive: a pencil sketch, a detailed pencil sketch, a toned pencil sketch (two colors or more on colored paper), a full color pencil sketch, an ink sketch, a detailed ink drawing, a detailed ink drawing colored in watercolor, a watercolor painting, an acrylic or oil painting.

- ✤ **Size**: The bigger the size, the higher the cost.

Calendars

Since 1973, Tolkien's publishers have had an active calendar publishing program, drawing from the abundance of artwork that adorned the book covers and interior illustrations. Most of them have been the traditional wall calendar, with desk and locker calendars supplementing the main line.

Rather appropriately, the first calendar, published by Allen & Unwin in 1973, reprinted artwork by Tolkien. That same year, Ballantine Books published its first Tolkien calendar, which featured art by Tolkien, Pauline Baynes, and John Wyatt. The 1974 calendars from Allen & Unwin and Ballantine Books both featured art by Tolkien and Pauline Baynes, but in 1975, Ballantine Books broke new ground by publishing a calendar of all new material produced by a single artist—Tim Kirk, who had chosen *The Lord of the Rings* as the subject for his master's thesis in art. Up until then, all the calendars were simply titled "The J.R.R. Tolkien Calendar."

In the years that followed, thematic Tolkien calendars were published—*The Hobbit*, *The Lord of the Rings*, and *The Silmarillion*—but, over the years, the mainstay has been "The J.R.R. Tolkien Calendar."

Though U.S. artists have been represented in the calendar publishing program—notably Tim Kirk, the Brothers Hildebrandt, Michael Hague, Michael Kaluta, and Stephen Hickman—the art has predominantly been British, drawing on the work of Ted Nasmith, Roger Garland, and Alan Lee. John Howe is a notable Canadian artist.

"The J.R.R. Tolkien Calendar" for 2004 (Harper Entertainment), featuring artwork by Ted Nasmith, is appropriately themed around *The Return of the King*, to celebrate the final film in the Peter Jackson trilogy.

Supplementing the pictorial line of calendars from HarperCollins, Cedco publishes a weekly calendar and a student planner with images from the movies. In addition, New Line Cinema publishes the movie tie-in calendars with stills from its three films.

The other alternative is the first of four calendars by the Brothers Hildebrandt, who previously published the 1976–78 Tolkien calendars in the United States, from Ballantine. A 16-month calendar, "The Tolkien Art of the Brothers Hildebrandt" (Ronnie Sellers, $13) includes 14 paintings from those previously published calendars.

For obvious reasons, calendars—unlike books—have a limited shelf life. They are put up for sale in retail stores by early fall, usually starting in August, and typically sell best during the Christmas season. After the New Year, existing stock is marked down by half (or more) to clear the inventory.

Because of their smaller print runs, the early calendars are difficult to find and have become collectibles in their own right, costing $100–$125. The best place to find these is eBay, but be sure to read the descriptions carefully—some of them may be marked from original use.

The cover of the 2002 Fellowship of the Ring *movie tie-in calendar.*

The cover of the 2003 Two Towers *movie tie-in calendar.*

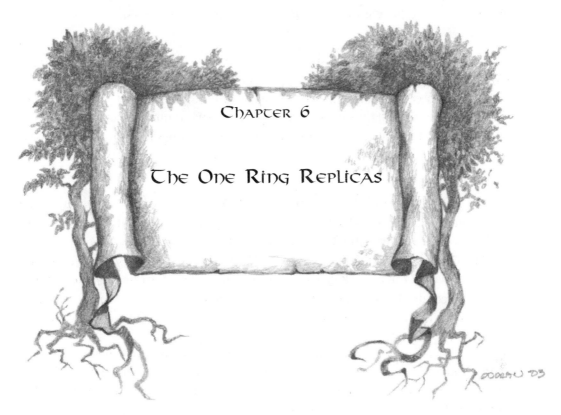

Chapter 6

The One Ring Replicas

It appears to be a plain, gold band, a simple piece of jewelry, but looks can be deceiving. A Ring of Power, it is the Master Ring that, if wielded by its creator, Sauron, will give him dominion over all of Middle-earth. As any of the long history of ring-bearers might tell you, one does not so much possess the ring as be possessed *by* it.

For Tolkien fans who have wanted a faithful reproduction of the One Ring that holds dominion over the other, lesser rings of power—three for the elf kings, seven for the dwarf lords, and nine for men—the ring was simply not available legally because no authorized reproduction had been licensed by Tolkien Enterprises.

In 2001, when the movie version of *The Fellowship of the Ring* predictably created a resurgence of interest in rings and all things Tolkien, the timing was right to release ring replicas, and lo, they were forged.

So rare—and so sought after—was the One Ring that the cheaply made $18.95 ring from Applause commanded over $100 on eBay when initially released, because demand was high, but stock was low. Not surprisingly, when an even more expensive ring appeared—a handsome $299.95 replica from the Noble Collection— unscrupulous sellers, who offered to sell their rings on eBay, deliberately avoided mentioning the manufacturer, because the rings were open editions, available directly from the source for hundreds of dollars less than what the rings would get on eBay from customers ignorant of its general availability.

Even the official movie Website's store at *www.lordoftherings.net* did not carry the Noble Collection replica until months afterward. (I speak with authority on this because I talked to the people running the Website store and learned that they did not even know of the existence of the One Ring manufactured by the Noble Collection. Soon afterward, the official Website began stocking it, by which time the speculators had left, having made their ill-gotten gains on eBay and slunk away.)

The supply has now caught up with the demand, and rings in all sizes with various metals are plentiful, with prices ranging from $16.95 to $1,500 (in platinum).

The One Ring From Applause LLC

From Applause, for $16.95, is a metal ring plated with gold coloring. With chain, this ring features the Tengwar inscription.

The first edition, released in time for *The Fellowship of the Ring*, featured the ring with chain set in a black cylindrical box, with Tengwar around its perimeter.

The second edition, released in time for *The Two Towers*, features the ring with chain set in a resin base resembling lava and lava rock from Mount Doom, from whence it came.

The size-seven ring is not intended for finger placement; it is intended to be worn around the neck on its 21-inch chain. More a souvenir than a collectible because of its toy origins and cheap metal, it is $14.99 and can be ordered from New Line Cinema's store at *www.lordoftherings.net*.

The One Ring From Schmuck-Uhren-Noll

From Schmuck-Uhren-Noll, with a price ranging from $199 to $639, depending on the precious metal used, this model uses laser technology to etch the Tengwar inscription on the inside and outside of the ring itself. Designed to be finger worn, the ring comes with a leather pouch. It is available in a variety of sizes.

→ **The sterling silver ring** is the least expensive. It comes stored in an unmarked, dark green pouch, for $199.

→ **The 8-karat gold ring**, stored in a black velvet pouch with gold overprinting, costs $399.

→ **The 14-karat gold ring**, stored in a black velvet pouch with gold overprinting, is priced at $499.

→ **The 18-karat gold ring**, stored in a black velvet pouch with gold overprinting, retails at $639.

Order from *www.theonering-shop.com*.

The One Ring From Badali Jewelry

An independent jeweler, Paul Badali began manufacturing his replica ring for sale in 1998. Wrote Badali on his Website (*www.baladijewelry.com*): "I had no idea that anyone owned the trademarks to J.R.R. Tolkien's works when I started selling the rings. A customer asked if I was licensed with Tolkien Enterprises soon after I started, and I responded 'Who is Tolkien Enterprises?'"

Badali wisely secured a license and began selling two versions of the One Ring, as well as some the lesser Rings of Power.

➤ **The Gollum Gold Ring with Necklace**. A bronze ring plated with 24-karat gold, size 9 3/4, with a 24-inch, gold-plated chain. Comes packaged in a burgundy drawstring pouch. In plain script ($39.95), black script ($49.95), and red script ($49.95).

➤ **The One Ring** is available in 10-karat ($480), 14-karat ($590), 18-karat ($739), and 22-karat ($896), with plain lettering, black antiqued lettering, and red enamel lettering. (A plain gold ring with no script is available from $305 and up.) The ring comes in a decorative ring box.

Order from *www.badalijewelry.com*.

The One Ring From the Noble Collection

This company principally markets its wares through its direct-mail catalog, though New Line Cinema's Website carries most of its Tolkien-related items.

➤ **The sterling edition** is cast in sterling silver, with laser etching of the Tengwar inscription. This size-10 ring comes in a small wooden box with a 20-inch chain and a certificate of authenticity, for $129.

➤ **The solid gold edition** features laser etching of the Tengwar inscription. This size-10 ring comes in an ornate wood box—a handsome, if gaudy, presentation, for $295.

Order from *www.noblecollection.com* or from *www.theonering.net*.

The Jens Hansen Gold & Silversmith

In the window of a jewelry store in New Zealand, a small sign states, simply, that Jens Hansen made the One Ring—a singular distinction, because Peter Jackson had hand-picked him to manufacture what is unarguably the most important prop for the movie.

The late Jens Hansen designed several versions, from which one was selected; from that, several sizes were made, as required by Jackson. The result was a plain gold ring, stunning in its simplicity, its elegance—the hallmarks of a Hansen piece of jewelry.

Sadly, Jens Hansen never lived to see his ring replicas on the big screen.

Jens Hansen's son, Thorkild, continues the fine work of his father and now offers replica rings in various precious metals, with prices ranging from $80 to $1,500:

- → In sterling silver, $80.

- → In 9-karat white gold, $260.

- → In 14-karat white gold, $475.

- → In 18-karat white gold, $725.

- → In platinum, $1,500.

- → In 8-karat gold, $240.

- → In 14-karat gold, $385.

- → In 18-karat gold, $530.

Order from *www.jenshansen.com*.

 The Hansen Ring

Among the replicas, if there is one ring that rules them all, it is the Hansen ring. As Hansen's son, Thorkild, points out on the company's Website, their ring—among all the rings currently available—is closest to what Tolkien had envisioned:

Gandalf held it up. It looked to be made of pure and solid gold.

"Can you see any markings on it?" he asked.

"No," said Frodo. "There are none. It is quite plain, and it never shows a scratch or sign of wear."

And so, too, is the Hansen ring. Unlike the other rings with the Elvish script—in the movie, the Hansen ring was visually enhanced by special effects—this one is quite plain, and as manufactured and presented in its wooden box, it shows neither a scratch or sign of wear.

A reproduction of the One Ring, manufactured by Jens Hansen (New Zealand), the firm that designed the One Ring in various sizes for the movie trilogy.

Though some will undoubtedly prefer the more gaudy replica rings with the inscription emblazoned around their bands, I think most Tolkien purists would appreciate the beauty of the Hansen ring, which is a lovely piece of jewelry, its literary significance notwithstanding.

From the Jens Hansen Website (*www.jenshansen.com*):

The movie's Art Direction team (later nominated for an Academy Award for their work on the set) first approached Jens Hansen in March 1999. From here, 15 prototypes were submitted. They all boasted the same elegant simplicity but came in a variety of weights and finishes. From this extensive collection, a decision was made and the final design for the One Ring was selected.

Jens and his son Thorkild then had to make the One Ring scaled for different scenes and sized to suit the various owners of the Ring. We all know that there is only One Ring, but for the film more than 40 variations were needed, from smaller, solid gold versions that perfectly fit Hobbit's fingers, to the one seen in the prologue, spinning and turning through the air. With a diameter of a massive 8 inches, this ring obviously couldn't be made of solid gold, so steel was used, it was cut on a lathe and then plated.

We are not an authorized or official licensee for any of *The Lord of the Rings* movie jewelry or merchandise, and we would hate to add to any confusion regarding the marketing or ownership rights of the One Ring. However, since the high profile launch of *The Fellowship of the Ring*, and the impending premier of *The Two Towers* movie release, interest and requests from discerning individuals has been so high, that we have decided to make faithful replicas for those who wish to own the genuine article.

Chapter 7

Licensed Movie-
Related Collectibles

Decorative Items

Candle Holders

LotR: **Witch-king Candle Holder** (The Noble Collection, $21.95). A votive holder, with four sword-shaped pieces attached to the crown, extending it to 11 inches tall.

LotR: **Balrog Candle Holder** (The Noble Collection, $39.95). Made of resin, this 8.5-inch high holder glows when a candle is lit and placed in its holder.

Ornaments

LotR: **Frodo and Bilbo Ornament** (Department 56, $9.95). Measures 2.5 inches high, this shows Frodo and Bilbo together, with a large One Ring at its base.

LotR: **Saruman Ornament** (Department 56, $9.95). Measuring 3.5 inches, this resin ornament shows Saruman holding his staff, with the One Ring at the base.

LotR: **Arwen Ornament** (Department 56, $9.95). Measuring 3.5 inches high, this ornament shows Arwen astride her horse.

Globes

LotR: **Galadriel Waterglobe** (Department 56, $24.95). Made of resin and glass, measuring 6.25 inches tall, this figurine of Galadriel is mounted atop a sculpted base.

LotR: **Hobbits in Hiding Waterglobe** (Department 56, $39.95). Made of resin and glass, measuring 7.5 inches tall, this shows the hobbits hiding from a Ringwraith. The design is ingenious—the hobbits are in a protective ledge, encircled by a globe, which is seemingly held in place from above, by the large, ominous hand of a Ringwraith.

LotR: **Gollum Encounter Snow Globe** (Department 56, $44.95). Measuring 6 inches tall, this resin and glass snow globe is the best this company offers: Gollum is reaching down to Frodo and Sam; the globe itself rests on a rocky base. Very imaginative, very attractive.

Clothing and Apparel

All of the shirts and hats mentioned in the following sections are official movie tie-in merchandise, distributed solely by New Line Cinemas (*shop.newline.com*). The costumes listed are manufactured and distributed by Rubie's Costume Company (*www.rubies.com*).

Shirts

LotR **Arwen babydoll shirt** ($16.95). Blue design of Arwen's pendant against a black background. Babydoll t-shirt.

Frodo Lives T-shirt ($16.95). Tan T-shirt with "Frodo Lives" and the first film's release date on the front, the "One Ring to rule them all..." poem on the back, and the movie on the left sleeve. A limited edition (though no limitation notice stated).

LotR **Crow Symbol T-shirt** ($15.95). Black T-shirt with a gray silhouette of a crow on the front, with the words "The Lord of the Rings: The Two Towers" in silver. The back has the poem, "One Ring to rule them all...."

LotR **Orc Trio youth T-shirt** ($14.95). Sized for youngsters only, three orcs on the front against a black background.

LotR **Eye of Sauron T-shirt** ($15.95). On the front, the symbol of Sauron, with the legend, "The Lord of the Rings: The Two Towers." On the back, a large image of the flaming, unblinking red eye of Sauron.

LotR: The Two Towers **adult sweatshirt** ($29.95). On the front, an image of the One Ring, with the legend, "The Lord of the Rings: The Two Towers." A cotton/polyester blend (90 percent/10percent).

LotR: The Two Towers **movie montage T-shirt** ($15.95). On the front is printed "The Two Towers" and an image of the One Ring. On the back, the One Ring is surrounded by a montage of heroes from the film. **Note:** A kid's version is available as well ($13.95).

Baseball Caps

Frodo Lives baseball cap ($15.95). White lettering on black, adjustable cloth closure in back.

***LotR* logo baseball cap** ($14.95). Gold stitching on black, adjustable cloth closure in back.

Faramir logo baseball cap ($14.95). The most visually attractive baseball cap offered. Features the logo of Faramir of Gondor, embroidered in light gray with gold stitching against a dark background, adjustable cloth closure in back.

***The Two Towers* logo baseball cap** ($15.95). Yellow-orange logo on the front, adjustable cloth closure in back.

Hobbit tree baseball cap ($15.00). Green cap with tree logo on the front, *LotR* movie logo on back, adjustable cloth strap with metal clasp.

Orc Flag baseball cap ($15). Black cap with gray Orc logo on front, *LotR* movie logo on back, adjustable cloth strap with metal clasp.

Costumes

Gandalf Kids' Costume (Rubie's Costume, $31.95). Costume includes hat, robe, satchel, and belt. (Wig, beard, and staff not included.)

Gandalf Kids' Costume Set (Rubie's Costume, $44.95). Costume includes hat, robe, satchel, belt, wig, and beard. (Staff not included.)

Hobbit Kids' Costume (Rubie's Costume, $29.95). Costume includes hooded cloak, vest, and satchel. (Pants and shirt not included.)

Moria Orc Mask (Rubie's Costume, $49.95). For teens or adults, this latex mask has a very authentic paint job—detailed, very convincing. The perfect thing for Halloween.

Ringwraith Kings Costume Set (Rubie's Costume, $32.95). Costume includes shredded black robe with matching hood and "see-out-only" mesh drape for the face.

Jewelry

The watches listed here have been manufactured for exclusive distribution through New Line Cinema's official Web store or through its official fan club Web store.

***LotR*: Middle-earth Adult Watch** (Fossil, $95). Limited to 2,000 pieces, this watch comes in a wooden keepsake box, within which is a map of Middle-earth; a limitation notice is attached to the inside lid. The watch, run by a quartz movement, has three hands and a leather band.

LotR: The Two Towers **Eye of Sauron Fossil Watch** (Fossil, $125). Limited to 3,000 pieces. Comes in a molded silver case, packaged in a polyresin replica of the tower at Barad-dûr. Its certificate of authenticity is etched in its base.

LotR **watch: Frodo** ($49.95). A unisex design with a black leather band and three hands. Shows Frodo holding the One Ring. Comes in a decorative tin.

LotR **watch** ($49.95). A unisex design with a black leather band and three hands. Shows a map of Middle-earth. Comes in a decorative tin.

LotR **watch** ($49.95). A unisex design with a black leather band and three hands. A black face with gold lettering, the inscription, in Elvish, is the "One Ring to rule them all..." poem.

LotR: **Argonath Adult Watch** ($49.95). The face of the watch has an image of the Argonath. The gold-colored watch, with the "One Ring" inscription on its perimeter, has a black leather band and comes in a gift tin.

Standups

These are life-size cardboard cut-outs of favorite characters from the movies. (If you want to impress your friends, tell them you hobnob with wizards and hobbits. Take your picture standing next to a Gandalf or Frodo standup, but use a flash to flatten the lighting to make it look more convincing, though only fools of a Took will be taken in by this ruse!)

Life-size Frodo Standup (Advanced Graphics, $29.95). Frodo (actor Elijah Wood) dressed in his walking garb (green cloak, brown jacket/shirt and pants), he is holding Sting. Height: 4 feet, 2 inches.

Life-size Gandalf Standup (Advanced Graphics, $29.95). Gandalf the Grey (actor Ian McKellen) holding his wizard's staff. Height: 5 feet, 11 inches.

Life-size Hobbit Standup (Advanced Graphics, $39.95). This standup is one single piece depicting the four hobbits: Frodo Baggins (actor Elijah Wood), Sam Gamgee (Sean Austin), Peregrin "Pippin" Took (Billy Boyd), and Meriadoc "Merry" Brandybuck (Dominic Monaghan). Height: 4 feet, 5 inches.

Life-size Saruman Standup (Advanced Graphics, $29.95). Saruman (actor Christopher Lee) holding his wizard's staff. Height: 6 feet, 3 inches.

Life-size Talking Gollum Standup (Advanced Graphics, $39.95). Height: approximately 3 feet. This standup has a motion-detecting voicebox that emits three phrases: "My Precious!", "You filthy little thieves!", and "You stole it, My Precious, and we wants it!" (This one's perfect for the porch on Halloween.)

Gollum and Sméagol Talking Life-size Standups (Advanced Graphics, $59.95). Gollum is approximately 3 feet tall, Sméagol 3 feet, 4 inches, both pictured together on this standup. Nasty Gollum utters three phrases (same as the talking Gollum standup), but nice Sméagol says, "Rock and pool, is nice and cool, so juicy sweet!"

Life-size Aragorn Standup (Advanced Graphics, $29.95). Aragorn, a.k.a. Strider, (actor Viggo Mortensen) holding his sword. Height: 5 feet, 9 inches.

Life-size Gandalf the White Standup (Advanced Graphics, $29.95). No longer Gandalf the Grey, Gandalf (actor Ian McKellen) is now dressed in white and is the head of the council. Height: 5 feet, 11 inches.

Life-size Gimli and Legolas Standup (Advanced Graphics, $29.95). This single standup pictures both Gimli the Dwarf (actor John Rhys-Davies) and Legolas the Elf (actor Orlando Bloom). Height: 5 feet, 10 inches.

Life-size Legolas Standup (Advanced Graphics, $29.95). Legolas Greenleaf (actor Orlando Bloom) stands peering into the distance. Height: 5 feet, 10 inches.

Life-size Talking Sméagol Standup (Advanced Graphics, $29.95). Stands 3 feet, 4 inches. Uses a motion-detecting voicebox that utters, "Rock and pool, is nice and cool, so juicy sweet! My only wish, to catch a fish, so juicy sweet!"

Action Figures and Dolls

Toy Biz

Manufactured by a division of Marvel Comics, Toy Biz offers the collector an affordable set of articulated, poseable figures (that is, "dolls") in collector's boxes. Unlike the Sideshow/Weta line with limited runs, the Toy Biz line is geared toward the mass market, with distribution through major toy-store chains and other high-volume retail outlets.

These action figures are poseable and are designed for action play; the Elrond figure, for instance, has a sword attack action.

From Toy Biz, a Black Rider and his steed.

The Fellowship of the Ring

6-inch Action Figure Assortment #1

1. **Frodo**, with sword attack action and Ringwraith base.

2. **Strider**, with sword-drawing and slashing actions.

3. **Newborn Lurtz**, with realistic battle attack action.

4. **Legolas**, with dagger-slashing and arrow-launching action.

5. **Witch-king Ringwraith**, with sword-lunging action.

6-inch Action Figure Assortment #2

1. **Samwise Gamgee**, with Moria Mines goblin battle base.

2. **Gandalf**, with light-up staff action.

3. **Saruman**, with magic-floating Palantir on base.

4. **Gimli**, with battling axe-swinging action.

5. **Orc Overseer**, with dungeons of Isengard newborn Uruk-Hai.

6-inch Action Figure Assortment #3

1. **Traveling Bilbo**, with Bag End diorama and traveling gear.

2. **Strider**, with arrow-launching action.

3. **Elrond**, with Elven sword-attack action.

4. **Orc Warrior**, with axe-hacking and arrow-launching actions.

6-inch Twin Packs Assortment #1

Two action figures from a pivotal movie scene.

1. **Lurtz**, with bow-attack action vs. **Boromir**, with battle-attack action.

2. **Merry and Pippin**, vs. **Moria Orc**, with Moria Mines battle attack action.

6-inch Twin Packs Assortment #2

1. **Samwise Gamgee and Frodo**, with Elven boat accessory.

2. **Uruk-Hai Warrior**, with sword & shield battling action vs. **Gimli** with axe-throwing action.

Collector Series Assortment #1

1. **Gandalf**.

2. **Frodo**.

3. **Arwen**.

Collector Series Assortment #2

1. **Aragorn**.

2. **Galadriel**.

3. **Gimli**.

From Toy Biz, Arwen Evenstar and Frodo "Deluxe Horse and Rider Set."

Other

1. Deluxe Horse and Rider Assortment.

2. Electronic 10-inch Cave Troll.

3. Bow 'n Arrow.

4. Electronic Middle-earth Sword.

5. Light 'n Sound Sting Sword.

6. *Lord of the Rings* Deluxe Gift Pack.

The Two Towers: **Gandalf the White** (Toy Biz, $11.95). Fully articulated, poseable character replica, 6 inches high.

The Two Towers: **Gondorian Ranger** (Toy Biz, $11.95). Fully articulated, poseable character replica, 6 inches high.

The Two Towers: **Aragorn and Brego** (Toy Biz, $24.95). A set of two pieces, each articulated and poseable. Aragorn and his horse, Brego, each 6 inches high.

The Two Towers: **Bilbo Figure** (Toy Biz, $28.95). An articulated piece, Bilbo is drawing Sting from its sheath, 12 inches high.

The Two Towers: **Legolas Figure** (Toy Biz, $28.95). An articulated piece, Legolas prepares for battle, arrow and bow in hand, 12 inches high.

The Two Towers: **Talking Treebeard** (Toy Biz, $35.95). An articulated, poseable action figure. It requires three AA batteries and, with its voice chip, speaks several digitized phrases: "Treebeard, some call me!", "I told Gandalf I would keep you safe, and safe is where I'll keep you!", "I am not a tree, I am an Ent!", "Little orcs, burarum," and "Burarum, don't be hasty!"

The Two Towers: **Witch-king Ringwraith** (Toy Biz, $28.95). An articulated, poseable action figure, 12 inches high.

Plush Replicas and "Bobbing Head" Dolls

Note: Regarding "bobbing head" dolls—what would J.R.R. Tolkien have thought?

Frodo Plush Character Replica ($24.95). Distributed by New Line Cinema, this plush doll, with molded plastic arms, legs, and head, measures 12 inches high.

Aragorn (Strider) Bobbing Head Doll (Upper Deck, $14.95). Packaged in a character-specific window box, 7 inches tall.

Boromir Bobbing Head Doll (Upper Deck, $14.95). Packaged in a character-specific window box, 7 inches tall.

Frodo Bobbing Head Doll (Upper Deck, $14.95). Packaged in a character-specific window box, 6 inches tall.

Gandalf Bobbing Head Doll (Upper Deck, $14.95). Packaged in a character-specific window box, 8 inches tall.

Gimli Bobbing Head Doll ($14.95). Packaged in a character-specific window box, 7 inches tall.

Merry [Merriadoc Brandybuck] Bobbing Head Doll ($14.95). Packaged in a character-specific window box, 6 inches tall.

Pippin [Peregrin Took] Bobbing Head Doll ($14.95). Packaged in a character-specific window box, 6 inches tall.

Sam [Samwise Gamgee] Bobbing Head Doll ($14.95). Packaged in a character-specific window box, 6 inches tall.

Board Games and Puzzles

The Fellowship of the Ring **Board Game** (Reveal Entertainment, $23.95). Game contains a playing die, 14 game tiles, 74 ring cards, 12 character cards, and 6 metalized rings.

The Lord of the Rings **Chess Set** (Hasbro Games, $39.95). The cardboard chess board measures 15 x 19 inches; the pieces, made of plastic, are tinted pewter (heroes) or bronze (villains), and stand approximately 3 inches high. For the heroes, the pieces include: Sam Gamgee as the pawn pieces, Boromir as the rooks, Aragorn as the knights, Frodo as the bishops, Galadriel as the Queen, and Gandalf as the King. For the villains, the pieces include: an orc warrior as the pawns, an orc overseer as the rooks, Lurtz as the knights, the Cave Troll as the bishops, a Ringwraith as the Queen, and Saruman as the King.

Risk, *The Lord of the Rings* **Edition** (Hasbro Games, $34.95). Modeled after the classic board game Risk, this is the battle not for Earth, but Middle-earth.

Frodo & Sam Poster Puzzle (Wrebbit, $14.95). A collage of images featuring Frodo and Sam. When completed, this 500-piece puzzle measures 25 x 36 inches.

Gandalf the White Poster Puzzle (Wrebbit, $14.95). A collage of images featuring Gandalf the White. When completed, this 500 piece puzzle measures 24 x 36 inches.

The Lord of the Rings **Golden Hall, Edoras 3-D Puzzle** (Wrebbit, $24.95). This is a 3-D jigsaw puzzle of the home of King Théoden. When assembled, this 700-piece puzzle measures 9 inches high x 18 inches wide x 20.5 inches long.

The Lord of the Rings **Orthanc Tower, Isengard 3-D Puzzle** (Wrebbit, $19.95). This is a 3-D jigsaw puzzle of 409 pieces that, when assembled, measures 6 inches wide x 6 inches long x 27 inches high.

Computer Software

The Lord of the Rings: The Fellowship of the Ring **CD-ROM Activity Studio** (IMSI, $24.95). For Windows PC only, this CD-ROM includes: a print room, in which you can print out color images from the movie as various printed product, such as bookmarks and posters; a Character Profile section, with info on all the major characters and printable scroll posters of each; screensavers and wallpaper for your computer; video extracts from the film; Web links; and the Paint and Create studio, where character line drawings can be printed as greeting cards, posters, and so on.

***The Lord of the Rings: The Two Towers* CD ROM, Mousepads, and Bookmark Souvenir Set** ($24.95). Available exclusively through New Line Cinema, this CD-ROM (for Windows PC only) includes a desktop calendar and personal organizer, three screensavers, and a selection of desktop wallpapers. Also included are a fan folder and two mouse pads.

***The Lord of the Rings: The Two Towers* Activity Studio** (IMSI, $24.95). For Windows PC only, this Activity Studio is similar to *The Fellowship of the Ring* edition, featuring a print room (to print out images as various products), character profiles, an interactive map of Middle-earth, screen savers, wallpaper, puzzles, a quiz, a paint-and-create studio, and a video trailer of *The Two Towers* movie.

CD Cardz Set 1: Frodo, Gandalf, Aragorn, and Ringwraiths (SeriousUSA, $19.95). Designed for insertion in a computer, these CD-ROMs shaped like trading cards include "highlights, screensavers, film trailers, and sound effects." Because of the unconventional shape, these will not play in a slot-loading computer tray.

CD Cardz Set 2: *The Two Towers* (SeriousUSA, $14.95). Another set of four, with images of Frodo, Gandalf, Aragorn, and the Rightwraiths. These CD-ROM "cards" feature "character bios, photo gallery, behind the scenes, postcards, screensavers, wallpaper, and more."

A CD-ROM card for The Lord of the Rings: The Two Towers.

Sideshow/Weta

The Weta Workshop has been immersed for the last five years in the conceptualizing, creation and on-set operation of the creatures, miniatures, armor, weapons and special make-up effects for the three epic films. Weta's focus has been to create a unified look throughout the three films while capturing the essence of the books.... It is the same Weta designers and technicians that have created the different armies and creatures within Middle-earth that have chosen to create the high quality collectibles under the Sideshow/Weta brand. The integrated experience that these designers and technicians have resulted in the most authentic figure and miniature collectibles possible.

—From the series 4 brochure

The film has spawned numerous tie-in products, running the gamut of the silly (bobbing head dolls) to the predictable (One Ring replicas), but this line of hand-painted collectible busts and figures, produced in limited runs, are collectibles of the highest possible quality. Ranging in size from miniatures to 17-inch figures, Sideshow/Weta is now offering high-end collectibles, including a hand-painted bronze sculpture of Gandalf ($4,995), limited to 36 pieces.

A display of Sideshow/Weta collectibles at the 2002 San Diego Comicon. (Photo courtesy of Colleen Doran.)

For fans who want a truly memorable collectible with which to remember the films, a selection of busts and figures from this collection are certifiably collectibles. They have intrinsic value and will rise in price over time after their retirement.

The Fellowship of the Ring Series 1

Gandalf the Grey Figure ($125). Constructed of polystone, 12.5 inches high, weighs 10 pounds.

Gandalf the Grey Bust ($60). Constructed of polystone, 9.25 inches high, weighs 5 pounds.

Orc Crowfaced Helm ($25). Metal helm, approximately 4 inches high, weighs 3 pounds.

Orc Squinter Helm ($25). Metal helm, approximately 5 inches high, weighs 3 pounds.

Orc Trapjaw Helm ($25). Metal helm, approximately 5.5 inches high, weighs 3 pounds.

Orc Hide Helm ($25). Metal helm, approximately 5 inches high, weighs 3 pounds.

Aragorn, Son of Arathorn Bust ($60). Polystone, 8.5 inches high, weighs 5 pounds.

Frodo Baggins Bust ($50). Polystone, 6.75 inches high, weighs 2 pounds.

Frodo Baggins Figure ($100). Polystone, 9 inches high, weighs 3 pounds.

Lurtz Figure ($125). Polystone, 14.5 inches high, weighs 5 pounds.

Moria Orc Swordsman Bust ($60). Polystone, 7.5 inches high, weighs 3 pounds.

Orc Overseer Bust ($60). Polystone, 6.5 inches high, weighs 3 pounds.

Orc Overseer Figure ($125). Polystone, 10.5 inches high, weighs 5 pounds.

Peregrin Bust ($50). Polystone, 6.75 inches high, weighs 2 pounds.

Series 2

Legolas Greenleaf Figure ($125). Polystone, 12.5 inches high, weighs 6 pounds.

Gimli's Helm ($25). Metal helm, 5 inches high, weighs 3 pounds.

High Elven Infantry Helm ($25). Metal helm, 6 inches high, weighs 3 pounds.

Númenorian Infantry Helm ($25). Metal helm, 6 inches high, weighs 3 pounds.

Orc Iron Cap Helm ($25). Metal helm, 5 inches high, weighs 3 pounds.

Boromir, Son of Denethor Bust ($60). Polystone, 8 inches high, weighs 4 pounds.

From Sideshow/Weta, a close-up of the Legolas Greenleaf sculpture.

Gimli, Son of Glóin Bust ($60). Polystone, 7.5 inches high, weighs 5 pounds.

Lurtz, Uruk-Hai Captain Bust ($60). Polystone, 6.5 inches high, weighs 6 pounds.

Moria Orc Swordsman Figure ($125). Polystone, 9.5 inches high, weighs 6 pounds.

From Sideshow/Weta, a sculpture of an orc swordsman.

Númenorian Infantryman Bust ($60). Polystone, 9.25 inches high, weighs 5 pounds.

Orc Pitmaster Figure ($125). Polystone, 10.25 inches high, weighs 4 pounds.

Orc Warrior Figure ($125). Polystone, 8.38 inches high, weighs 5 pounds.

Samwise Gamgee Bust ($50). Polystone, 6.5 inches high, weighs 2 pounds.

Uruk-Hai Scout Bust ($60). Polystone, 9.25 inches high, weighs 6 pounds.

Series 3

Elendil's Helm ($25). Metal helm, 5.5 inches high, weighs 3 pounds.

Gandalf's Hat ($25). Polystone, 6.5 inches high, weighs 3 pounds.

Isildur's Helm ($25). Metal helm, 5.75 inches high, weighs 3 pounds.

From Sideshow/Weta, a close-up view of the head of a Black Rider steed.

Moria Orc's Helm ($25). Metal helm, 5 inches high, weighs 3 pounds.

Bilbo Baggins Bust ($50). Polystone, 6.25 inches high, weighs 2 pounds.

Cleaved Orc Bust ($60). Polystone, 6.5 inches high, weighs 3 pounds.

High Elven Infantry Bust ($60). Polystone, 9.75 inches high, weighs 4 pounds.

Meriadoc Figure ($100). Polystone, 9.5 inches high, weighs 3 pounds.

Merry Brandybuck Bust ($50). Polystone, 6.25 inches high, weighs 2 pounds.

Nazgûl Steed Bust ($75). Polystone, 12 inches high, weighs 7 pounds.

Orc Brute Figure ($125). Polystone, 11.5 inches high, weighs 8 pounds.

Orc Soldier Bust ($60). Polystone, 7.25 inches high, weighs 3 pounds.

Samwise Gamgee and Bill the Pony Figure ($150). Polystone, 9.5 inches high, weighs 14 pounds.

Saruman the White Figure ($150). Polystone, 12.75 inches high, weighs 14 pounds.

From Sideshow/Weta, a sculpture of Saruman the White, as he communicates with the Dark Lord, Sauron, using a Palantir.

Series 4

Aragorn, Son of Arathorn Figure ($125). Polystone, 11.5 inches high, weighs 5 pounds.

Arwen Evenstar Bust ($60). Polystone, 11.5 inches, weighs 5 pounds.

Arwen Evenstar Figure ($125). Polystone, 11.5 inches high, weighs 5 pounds.

Dwarven Lord Bust ($60). Polystone, weighs 3 pounds, size not available.

Moria Orc Archer Bust ($60). Polystone, weighs 3 pounds, size not available.

Moria Orc Archer Figure ($125). Polystone, 9.5 inches high x 9 inches deep x 5 inches wide, weight not available.

Ringwraith Bust ($65). Polystone, 9 inches high, weighs 5 pounds.

Uruk-Hai Scout Swordsman Figure ($125). Polystone, 11.75 inches high, weighs 6 pounds.

From Sideshow/Weta, a sculpture of an orc archer in the Mines of Moria.

From Sideshow/Weta, a sculpture of an Uruk-Hai swordsman.

Series 5

(Announced but no details.)

The Two Towers Series 1 Busts

Gríma Wormtongue Bust ($60). Limited edition of 2,000 hand-numbered pieces. Polystone, 7.75 inches high, weighs 4 pounds.

Lady Galadriel Bust ($60). Limited edition of 2,000 hand-numbered pieces. Polystone, 8 inches high, weighs 3 pounds.

Legolas Greenleaf Bust ($60). Limited edition of 3,000 hand-numbered pieces. Polystone, 8.25 inches, weighs 6 pounds.

Saruman the White Bust ($60). Limited edition of 3,000 hand-numbered pieces. Polystone, 8.5 inches, weighs 6 pounds.

The Two Towers Series 1 Figures

Easterling Soldier Figure ($125). Limited edition of 2,000 hand-numbered pieces, sculpted by Gary Hunt. Polystone, weighs 10 pounds, size not available.

Gimli, Son of Glóin Figure ($125). Limited edition of 2,000 hand-numbered pieces, sculpted by Jamie Beswarick. Polystone, 9 inches high x 6.5 inches wide x 12 inches deep, weighs 6 pounds.

From Sideshow/Weta, a sculpture of an Easterling Soldier.

From Sideshow/Weta, a sculpture of Gandalf the White bearing his wizard's staff.

Gandalf the White Figure ($125). Limited edition of 3,000 hand-numbered pieces, sculpted by Gary Hunt. Polystone, weighs 10 pounds, size not available.

The Two Towers Series 2 Busts

Galadhrim Soldier Bust ($60). Limited edition of 2,000 hand-numbered pieces, sculpted by Heather Kilgour. Polystone, 9.75 inches high, weighs 7 pounds.

Gandalf the White Bust ($60). Limited edition of 2,000 hand-numbered pieces, sculpted by Gary Hunt. Polystone, weighs 8 pounds.

Grishnákh Bust ($60). Limited edition of 2,000 hand-numbered pieces, sculpted by Jamie Beswarick. Polystone, 6.25 inches high, weighs 5 pounds.

Uruk-Hai Berserker Bust ($60). Limited edition of 2,000 hand-numbered pieces, sculpted by Jonny Brough. Polystone, 10 inches high, weighs 8 pounds.

The Two Towers Series 2 Figures

Galadhrim Archer Figure ($125). Limited edition of 2,000 hand-numbered pieces, sculpted by Roger Lewis. Polystone, 17.25 inches high, weighs 12 pounds.

From Sideshow/Weta, a bust of an Uruk-Hai Beserker, the front-line "shock" troops, who were first into battle.

Gríma Wormtongue Figure ($125). Limited edition of 2,000 hand-numbered pieces, sculpted by Mike Asquith. Polystone, 11.5 inches high, weighs 10 pounds.

Ugluk, Uruk-Hai Captain Figure ($125). Limited edition of 2,000 hand-numbered pieces, sculpted by Mike Asqith and Jamie Beswarick. Polystone, 11.25 high, weighs 10 pounds.

From Sideshow/Weta, a sculpture of a Galadhrim Archer.

The Two Towers Series 3 Busts

Éomer Bust ($60). Limited edition of 2,000 hand-numbered pieces, sculpted by Greg Tozer. Polystone, 8 inches high, weighs 5 pounds.

King Théoden Bust ($60). Limited edition of 2,000 hand-numbered pieces, sculpted by Virginia Lee. Polystone, 8.25 inches tall, weighs 5 pounds.

Uruk-Hai Swordsman Bust ($60). Limited edition of 2,000 hand-numbered pieces, sculpted by Greg Tozer. Polystone, 9 inches tall, weighs 5 pounds.

The Witch-king of Angmar Bust ($60). Limited edition of 1,500 hand-numbered pieces, sculpted by Mike Asquith. Polystone, 11.5 inches high, weighs 3 pounds.

Exclusives

The Watcher in the Water Statue ($250). Limited edition of 750 pieces. Polystone, 10.5 inches high, 15.75 inches wide and 10.5 inches deep, weighs 20 pounds.

Bilbo Baggins Statue ($100). Limited edition of 1,000. Polystone, 8.5 inches high, weighs 5 pounds.

Boromir, Son of Denethor Statue ($125). Limited edition of 2,000. Polystone, 11.5 inches high, weighs 6 pounds.

From Sideshow/Weta, a sculpture of the Witch-king, the Lord of the Nazgûl.

From Sideshow/Weta, a sculpture of the Orthanc Tower, occupied by Saruman.

Witch-king of Angmar Statue ($150). Limited edition of 1,000, sculpted by Xander Forterie. Polystone, 16 inches high, weighs 18 pounds.

Orc Legion Helm ($25). Metal helm, 6.75 inches high, weighs 3 pounds.

Orthanc ($95). Limited edition of 750 copies. Polystone environment, 11.75 inches tall, with 5.5 inch wide sculpted base, weighs 6 pounds.

"No Admittance Except on Party Business" Bookends ($60). Sculpted by Oluf W. Hartivgson and Mary MacLachlan, each polystone bookend measures 6.5 inches high and 5.25 inches deep. (Note: The bookends are discontinued because Houghton Mifflin is selling these with a one-volume edition of *The Lord of the Rings* for $75.)

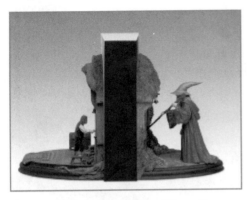

A one-volume movie tie-in edition of
The Lord of the Rings, *by Houghton
Mifflin, buttressed by a pair of Sideshow/
Weta bookends with Bilbo Baggins and
Gandalf the Wizard.*

*A close-up of a wall plaque showing the
four hobbits hiding from a Black Rider,
who is searching for them. The plaque
was sculpted by Virginia Lee, daughter of
Tolkien artist Alan Lee.*

"Escape off the Road" Wall Plaque ($150). Limited edition of 5,000 copies,
sculpted by Virginia Lee (daughter of Alan Lee, Tolkien artist and conceptualizer
for the movies). The piece is signed by Virginia Lee and Weta director Richard
Taylor. Polystone plaque, 15.75 inches wide x 9.5 inches high, weighs 12 pounds.

Ringwraith and Steed Statue ($275). Limited to 5,000 copies. Polystone, 15 inches
high x 16 inches wide x 9 inches deep, weighs 17 pounds.

*From Sideshow/Weta, a
saddled Black Rider and
his steed.*

*A close-up of the steed
ridden by a Black Rider.*

*A back view of the Black
Rider on his steed sculpture.*

The Alan Lee Lithograph and Filmstrip Collectible ($599). A limited edition of 1,000 (and 150 artist proofs) signed by director Peter Jackson, Weta director Richard Taylor, and illustrator Alan Lee. A lithograph of the conceptual art of Rivendell by Lee, with four frames cut from an actual reel of film donated by Jackson, this matted and framed print measures 29 x 29 inches. (**Note:** The film frames are backlit with a lighting device.)

From Sideshow/Weta, a numbered, limited edition color lithograph, matted and framed with a piece of authentic The Lord of the Rings *film and signed by Alan Lee (artist), Peter Jackson (director), and Richard Taylor (Weta creative director).*

Cave Troll Bust ($70). Limited to 10,000 pieces. Polystone, weighs 8 pounds, size unavailable.

The Balrog Statue ($300). Limited to 1,000 pieces. Heavy-weight polystone on a sculpted base, 13.5 inches high, weighs 25 pounds.

The Cave Troll Figure ($300). Limited to 750 pieces, sculpted by Jamie Beswarick. Polystone, 14.25 inches high x 10.25 inches wide x 18 inches long, weighs 25 pounds.

The Stone Trolls Statue ($300). Limited to 750 pieces. Polystone, 8 inches high x 10.5 inches deep x 16 inches long, weighs 30 pounds.

Gollum Bust ($250). Polystone, 12.5 inches high x 7.75 inches deep x 7.5 inches wide, weighs 12 pounds. The Gollum nameplate bears the movie logo of "The Lord of the Rings" and a hand-numbered edition size.

From Sideshow/ Weta, a bust of Gollum.

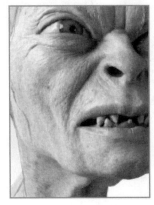

A close-up view of the Gollum bust.

Treebeard Bust ($300). Limited to 1,500 pieces. Heavy-weight polystone, hand-painted, on a base. Sculpted by Brigitte Wuest and Daniel Falconer, 17.75 inches high x 13 inches deep, weighs 15 pounds.

The Lord of the Rings Weapons Sets

The Arms of Aragorn ($40). Limited edition of 2,500 pieces. A polystone weapon set, hand-numbered, the weapons are permanently mounted on the display plaque and sit on an oval display base. Stands 9.5 inches high x 5.74 inches wide, weighs 3 pounds.

The Arms of Lurtz ($40). Limited edition of 2,500 pieces. A polystone weapon set, hand-numbered, the weapons are permanently mounted on the display plaque and sits on an oval display base. Stands 11.5 inches high x 7.25 inches wide, weighs 3 pounds.

The Arms of the Fellowship 1: Frodo, Gandalf the Grey, and Aragorn ($40). Limited edition of 2,500 pieces. A polystone weapon set, hand-numbered, the weapons are permanently mounted on the display plaque and sit on an oval display base. Stands 11.5 inches high x 7.25 inches wide, weighs 3 pounds.

The Arms of the Fellowship 2: Boromir and Merry ($40). Limited edition of 2,500 pieces. A polystone weapon set, hand-numbered, the weapons are permanently mounted on the display plaque and sit on an oval display base. Stands 9.5 inches high x 5.75 inches wide, weighs 3 pounds.

The Arms of Gimli ($40). Limited edition of 2,500 pieces. A polystone weapon set, hand-numbered, the weapons are permanently mounted on the display plaque and sit on an oval display base. Stands 11.75 inches high x 7.25 inches wide, weighs 3 pounds.

The Arms of Legolas, Collection #1 Weapon ($40). Limited edition of 2,500 pieces. A polystone weapon set, hand-numbered, the weapons are permanently mounted on the display plaque and sit on an oval display base. Stands 9.25 inches high x 5.75 inches wide, weighs 3 pounds.

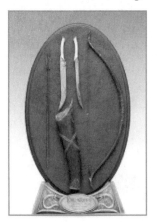

The Arms of the Moria Orcs ($40). Limited edition of 2,500 pieces. A polystone weapon set, hand-numbered, the weapons are permanently mounted on the display plaque and sit on an oval display base. Stands 11.75 inches high x 7.5 inches wide, weighs 3 pounds.

From Sideshow/Weta, a miniature reproduction of the weapons carried by Legolas Greenleaf: a bow and arrow and a pair of hunting knives, permanently mounted on a plaque, set on a decorative base.

The Arms of the Hobbits, Collection #1: Frodo, Samwise, Merry, and Pippin ($40). Limited edition of 2,500 pieces. A polystone weapon set, hand-numbered, the weapons are permanently mounted on the display plaque and sit on an oval display base. Stands 9.25 inches high x 5.75 inches wide, weighs 3 pounds.

The Lord of the Rings Medallions

The certificate of authenticity, numbered and signed by the artist, that accompanies each medallion.

Designed by Weta Workshop, the medallions are hand-finished with a faux bronze patina, and are accompanied with a Certificate of Authenticity. Numbers 1 through 8 are *The Fellowship of the Ring* medallions, while 9 through 16 are for *The Two Towers*.

Medallion #1: The Orcs of Moria ($25). A limited edition of 10,000 pieces. Made of polystone, 6 inches in diameter, weighs 2 pounds.

Medallion #2: The Nazgûl ($25). A limited edition of 10,000 pieces. Made of polystone, 6 inches in diameter, weighs 2 pounds.

Medallion #3: The Industry of Isengard ($25). A limited edition of 10,000 pieces. Made of polystone, 6 inches in diameter, weighs 2 pounds.

Medallion #4: The Last Alliance ($25). A limited edition of 10,000 pieces. Made of polystone, 6 inches in diameter, weighs 2 pounds.

Medallion #5: The Birth of the Uruk-Hai ($25). A limited edition of 10,000 pieces. Made of polystone, 6 inches in diameter, weighs 2 pounds.

From Sideshow/Weta, a medallion of orcs in profile, titled "The Orcs of Moria."

Medallion #6: The Soldiers of the White Hand ($25). A limited edition of 10,000 pieces. Made of polystone, 6 inches in diameter, weighs 2 pounds.

Medallion #7: The Cave Troll ($25). A limited edition of 10,000 pieces. Made of polystone, 6 inches in diameter, weighing two pounds.

Medallion #8: The Watcher in the Water ($25). A limited edition of 10,000 pieces. Made of polystone, 6 inches in diameter, weighs 2 pounds.

Medallion #9: The Uruk-Hai Beserkers ($25). A limited edition of 1,000 pieces. Made of polystone, 6 inches in diameter, weighs 2 pounds.

The base of the "Orcs of Moria" medallion, numbered and signed by the artist.

Medallion #10: The Ambitions of Grishnákh ($25). A limited edition of 1,000 pieces. Made of polystone, 6 inches in diameter weighs 2 pounds.

Medallion #11: The Return of King Théoden ($25). A limited edition of 1,000 pieces. Made of polystone, 6 inches in diameter, weighs 2 pounds.

Medallion #12: The Warg Riders ($25). A limited edition of 1,000 pieces. Made of polystone, 6 inches in diameter, weighs 2 pounds.

Medallion #13: The Master of Fangorn ($25). A limited edition of 1,000 pieces. Made of polystone, 6 inches in diameter, weighs 2 pounds.

Medallion #14: The Dilemmas of Sméagol ($25). A limited edition of 1,000 pieces. Made of polystone, 6 inches in diameter, weighs 2 pounds.

Medallion #15: The Easterlings ($25). A limited edition of 1,000 pieces. Made of polystone, 6 inches in diameter, weighs 2 pounds.

Medallion #16: The Duel of Light and Fire ($25). A limited edition of 1,000 pieces. Made of polystone, 6 inches in diameter, weighs 2 pounds.

High-End Collectibles

From Sideshow/Weta, a limited edition bronze sculpture of Gandalf the Wizard.

Gandalf the Grey Bronze Statue. Sideshow/Weta has moved into the realm of high-end collectibles with the production of its first bronze statue. A limited edition of only 36 pieces (and four artist proofs), with its edition number engraved on the piece and signed by sculptor Gary Hunt, the sculpture itself is 24 inches high (with its marble base, 27 inches) and weighs 75 pounds.

The choice for the first statue—one of many to come, I imagine—is an excellent choice: Gandalf the Grey, as he battles the Balrog. Made by the traditional "lost wax" process, the bronze piece is priced on a sliding scale—copies 1–9, $4,995; 10–18, $5,495; 19–27, $5,995; and 28–36, $6,495.

Made to order with a 4–6 week delivery schedule, the bronze statue has a special acid-washed patina on Gandalf's cloak, giving it a weathered look.

Appealing to well-heeled collectors who want the very best, the Gandalf bronze fills the need for the high-end market, which has largely been ignored by the licensing effort. One hopes that the program will expand to include bronzes of other notable characters and creatures, including the Balrog, a Nazgûl, Treebeard, Gandalf the White when he dramatically reappears before the Fellowship, and so on.

A close-up of the Sideshow/Weta bronze Gandalf sculpture.

Supreme Edition Gollum Replica from Rubies ($250). Although this replica is not from Sideshow/Weta, it is an amazing high-end collectible well worth mentioning. Three feet tall and mounted on a base, this is a prop replica that looks and feels very real.

The Return of the King

At present time, images and information about the tie-in collectibles for the third movie have not yet been released. So far, four have been announced:

Elrond, Herald of Gil-Galad ($125). Limited to 2,000 pieces. Heavy-weight polystone, hand-painted, on a base. Statue is 13 inches high x 5 inches wide x 6.25 inches deep, weighs 7 pounds.

Fell Beast and Morgul Lord ($150). Limited to 3,000 pieces, in heavy-weight polystone, sculpted by Jamie Beswarick and Brigette Wuest. This statue is 10.5 inches high x 5 inches wide x 8.5 inches deep, weighs approximately 7 pounds.

King Elessar Statue: Aragorn, King of Gondor Statue ($125). Limited to 2,000 pieces, in heavy-weight polystone, hand-painted, on a base. Sculpted by Gary Hunt, 12.5 inches high x 5.25 inches wide x 8.5 inches deep, weighs 7 pounds.

Théoden Statue ($125). Limited to 2,000 pieces, in heavy-weight polystone, hand painted, on a base. Sculpted by Brigette Wuest, 16.5 inches high x 5.5 inches wide x and 8.25 inches deep, weighs 12 pounds.

Sideshow Collectibles: Going, Going, Gone!

Sculpture that is no longer being manufactured is termed "retired." Furthermore, once the remaining stock is sold out, it is not available through retail outlets. At that point, the piece has moved in status from "retired" to "sold out" and is generally not available on the retail market. However, it will likely resurface in the secondary collectibles market, albeit at a higher cost.

Sideshow/Weta posts on its Website (*www.sideshowtoy.com*) a section that lists the retired pieces from *The Lord of the Rings* collection. That notice should serve as a final warning for fans who are interested in a piece but haven't yet bought: Buy it now, or pay higher prices if and when it can be located through other sources.

Swords by United Cutlery

Blades are United Cutlery's sole business. Tolkien fans will be delighted to learn that, in addition to an impressive line of existing swords and scabbards, the product line will be fleshed out with hunting knives, fighting knives, staff replicas, helmet replicas, the Sauron collection, Gimli's axe replicas, bows, shields, spears, pikes, crowns, and tiaras.

The designs are by Weta Workshop, which took on the formidable task of literally outfitting an army of actors—men, dwarves, elves, orcs, and hobbits—with weapons that had to be designed from scratch. In Sibley's *The Lord of the Rings: The Making of the Movie Trilogy*, Richard Taylor said that "We designed and made 48,000 pieces of armor and had four people working 10 hours a day just producing chain mail. We also produced 2,000 weapons, including swords, spears, pikes and maces, longbows, crossbow, daggers, knives and axes."

The goal, said Taylor, was to give the weapons distinctive looks—no generic weapons, as is often the case with fantasy movies that are usually short of budget and imagination, as well. The result: works of art reproduced as replicas that, like the Sideshow/Weta line of sculpture, are worth collecting.

Blades

Hadhafang: Sword of Arwen ($310.99). Overall length, 38.125 inches; blade length, 30 inches; blade thickness, 0.25 inches; blade material, tempered 420 J2 stainless steel, sharpened; hand grip, wood with an Elven design, solid metal pommel, rat-tail tang construction. Rests on a wood display base, silk-screened with an Elven design. Accompanied by a Certificate of Authenticity printed on parchment.

Hadhafang Display.

On the blade, in Sindarin, is Elvish text that translates to: "this blade is called Hadhafang, a noble defense against the enemy throng for a noble lady."

Hadhafang Handle.

A striking blade, this is wielded by Arwen Evenstar, most notably in a scene from *The Fellowship of the Ring* in which she draws it to protect herself and Frodo, as Ringwraiths draw their dark blades and attempt to cross the river to reach them. "If you want him," she says, pulling the sword and holding it over her head, "come and claim him!"

The Sword of Strider.

Shards of Narsil.

Narsil

The Sword of Strider ($348.99). Overall length, 47.25 inches; blade length, 36 inches; blade thickness, 0.25 inches; blade material, tempered 420 J2 stainless steel; handle material, metal crossguard and pommel, antique metal finish, genuine leather-wrapped grip, rat-tail tang construction. Displayed on a wall plaque with a silkscreened heraldic insignia of the Kingdom of Gondor.

Accessory: A matching sword scabbard with companion knife (forthcoming).

Shards of Narsil ($374.99). A limited edition of 5,000 pieces. Overall length (mounted on wall plaque), 47 inches; blade material, solid metal, antiqued metal finish, false edged; handle material, solid metal crossguard and pommel, antique silver-plated finish, 24-karat gold-plated fittings, engraved Elven runes, leather-wrapped grip, rat-tail tang construction. The Certificate of Authenticity is signed by movie production artist, John Howe.

This is historically the most famous sword in Middle-earth. In a battle against Sauron—the Last Alliance of Elves and Men—this sword was wielded by Elendil and broken in battle. Elendil's son, Isildur, picked up the broken hilt and used it to cut off the One Ring from Sauron's hand. After the battle, the shards were collected and subsequently stored in Rivendell, because legend foretold that it would one day be reforged when the king (Aragorn) would return. On the blade, in Sindarin, is engraved: "Narsil is my name, a mighty sword; Telchar made me in Nogrod."

Narsil ($348.99). Overall length, approximately 53 inches; blade thickness, 0.25 inches; blade material, tempered 420 J2 stainless steel, false edged; handle material, solid metal crossguard and pommel, antique silver-plated finish, 24-karat gold-plated fittings, engraved Elven runes, leather-wrapped grip with rat-tail tang construction. Mounted on a wooden plaque with Elven runes, accompanied by a Certificate of Authenticity.

As legends foretold, the blade that was broken would be restored. Shattered into shards during battle against Sauron, this is the restored sword.

Uruk-hai.

Uruk-Hai Scimitar ($148.99). Overall length, approximately 32 inches; blade thickness, 0.1875 inches; blade material, high carbon steel, battle worn, with a tarnished finish, and false edged; hand grip, leather-wrapped, laminated wood, full tang construction. Rests on a wall plaque. Accompanied by a Certificate of Authenticity.

Forged in the mines of Orthanc, this is the sword wielded by the Uruk-Hai, the special breed of Orcs who comprise part of Saruman's army. (These Orcs bear on their shields the symbol of Saruman's white hand.)

Sword of the Ringwraiths ($348.99). Overall length, 53 inches; blade thickness, 0.25 inches; blade material, acid-etched, tempered, 420 J2 stainless steel, false edged; hand grip, battle-worn solid metal crossguard and pommel, with a leather grip, and rat-tail tang construction. Rests on a wall plaque with runes.

This is the weapon carried by the dreaded Ringwraiths, formerly kings of men, corrupted by evil—known as the Dark Riders of the Nazgûl, their swords were forged in Mordor.

Sword of the Ringwraiths.

Sting ($223.99). Overall length, 22 inches; blade length, 15 inches; blade thickness, 0.25 inches; blade material, tempered 420 J2 stainless steel with etched Elven runes; handle material, hardwood handgrip adorned with an Elven design, solid metal guard and pommel with antiqued metal finish, rat-tail tang construction. Mounted on a wall plaque with Elven runes.

This is the sword discovered by Bilbo Baggins (in *The Hobbit*) and given to his nephew, Frodo Baggins. The blade has a unique quality: It glows

Sting on wall plaque.

Sting.

Sting Scabbard.

blue in the presence of orcs. Its inscription is in Sindarin and states, "Maegnas is my name, I am the spider's bane." (This proves to be true, when Samwise uses Sting to impale the giant spider Shelob in *The Two Towers*).

Sting scabbard ($73.99). Overall length, approximately 18 inches; scabbard material, solid metal collar and tip, antiqued metal finish, Elven vine design, genuine leather wrap.

Sting scabbard belt ($45). Belt measures 1 inch x 6 feet, with scabbard support hangers. (This was manufactured by Blades by Brown, not United Cutlery.)

Glamdring.

The Sword of the Witch-king.

Glamdring ($348.99). Overall length, approximately 48 inches; blade length, 36 inches; blade thickness, 0.25 inches; blade material, tempered 420 J2 stainless steel; handle material, solid metal crossguard and pommel, with antiqued metal finish and engraved Elven runes, leather grip with rat-tail tang construction.

This is the sword wielded by Gandalf, who used it to kill a Balrog in *The Fellowship of the Ring*. The Elven runes states that this sword was forged for Turgon, the King of Gondolin.

The Sword of the Witch-king ($348.99). Overall length, approximately 55 inches; blade length, approximately 40 inches; blade thickness, 0.25 inches; blade material, tempered 420 J2 stainless steel; handle material, genuine leather-wrapped handgrip, solid metal cross guard and pommel with antique metal finish and engraved designs, rat-tail tang construction. Mounted on a wall plaque with Nazgûl designs.

As befitting his most evil stature, this sword is wielded by the Lord of the Nazgûl, the leader of the nine Ringwraiths.

Miniatures

The Shards of Narsil ($59.99). A hand-painted, cold cast porcelain statue of an Elven princess with the sword's shards on a shield. Measures approximately 7.25 inches high x 8 inches wide x 6 inches deep.

The Shards of Narsil Miniature.

Narsil ($44.99). The sword is upright, its tip imbedded in a cold-cast porcelain base. The sword measures approximately 11 inches and the base measures 2.5 inches high.

Sword of the Ringwraiths ($44.99). The sword is upright, its tip imbedded in a cold-cast porcelain base. The sword measures approximately 11 inches and the base measures 2.5 inches high.

Sting ($44.99). The sword is upright, its tip imbedded in a cold-cast porcelain base. The sword measures approximately 7 inches high and the base measures 2.5 inches high.

Glamdring ($44.99). The sword is upright, its tip imbedded in a cold-cast porcelain base. The sword measures approximately 7 inches and the base measures 2.5 inches high.

Sword of the Witch-king ($44.99). The sword is upright, its tip imbedded in a cold-cast porcelain base. The sword measures approximately 11 inches and the base measures 2.5 inches high.

Sting Miniature.

Forthcoming

Timed for release in conjunction with the movie, *The Return of the King*, United Cutlery will be shipping six new products:

➤ **Anduril: The Sword of Aragorn** (a limited edition).

➤ **Fighting Knives of Legolas** (set of two).

➤ **Elven Knife of Strider**.

➤ **The Sword of Strider Scabbard** (with companion knife and sheath).

➤ **Helm of Gimli** (a limited edition).

➤ **Helm of King Elendil** (a limited edition).

Anduril.

Fighting Knives of Legolas.

Elven Knife of Strider.

Helm of Gimli.

Helm of King Elendil.

Stamps

The stamps listed here are of New Zealand currency and were designed by Weta Workshop.

***LotR: The Two Towers* Miniature Sheet First Day Cover Stamp and Envelope Set** ($14.95). Six New Zealand stamps in various denominations, with key scenes from the movie; the illustrative envelope for each depicts Éowyn.

***LotR: The Two Towers* Set of New Zealand Postcards and Official Stamps** ($14.95). This set includes six New Zealand stamps and six "Maximum" postcards (4 x 5.75 inches).

***LotR: The Two Towers* Stamp Book** ($19.95). Two sets of six stamps in various denominations. The stamp sets come with a booklet.

***LotR: The Two Towers* Stamp Presentation Pack** ($32.95). A folio (9.5 x 8.25 inches) inside which are 18 stamps.

LotR: The Two Towers **Ultimate Stamp Collection** ($306.95). The complete set of *The Two Towers* stamps, including: 12 gummed and self-adhesive stamps, six gummed stamp sheets, stamp booklet of 10 self-adhesive stamps, set of six miniature sheets, set of six "Maximum" cards, two first-day covers, set of six miniature sheet first day covers, and *The Two Towers* Presentation Pack, containing all the limited edition commemorative official stamps.

LotR **Framed Stamp Sheets** ($39.95). Measuring 8 x 10 inches, with an original New Zealand stamp sheet, each is matted and framed. Sheets include: Strider, Boromir, Gandalf and Saruman, Frodo and Sam, Galadriel, and The Guardian of Rivendell.

Coins

ReelCoinz

ReelCoinz offers two series of *LotR* collectible coins:

→ *LotR: The Fellowship of the Ring* **Collectible Coins** (ReelCoinz, $14.95). Five silver-colored medallions featuring, on the front, a character (Gandalf, Strider, Frodo, Legolas, Gimli) and, on the back, a circle of Elvish script. The 1-inch diameter coins are set in a cardboard holder accompanied with a color booklet and reusable stickers. (**Note:** These coins are collectibles, not currency.)

→ *LotR: The Two Towers* **Collectible Coins** (ReelCoinz, $14.95). Designed by The Royal Canadian Mint, five nickel alloy medallions featuring, on the front, casts of Gandalf, Frodo, Sam, Éomer, and Éowyn and, on the back, the official *LotR* logo. The medallions are set in a cardboard case accompanied with reusable stickers.

The British Royal Mint

The British Royal Mint has released a series of coins bearing designs by engraver Matthew Bonaccorsi, who created 44 different designs. The coins were introduced at the 2003 American Numismatic Association's World Fair of Money. The coins are offered in sets, priced for every budget:

→ Low end: An 18-coin set struck in cupronickel, consisting of uncirculated 50-cent coins (50¢).

→ Mid-range: A 24-coin set struck in silver, consisting of uncirculated $1 coins ($1, New Zealand currency).

→ High end: A three-coin set struck in gold ($10, New Zealand currency).

Pobjoy Mint

Pobjoy Mint (*www.pobjoy.com*) offers a number of *The Lord of the Rings* coins, including:

- → Gandalf the White on his horse, Shadowfax: 1-ounce Crown, fine 999.9 gold.

- → Gimli the dwarf brandishing two battle-axes: 0.50-ounce Crown, fine 999.9 gold.

- → Legolas the elf, aiming his bow: 0.20-ounce Crown, fine 999.9 gold, 2,500 minted, $199 (U.S.).

- → Aragorn, son of Arathorn: 0.10-ounce Crown, fine 999.9 gold, 3,500 minted, $119 (U.S.).

- → Frodo brandishing Sting: 0.04-ounce Crown, fine 999.9 gold, 5,000 minted, $59 (U.S.).

- → The Fellowship, Arwen, and Galadriel: in Sterling Silver Proof (10,000 minted; $59 U.S.) and Uncirculated Cupro Nickel (100,000 minted; $17 U.S.).

Note: The five gold coins are available in a limited edition set of 1,000 ($1,899 U.S.); the presentation box is circular, with a 9-karat replica of the One Ring, surrounded by the five gold coins.

Miscellaneous Collectibles

Magnets

These magnet sets were all produced for exclusive distribution by New Line Cinemas.

The Lord of the Rings **Heroes Magnet Set** ($19.95). Five magnets: the group of four hobbits, Gandalf and the Fellowship, and three of Frodo.

The Lord of the Rings **Villains Magnet Set** ($19.95). Five magnets: Saruman, a collage of the movie's villains, Lurtz, and two of orcs.

The Lord of the Rings **Oversized Magnet Set** ($9.95). Five larger-sized magnets (5 inches each): Frodo, Gandalf, Aragorn, Gimli, and Legolas.

The Two Towers **Magnet Set A** ($19.95). Five magnets (2.5 x 3.5 inches): the final movie poster, Sauron's Orthanc Tower, Sauron's fortress (Barad-dûr), Legolas, Aragorn, and Merry and Pippin being carried by Treebeard.

The Two Towers **Magnet Set B** ($19.95). Five magnets (2.5 x 3.5 inches): Frodo with Sting drawn, Gandalf the White, the Fellowship, Éowyn, and Uruk-Hai troops.

Key Chains

The Lord of the Rings **Key Chain Set A** (Applause LLC, $9.95). Three key chains each feature a scene from the movie—Frodo, Bilbo, and the Fellowship. The key chains measure 2.5 x 3.5 inches.

The Lord of the Rings **Key Chain Set B** (Applause LLC, $9.95). Three key chains each feature a portrait from the movie—Aragorn, Arwen, and Legolas. The key chains measure 2.5 x 3.5 inches.

The Lord of the Rings **Key Chain Set C** (Applause LLC, $9.95). Three key chains each feature a portrait—Saruman, Lurtz, and the Orcs. The key chains measure 2.5 x 3.5 inches.

The Fellowship of the Ring **Key Chain Set** (Applause LLC, $9.95). This set consists of two metal medallions, each measuring 2.25 inches in diameter. One shows the Elvish brooch worn by the members of the Fellowship, the other shows the Eye of Sauron.

A key chain bearing an Elven leaf design, a tie-in product of The Fellowship of the Ring.

A key chain that shows "One Ring to rule them all..." and a decoration in the center (shown); on the back, the Eye of Sauron.

The Two Towers **Key Chain Set** ($12.95). A set of three key chains: the Kingdom of Rohan, the Uruk-Hai Warriors, and the Eye of Sauron.

Trading Cards

The Fellowship of the Ring **Card Set** (Topps, $20). Includes 90 foil-stamped images from the movie.

Playing Cards

The Fellowship of the Ring **Playing Cards with Collector's Tin** ($9.95). Distributed by New Line Cinemas, features two decks of playing cards—a set of heroes and a set of villains—in a limited edition, numbered, tin case, measuring 3.5 x 6 inches.

Candy

LotR **mints** ($1.50). A 1.5-ounce pack of mints, in packets with film photos.

LotR **sour gummies** ($2.50). A 3.5-ounce pack of sour gummies, in packets with film photos.

Movie Prop Auctions

At *www.LordoftheRingsauction.com*, you can bid on actual props, cutting room footage, and other movie memorabilia, unavailable anywhere else.

The bidding mechanism is, of course, eBay, which has become *the* place where auction houses specializing in collectibles go to sell their wares.

In the early days, film memorabilia—if not thrown out for lack of storage space—was given away to interested fans as souvenirs. Disney cels, for instance, were literally sold in open stacks at Disneyland for $5 each. (Now, these same cels are being auctioned off at Sotheby's for many thousands of dollars!)

The advantage of bidding at an authorized site like this is that you can be assured you are getting the genuine article. Everything is sold with a letter of authenticity. Buying from the source obviously ensures the provenance of the piece.

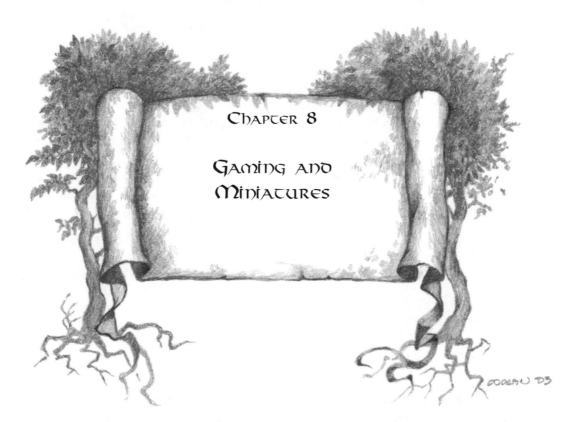

Chapter 8

Gaming and Miniatures

Most moviegoers will be content to see the movie trilogy once, on the large screen, when it first comes out; a certain percentage of those will buy the VHS or DVD, because they want their own copy. A smaller percentage will be interested enough to buy *The Lord of the Rings* and, possibly, *The Hobbit*, but go no further. And then there are those who will want to literally immerse themselves in Middle-earth by becoming active participants and play board games, role-playing games, card games, computer games, or participate in a world-wide online game.

Metal miniatures of Gríma Wormtongue and Saruman, designed to be hand-painted and used for role-playing games.

Welcome to the world of games about Middle-earth.

It's an all-encompassing world in which one can become totally immersed, spending hours, possibly days, at one of the major tournaments worldwide where fans—almost exclusively males, and predominantly young males—gather for a battle royal for significant cash prizes and, just as significant, bragging rights.

A detailed discussion about Tolkien and the various games his work has inspired is, properly, the subject of a separate book. For most readers of this book, here's a basic overview of the key players in the field, so to speak.

Fantasy Flight Games (*www.fantasyflightgames.com*)

The Lord of the Rings ($44.95). Board game. Played on four boards, five players take on their roles as hobbits—Frodo, Sam, Merry, Pippin, and Fatty—working to prevent the Ringbearer from being corrupted. As the hobbits move across the boards, Sauron is on the move, too, toward them, corrupting any hobbit he meets, causing him to drop out of the game. (If Sauron meets the Ringbearer, he is corrupted and the game ends.) Players can call on Gandalf for help or take matters in their own hands by using the Ring, which carries its own risk—corruption.

The Hobbit ($42.95). Board game. The goal is to safely traverse the terrain—Edge of the Wild, the Misty Mountains, the Carrock, Mirkwood, Long Lake, and Desolation of Smaug (the areas scorched by his breath, Erebor and Dale)—to emerge victorious.

***The Lord of the Rings* Trivia** ($39.95). A board game in which you (or your team) take on the role of Frodo Baggins and must travel through 14 areas of Middle-earth, where you are required to answer questions (prepared by Tolkien experts). There are 400 trivia cards, with 1,200 questions.

Friends & Foes Expansion ($21.95). Board game. Find friends to help you conquer challenges (Treebeard, Strider, Tom Bombadil, Glorfindel), as you're pitted against 30 foes sent to bedevil you (spiders of Mirkwood, orcs of the Red Eye, cave-trolls, wolf riders, and barrow-wights). Two new scenario boards have been added (Bree and Isengard).

Sauron Expansion ($24.95). Board game. The tables are turned! One player is Sauron and seeks to thwart the Fellowship.

***The Lord of the Rings:* The Confrontation** ($19.95). For two players. One player controls the nine members of the Fellowship, and the other controls Sauron's minions. Opposing the Fellowship seeking to bring Frodo to Mordor, the dark forces seek to capture him and save the One Ring from destruction.

Games Workshop: Strategy Battle Games (*us.games-workshop.com*)

This company manufactures the licensed tie-in games, which includes *The Lord of the Rings* Battle Game, *The Fellowship of the Ring, The Two Towers, The Return of the King,* and a supplement game, Shadow and Flame.

These are tabletop battles using miniature figurines and dice to determine the outcome of an encounter, be it a one-on-one engagement or a large-scale engagement.

Part of the fun is that, although many of the pieces are metal, some are in plastic and come with paint sets, so you can literally put on the "war" paint—especially handy for the minions of evil, like the Uruk-Hai, for which customized paint jobs are the order of the day.

For those new to strategy battle gaming, Games Workshop provides a brief tutorial on what to expect, using the example of a Rider of Rohan who has spotted a Uruk-Hai scout warrior in advance of a raiding party. A player rolls his dice to determine who goes first in all three phases of the turn—the move phase, the shoot phase, and the fight phase.

In each phase, the roll of the dice determines the outcome—the movement of the pieces, the right to use a weapon, and the result of the battle itself.

Unlike real war, in which anything goes and all's fair, this mock-battle relies on rules specified in the rules manual—to impose order on war, an admittedly chaotic event. Lives (and fortunes) are won, or lost, with a throw of the dice.

Beyond the rulebook, there are several resources upon which to draw: battle scenarios, rules for specific peoples, clarifications, and playsheets. In other words, a strategy battle game offers levels of complexity and player commitment.

The Fellowship of the Ring

The principal game is *The Lord of the Rings: The Fellowship of the Ring* Strategy Battle Game ($40). Designed for two or more players, it includes a 128-page rulebook, dice, and 48 unassembled and unpainted plastic miniatures (8 Men of Gondor, 16 Elves and 24 Moria Goblins), and a ruined building.

The forces can be expanded through box sets (all listed miniatures are unassembled and unpainted):

Ambush at Amon Hen ($40). Plastic miniatures include: Aragorn, Legolas, Gimli, Lurtz, dying Boromir, 1 Uruk-Hai with Merry, 1 Uruk-Hai with Pippin, and 3 more Uruk-Hai.

Attack at Weathertop ($40). Plastic miniatures include: Frodo, Sam, Merry, Pippin, Aragorn, the Witch-king, 4 Ringwraiths, and the Weathertop campfire.

Battle at Khazad-dûm ($45). Plastic miniatures include: Gandalf, and the Balrog.

Escape from Orthanc ($40). Plastic miniatures include: Saruman, the Palantir, Gandalf, and Gwaihir.

The Fellowship of the Ring **Box Set** ($40). Recreates the journey of the Fellowship. Plastic miniatures include: Gandalf, Frodo, Sam, Pippin, Merry, Aragorn, Boromir, Legolas, and Gimli.

Warriors of the Last Alliance Box Set ($20). Reenacts the Last Alliance of Elves and Men, at which Sauron is the central figure. This set includes: 8 High Elf Warriors, 8 High Elf Bowmen, and 8 Men of Gondor.

Moria Goblins Box Set ($20). Includes 24 Moria goblins under the command of Sauron.

Sauron Box Set ($25). Plastic miniatures include: Sauron, Isildur, Elendil.

The Free Peoples of *The Fellowship of the Ring*

(**Note:** all are metal figurines, unassembled and unpainted.)

→ Arwen ($8).

→ Bilbo Baggins ($8).

→ Dwarf Kings ($9)—2 figurines.

→ High Elves with spears ($9)—
   3 figurines.

→ Elrond ($15).

→ Gil-Galad ($8).

→ Galadriel and Celeborn
   ($15)—2 figurines and 1 figure
   (Galadriel's Mirror).

→ Haldir ($8).

→ Elendil and Isildur ($15)—
   2 figurines.

→ Kings of Men ($9)—2 figurines.

→ Lorien Elf Bowmen ($9)—
   3 figurines.

→ Men of Gondor Bowmen ($9)—
   3 figurines.

→ Men of Gondor Spearmen ($9)—
   3 figurines.

→ Mounted Arwen with Frodo ($9).

→ Mounted Boromir ($9).

The Forces of Darkness of *The Fellowship of the Ring*

(**Note:** all are metal figurines, unassembled and unpainted.)

→ Cave Troll with Spear and
   Chain ($15).

→ Lurtz ($8).

→ Moria Goblin Bowmen ($9)—
   4 figurines.

→ Moria Goblin Warriors ($9)—
   4 figurines.

→ Mounted Ringwraiths ($9).

→ Orc Bowmen ($9)—4 figurines.

→ Orc Warriors ($9)—
   4 figurines.

→ Ringwraiths ($8).

→ Saruman ($8).

→ Twilight Ringwraiths ($8).

→ Uruk-Hai Bowmen ($9)—
   3 figurines.

→ Uruk-Hai Warriors ($9)—
   3 figurines.

The Two Towers

The Lord of the Rings: The Two Towers **Strategy Battle Game** ($40). Continues the main action through the events in the second volume. It includes a 160-page rulebook, 12 Riders of Rohan, 20 Fighting Uruk-Hai, ruins, and two different-colored sets of dice.

The Lord of the Rings: The Two Towers—**The Helm's Deep Fortress** (sold out, no longer in production). Recreates the siege at Helm's Deep between the free peoples of Middle-earth and Saruman's fighting Uruk-Hai.

The Lord of the Rings Miniature Figures and Sets

→ Riders of Rohan boxed set ($20)—6 warriors on horseback.

→ Heroes of Helm's Deep ($40)—Aragorn, Gimli, Legolas, Éowyn, Théoden, Gamling, Haldir, and a Wood Elf Standard Bearer.

→ Éomer ($8). Metal figurine, unpainted, in blister pack.

→ Merry and Pippin vs. Grishnákh ($9)—3 metal figurines, unpainted, in blister pack.

→ Haldir's Elves with swords ($9)—3 metal figurines, unpainted, in blister pack.

→ Haldir's Elves with bows ($9)—3 metal figurines, unpainted, in blister pack.

→ The Warriors of Rohan Boxed Set ($20)—24 plastic figurines, unpainted and unassembled.

→ Gandalf on Shadowfax ($9). Metal figurine, unpainted and unassembled.

→ Warg Attack Box ($40). Plastic figurines, unpainted and unassembled, including 2 Warg Riders, a Mounted Aragorn, a Mounted Théoden, and a Mounted Sharku.

→ Gollum, Sam, and Frodo ($9). Metal figurines, unpainted and unassembled.

→ Gandalf the White ($8). Metal figurine, unpainted and unassembled.

→ Treebeard, Mighty Ent carrying Merry and Pippin ($40). Metal figurine, unpainted and unassembled.

→ Captured by Gondor ($40)—5 Rangers (Faramir's men), Faramir, Gollum, Sam, and Frodo. Metal figurines, unpainted and unassembled.

→ Faramir's Rangers ($9)—3 metal figurines, unpainted and unassembled.

→ Gamling: Rohan Royal Standard Bearer ($8). Metal figurine, unpainted and unassembled.

→ Legolas and Gimli on Horseback ($9). Metal figurine, unpainted and unassembled.

→ Rohan Royal Guard on Foot ($9). Metal figurine, unpainted and unassembled.

→ Rohan Royal Guard Mounted ($8). Metal figurine, unpainted and unassembled.

The Two Towers: Forces of Darkness

→ The Fighting Uruk-Hai Boxed Set ($20)—10 warriors with pikes and 10 with swords and shields. Plastic figurines, unpainted and unassembled.

→ Warg Riders ($40)—5 wargs with riders. Metal figurines, unpainted and unassembled.

→ Saruman ($8). Metal figurine, unpainted and unassembled.

→ Uruk-Hai Siege Troops ($20)—8 engineers, 2 beserkers, 2 demolition charges, and 4 ladders.

→ The Uruk-Hai Siege Assault Ballista Box Set ($35)—1 Ballista, 1 loader, 1 winch operator, and 1 spotter. Metal figurines, unpainted and unassembled.

→ Uruk-Hai Beserkers ($9)—3 metal figurines, unpainted and unassembled.

→ Uruk-Hai with Crossbows ($9)—3 metal figurines, unpainted and unassembled.

→ Uruk-Hai Battering Ram ($20)—1 metal battering ram figure and 4 Uruk-Hai figurines, unpainted and unassembled.

→ Uruk-Hai Commanders ($9)—2 metal figurines, unpainted and unassembled.

→ Wildmen of Dunland ($9)—3 metal figurines, unpainted and unassembled.

→ Gríma Wormtongue ($8). Metal figurine, unpainted and unassembled.

→ Ringwraith on Fellbeast ($40)—2 metal figurines: the Ringwraith mounted on the flying Fellbeast, with Frodo Baggins. Unpainted and unassembled.

Shadow & Flame Expansion Board Game

A supplemental game, to play Shadow & Flame requires the rulebook for *The Lord of the Rings: The Fellowship of the Ring* and/or *The Lord of the Rings: The Two Towers* strategy battle games. The game includes four scenarios: the Dwarves fighting Goblins and a Balrog, Good vs. Evil in Rivendell, at the Barrow-Downs, and Fangorn Forest.

The *Supplement* is the basic document, containing the rules, detailing the scenarios, and providing painting tips ($15).

Shadow & Flame Packaged Subsets

→ Balin and Khazad Guard Boxed Set ($35)—Balin and 8 Khazard Guards. Metal figurines, unassembled and unpainted.

➔ Fog on the Barrow-Downs ($35)—Tom Bombadil, Goldberry, 2 Barrow-wights, and 4 paralyzed Hobbits. Metal figurines, unassembled and unpainted.

The Free Peoples: Shadow & Flame

(**Note:** all are metal figurines, unassembled and unpainted.)

➔ Dwarf Bowmen ($9)—3 figurines.

➔ Dwarf Warriors ($9)—3 figurines.

➔ Ellandan and Elrohir ($15)—2 figurines.

➔ Glorfindel ($15).

➔ Khazad Guard ($10)—3 figurines.

➔ Radagast the Brown ($18).

The Forces of Darkness: Shadow & Flame

(**Note:** all are metal figurines, unassembled and unpainted.)

➔ Barrow-wights ($9)—2 figurines.

➔ Goblin King of Moria ($8).

➔ Moria Goblin Drummers ($9)—3 figurines.

➔ Moria Goblin Shaman ($8).

➔ Uruk-Hai Shaman ($8).

The Return of the King

(Figures and information not yet available at the time of this writing.)

Sabertooth Games (*www.sabertoothgames.com*)

The Lord of the Rings Tradeable Miniatures Game (November 2003). Prepainted miniatures, 40 mm in height, with a hexagonal base are placed on a fold-out hexagonal-gridded board. Similar to trading card games, this game is expandable, with booster packs and expansion sets. The starter game comes with a board, 120 starter pieces, and dice.

On the hexagonal base of each character you'll find his attributes and, for combat play, his point value—the higher the point value, the more valuable he is: He's simply harder to kill.

Middle-earth Online:
Vivendi Universal and Turbine Entertainment
(*www.lordoftherings.com*)

This much-anticipated, long-awaited, massively multiplayer (MMP) game will debut in late 2004 for the Windows PC platform only. It is a subscription fee-based game. A 3-D role-playing game that allows you to choose your character from among the Free Peoples of Middle-earth—men, elves, or dwarves—the graphics (judging from early screenshots) are state-of-the-art. You, as a character, will literally walk through Tolkien's Middle-earth. Moreover, in contrast to the restrictive choices found in similar games, this game doesn't lock the player on predetermined paths. Instead, it allows the player to branch out on various paths and enjoy different endings based on the choices he makes.

The key word here is "choices," because every decision you make will ultimately have a bearing on your fate, which, in the end, puts you squarely on the path for good...or evil. Again, your choice.

What will make this game so compelling is the extent to which you can customize your character. You can choose his physical characteristics (face, height, skin color, and so on); craft appropriate armor, weapons, and accessories; and purchase homes, which can be customized and provide limited off-character storage.

In terms of story lines, the first scenario begins after the Fellowship emerges from the Mines of Moria. Successive product expansions include the journey from the Shire to Mirkwood, Mirkwood, the Lonely Mountain, and distant lands in Middle-earth that have not been explored, such as Umbar and Rhûn.

The word *immerse*—used too often to describe games such as this—is certainly appropriate in this instance. Of course, you, as a player, can choose your level of immersion—a few hours a week or, if you're a hard-core player, many more hours, which comes with its own gaming rewards.

In terms of game-playing audience, quite literally, all the world's a stage. You will be able to go online and play with others anywhere in the world.

With its dazzling computer-generated graphics, customization features, and scope of geography and scenarios, Middle-earth Online will soon be populated by ordinary people who want to vicariously live an extraordinary life. The battle for Middle-earth begins in late 2004.

Electronic Arts (*www.ea.com*)

EA currently has available *The Two Towers*, with *The Return of the King* and an ambitious trilogy game in the works.

These games are playable on multiple machines (Sony PlayStation 2, Nintendo GameBoy Advance and GameCube, and Microsoft Xbox). Typically, you assume the role of a third-party character, who fights his way through multiple levels of 3-D environments to advance the gameplay.

For instance, in *The Two Towers* ($49.99), you must choose your character (Aragorn, Legolas, or Gimli), whom you must direct in battle using sword-play to advance through 13 levels of gameplay—all rendered in lifelike, 3-D computer animation.

Black Label Games (*www.lotr.com/frame_games.jsp*)

This company publishes action/adventure games playable on multiple systems: PlayStation, PlayStation 2, Nintendo GameCube, PC CD-ROM, and Xbox.

The games include:

The Hobbit (not yet released). From the Website (*www.lotr.com/frame_hobbit.jsp*):

> *The Hobbit* is an action adventure game in which the player assumes the role of Bilbo Baggins. The player will control Bilbo from his peaceful Hobbit hole in Hobbiton into the dark and harrowing Mirkwood forest and finally to the Lonely Mountain, in which lies Smaug the dragon. Sent on a journey by Gandalf the wizard, along with Thorin the dwarf and his stout and sturdy cohorts, Bilbo will acquire items, knowledge, and in the case of a Hobbit, courage to help him complete the quest as he comes face to face with elves, trolls, orcs, spiders, wolves, and more.

The Fellowship of the Ring ($49.99). **Note:** This follows the book, not the movie.

The Treason of Isengard (canceled). In an interview on the manufacturer's Website (*www.gamespot.com*), it stated: "We were due to ship *Treason of Isengard* this November, but the game wasn't going to deliver the experience that our fans demand, so we knew the right choice was to cancel the project and move on."

The War of the Ring (upcoming for spring 2004). The early screenshots show exquisite rendering, very detailed and wholly convincing. This is a real-time strategy game, not a third-person engagement game. From *www.lordoftherings.com*:

> Massive battles will erupt as the peoples of Middle-earth fight for control of Tolkien's World. Play as the forces of good and valiantly fight for the One Ring's destruction or play as the forces of evil to claim control over Middle-earth forever.
>
> Highlights:
>
> · Play as the forces of Good or Evil using multiple types of character units.
>
> · Single or Multi-player campaigns
>
> · Character units gain experience and visual enhancements as they destroy enemy units—strategic use of units is key to success.

- Real world environment and terrain effects alter the outcome of skirmishes and battles.

- Some hero units will aid other units' morale, increasing the chances for victory in battle.

Decipher (*www.decipher.com*)

For new fans trying to decipher just what a role-playing game is, the best way to get your feet wet, so to speak, is to go to a local retailer who sells these games and hang out when players show up to compete.

At the core of role-playing is imagination. Rather than a board game, in which players are typically on a fixed route and the roll of the dice determines outcomes as players work toward an end goal, a role-playing game is more complex, with an open architecture that allows expanding play through supplement volumes—books with detailed information about the character, places, and imaginative world in which you are playing.

Players interact through a Game Moderator (GM), who oversees the play of the game itself. As players make decisions on questions to ask or actions to take, the GM decides the outcome of those actions. In other words, unlike a traditional board game, a role-playing game is about the journey, not the destination.

If your interest is Tolkien, the best place to start is an entry-level game that will likely whet your appetite for the bigger, more expansive games. Decipher offers two introductory role-playing adventure games:

Through the Mines of Moria Adventure Game ($29.95). This game begins at the doors of Moria, which Gandalf opens by saying "friend" (in Elvish) and entering. In this game, players choose roles among the Fellowship. This game then puts the players through several close encounters with servants of the Shadow and, finally, pits them against the Balrog.

The contents of the game are specifically designed to ease a newcomer into the role-playing fantasy world of Tolkien's, with a 32-page adventure, taking the Fellowship through the Mines of Moria; a 24-page introductory guide to Middle-earth, called "Welcome to Middle-earth"; a booklet explaining—for the newcomer—just what role-playing is; four tactical maps to guide the major action sequences; character and monster cut-outs with which to play the game; and a poster map of Middle-earth.

An excellent way to enter Tolkien's role-playing world, going through the Mines of Moria is not a shortcut in the end, but that which doesn't destroy you will make you stronger.

***The Two Towers* Adventure Game** ($29.95). Like Through the Mines of Moria, this is the next step for new players. It's a boxed adventure game that, timewise, takes place after the Fellowship has been broken up and continues to the Battle at Helm's Deep. This set contains an adventure booklet, character sheets, tactical maps, counters, and dice.

Newcomers are advised to try a game like this before proceeding to the more complex and demanding world that awaits in the Full Game System.

The Lord of the Rings Role-Playing Game (RPG) [Full Game System]

A good role-playing game explores a universe so fully realized that one can literally be immersed in its secondary reality. Decipher, which has developed an entire line of RPGs (Star Trek, Star Wars, and of course, Middle-earth), constantly expands its respective universes.

The Lord of the Rings RPG Core Book ($39.95) is the basic document. Designed for extensive handling, it's the prime reference book. You get to choose any character you wish, and through that character you make your way through Middle-earth. (For hardcore collectors, a limited edition core book is also available, for $80. It's a "premium printing," packaged in a slipcase, including a limited edition guide to hobbits and the Shire.)

Because the world of Middle-earth was so fully realized by Tolkien, it's ideal for role-playing, because, in his books, the scale of time encompasses four Ages, with a cast of characters that number in the hundreds. In other words, Decipher could spend decades expanding Tolkien's universe with supplemental material such as sourcebooks, maps, and journals, as players take on roles from Morgoth (from the First Age) to Samwise (at the end of the Third Age). Just as Tolkien's fictional universe was limited only by his imagination, its role-playing universe is also limited only by the imagination of the players, and the imagination of the game designers that develop the overall game plan.

Note: Decipher publishes the role-playing game and trading-card game based on Tolkien's Middle-earth; the distinction is that the former is based on the book, where the latter is based on the movies.

Beyond the core book, which is the "must have" document, the full game system of *The Lord of the Rings* RPG currently includes:

Maps of Middle-earth ($29.95). Drawn by Daniel Reeve, these six maps measure 17 x 22 inches, and the set includes a 32-page guide to the lands of Middle-earth.

Narrator's Screen ($18.95). This fold-out screen, with reference tables from the Core Book, includes character sheets and a 16-page adventure ("The House of Margil").

The Fellowship of the Ring Sourcebook ($24.95). This is a 128-page, full-color hardback book detailing everything from the book *and* the movie. It provides a detailed timeline, a guide to story events, game statistics, and 15 illustrated maps.

Hero's Journal ($9.95). A useful accessory, this booklet is designed for recording information about your character attributes and background. It includes step-by-step instructions on how to build your character, provides 14 pages of charts for character skills, offers information on *The Lord of the Rings*, and provides specific RPG strategies.

Fell Beasts and Wondrous Magic ($24.95). A 96-page hardback book in full color. This exhaustively details the beasts of Middle-earth, as well as magical places.

Moria ($34.95). A boxed set with a 96-page book, a 32-page book, and maps. Details the world of Moria, the domain of the dwarf lords. Described as a "subterranean adventure with lots of twists, traps, and caverns, the Fellowship will be tested at every turn as they journey through the twisted underground mazes of Moria."

The Two Towers Sourcebook ($29.95). This 128-page, full-color hardback book, with detailed information about everything in the book *and* film, provides expanded rules for large-scale combat engagements, and detailed write-ups on Rohan, Edoras, Meduseld, Isengard, Fangorn and the Ents, Gondor, Helm's Dike, and the Glittering Caves of Aglarond.

Maps of Middle-earth, Set 2: Cities and Strongholds ($29.95). A boxed set with a 32-page paperback book that includes in-depth background information on the locations found on the six maps depicting Minas Tirith, Helm's Deep, Rivendell, Isengard, Edoras, and Umbar.

Helm's Deep Sourcebook ($24.95). A 96-page, hardback book, in color, with in-depth information about this fortress at which the Free Peoples of Middle-earth make a stand against Saruman's army.

Paths of the Wise: The Guide to Magicians & Loremasters ($24.95). A 96-page, hardback book, in full color, this is the reference manual to learn about the magician and loremaster orders. Includes information on new abilities, skills, traits, and also elite orders.

The Lord of the Rings Trading Card Game

This is based on the movie, not the book. Sometimes abbreviated TCG (Trading Card Game) or CCG (Customizable Card Game), the cards number in the hundreds, packaged in expansion sets that increasingly enlarge the gameplay by introducing new characters and scenarios.

A trading card game from Decipher. Pictured are the cards, the box, the rulebook, and playing pieces.

The best way of getting started is buying a starter set, to introduce you to the game. As you gain experience, buy booster packs to expand your collection.

If you're really good at it, consider entering a local tournament or—if you're the kind of person who sets his sights high—there's always the World Cup Teams. For most people, however, playing with friends or others at a gaming store (a popular place to meet fellow gamers) will likely be the extent of involvement.

The list of individual cards is too extensive to reprint here (see related links on page 144 for more information), but the existing sets of cards include:

- *The Fellowship of the Ring* (365 cards).

- Mines of Moria (122 cards).

- Realms of the Elf-lords (122 cards).

- *The Two Towers* (365 cards).

- Battle of Helm's Deep (128 cards).

- Ents of Fangorn (128 cards).

- *The Fellowship of the Ring* Anthology (18).

- *The Return of the King* (approximately 365 cards).

- Siege of Gondor (approximately 122–128 cards).

- Mount Doom (approximately 122–128 cards).

From Decipher, an oversized trading card. This one is inscribed to Colleen Doran from Lawrence Makoare (Lurtz). (Photo courtesy of Colleen Doran.)

From Decipher, an oversized trading card. This one is inscribed to Colleen Doran from Sala Baker (Sauron). (Photo courtesy of Colleen Doran.)

Forthcoming Sets:

- Shadows.

- Black Rider.

- Bloodlines.

- *The Return of the King* Anthology.

- The Hunters.

- Rise of Saruman.

- Treachery and Deceit.

- The Great Eye.

- Shelob's Lair.

- Age's End.

Decipher Links

Recognizing that a large number of people will have experienced Tolkien's world through the film and not the book—and these games are directly linked to the film—Decipher has provided numerous links on its Website to acquaint first-timers on the basics of what a trading card game is, how to play it, and what to expect:

➼ An explanation of what a trading card game is:

www.decipher.com/gettingstarted/

➼ A video tutorial:

www.decipher.com/lordoftherings/gettingstarted/videotutorial.html

➼ A printout of the video tutorial:

www.decipher.com/lordoftherings/gettingstarted/videotranscript.html

➼ General references and resources and a sample game in play:

www.decipher.com/lordoftherings/gettingstarted/samplegame.html

➼ *The Two Towers* starter rulebook (in Adobe PDF format). Designed for new players, with a discussion of the basic rules:

www.decipher.com/lordoftherings/gettingstarted/

➼ *The Two Towers* downloadable starter decks. Download these and print them out for gameplay. A good way to "try before you buy":

www.decipher.com/lordoftherings/downloads/index.html

Chapter 9

The Noble Collection

The Noble Collection's line of collectibles is available only by mail order and online order. Although readers of this book will be principally interested in the Tolkien film-related offerings, the collectibles company offers other merchandise, with an emphasis on fantasy- or historical-related objects.

The Tolkien film-related product line is divided into jewelry, "treasures," and weapons. The designs are based on the props constructed especially for the movie.

Where applicable I've indicated the jewelry's provenance and also provided a little background information on who wore it and its historical significance. When the Noble Collection calls the piece a "reproduction," it means that it is a facsimile of the item as seen in the movie. When it states that it was "inspired" by the movie, then it exists only as a replica and may not necessarily have any linkage to the movie or the book.

Note: Jasmine Watson, who designed much of the jewelry for the movie trilogy, was a consultant for the Noble Company, because most of the jewelry the company sells is based on her original designs. (Her Website is at *www.jasminewatson.com*).

Jewelry

The Evenstar Pendant of Arwen ($95). A reproduction made of sterling silver, this is the pendant that, in the film, Arwen gives to Aragorn as a sign of her undying love for him.

In the book: Daughter of Elrond and Celebrían, Arwen is an Eldarin princess and chooses mortal love instead of joining her people as they leave Middle-earth to go across the Sea.

The Elven Brooch ($65). A reproduction, this brooch is designed in the shape of a green leaf.

In the book: In Chapter 8 (Farewell to Lórien), each member comprising the Fellowship is given a hood and cloak, fastened at the neck "with a brooch like a green leaf veined with silver."

The Fellowship necklace ($75) **and earrings** ($59). Inspired pieces that match the Elven Brooch.

The One Ring: Gold Edition ($295). A reproduction made of 10-karat gold, a laser process is used to etch the Elvish writing. The ring is presented in an ornate and (in my opinion) gaudy red box with silver highlights. This is available in one size and not intended as fingerwear. No chain is provided on which to carry it around the neck.

A reproduction of the leaf brooch worn by members of the Fellowship in The Fellowship of the Ring, *manufactured by the Noble Collection.*

In the movie and the book: Though the writing (only visible when subjected to heat) is Elvish, the language is not. It is the language of Mordor and, translated, the inscription is two lines from a longer verse. The inscription, roughly translated, means "One Ring to bring them all and in the darkness bind them," for this is the One Ring, the Ruling Ring, the Master Ring that binds all the lesser Rings of Power.

The One Ring: Sterling Silver Edition ($129). A reproduction plated in "pure gold," this ring is actually constructed of sterling silver, which is why the engraved laser-etched Elvish inscription shows through in silver, instead of gold (as with the $295, 10-karat gold ring). The ring comes with a 20-inch chain and is mounted in a simple wooden display box.

The Revolving Elvish Script Ring ($75). A replica intended as fingerwear, this is available in even sizes only, from 6 to 14. Made from sterling silver with the Elvish inscription in black, etched by laser, the ring itself revolves around its simple silver band. It is, however, the only such product of its kind offered by the Noble Collection that's actually designed to be worn.

The Headdress of Elrond ($195). A reproduction, this is an elegantly simple, flowing headdress worn by Master Elrond, as befitting his royal stature among the Elves. This headdress is made of solid sterling silver and rests on a blue presentation pillow.

The Ring of Elrond ($295). A reproduction made of 10-karat gold and available in sizes 6–14, this is designed to be worn. Called Vilya (the Ring of Air), it is the greatest of the Three Rings of the Elves and was given to Elrond by Gil-Galad, whose banner he carried in the war of the Last Alliance.

This design is historically accurate. In the book, the ring is described as made of gold and set with a sapphire.

The Elven Necklace ($129). A replica made of sterling silver, it is set with crystal cabochons (a highly polished, unfaceted gem). Not in the movie or the book, this was designed especially for the Noble Collection.

Jasmine Watson: Jewelry Designer Extraordinaire

Even if you do not know the name, you know her work, and that's more important. Jasmine Watson—then living in New Zealand, now living in England—is the one responsible for designing and creating the jewelry used in Peter Jackson's movie trilogy.

Though her *LotR* pieces are not available directly from her—The Noble Collection has issued the jewelry replica line, with her as a consultant—she does have a singular piece for sale on her Website (*www.jasminewatson.com*).

A silver leaf pendant with chain ($124.95) is the first piece in her 2003 collection. Limited to 2,000 pieces, each numbered and stamped, this silver pendant is 1.5 inches in length, suspended from a sterling silver Prince of Wales chain, and presented in a green-velvet case.

The Elven Choker ($97.50). A replica, this is a black velvet and sterling silver choker, with inlaid crystals. Not in the movie or the book, this was designed especially for the Noble Collection.

The Necklace and Earrings of Arwen ($95/$65). Replications that match her Evenstar Pendant (see the first item).

The Necklace and Earrings Set of Éowyn ($395). Reproductions from the movie, this set is made of 14-karat gold set with crystal cabochons.

Éowyn, daughter of Éomund and Théodwyn, hails from Rohan and falls in love with Aragorn. In *The Return of the King*, at the Battle of the Pelennor Fields, she is disguised as a man and kills both the Lord of the Nazgûl—the Witch-king of Angmar—and his mount.

The Brooch of King Théoden ($59). A replica worn by the 17th King of Rohan, cast in sterling silver, plated in 14-karat gold, set with an onyx in its center.

King Théoden, under the evil influence of Saruman working through counselor Gríma Wormtongue, is restored to his former self after Gandalf the White exorcises Saruman. King Théoden falls in battle, killed by the Lord of the Nazgûl, in the Battle of the Pelennor Fields.

The Rohan Brooch ($75). A reproduction made in sterling silver, it is a stylized symbol of a horse—appropriate, of course, because these are worn by the Riders of Rohan, who bred and raised horses.

The Ring of Aragorn ($129). A reproduction made of sterling silver, with gold accents and set with a green crystal. The product description notes that this was "Known as the Ring of Barahir."

In the book, the Ring of Barahir is an Elven ring given by Finrod to Barahir in the First Age and then recovered by Beren. It survived to the Third Age. Though Aragon didn't wear this ring—a bit of film license—the replica is historically accurate, with its design of twin serpents, though Tolkien states the serpents' eyes are made of emerald, whereas this ring has a large emerald-green crystal set in the middle of its design.

The Brooch and Headdress of Arwen ($145). Reproduction made of sterling silver, these are worn by Arwen.

The Brooch of Galadriel ($97.50). A reproduction. Galadriel is the Queen of Lórien. She is freely offered but refuses the One Ring from Frodo Baggins. To aid the Fellowship, she gives them provisions for their journey and individual gifts.

The Ring of Galadriel ($129). A reproduction made of solid sterling silver and set with a crystal.

In the book, this is the second of Three Rings of the Elves, and is made of mithril (the chain mail that protects Frodo Baggins is also made of this priceless metal—a gift from Bilbo Baggins).

The Elven Star Necklace and Earrings ($75). Replicas made of sterling silver, set with faceted crystals.

The Dwarven Ring of Power ($97.50). A replica made of sterling silver set with a blue crystal. Designed to be worn, it comes in full sizes from 6 to 14.

In the book, the race of dwarves is given seven of these Rings of Power.

The King of Men Ring ($97.50). A replica made of sterling silver and set with a cornelian.

The Ring of the Witch-king [of Angmar] ($97.50). A reproduction made in solid sterling silver and set with a cabochon, it is the Ring worn by the Lord of the Nazgûl.

The Ring and Brooch of Gandalf (ring, $295; brooch, $129). No indication as to whether these are reproductions or replicas, the ring is made of 10-karat gold and set with a red crystal. The brooch is made of sterling silver.

Treasures

The Staff of Gandalf: Votive Candle Holder ($59). A rather curious reproduction, the top of the staff is cut off and mounted on an ornate base. Get the staff of Gandalf instead.

The Staff of Gandalf the Grey ($295). A 66-inch reproduction of his wooden walking staff, replete with a mirror-backed display plaque.

In the film and the book, Gandalf's staff is not what it seems. To the unknowing, it appears to be a simple walker's aid, appropriate for an aged man; but in the hands of a wizard, it is a powerful weapon, as the King's counselor, Gríma Wormtongue, knew when he gave instructions to the guards to confiscate it before allowing Gandalf to see King Théoden.

The Lord of the Rings Collector's Chess Set ($495). The most expensive item in the catalog, and certainly the most elaborate, this chess set features playing pieces bearing the likenesses of the actors—"personally approved," we are told, "by the individual actor."

The individual pieces are up to 3 inches in height, the board itself measures 15 x 15 inches and rises 4 inches, and the face of the board is a map of Middle-earth.

The two armies are imaginatively interpreted. The forces of good show hobbits as pawns and the main characters as rooks, knights, and bishops, with Gandalf, rather than Aragorn, as the King. Representing the forces of evil, the pieces include the Tower of Orthanc as rooks, Black Riders as Knights, battle orcs as pawns, and so on.

Mines of Moria Goblet ($59). At a height of 7 inches, this manufactured collectible, made of solid pewter, bears an image of Gandalf holding a book.

At the Shire Goblet ($59). More than 7 inches in height, this pewter goblet shows Bilbo Baggins in two scenes—his holding forth at his birthday party, and his holding the One Ring.

Quest for the Ring ($97.50). A manufactured collectible, this sculpture is 7 inches tall and shows Ringwraiths on their black steeds, with a pillar, on which rests a globe embedding the One Ring.

My Precious ($97.50). A manufactured collectible, this sculpture shows Gollum staring at his coveted precious, the One Ring, which is suspended in a globe sitting on a base of rocks. The sculpture is 7 inches high.

The One Ring: Mirage Holographic Image Chamber ($97.50). A curious item— an ornate circular chamber, more than 7 inches in diameter, which projects an image of the One Ring that can be seen but not physically touched.

Weapons

Sting: The Sword of Frodo ($295). A reproduction with a wall-mounted plaque (Optional: a $55 scabbard).

In *The Hobbit*, Bilbo Baggins discovers this in a troll-cave along with other booty. Named Sting by Bilbo, he gave it to Frodo as a gift—a most useful one, because it glows with a blue light when orcs are nearby. Sting is also used by Sam to wound the giant spider, Shelob, in *The Two Towers* (the book, not the movie).

Glamdring: The Sword of Gandalf ($295). This 47-inch reproduction comes with a mirror-backed wall plaque for display purposes. *Glamdring*—translated "foe-hammer," and called by the orcs "Beater"—is an elf sword and, like Sting, glows with a blue light when orcs are nearby.

The Axe of Gimli ($129). A reproduction measuring 34 inches in length, this two-headed axe is the principal weapon of Gimli, who is one of the members of the Fellowship and who distinguished himself in combat in subsequent battles during the War of the Ring.

Narsil: The Broken Sword ($245). A reproduction, this shard is mounted on a wooden wall plaque.

Chapter 10

Smaug's Stash:
Tolkien Treasures

The notion of what is truly collectible and what is simply merchandised product is an important distinction, because the former has intrinsic value and the latter has little or none.

By definition, a true collectible's worth is driven by scarcity and demand, compounded by time. Judged by that standard, most of what is manufactured or published falls by the wayside: fool's gold. But the real treasures—Smaug's dragon-hoard, as it were—appreciate in value with each passing year.

Because Tolkien fans are principally interested in the text and its creation, manuscripts (holographic and typescript), letters, first editions, and limited editions are of prime interest.

Unfortunately, the rigorous examination of collectibles as offered through antiquarian booksellers does not necessarily apply to public auction houses such as eBay, so descriptions therein are not necessarily accurate. These days, more than ever, it's important to know what you are buying, and from whom.

In terms of key Tolkien collectibles, which began with the publication of *The Hobbit* in 1937, the gold standard—scarcity + demand + time's passage—has proven to be a reliable barometer. Tolkien is among the most collectible authors in our time, challenged only by another British fantasy writer, J.K. Rowling.

For the serious Tolkien investor/collector, there are several factors that make Tolkien a blue chip stock:

1. The enduring popularity of *The Hobbit* and *The Lord of the Rings*. In numerous reader's polls—BBC, The Folio Society, Amazon.com, Waterstone's, and others—Tolkien's *The Lord of the Rings* ranked first,

to the dismay of some critics and academicians who feel strongly that the book is overrated. Despite what they think, the fact remains that among fantasy authors, Tolkien's two major books—*The Hobbit* and *The Lord of the Rings*—remain at the top of any list for fantasy lovers. Published decades ago in relatively small quantities in England, copies are scarce and, when found, expensive.

2.   Tolkien was not a publicity-seeking author. Unlike other authors who routinely took every advantage to promote and sell their books by seeking media coverage and autograph opportunities at bookstores, Tolkien granted few interviews and did not promote his books in bookstores with personal appearances. Consequently, signed copies of his books are hard to come by.

3.   The first printings of *The Hobbit* and the three volumes of *The Lord of the Rings* were modest: *The Hobbit*, 1,500 copies, according to Douglas A. Anderson. Similarly, the three volumes of *The Lord of the Rings*, as originally published by Allen & Unwin, went to press with relatively low print runs, as well: 3,000, 3,250, and 7,000 copies, respectively.

4.   Tolkien, who passed away in 1973, never came to the United States, his biggest book market.

5.   In 2001, Peter Jackson's film adaptation of *The Fellowship of the Ring*, which grossed a billion dollars worldwide, created a resurgence of interest from fans who otherwise would not have been interested in Tolkien.

6.   Collectible Tolkien material, previously available from antiquarian book dealers and auction houses, is now available worldwide because of the Internet. Book dealers, traditional auction houses such as Sotheby's, and the emergence of eBay as a dominant force means that more people are afforded the opportunity to buy these offerings. Low supply and high demand, fueled by a worldwide audience, means increasing prices for Tolkien treasures.

The bottom line is that the truly rare Tolkien treasure, a fitting gift for a king, will command princely prices.

In general terms, the rarest commodities include manuscripts, original art, first editions, and letters/postcards. These are the most desired Tolkien treasures, some of which are available—if you know where to look and are willing to invest accordingly.

Original Manuscripts

Tolkien wrote books the old-fashioned way, not with a computer (because they didn't exist at the time) but by hand, in several drafts (up to three per book), and a typescript draft followed by a final typescript for submission.

What most people don't know is that the manuscripts for *The Hobbit*, *The Lord of the Rings*, *Farmer Giles of Ham*, and *Mr. Bliss* were sold by Tolkien himself, in 1956, to Marquette University, for an average price of 70¢ per leaf (manuscript page). What is even more surprising is that Marquette University found itself the only party interested in acquiring the original manuscripts, so there was no competitive bidding.

If you want to get an idea of what a bargain Marquette University had gotten, consider this: A single letter from Tolkien, in which he discussed *The Lord of the Rings*, sold at auction in the United Kingdom, in 2002, for $7,672.

Put differently, at current market valuation, Marquette University could have only afforded to buy *two* pages of original manuscript. But the University bought wisely and well, and their dragon-hoard of Tolkien manuscripts—based on $7,672/page—is conservatively worth $79 million dollars. And because these were not merely letters talking *about* the manuscripts, but in fact were the actual manuscripts, intact, with all drafts, $100 million would be closer to the mark.

Tolkien could hardly be considered a fool of a Took for selling the pages for $15,000, because he got the best price he could for a commodity that, as I pointed out, had attracted no other buyers. And, like most authors, he simply needed the money, as Clyde S. Kirby wrote, in *Tolkien and the Silmarillion*.

At this very late date, the only hope for those seeking an original manuscript lies in the possible sale of fragments currently in the hands of Christopher Tolkien, who edited *The Silmarillion* and the 12 volumes of *The History of Middle-earth*. But don't hold your breath. Christopher Tolkien—reportedly a recluse who lives in a guarded estate in France, and who only visited England once in recent years—has not yet offered for sale any of his father's manuscripts, nor is it likely. (My guess is that they will not appear on the open market but, instead, be deposited at the Bodeleian Library at Oxford.)

First Editions

In lieu of original manuscripts, the next best thing would be first editions of *The Hobbit* and *The Lord of the Rings*. An Internet search turned up several copies of each book, but be warned: Sticker shock may result!

Tolkien's first book, *The Hobbit*, was published in 1937 by George Allen & Unwin, in England, with a first printing of 1,500 copies, according to Douglas A. Anderson. It had black-and-white pen-and-ink illustrations by Tolkien himself. Depending on condition, prices vary. A jacketed copy, auctioned off by Sotheby's in 2002, went for $68,767.

On the Internet, as of this writing, a U.S. book dealer is offering a fine copy with jacket for $85,000. Another dealer is offering a second impression (second printing) for $71,978—an edition distinctive for its inclusion of color art by Tolkien; only 2,300 copies were printed, of which 423 copies were destroyed in the bombing of London in 1940, according to Douglas A. Anderson.

Even a jacketless copy of the first edition can fetch $13,995. Of course, a signed copy—Tolkien usually inscribed them to family and friends—adds a premium price. One bookseller estimated that a first edition with jacket in fine condition, if inscribed by Tolkien, would fetch up to $100,000, because he likely signed very few of them.

Though *The Hobbit* has the virtue of being the first major Tolkien book and is thus the most collectible of all his books, Tolkien collectors recognize that, in terms of story, it whets the literary appetite, so to speak, for the larger, more ambitious work that followed: *The Lord of the Rings*.

Though often referred to as a trilogy, *The Lord of the Rings* is, in fact, a single book that was *published* as a trilogy for the convenience of its publisher. (Subsequently, one-volume editions were published, which is what Tolkien originally intended.) Issued as trade hardbacks with uniformly designed dust jackets, *The Fellowship of the Ring* was published in 1954, followed by *The Two Towers* and *The Return of the King*, both published in 1955.

Allen & Unwin was rightly concerned about the economics of publishing a single volume of *The Lord of the Rings*—its cost was prohibitive, and it was risky business—so the idea was to issue three separate volumes, taking into account how well each volume did, so the print run of the next book could be adjusted accordingly.

Current market prices vary as to condition, of course. A U.S. bookseller has a set of the three books in fine condition for $47,500, with the caveat that the dust jackets have had minor repairs done by a paper conservator.

A signed set of *The Lord of the Rings* commands a commensurately higher price, of course, especially if all three volumes have been signed, as opposed to only one of them.

Alternative choices: Consider buying one of his other works of fiction. A signed copy of *Farmer Giles of Ham* (U.K. first edition, 1949) is currently being offered for $12,000. Or consider buying a book that he's inscribed, though he was not the author; A bookseller is currently offering, for $1,519, a copy of Humbert Wolfe's *London Sonnets*, which bears the inscription: "S.R.T. / Because he doesn't, / either to you or me, / I do to you / J.R.T. 22.2.20."

For those who absolutely must have a book signed by Tolkien, consider purchasing one of the books from his personal library, signed by him—some with handwritten notes in the margins. One bookseller had copies for as little as $400, but they have since sold out. Now copies are commanding up to $2,000.

Signed Letters

A first edition of *The Hobbit* or *The Lord of the Rings* is understandably out of reach for most people, so consider the purchase of a signed letter by Tolkien—not cheap, but a collectible guaranteed to rise in value. As Humphrey Carpenter wrote in the Introduction to *The Letters of J.R.R. Tolkien*:

An immense amount of Tolkien's time was taken up with the written word: not just his academic work and the stories of 'Middle-earth', but also letters. Many of these had to be written in the way of business, but in any case letter-writing was on most occasions a favourite activity with him.

A goodly number of letters are in response to his readers, who often wrote and asked him specific questions about Middle-earth, its inhabitants, and its languages—subjects that Tolkien could discuss at length.

 The Bodeleian Library

In the matter of Tolkien manuscripts, foresight trumped hindsight. William Ready recognized that *The Hobbit* and *The Lord of the Rings* were classics and wasted no time in contacting Tolkien, who reportedly had a tax bill to pay and could use the unexpected but welcomed offer. The deal was brokered through a London bookseller; soon thereafter, Ready's employer, Marquette University, acquired the crown jewels—seven feet of manuscripts that included the originals and all drafts of *The Hobbit*, *The Lord of the Rings*, and *Farmer Giles of Ham*.

Tolkien, I'm sure, would have preferred that his alma mater had asked for the papers, but the Bodeleian Library at Oxford never asked until years later, when it realized that Tolkien was a national literary treasure.

Since that time, the Bodeleian Library has wisely pursued collecting Tolkien's papers, and in its collection can be found his personal and academic papers and the manuscripts to *The Silmarillion* and "Leaf by Niggle." In time, it's expected that Christopher Tolkien may turn over additional papers—the notes, drafts, and final copies of the papers that comprise *The History of Middle-earth*—but this means that the Tolkien scholar wishing to see his principal works must journey not only to England, but to Wisconsin, where Marquette University is located.

The Bodeleian Library has published several Tolkien items worth your attention: seven postcards, three posters, and a catalog, available by mail or online.

The postcards include the dust jacket art for *The Hobbit* and *The Two Towers* and four whimsical cards: a "Maddo" postcard, a "Code Letter" postcard, a "Motor Bus" postcard, and a postcard with an owl design—the "Owlamoo."

The three posters, all in color and all from *The Hobbit*, include "The Hill: Hobbiton-across-the-Water," "Bilbo comes to the Huts of the Raft-elves," and the dust jacket to *The Hobbit*.

The real prize is a catalog of a Tolkien exhibition in 1992, *J.R.R. Tolkien: Life and Legend* (£14.95: Oxford, Oxford Bodeleian Library, trade paperback). In full color, its 96 pages chronicle 250 items on exhibit, including original letters, artwork, and a rebus, as well. A great souvenir of the exhibit, especially if you were not fortunate enough to see it at the time.

Whether written in his own hand (ALS: Autograph Letter, Signed) or type-written, Tolkien's letters ranged in length from one page (simple declinations, invitations, or generic thank-you notes) to dozens of pages.

The price of Tolkien letters varies widely, depending on condition, whether or not a matching envelope is present, the length of the letter, whether it is handwritten or typed, and most important of all, its contents. A "bare bones" letter, written in 1966, sold for $2,333. On eBay, another such letter, thanking a U.S. reader for her interest in his books, went up for auction—and did not sell—for its minimum of $2,500.

More substantiative letters sell for correspondingly more, of course. A one-page, handwritten letter to Ace Books publisher Donald A. Wolheim, regarding its pirated edition, was offered for $6,500. In March 2002, the BBC reported that a handwritten letter dated 1955, in which Tolkien discussed his difficulties in completing *The Lord of the Rings*, sold at auction for $7,672—twice its original estimate. In recent bookseller catalogs, a Tolkien letter generally sells for an average of $7,500.

Demand for prime Tolkien material will continue to increase, because the popularity of Peter Jackson's film adaptations have had a salutary effect on all things Tolkien.

Collectible Tolkien Books

To rephrase a truism, nothing exceeds like excess, especially in the case of the Tolkien movies and the extensive line of tie-in products—from the sublime to the ridiculous—almost all of which use the word "collectible" with abandon.

What, then, is the new Tolkien fan to buy?

First, let's agree on what the word "collectible" means. According to *The American Heritage Dictionary*, the word means "worthy of being collected." Put differently, it infers that there is an *intrinsic* value in the item, as opposed to a manufactured value or, worse, plain marketing hype.

With the hundreds of movie tie-in products, and more on the way, the new collector—looking to buy true collectibles—is best advised to stick to the tried and true: books by Tolkien.

Book Condition

The condition of the book is a key factor in its value. *AB Bookman's Weekly* uses four criteria:

1. "As New" should "be used only when the book is in the same immaculate condition in which it was published." In other words, even though you are buying a *used* book, its condition is comparable to what it would be if it came directly out of the shipping carton from its publisher. (Some people prefer the term "mint" to indicate a flawless copy, but booksellers prefer "as new" because it is more properly descriptive.)

2. "Very Good" describes "a used book that does show some small signs of wear—but no tears—on either binding or paper."

3. "Fair" describes "a worn book.... Binding, jacket (if any), etc., may also be worn."

4. "Poor" describes "a book that is sufficiently worn that its only merit is as a Reading Copy...."

AB Bookman's Weekly presumes that all listings in its magazine also clarify other important considerations: Is it an ex-library copy? Is it a book club edition? What (if any) are its defects? And (if thus issued) is the dust jacket present?

Furthermore, the presumption is that nothing is *added* by the book owner—no bookplates and no handwriting.

Factors That Affect Valuation

These are the things that you should *not* do:

→ Do *not* discard the dust jacket. Because it is an integral part of the book, the overall value will be determined accordingly.

→ Do *not* clip the price off the corner of the dust jacket. (This is commonly done when bought as a present, so the recipient doesn't know what the giver has paid.)

→ Do *not* paste in your own bookplate. (These are usually glued in and cannot be removed.)

→ Do *not* sign your name in the book, *Unless* you are the author. (In this case, the preferred place is the title page on which your name appears.)

→ Do *not* store the book in a place with high humidity, such as an attic or an outside storage unit with no temperature control.

→ Do *not* buy book club editions except for reading copies, because these are usually inexpensive reprints and have no real collectible value.

→ Do *not* buy ex-library copies except for reading copies only, because these are usually well-read, shopworn, and likely in poor—or, at best, fair—condition, with stampings and envelopes pasted in.

→ Do *not* shrink-wrap a book, because shrink-wrapping can literally warp a book over time.

→ Do *not* put books where they are accessible by pets. (I have a friend whose "As New" copy of a valuable Tolkien book was damaged when her cat knocked a vase and water-stained its cloth binding—a non-repairable flaw that significantly affects its value.)

These are the things that you *should* do:

➔ Buy from a reputable book dealer, preferably one who specializes in antiquarian books, because he will know what he is selling, describe it accurately, and ask a fair price.

➔ Be wary of signed Tolkien books or ephemera offered on general auction Websites, such as eBay, where anyone can sell anything at any price, and the provenance may be questionable. (That said, I have seen signed letters by Tolkien on eBay that are incontrovertibly the real thing. However, while forging the real One Ring is the stuff of fiction, forging signatures is much easier!)

➔ Carefully inspect your copy for damage before storing it.

➔ Store books upright on a bookshelf. (Don't do what a friend of mine did: He painted his bookshelves white, and then put books on them before proper drying. Since then, his books literally have "glued" to the shelf!)

➔ Protect the dust jacket by using a Gaylord or Brodart acetate cover, such as libraries use.

➔ On the bookshelf, do not cram books together to make them fit, which can compress them.

➔ Consult a descriptive bibliography to ensure that the book you have bought is, in fact, the edition you expected: *J.R.R. Tolkien: A Descriptive Bibliography* by Wayne G. Hammond and Douglas A. Anderson is indispensable.

➔ Store the book in a room with relatively low humidity.

Book Defects

These are the most common defects found in a book—defects that adversely affect its condition:

➤ Clipped price. If people routinely give you books for gifts, ask them *not* to clip the price or inscribe the book with a cheery celebratory greeting.

➤ Tears. Small tears turn into large tears. Be especially careful to inspect the edges of the dust jacket and the interior pages of the book, because book manufacturing cannot guarantee trouble-free printing and binding for 100 percent of the copies printed. (Bloomsbury, the U.K. publisher of J.K. Rowling's popular Harry Potter novels, was surprised to discover that hundreds of books were printed with pages missing. It can happen.)

➤ Torn or ripped pages. This is usually accidental, but these are fatal flaws.

➤ Chipping. Book jackets are particularly susceptible to small chips, which can, like a tear, turn into a larger chip.

- Creasing. This is usually unintentional and often affects corners, but a crease *cannot be repaired*. It is a permanent flaw. (Sometimes people don't use bookmarkers—they just turn down the pages as convenient. This is particularly a problem with library books.)

- Trimmed dust jacket. Publishers make jackets to fit the book exactly, so why some people feel the need to trim them is a puzzlement. There's no rational reason to trim a book jacket!

- Tape. Often used to mend small tears, tape used by amateurs is usually acidic and will yellow over time. (Book conservators use tape sparingly and only an acid-free brand.)

- Adhesive sticker attached. This is the fault of the bookseller. The current worst offender is Books-a-Million, which computerizes its titles but affixes a fiendishly sticky label that, over time, actually becomes permanently bonded to the dust jacket! Even when carefully removed, as much as possible, a sticky residue remains.

- A close cousin of the adhesive sticker: a small plastic anti-theft device literally affixed to the dust jacket or the inside of a book. When stuck on, this device *cannot* be removed. (Barnes & Noble inserts these loose, placed randomly between the pages of the book.)

- Written markings, usually the price. Booksellers who specialize in used books often use a soft pencil to mark the price on the inside front cover—erasable, fortunately. Beware if the price is in ink.

- Stamped markings. A book owner may use a stamp to print his name, address, or phone number (or all three) in the book itself, presumably to prevent theft.

- An adhesive label. I actually bought a first edition of what turned out to be a very valuable book—*The Forever War* by Joe Haldeman—that bore the bookseller's adhesive address label permanently affixed to the inside front cover! It's a form of advertising for him, but it did detract from the value of the book when I eventually resold it.

- Excessive wear. Obviously more of a problem with used books, but because new books are returnable and some have been manhandled before being sent back to the distributor or publisher, who in turn will reship it out as a new book, beware. Inspect the book carefully.

- Water stains. Books are very susceptible to water damage and, in fact, cannot be repaired when significantly wet. (After a water heater on the third floor of my home burst, flooding the lower two levels, including the air-conditioned storage area where some of my books are stored, three boxes of books were literally soaked with water. The insurance adjuster couldn't believe that these books had no resale value—waterlogged with pages literally stuck together, the books could not be salvaged.)

➤ Embossing. A favorite book tool is the customized hand-embosser, which imprints in raised lettering your name, or initials, in a circular seal, "This book is from the library of ____." This physically damages the book beyond repair, because the page itself has been permanently altered.

➤ Removed pages. This is usually a binding problem, and not always from old age. New books, improperly bound, may have signatures falling out, as was the case with a recently published 415-page book of Marilyn Monroe collectibles.

➤ Bumped corners. Books, if dropped, will inevitably land on a corner, permanently bumping it. Must be a law of physics.

➤ Remainder marks. These are designed to be nonremovable, because books are returnable, and a book without an indelible marking could—if in the hands of an unscrupulous bookseller—be purchased for pennies on the dollar and returned for full value. For this reason, remainder marks usually bear the stamp seal of the publisher or heavy black permanent ink marked as a solid line across a book's bottom edge.

➤ Annotated pages. Some people write in the margins. This can sometimes be a real problem with collectible books that are used.

➤ Page discoloration. Usually a problem with older books, it can also be a problem with new books if left in the sunlight—a sure way to fade the dust jacket or cloth binding.

➤ Spine defects. A book's spine is designed to hold the book together when it is stored properly—upright, without too much compression, with books on either side. If improperly stored, a book's spine may crack, slant, or become loose. This is repairable, but restoration is expensive and often easier to prevent than to correct after the fact.

Terms Used to Identify Books

As in any other specialized profession, booksellers have their own vocabulary. The following terms are what you will most likely encounter when reading descriptions for used books. If you understand the vocabulary, you'll be in a better position to know exactly what you're buying.

➤ **Proof copy**. This is most commonly bound as a trade paperback and marked "proof" or "proof copy" and is usually the uncorrected, typeset text that's published in small runs and given out to book reviewers who need long lead times. (Time doesn't permit the nicety of providing a typographically accurate edition.) Because the text may change significantly, as the author makes revisions, there's usually a standard disclaimer to the effect that any quoted text should be checked against the final printed book and not this proof copy. Printed in relatively small runs, these are not sold, but some do find their way into the hands of secondhand booksellers.

➤ **Limited edition**. For the most part, Tolkien has not had limited editions published, which are usually signed and numbered by the author, artist, or both. What few limited editions I've seen in the Tolkien market have been issued by his British publisher, HarperCollins. For example, to celebrate the 60th anniversary of *The Hobbit*, 600 copies were specially bound and signed by artist Alan Lee; to celebrate the centenary of Tolkien's birth, 250 copies of the three volumes of *The Lord of the Rings* were published, each volume individually signed and numbered by Alan Lee; and 500 copies of *The Silmarillion*, specially bound and slipcased, signed by Christopher Tolkien and Ted Nasmith.

➤ **First edition**. This is the most desired state—the first published copies of the book. The edition is normally marked on the "legal" page, along with the number of its printing. (As the book sells out and goes back to press, the publisher notes which printing the book is currently in.) For instance, the First American Edition of *The Silmarillion*, published in 1977, states "First American Edition" and, at the bottom, bears a line of numbers; on the far right, the number "1" indicates it is the first edition, first printing—the most valuable edition. (When the book is reprinted, the number "1" is removed and the number "2" shows—in this instance, a first edition with a second (or subsequent) printing. *It's an important distinction, because the first printings of the first edition are the most collectible.*

➤ **Second edition, first printing**. This means the book has been revised, so it's in fact a *new* edition of the book. In this instance, the publisher usually indicates on the cover, "revised" or "expanded" edition. The "legal" page will also reflect the fact that the text has been altered.

➤ **Second edition, second (or subsequent) printing**. This means the book has been revised and has gone back to press; the lowest number will indicate how many printings the book has had.

Specific Terms

➤ **Association copy**. This is a copy of the book given to someone close, personally or professionally, to the author. Typically, association copies are first editions and very warmly inscribed, as well. Obviously, the stronger the association, the more valuable the book. A first edition copy of *The Hobbit*, given by Tolkien to his aunt Jane on his mother's side (Emily Jane Suffield) fetched $66,630 at a Sotheby's auction in 2002. (She was the one who urged him to write a book about Tom Bombadil—the result, *The Adventures of Tom Bombadil*.)

➤ **First edition**. I've discussed this earlier but want to emphasize that there is no standardized method of identifying first editions; each publisher has his own method, which complicates things needlessly for all in the book trade. The key thing to remember is that the *lowest* number indicates its printing; thus, if a book is marked "First Edition," the number "1" indicates the first printing of that first edition, the number "2" indicates a second printing of that first edition, etc.

✦ **Inscribed copy**. When Tolkien gave out books, he often inscribed them, writing a warm note, signing his name, and dating it. Typically, an author, especially if pressed for time or inscribing for a stranger, will write "Best Wishes" or something similar and short. A warmly inscribed copy to someone Tolkien knew is, obviously, more valuable than an inscribed copy to someone with whom he had no association—that is, a reader he didn't personally know, who had asked him to sign it.

✦ **Out of print**. This means the book is no longer available for sale in the book trade through normal book channels—distributors and wholesalers. (The book may still be available, as remaindered copies or as regular stock that's unsold.)

✦ **Paperback**. There are two varieties of paperback books, *mass market* and *trade*. Mass market are smaller, pocket-size books printed on low-quality paper. Trade paperbacks, sometimes called "quality" paperbacks, are usually printed on higher quality paper, have better covers, a larger trim size, and a price to match.

✦ **Trade hardback**. These are usually clothbound, with a dust jacket. Most of Tolkien's books have been issued in this fashion.

✦ **Publication date**. This is the actual date the book is allowed to be sold in the bookstore. (These days, to prevent premature sales, big-name books are released simultaneously on a specific day. For example, J.K. Rowling's *The Order of the Phoenix* was made available for sale worldwide one minute after midnight on the day of release—June 21, 2003.)

✦ **Remainder marks**. Indelible markings usually on the bottom edge of the book with black permanent ink, a stamp with the publisher's logo, or with spray paint—all impossible to remove. This indicates the publisher printed more than could be sold through normal book channels and, thus, marked them down and sold them to remainder companies that specialize in books. These copies usually show up at the chain stores on bargain tables or in specialty bookstores that carry remaindered books.

✦ **Slipcase**. Usually a cloth-covered case into which a book can be slipped. The cloth case usually matches the cloth of the book itself. Normally done for more valuable editions, such as the deluxe editions of *The Hobbit*, *The Lord of the Rings*, *The Silmarillion*, and *The History of Middle-earth* (three volumes, each slipcased, with the books printed on India paper).

On Autographs

Tolkien's signature can be found on both handwritten and typed letters, on copies of his books, and on books that were from his personal library.

Signed letters are the most affordable, especially if it's short (one or two paragraphs) and its contents bland (thanking a reader for enjoying his books, or declining an invitation). I've seen these come up for sale occasionally on eBay, for $2,500 and up, but for the most part I've seen copies for sale through antiquarian booksellers.

Christopher Tolkien also sold some books from his father's library—grammar books, in which J.R.R. Tolkien had signed his full name, with notes or grammatical annotations—but the last copies I've seen for sale sold in early 2003 for $650 and up. Those copies are now rapidly rising in value.

Considering Tolkien's enduring popularity, his importance in the fantasy field, and the fact that he (unlike many authors) did not generally support book signings, his signature is surprisingly obtainable—*if* money is not a major consideration and you know exactly where to look.

Tolkien's calligraphic signature.

The most valuable signatures are found on holographic letters in which he discusses his major works, such as *The Hobbit* and, especially, *The Lord of the Rings*. Likewise, his signature on first editions of any of his books—especially the prize, a set of *The Lord of the Rings* individually signed—will continue to command top dollar. (To one English reader who wrote and identified himself as "Sam Gamgee," after hearing he was in the story, Tolkien sent a signed set of all three volumes.)

In addition to listings in booksellers' catalogs, signed books and letters have, in recent years, shown up at major auction houses and, of course, on eBay—a reputable online "flea market" where it's especially important to know what you're buying and from whom. Unfortunately, there are some unscrupulous, greedy people who take advantage of others through the anonymity of the Internet and the gullibility of customers who can't distinguish between a real signature and a fake one.

I *have* seen two authentic letters by Tolkien for sale, and have not seen any fake signatures, but to borrow a line from Gandalf, don't be a fool of a Took! Know what you're buying and from whom, to avoid disappointment.

Generally speaking, booksellers know their inventory and know the current market values for the books they carry. Here's a sampling of some of the first editions for sale, with approximate prices culled from booksellers' catalogs and online listings.

→ *The Hobbit, or There and Back Again* (London: George Allen & Unwin, 1937). First edition, hardback, with first issue dust jacket: $85,000.

→ *The Lord of the Rings* (London: George Allen & Unwin, 1954/1955). First editions, hardback with dust jackets: $44,500.

→ *The Hobbit, or There and Back Again* (London: George Allen and Unwin, 1937). First edition, second printing, with dust jacket: $15,000. Although 2,300 copies were printed, 423 copies, in sheet form, were destroyed during World War II, when London was bombed. This edition has Tolkien's art in color, whereas the first edition has his art in black and white.

→ *Farmer Giles of Ham* (London: George Allan Unwin, 1949). First edition, with dust jacket, signed with Tolkien's full signature: $12,000.

❖ A set of the deluxe editions of *The Hobbit*, *The Lord of the Rings*, and *The Silmarillion* (London: Harper Collins): $6,000. *The Hobbit* was a limited edition of 600 copies; *The Lord of the Rings* was limited to 250 copies, signed by illustrator Alan Lee; and *The Silmarillion* was limited to 500 copies, signed by Christopher Tolkien and illustrator Ted Nasmith.

❖ *The Hobbit* (Boston: Houghton Mifflin, 1938). First edition. Hardback with dust jacket: $4,500.

❖ *The Road Goes Ever On: A Song Cycle* (Allen & Unwin, 1968). First edition, signed by Tolkien, hardback, with dust jacket: $4,000.

❖ *Smith of Wootton Major* (Allen & Unwin, 1967). First edition, proof copy, paperback: $3,000.

❖ *The History of Middle-earth* (12 volumes bound in three), *The Hobbit*, *The Lord of the Rings*, and *The Silmarillion*, all printed on India paper, with quarter-leather bindings, and slipcased: $2,000.

❖ *Anthology Oxford Poetry* (Oxford: B.H. Blackwell, 1915). Includes "Goblin Feet" by Tolkien (his first appearance in book form), paperback: $1,400.

❖ *The Hobbit* (Hatchard's of London, 1997). Half-leather in slipcase, each copy signed by its illustrator, Alan Lee: $1,200.

❖ *Farmer Giles of Ham* (London: Allen & Unwin, 1949). First edition, hardback, with dust jacket: $800.

❖ *The Adventures of Tom Bombadil* (London: Allen & Unwin, 1962). First edition, hardback, with dust jacket: $750.

❖ *Pictures by J.R.R. Tolkien* (Boston: Houghton Mifflin, 1979). First edition, hardback, with slipcase: $200–400.

❖ *Tree and Leaf* (London: Allen & Unwin, 1964). First edition, hardback, with dust jacket: $350.

❖ *On Fairy Stories* (London: Oxford University Press, 1947). First edition, hardback, with dust jacket: $300.

❖ *The Monsters and the Critics and Other Essays* (Boston: Houghton Mifflin, 1984). First edition. hardback, with dust jacket: $250.

❖ *The Road Goes Ever On: A Song Cycle, Music by Donald Swann & Poems by J.R.R. Tolkien* (London: Allen and Unwin, 1968). Hardback, with dust jacket: $250.

❖ *Smith of Wootton Major* (Boston: Houghton Mifflin, 1967). Hardback, with dust jacket: $200.

→ *Letters of J.R.R. Tolkien* (London: Allen & Unwin, 1981). Hardback, with dust jacket: $150.

→ *A Tolkien Family Album* (Boston: Houghton Mifflin, 1992). Hardback, with dust jacket: $150.

→ *The Road Goes Ever On* (Boston: Houghton Mifflin, 1967). Hardback, with dust jacket: $125.

→ *The Father Christmas Letters* (London: Allen & Unwin, 1976). Hardback, with dust jacket: $125.

→ *The Silmarillion* (Boston: Houghton Mifflin, 1977). Hardback, with dust jacket: $100.

→ *Mr. Bliss* (London: Allen & Unwin, 1982). Hardback, with dust jacket: $100.

→ *Unfinished Tales* (Boston: Houghton Mifflin, 1980). Hardback, with dust jacket: $100.

Letters

Set in small type and totaling 502 pages, *The Letters of J.R.R. Tolkien* is not definitive, as its editor, Humphrey Carpenter, points out: "Despite the length of this volume, and the great number of letters we have collected, there can be no doubt that much of Tolkien's correspondence still remains untraced."

According to Houghton Mifflin, Tolkien was "one of the 20th century's most prolific letter writers" and, from the prices realized today on the open market, one of the most collectible, as well.

Here are some of the letters offered for sale in the last half year, culled from bookseller catalogs:

→ A holographic letter, two pages, written in 1969: $13,000.

→ A holographic letter, on Merton College letterhead, 1954: $7,500.

→ A holographic correspondence card, with envelope, 1949: $7,300.

→ A holographic letter mentioning *The Hobbit*, 1969: $4,900.

→ A holographic letter to Tolkien biographer Humphrey Carpenter, 1968: $4,000.

→ A typed letter, 1966: $3,000.

→ A holographic letter (declining an invitation), 1956: $2,500.

→ A typed letter (declining to review a book), 1967: $1,750.

Chapter 11

Visions of Middle-earth: Tolkien Art

As a writer and an artist himself, Tolkien was very concerned about the art used for his books—especially cover art—and was vocal in raising his objections, politely but firmly. It's easy to understand Tolkien's frustrations, because the book publication process, as viewed from the publisher's perspective, is worlds apart from the author's perspective. The former looks to save time and cut costs in every way possible, but the latter imagines only the illustrative possibilities and the look of the book. As a result, the two perspectives may be very different, as was the case when Ballantine Books issued a mass market paperback of *The Hobbit* with a bulbous fruit-bearing tree surrounded by emus, which understandably upset Tolkien. Expressing his strong disapproval, he was told the artist hadn't had time to read the book and that the tree was meant to suggest a Christmas tree. Tolkien's understandable response was that he felt as if he had been shut up in a "madhouse."

Since the publication of *The Hobbit* in 1937, with Tolkien's own delightful illustrations, hundreds of artists—fan and pro—have attempted to visualize Tolkien's Middle-earth, with varying results. The Tolkien illustrator faces several formidable obstacles, not the least of which is the reader's individual vision as he imagines it in his mind's eye.

With the release of the Jackson film adaptations, yet another obstacle is created. The visuals from the films are firmly imprinted in one's mind, so when thinking of Frodo Baggins, an image of the boyish Elijah Wood may come to mind.

Beyond the force of the visual imprinting from the film adaptations, there is the subjective matter of individual visions from artists who clearly have their own perceptions of how the people, places, and things in Middle-earth ought to look.

Despite the formidable challenges involved in imagining and depicting Middle-earth, with all its varied landscapes populated by orcs, trolls, hobbits, ents, wizards, and elves (to name but a few), the best Tolkien artists rise to the occasion. Richly imaginative, technically accomplished, and able to go beyond mere illustration by evoking a sense of wonder, these artists know and love Tolkien's work and give us interpretations that ring true.

My personal favorite, about whom I've written at length elsewhere in this book, is Tim Kirk—a fantasy artist who has illustrated H.P. Lovecraft, Lord Dunsany, William Hope Hodgson, and, of course, Tolkien.

To date, four Tolkien art books have appeared: two collecting Tolkien's own work (*Pictures by J.R.R. Tolkien* and *J.R.R. Tolkien: Artist & Illustrator*) and two anthologies (*Tolkien's World: Paintings of Middle-earth* and *Realms of Tolkien: Images of Middle-earth*). Regarding the two anthologies, the art—in my estimation—runs the gamut in terms of quality.

We can consider Tolkien's own art as definitive, and all others interpretive, but all the artists share a considerable enthusiasm for Tolkien's imaginative fiction.

Any discussion of Tolkien artists—drawn from the hundreds of fan and pro artists who have illustrated his work—must, by necessity, be truncated. Rather than a subjective approach, I'm limiting it to the work of professional artists who have illustrated Tolkien's books or calendars, or books about Tolkien.

Tolkien Artists: A Selective Overview

American Artists

Donato Giancola. A classically trained artist, Donato Giancola has already propelled himself in the first rank of fantasy illustrators with a series of imaginative, boldly designed, and brilliantly executed book covers inspired not by previous fantasy illustrators but by Old World artists who excelled in draftsmanship.

Drawing in a realistic vein, Giancola's cover for *The Hobbit* is an impressive 38 x 68 inches. A similarly themed painting, a portrait of the Fellowship, was done for the Science Fiction Book Club edition of *The Lord of the Rings*, showing Aragorn sheltering Frodo in the Mines of Moria. On a smaller scale, measuring 8 x 10 inches, a rendition of the One Ring—a jewel-like painting done for a gaming card.

Complementing the book covers, a series of illustrations for gaming cards amply shows Donato's strong compositional skills and draftsmanship. (His portraits are, as you'd expect from someone inspired by the European masters, exquisitely rendered.)

The heir apparent to the title of "Best Professional Artist" in the science fiction and fantasy field, Giancola's the man to watch. His pieces of art are works of wonder.

Open edition prints of his Tolkien art are available from his Website, *www.donatoart.com*.

Michael Hague. A former greeting card artist for Hallmark Cards and Current Company, Michael Hague is best known for his watercolors illustrating children's classics, including *The Wizard of Oz*, *The Wind in the Willows*, *The Reluctant Dragon*, *Aesop's Fables*, and his series of children's books done in collaboration with his wife, Kathleen. Of special interest to Tolkien fans is Hague's work for *The Hobbit* (HarperCollins, $17.95, trade paperback), for which he rendered 48 color illustrations—seven of which were reprinted in *Tolkien's World: Paintings of Middle-earth*.

No official Website exists and no prints are available.

Stephen Hickman. Principally a paperback book cover artist, with more than 350 to his credit, Hickman's interpretations of Middle-earth strike a resonant chord in me. Two of his Tolkien-inspired paintings were published in *Realms of Tolkien* (HarperCollins, $30): from *The Fellowship of the Ring*, "The Black Rider," showing Gaffer Gamgee confronted by a Nazgûl on his black steed; and from *The Return of the King*, "The Siege of Gondor," a magnificent battle scene, awash in red, showing a horse-mounted Nazgûl directing the assault against the city.

Though long out of print, *The Art of Stephen Hickman* (originally published by The Donning Company) is worth hunting down because it shows an excellent selection of his cover paintings.

No prints of Hickman's Tolkien work are currently available. His Website is at *www.stephenhickman.com*.

Greg and Tim Hildebrandt. Commonly called the Brothers Hildebrandt (a nod, perhaps, to the Brothers Grimm?), Greg and Tim Hildebrandt are well known in Tolkien circles because of their three Tolkien calendars published in 1977, 1978, and 1979.

Fans interested in the story behind their pictures will find *Greg and Tim Hildebrandt: The Tolkien Years* (Watson-Guptill Publications) a fascinating read. Written by Gregory Hildebrandt, Jr., the book sheds light on how the Hildebrandts began their long association as Tolkien artists, when an editor at Del Rey Books gave Greg and Tim an assignment to do a cover for a mass market paperback edition of *Smith of Wootton Major/Farmer Giles of Ham* that recalled the art of Maxfield Parrish.

In September 2002, an expanded edition was published in trade paperback ($24.95) included 12 additional pages and a pullout poster, as well.

Giclée prints are available of many of their illustrations from the calendars.

A little bit of history here: *The Tolkien Years* bears a dedication from Tim Hildebrandt, who credits his wife for being the initial impetus to his Tolkien work:

> To my wife Rita, who made it possible for me to have illustrated the Ring calendars. She gave me the 1975 Tolkien calendar [illustrated by Tim Kirk] as a Christmas gift. On the back, there was an invitation for artists to contact the publisher if they were interested in illustrating *The Lord of the Rings*. If I hadn't received this present, I would never have called [on the publisher].

Their Website is at *www.brothershildebrandt.com*.

Michael Kaluta. A well-regarded artist, best known for his work in the comic book field, Kaluta has illustrated numerous major books, including *Batman* (DC Comics) and *Vampirella* (DC Comics); profusely illustrated an edition of *Metropolis* (Donning Company); published two major artbooks collecting his work; and has seen his Tolkien art published in calendar and book form. His Website is at *www.kaluta.com*.

Tim Kirk. A former greeting card artist for both Hallmark Cards and Current Company, Kirk has spent the bulk of his professional career as a senior designer at Imagineering for the Walt Disney Company. Currently a partner in Kirk Design Inc., Tim Kirk's name is well known in organized fandom because of his whimsical cartoons and illustrations for fanzines, prozines, and book covers for small presses and mainstream publishers, alike.

In 1980, a retrospective of his work, *Kirk's Works*, was edited by George Beahm. Published by Heresy Press, this book looks at Kirk's works predating his employment at Disney.

Kirk's artwork is distinctive, not only in appearance but in execution. With an art style uniquely his own, his lifelong interest in fantasy and affiliation with fandom led to numerous assignments from small presses such as Arkham House, Mirage Press, Whispers Press, and large publishers such as DAW Books.

An ardent Tolkien fan, Kirk illustrated the dust jacket for Robert Foster's *Guide to Middle-earth*, published by Mirage Press in 1971. But Tolkien fans know his work best from the "1975 J.R.R. Tolkien Calendar," which was the first Tolkien calendar to feature artwork by a sole artist (previous calendars had art by Tolkien and Pauline Baynes).

Kirk's Tolkien art came to the attention of Ian and Betty Ballantine, who saw an exhibit of the original art at Worldcon in southern California in 1972. The Ballantines then published the art to a worldwide audience. Of the 26 illustrations originally drawn to fulfill the requirements for his master's degree in art, 13 appeared in the calendar. For years a fan favorite, Tim Kirk's work is now known internationally in Tolkien circles.

What makes Tim Kirk unique among Tolkien artists is his unique vision and powerful imagination that combines to evoke a sense of wonder. Kirk's affinity for and love of fantasy makes him, in my estimation, *the* Tolkien artist whose work best visually depicts Middle-earth.

For information on some of his work, visit *www.FlightsofImagination.com*.

David Wenzel. As a book illustrator, Wenzel's principal influence is a turn-of-the-century British illustrator, Arthur Rackham (b. 1867). In terms of Tolkien work, Wenzel has the singular distinction of having illustrated the only graphic novel adaptation of any Tolkien book—*The Hobbit* (HarperCollins, $15), which was designed to appeal especially to younger readers.

Working in watercolor, Wenzel's Tolkien art is available as inkjet prints (13 x 19 inches, $60–90) and (to date) one lithograph, as well.

His work can be viewed at *www.davidwenzel.com*.

David Wenzel's art for his graphic novel adaptation of The Hobbit.

A watercolor painting by David Wenzel from The Hobbit, the graphic novel adaptation.

Michael Whelan. Best known for his cover art for major science fiction and fantasy authors, Whelan's sole contribution to the canvas of Tolkien art is a scene from *The Return of the King*, in which Frodo and Sam have achieved their arduous mission—to destroy the One Ring by casting it back into the Crack of Doom, from whence it was forged—and await their rescue by the eagles.

Titled "The Eagles are Coming," this pivotal scene is from *The Return of the King* ("The Fields of Cormallen").

Whelan's painting depicts Frodo and Sam on a volcanic outcrop, surrounded by rivers of lava, as swirling plumes of smoke rise; in the background, two towers are crumbling, and the light of day breaks through as the eagles—Gwaihir, Landroval, and Meneldor—come to rescue them.

Rich in symbolism—the crumbling towers juxtaposed against the light of hope—Whelan's draftsmanship is buttressed by his ability to think through a painting, determining the key image that best illustrates the work at hand. In this painting, Whelan chose wisely and well, for everything in *The Lord of the Rings* has been encapsulated in this painting. It is, simply, a masterpiece, though Whelan himself principally sees its flaws. Painted years ago, "The Eagles are Coming" is representative, he says, of what he could do back then. Now, he knows, he would approach the painting differently, bringing to bear additional years of knowledge and skill.

Most readers, I suspect, will look at the painting and gasp in delight. Whelan has given us an image that most of us have seen, however inadequately, in our collective mind's eye and concretized it: *This* painting is what I see when *that* scene comes to mind, which is the highest compliment I can pay.

Whelan's ability to think through a cover painting, by reading it thoroughly and picking a symbolic scene that encapsulates the entire work, is a rare gift. Also, Whelan's technical abilities as an artist—his composition, his color sense, and his draftsmanship—are second to none.

It's little wonder that Whelan has won more awards in the fantasy and science fiction field than any other artist in the history of the genre—14 Hugos; three

Howards (the maximum allowed by voting rules); and "Best Professional Artist," as voted on by the readership of the field's trade journal, *Locus*, for 21 years in a row.

The illustrator of Stephen King's first Dark Tower novel, *The Dark Tower: The Gunslinger* (Donald M. Grant, Publisher, Inc.), Whelan has come full circle by illustrating the seventh—and last—book in the Dark Tower series, simply titled *The Dark Tower* (Donald M. Grant, Publishers, Inc.).

With a few paperback covers for DAW Books due in 2004, Whelan is concentrating on his gallery work and private paintings in the short term.

Many of Whelan's prints are available through Glass Onion Graphics, *www.glassonion.com* (see Appendix A for more information), but, alas, for Tolkien fans, his signature piece of Frodo and Sam ("The Eagles are Coming") is available only in their original appearances: "The 1980 Tolkien Calendar: The Great Illustrators Edition" and *Michael Whelan's Works of Wonder* (both by Ballantine Books).

Canadian Artists

Ted Nasmith. Completing the circle of officially endorsed artists prominently featured on Tolkien's official book Website, Ted Nasmith's association as a Tolkien artist began in 1987, when four paintings were used in the two versions of the Tolkien calendar for that year (one published by Unwin Paperbacks, the other by Ballantine). He followed that up with full calendars in 1990 (Ballantine), 1992 (Ballantine), 1996 (HarperCollins), and 2003 (Harper Entertainment), supplemented by Tolkien diary art, a poster book collection, and a fully illustrated edition of *The Silmarillion*, designed as a companion book to Alan Lee's illustrated editions of *The Lord of the Rings* and *The Hobbit*. Sumptuously illustrated with 20 full-color plates commissioned especially for this edition, *The Silmarillion* complements the other two masterworks by Tolkien. (Nasmith is currently painting 26 more pieces for a reissue of *The Silmarillion*.)

His official Website is at *www.tednasmith.com*. Giclée prints and original art are available through Chalk Farm Gallery, *www.chalkfarmgallery.com* (see Appendix E for further information).

British Artists

Pauline Baynes. Perhaps best known for her 350 illustrations for C.S. Lewis's *The Chronicles of Narnia* (HarperCollins), Pauline Baynes has a rare distinction among Tolkien artists: She met him, by chance, at Allen & Unwin, when she went to submit an art folio. Rejecting another artist's folio for *Farmer Giles of Ham*, Tolkien embraced her art, calling it (according to Humphrey Carpenter's writing in *J.R.R. Tolkien: A Biography*) "...more than illustrations, they are a collateral theme."

Baynes's art is charming and delightful, the perfect visual complement to the lesser known Tolkien books, *Farmer Giles of Ham* (Houghton Mifflin), *Smith of Wootton Major* (Ballantine Books), *The Adventures of Tom Bombadil* (in *The*

Tolkien Reader, by Ballantine Books), and *Tree and Leaf* (Houghton Mifflin); most recently, she illustrated a short poem, *Bilbo's Last Song* (Alfred A. Knopf), which is more a showcase for her art than it is a showcase for Tolkien's poem.

Unfortunately, no official Website exists, and no prints are available of her work.

John Howe. At HarperCollins UK, the official Website of Tolkien's British publisher, only three artists—excluding Tolkien himself—are highlighted: John Howe, Alan Lee, and Ted Nasmith.

Howe's Tolkien-related credits are extensive and impressive. In addition to calendars, diaries, and related products, such as a poster collection and a postcard book, he was a conceptual artist for Peter Jackson's *The Lord of the Rings* film adaptation.

A fellow artist and conceptual artist for Jackson's Tolkien films, Alan Lee, wrote of John Howe, in an appreciation published on Howe's Website (at *www.john-howe.com/biography/afterword.htm*), that:

> His love and respect for Tolkien's world is apparent through the imaginative power of his illustrations and the integrity he brings to all aspects of his design work. Large tracks of Middle-earth are brooded over by John's awe-inspiring structures. His Barad-dûr, glimpsed through clouds of swirling vapour, will be an enduring image in many minds, as will his Gandalf striding purposefully through the Shire.

Pictures of Howe's Tolkien works are available in book form, including *Images of Middle-earth: Poster Collection* (HarperCollins UK, $22.95), *Myth and Magic Poster Collection* (HarperCollins UK, $24.95), and *Myth and Magic* (HarperCollins UK, $35), which feature art from *The Hobbit*, *The Lord of the Rings*, *The Silmarillion*, and *The History of Middle-earth*.

John Howe's Website is located at *www.john-howe.com*.

Alan Lee. In the collective mind of the public, if there is one artist who is most strongly identified with Tolkien, that would be Alan Lee, who is one of three artists featured on the official Website of Tolkien's British publisher.

In Lee's case, his singular distinction is that he is the only artist to have illustrated Tolkien's two most popular works: *The Lord of the Rings* and *The Hobbit*.

For *The Lord of the Rings*, he provided 50 paintings for a special one-volume edition celebrating Tolkien's 1892–1992 centenary (Houghton Mifflin, $70). The art was subsequently reprinted in a three-volume set printed with matte paper that enhanced the art reproduction.

Complementing his work on *The Lord of the Rings*, Lee illustrated *The Hobbit* for its 60th anniversary (Houghton Mifflin, $35), as well, providing black-and-white and color art.

Because of his work on these projects, he was hired by Peter Jackson as a conceptual artist for the film adaptation of *The Lord of the Rings*, further solidifying his position as the premiere Tolkien illustrator.

In 1994, Lee illustrated David Day's *Tolkien's Ring*, providing color plates and numerous black-and-white illustrations for an examination of ring-quest tales that inspired Tolkien when fashioning his own story.

Lee's artwork can also be found in three poster collections—*Tolkien Poster Collection* (HarperCollins UK, $22.95), *The Hobbit Poster Collection* (HarperCollins UK, $22.95), and two volumes of *The Lord of the Rings Poster Collection* (HarperCollins UK, $24.95 each)—as well as two diaries, an address book, a birthday book, and the 1999 calendar from HarperCollins, with art from *The Hobbit*.

Fans of Lee's evocative watercolor art will want to buy *The Mabinogion* (HarperCollins UK, £25), with its 50 illustrations, many appearing in print for the first time in this book.

Three poster book collections are in print, but no separate prints exist. There is no official Website, though a small portfolio of art exists on the official Tolkien Website, *www.tolkien.co.uk*.

J.R.R. Tolkien. It is rare that an accomplished writer is also a skilled artist, but when this happy happenstance occurs, it illuminates the text and provides a unique visual insight of the fiction—we literally see, through the artist/writer's eyes, a creative vision, pure and undimmed.

Such is the case with Tolkien's fiction. From his lesser-known works such as *Mr. Bliss* to the artwork for *The Hobbit*, the book cover designs for *The Lord of the Rings*, and its numerous illustrations—not to mention the devices and calligraphy—Tolkien's art is inseparable from his fiction, a felicitous marriage of text and art that combines to form a pleasing whole.

In *Pictures by Tolkien* (Houghton Mifflin), his previously published artwork, from the books and calendars, give an excellent overview to his skills as an artist— his own objections notwithstanding. In *J.R.R. Tolkien: Artist & Illustrator* (Houghton Mifflin), the wide range of his art is on full display. No question: Tolkien, a self-taught artist, modestly considered himself an amateur, someone who drew for the love of it, and never considered himself serious competition to professional artists who would be called upon to illustrate his fiction. Nonetheless, Tolkien himself provided illustrations for *The Hobbit* that have stood the test of time, despite his modest assertion in *Letters by J.R.R.* Tolkien (Houghton Mifflin) that "The pictures seem to me mostly only to prove that the author cannot draw." The pictures Tolkien provided included eight black-and-white illustrations and a distinctive cover illustration that, to my mind, are utterly enchanting and delightful, far preferable to an illustrated edition by any other artist.

Unfortunately, too few prints, posters, or poster books of Tolkien's own art are available, but perhaps an enterprising publisher will remedy this lamentable situation.

Interviews and Art by Select J.R.R. Tolkien Artists

In terms of exposure, the work of Tolkien artists—those who illustrate his works—are more likely to be seen than discussed. What, after all, *needs* to be discussed? To paraphrase Shakespeare, the picture's the thing, and should it not speak to the viewer?

Of course it does, but should not artists have the opportunity to speak directly to their audience in ways other than visual?

In this section I've deliberately sought out my favorite artists to explain why they've illustrated Tolkien and how they have gone about doing so. What they have to say about Tolkien and his art is fascinating, though I suspect most people will skip immediately to their art and only then read what they have to say.

I have heard Tim Kirk, Donato Giancola, and Colleen Doran talk extensively about Tolkien, Tolkien art, and their enthusiasm for the man and his work. I think you'd like to hear what they have to say, as well. My only regret is that these interviews aren't recorded on CD and bound in with this book, because that would truly give you a sense of how excited they are when discussing Tolkien.

I remember, especially, two lectures given by Donato at a Philcon in 2002. He took the stage, talked at length about his work and exhibited color slides, and later gave a demonstration of how he tackles a portrait—from a blank sheet of paper to the finished work.

People were fascinated by the process and, as Donato is enthusiastic and articulate, his passions are infectious. The crowd came alive, became animated, and began peppering him with questions.

For those of you who wonder just what artists are thinking before they sit down to create art, this section is a brief glimpse into the art of imagination.

Tim Kirk's Works

The late William Rotsler—a prolific fan cartoonist, among his other talents—termed Tim Kirk the "Wizard of Whimsey." There's certainly some truth in that, because Tim's creatures, no matter how other-worldly, curiously resemble ourselves.

I was in high school when I first discovered Tim's work, and by the time I was in college, I eagerly collected his work. By then, Tim was one of the most prolific and obviously talented fan artists contributing to the major fanzines of his time.

Fantasy illustrator Tim Kirk, in front of his house, holds "Frodo Meditates"—one of his original paintings from his "1975 J.R.R. Tolkien Calendar."

An oil painting of Gandalf the Wizard and Bilbo Baggins, published in his "1975 J.R.R. Tolkien Calendar."

It didn't take long for Tim to make the leap from fan to pro. Tim's work adorned book covers, interiors, and magazines, and in all of it you could see his obvious love for fantasy books and illustration. Indeed, his library is jam-packed with books under the imprints of Arkham House; Donald M. Grant, Publisher, Inc.; Mirage Press; Whispers Press—all the specialty houses in the fantasy field that knew Tim was an artist of the first rank and quickly hired him for cover and interior illustrations.

To me, what Tim brings to fantasy illustration, especially when illustrating Tolkien, is a visual affinity for "high" fantasy: Lord Dunsany, Mervyn Peake, H.P. Lovecraft, Clark Ashton Smith, and, of course, Tolkien.

My great enthusiasm and unbridled admiration for Tim resulted in our collaborating on an art index to his work, *Kirk's Works*, published by Heresy Press, helmed by Cuyler W. Brooks, Jr., who is the man responsible for introducing me to organized fandom and who, incidentally, has one of the best private collections of illustrated fantasy books I've ever seen.

For many years Tim was well known in fantasy circles—in fact, he was a multiple recipient of the Hugo award for best fan artist—but in 1973 a happy coincidence resulted in the publication of his paintings for *The Lord of the Rings* as the first Tolkien calendar that was comprised wholly of art by a single artist.

The calendar, published in August 1974, for the calendar year of 1975, quickly became a collector's item. It not only sold out, but now commands collector's prices.

Building on his success, after completing his postgraduate work and receiving a master's degree in Art, he moved from California to Kansas City, where he worked for Hallmark Cards, then subsequently moved to Colorado Springs to briefly work for Current Cards, on the recommendation of Michael Hague, who was his next-door neighbor. His last move was back to California, where his brother, Steve, urged him to join Walt Disney's Imagineering, where he finished a career of more than 20 years as a senior designer. Tim currently lives in Long Beach, his hometown.

Art by Tim Kirk, published in his "1975 J.R.R. Tolkien Calendar."

Currently a partner with his brother in Kirk Design Inc., Tim is designing the Science Fiction Experience, the first museum of its kind in the world, to open in the summer of 2004 in Seattle.

So, you ask, just how good is Tim Kirk? I think his art speaks for itself, but let me call in my first and only witness—Michael Whelan.

About a year ago, I had asked Michael Whelan to inscribe for Tim a copy of his second art book, a collection of his covers for DAW Books. Michael, who can inscribe a book quickly, deliberated and then began writing...and writing...and writing. He had written several paragraphs and then closed the book cover.

"Michael, you didn't need to *write* a book," I jokingly said, and he just smiled.

Titled "The Riddle Game," this oil painting by Tim Kirk, of Bilbo Baggins and Gollum, was published in his "1975 J.R.R. Tolkien Calendar."

Weeks later, when I delivered the book to Tim, I saw Tim's face light up when he read what Michael had written. The gist of it was that Michael expressed his admiration for Tim's art and stated unequivocally that Tim's illustrations of *The Lord of the Rings* were the best he had ever seen, bar none. High praise, we both knew, from the artist who has gotten more Hugo awards as pro artist than any other in the field. *That's* how good Tim Kirk is, and that's why I'm pleased—after too long an absence from the fantasy/science fiction community—to see him back, as he picks up his paintbrush and shows us new visions of Middle-earth.

A historical note: Tolkien fans worldwide know of Tim Kirk because of his work for the Tolkien calendar in 1975, but not many of them realize that Tim, in fact, had published a Tolkien calendar in 1969. Consisting of a cover and six plates, each printed in a different color, the calendar sold for 50¢ and was available through a southern California fanzine publisher, Ken Rudolph, who shipped it out with his Tolkien zine, *Mythlore*. The calendar plates illustrated Caradhras, Théoden's Hall, The Nimrodel in Lothlórien, The Gates of Gondor, Bilbo's Birthday Party, and The Stairs of Cirith Ungol.

An oil painting by Tim Kirk, titled "Road to Minas Tirith," published in his "1975 J.R.R. Tolkien Calendar."

An Autobiographical Note From Tim Kirk

I first read *The Lord of the Rings* in 1964—in high school—on a friend's recommendation. I was hooked, of course. When I'd finished, I immediately reread the entire thing, out loud, to my younger brother over the course of that summer—I just had to share it with someone! On a trip to England in 1967, a clerk at the wonderful Oxford bookstore, Blackwell's, gave me Tolkien's address, and I made a pilgrimage to Professor Tolkien's former home in an Oxford suburb.

I went out to Professor Tolkien's house just to stand worshipfully in front of it. I was certainly awestruck. I took a snapshot, which I've managed to misplace, and went back to the bus stop. I wouldn't have dared to knock on the door, or even step onto the front path, afraid of being struck by lightning, I suppose! (Not until much later did I find out he had moved some time before to get away from pesky, adoring fans like me!)

I joined the Mythopeic Society, a southern California-based group devoted to the work of Tolkien, C.S. Lewis, and Charles Williams, and began doing illustration work for their publications, *Mythlore* and *Mythprint*. I even went so far as to design and build an orc costume, which I wore in the broiling summer heat to a Renaissance Faire.

When the time came in 1971 for me to choose a subject for my master's thesis project in illustration at California State University at Long Beach, the choice was an easy one: a series of paintings based on *The Lord of the Rings*.

My Master's Show was a lot of fun. We listed it in the program book of a small regional Tolkien convention in 1972, and several of the attendees came to the show in costume.

After graduation, I exhibited the complete project of 26 paintings at the World Science Fiction Convention in Los Angeles that year. Ian and Betty Ballantine of Ballantine Books saw the collection and liked it well enough to publish 13 of the 26 pieces as the "1975 J.R.R. Tolkien Calendar."

One of the most important things Professor Tolkien achieved with *The Lord of the Rings* was his creation of a totally believable, completely immersive world—a unique synthesis that has inspired a host of (less inspired) imitators. It is this uniqueness and vivid imagery that also makes *LotR* such a challenge—and ultimately a joy—to illustrate. The results are bound to be intensely personal and heartfelt—and controversial! Everyone who reads the books has her or his own vision of Frodo, Gandalf, Minas Tirith and Mordor.

I was delighted with Peter Jackson's take on the books—it was obvious, from the beginning, that the films were a labor of love for him, his production company, and New Line Cinema. Frankly, I can't imagine a better result; turning any complex literary work into a film, with the inevitable editing that results (witness Ray Bradbury's heroic struggle with John Huston and "Moby Dick"!), is a monumental task at best. I am very, very happy that this production came together the way it did.

Unless you happened to have been at the southern California convention where Tim exhibited all of these paintings, you've only seen roughly half of them, which were published in his Tolkien calendar.

In book form, there are only a half dozen copies showing *all* the pictures, though these are reproduced in black and white, because Tim's master's thesis was bound in hard boards (that is, the illustrations are pasted in).

As Tim explains, the thesis was a way to experiment with different media and in different sizes; and, as Tim is quick to point out, some pieces are more successful than others. (Beyond these, there are a dozen more that have never seen the light of day—the "also rans" that Tim felt were not sufficiently developed, conceptually, to warrant a further investment of time.)

As with any artist, Tim is his harshest critic—indeed, only very recently, he refused to hang his own art on the walls of his home, but his wife, Linda, convinced him otherwise—and though there are some favorites in this set, Tim would prefer to go back to Middle-earth to render new paintings, with the benefit of 25-plus years of more experience at the drawing board. Just imagine how wonderful *that* would be!

In the interim, as we hope and dream that he gets another opportunity to do a new calendar or an art book, we can enjoy these timeless images that show us Tolkien in a new light.

The complete list of paintings:

- *Gandalf & Bilbo.*
- *Rivendell.*
- *The Riddle Game.*
- *Mirkwood.*
- *Smaug.*
- *Fire and Water.*
- *Pipeweed.*
- *Frodo Meditates.*
- *Maggot's Farm.*

- *Tom Bombadil.*
- *The Well in Moria.*
- *The Balrog.*
- *The Mirrormere.*
- *Galdadriel.*
- *Barad-dûr.*
- *Treebeard.*
- *In the Emyn Muil.*
- *Shelob.*

- *The Road to Minas Tirith.*
- *The Temptation of Gandalf.*
- *The Watchers.*
- *Two Orcs.*
- *Mordor.*
- *The Cracks of Doom.*
- *Farewell to the Grey Havens.*
- *The Last Shore.*

Current Projects

Kirk Design Inc. is currently (as of August 1, 2003) the principal design group on two large projects: Paul Allen's "Experience Science Fiction" Museum in Seattle, the first museum in the world devoted exclusively to the world of science fiction; and Lotte Dome Theater, a major theme park planned for Tokyo, Japan. The company has also done work for a variety of other clients and venues, including the Aquarium of the Pacific (Long Beach, Calif.), Busch Gardens, Walt Disney Pictures ("The Haunted Mansion," to be released November 2003), and the Ronald Reagan Presidential Foundation.

Colleen Doran: Drawn to Please

Colleen Doran is the best Tolkien illustrator you've never seen. Let me explain: Though she has hundreds of publishing credits for companies such as Marvel, DC Comics, LucasFilm, Walt Disney, and more small and independent presses than you can shake a mallorn leaf at, she's not yet had the opportunity to illustrate any of Tolkien's work.

More's the shame, because she brings to the field of Tolkien illustration a distinct and elegant look that bespeaks her great interest in fantasy and in art.

She's a Tolkien geek: her bookshelves groan under the weight of Tolkien tomes, Sideshow/Weta statues and figures, and Toy Biz "dolls" of Arwen and Frodo. Given a choice, she'd want to live in Rivendell or perhaps Hobbiton, as she loves gardening.

Actor Craig Parker (Haldir, in The Two Towers) *and Colleen Doran at* The Two Towers *Oscar night party sponsored by* TheOneRing.net, *in Hollywood, California.*

I first encountered her when, at a local science fiction convention in the late 1970s, she took to the stage for a costume contest; dressed in a white gown as Lady Galadriel, she sang beautifully and stole the show. I don't think anyone gave any of the Trekkies in costume a second look after her performance.

A petite powerhouse with a lot of artistic talent, Colleen has always commanded attention in the comics field—a male-dominated industry with a long-established, old-boys network that worked to keep her in her place. Colleen understandably bristles when fanboys call her the "little woman," or question her as to whether or not she, in fact, has drawn the art for her own books. What's even more bizarre, some misguided souls see her as the ideal trophy girlfriend or wife. (Sorry, guys, but just because she's pretty as a picture and can draw them, she has no place in *your* fantasies. *Her* fantasies are more grounded in reality—putting pen to paper and bringing to life imaginative art the likes of which you've never seen and could never imagine.)

At the aforementioned local science fiction convention, when I first met her, the day after the costume contest, I struck up a casual conversation with her, and she showed me pages from her epic fantasy, which would eventually be published as *A Distant Soil*. In her early work—pencil drawings for pages of *A Distant Soil*— I could see the promise of more mature and better work to come. She would either fulfill the promise...or join the ranks of frustrated artists who, for whatever reasons, never bridged the gap from fan to pro. That was years ago.

This is now: Colleen is arguably the most visible woman in the comic book field today. Sought after as a convention guest and for interviews—in print, online, and in DVDs—she's personable, articulate, and, unlike most artists and writers who wilt before a TV camera, comfortable in the spotlight. It is, she says, part of her job. But given her druthers, she'd much prefer her cozy studio, with its over-sized drawing table, as Howard Shore's soundtrack plays in the background and she draws up a storm, producing page after page of beautiful art. (When the soundtrack isn't playing, the appendices of the DVD to *The Fellowship of the Ring* is playing, because she's inspired by other creators who talk about their work, who share her obvious joy in creating art.)

A world-builder by inclination, Colleen is nearing the end of her long-running series, *A Distant Soil*, which she began drawing when she was 15 years old. Despite ups and downs in the comics field, as the book has changed publishers several times, she's stuck to it and expects to see its completion within a year—possibly two. What then?

Well, if the recently published *Orbiter* is any indication, and if the preview pages from *Reign of the Zodiac* are reliable road marks (and I think they are), then we are seeing the continued evolution of an artist who enjoys to push the envelope and break new ground. Frankly, I think she's a world-class conceptualizer, which makes her the ideal candidate for film work, or for specialized book projects involving extensive design work, illustrations, and imaginative packaging. (One wonders what she would have created as the costume designer for *The Lord of the Rings*, or as a conceptual designer for the movies as a whole.)

At this writing I have not seen all the art she's done for this book, but from what I've seen—pieces here and there—I think you'll be surprise and pleased; and my prediction (a safe one, I think) is that in time she will assume a position in the first rank of Tolkien illustrators, because she is *that* good.

I am, of course, prejudiced; I am a big fan of her work, and a bigger fan of her as a person, but those weren't, professionally, sufficient reasons for her to illustrate this book: The sole reason is that I think she's the perfect artist for the job, bar none. On that note, Colleen's Tolkien work not only sings and soars, but they comprise a visual symphony: she gives us world unimagined and makes them real, doing what only the best artists can do—instill in us a sense of wonder.

An Interview With Colleen Doran

**George
Beahm:**   Please give us a brief professional bio and what you're currently working on.

**Colleen
Doran:**   I like to keep busy—I am working on a number of projects at the
moment. I created, as well as write and draw, the series *A Distant Soil*
for Image Comics, and I am a cocreator of the new series *Reign of the
Zodiac* for DC Comics, which I illustrate and is written by Keith Giffen.
I have a new graphic novel out from DC Comics's Vertigo division called
Orbiter, which is written by Warren Ellis. I am always doing various
projects off and on. I was the conceptual designer for an animated
science fiction show created by Warren Ellis, which is in development
limbo right now, and I am working on a new project for Image Comics
called *Meanwhile*, cowritten by me and Keith Giffen and illustrated
by me. I am also working on new illustrations for a Tolkien exhibit at
Storyopolis, in Los Angeles, in December 2003.

GB: When did you first read Tolkien's *The Lord of the Rings* and what was
your initial response?

CD: I first read it when I was about 10 years old. I remember it very well. It
was difficult going for a 10-year-old, but I had just read Malory's *La
Morte D'Arthur* and was determined to get through *The Lord of the
Rings*, as well. I was struck by the extraordinary detail and sense of time
and place. I had very vivid memories of the places in the book that
were so real I felt as if I had been to them. The sights and smells and
feel of Middle-earth were presented with such exacting and loving attention that, to this day, I feel as if I have been there.

GB: What, in your opinion, makes Tolkien unique among fantasy writers?

CD: Tolkien does something that very few fantasy writers can pull off: He is
a true world-builder. His world is so well-realized on every level that
he makes almost every other work of fantasy ever written look shallow
by comparison. Tolkien spent years working on this story for his own
enjoyment. It is like an extraordinary piece of outsider art, a work created wholly outside the art and entertainment system and all its commercial considerations.

It is deeply personal and moving in a way that most modern commercial writers can't even touch. That, combined with the purity and
goodness of the work, the deep ethical sensibility, combined with a true
sense of charity for mortal flaws, makes it a book of enormous heart
that touches deep truths and needs in every human heart. Its goodness
and beauty can be appreciated by many people. It is truly a universal
work of literature.

GB: What makes Tolkien such a challenge to illustrate?

CD: I don't find it a challenge in technical terms because I love it so much and love to spend time in Middle-earth. I have been drawing Tolkien pictures ever since I was a kid! My internal vision of the Tolkien world is complete and very vivid. It is a *wonderful* place to visit.

I   The only challenge is conveying that sense to other people, who also have extremely vivid mental images of Tolkien's world. For that reason, a lot of illustrators shy away from even trying to convey the characters—they stick to landscapes. I am not afraid of drawing the characters, because I never get offended or upset if another artist's vision doesn't match mine.

I   I was nervous when I went to see the film, wondering if I would actively dislike the casting. I worried that the visions of the artists who worked on the film might differ from my own so profoundly that I would find my own internal vision poisoned. Every artist worries about doing the same thing! But frankly, the vision of Middle-earth in the films was so close to my own vision in so many ways that I was utterly delighted! For example, when Hugo Weaving came on the screen, I practically jumped up and screeched "It's Elrond!" He looked exactly as I had pictured him!

I   I had drawn a picture of Thranduil that was on display at the San Diego Comicon in July 2003, and, though it was not captioned, Tolkien fans immediately recognized the character as Thranduil, with no prompting from me. That tells me I have done my job—reached into the book and pulled out the mental image for the reader. Some writers I have worked with have told me that I am reading their minds! I don't know if that's true, but I pay attention to the text. I try to get into the writer's mind and give visual expression to his words.

I   I obviously never had the opportunity to talk with Tolkien, but I took the time to read his diaries and letters. I truly want to know what the writer was thinking, what he meant, on every level. Tolkien was thinking a heck of a lot! So there's a lot of studying to do when illustrating Tolkien.

GB: Given the commission to illustrate *The Lord of the Rings*, with covers and interior illustrations, how would you approach the task of selecting what to illustrate and how many paintings/drawings would you feel is necessary to adequately illustrate the three books?

CD: The primary consideration would be deadline. Given my druthers, I would like years to do hundreds of pictures! Of course, I am unlikely to get that, but because I have spent most of my career working as a cartoonist, which is the most grueling and demanding of all the illustration disciplines, I am accustomed to working under high pressure and producing high volume.

One consideration would be to avoid the standard images everyone else has already tackled. I would try to go for characters and situations that are often overlooked. We rarely see characters like Radagast, Elladan and Elrohir, Imrahil, Gildor, Elanor Gamgee, and a dozen others I could name. I would want to do some of the major characters of course, but it is so easy to do another shot of Gandalf that it is almost cliché.

I would also love to do a large number of spot illustrations, little decorative pieces of things from Middle-earth such as mallorn leaves, elven bows, or a Rohirrim helmet. My dream is to do an edition in the highly decorated tradition of turn-of-the-century books, heavily illustrated, heavily decorated, and designed from top to bottom as a piece of art, a keepsake book with illuminated letters, the way great illustrators like Walter Crane decorated books.

GB: What did you think of the Peter Jackson movie trilogy?

CD: The films were so beautiful. They were incredibly close to my internal vision of the books that I almost couldn't believe it. Hobbiton looked *exactly* as I dreamed!

In the months following the release of the first film, I had a brutal seven-days-a-week work schedule and could only afford to take a half day off each week, so my treat was a trip to Middle-earth every Friday, for nine weeks straight. It completely transported me and allowed me to relax through the vision of another world. I loved everything about it—the casting, direction, the costume and set design. Every once in a while I would think to myself, "I would have done it *this* way, but *that's* a great idea—it really looks good, too." Sometimes I watch the first part of the film when I want to relax. The vision of Hobbiton feels like home to me.

Moreover, the changes from the books are interesting and respectful. I have rarely seen a film adaptation that showed so much devotion to the source material.

GB: Beyond *The Lord of the Rings*, what would you have liked to illustrate from J.R.R. Tolkien's other works?

CD: *The Silmarillion*. If nothing in the *The Lord of the Rings* cycle is allowed, then *Sir Gawain and the Green Knight*.

Steve Hickman: The Art of Imagination

Before I talk about the artist, let me tell you about the art. If you own a copy of *Realms of Tolkien: Images of Middle-earth* (HarperCollins UK), look at the back cover. The art is by Steve Hickman, and it's a memorable scene from *The Fellowship of the Ring*: Samwise's father, Gaffer Gamgee, is at the gate of his home and a mounted Black Rider from Mordor is looking down at him, etched against a sky with boiling clouds. Gamgee knows something is amiss—the Big People, as the hobbits call men, are seldom seen in Hobbiton, but now an emissary from Mordor has appeared, asking pointed questions about Frodo Baggins. Gaffer Gamgee cleverly misdirects the Black Rider to Bucklebury, and passes a cautionary word on to his son.

Another painting from the book—a battle scene, from the Siege of Gondor—painted in yellow and red, depicts a giant battering ram being brought forth, directed by the Black Captain, who is astride his black steed.

Both paintings by Steve Hickman show superb draftsmanship, compositional skills, and a rich imagination—no surprise to those who have seen his work on paperback covers, or to those who have

An oil painting by Steve Hickman, "The Black Rider," published in Realms of Tolkien, *an original anthology of Tolkien art.*

seen his first art book collection, *The Art of Stephen Hickman* (The Donning Company), which unfortunately is out of print. (I remember that book well, especially because I suggested the idea to Steve and recommended it to my publisher, The Donning Company, where it was published as a handsome hardback, with a lengthy introduction by Harlan Ellison.)

There's been a lot of water under the bridge since then (back in 1987) but what hasn't changed is that Steve is one of the nicest guys you'd ever want to

meet, a convention favorite, and not only prolific—his list of publishing credits is far too long to reprint here—but, with his paperback cover art, he has endeared himself to a score of fantasy writers whose books are grabbed off bookshelves just so a closer look at the cover art can be had. (Forget the hype, but even with the art obscured by cover text, Steve's art shines through.)

Akin to other artists who love fantasy and, especially, Tolkien, he brings an enthusiasm and a freshness of vision that makes his work in *Realms of Tolkien* so memorable.

An unpublished oil painting by Steve Hickman of Ents at the entmoot.

An Autobiographical Note From Steve Hickman

After attending art school at the Richmond Professional Institute, in the company of Michael Kaluta, Charles Vess, and Phil Trumbo—and incidentally reading the Tolkien books as part of the mythos of the times—I did a very brief stint in the comics business. At that time, the industry was so moribund that I drifted into doing private commissions to make ends meet, and working on my oil painting technique.

Then I landed a job with an emerging local T-shirt company doing designs for their line. That was a blast and kept me working until I could get my painting portfolio together to find work doing paperback covers, which is what, in my secret heart, I had wanted to do all along since seeing the magical covers painted by Roy Krenkel, Jr., and Frank Frazetta for the Ace editions of Edgar Rice Burroughs. In fact, Ace Books was the first company I started working for. I sold the printing rights to a piece in my portfolio, and then another, and then I got my big chance: I was assigned to do the cover for the reprint of *The Brain Stealers* by Murray Leinster; I must have worked on that cover for a month.

Steve Hickman

So I did reprint covers for Ace Books for a while, learning on the job, so to speak—art school did nothing to prepare me for earning a living as an illustrator—and did private commissions now and then. During this time, I was contacted by Chris Zavisa of Land of Enchantment to do a series of Tolkien-inspired scenes for posters, and did four pictures that are still being sold to this very day.

And that is essentially what I've been doing ever since, with the occasional foray into writing fantasy fiction, sculpture, and a series of stamps for the U.S. Postal Service: The Space Fantasy Commemorative Stamp Booklet, for which I won my first, and to date only, Hugo Award.

My earliest associations with Tolkien are linked with my days in Richmond, Virginia, in 1967. At the time, I was reading a lot of

Victorian fantasy—H. Ryder Haggard, Arthur Conan Doyle, Christopher Percival Wren, and the like—and Tolkien's writing style interested me, because I felt at home with the British usages and loved the way he could change his prose to classical voicings when a more formal tone was required—the Council of Elrond segment, for instance—or his use of alliteration in the King James Bible in moments of greatest tension.

Later on, when my visual imagination had become more vivid, the thing which drew me further into the mythos was the power Tolkien had of evoking images in my mind, scenes both directly described or implied, which I have worked at developing over the 25 years since I first read these books.

To my way of thinking, the aspect of Tolkien's writings, which make him pre-eminent among fantasists, and which, incidentally, make him a supreme challenge to illustrate properly, is the intensely poetic quality of the writing. In the beauty of the names, in the creation of beautiful evocative languages or harsh horrifying languages, or in worthy rustic languages, he is absolutely the master. If the sounds of these names do not evoke in you a magical sense of reality, if you do not feel the yearning of the places that you visit in these stories, or are not moved to awe by the beauty or the poignancy of these scenes and situations, then one should consider illustrating other material, until these feelings become stronger over the years of rereading.

The main difficulty is that Tolkien uses standard fantasy properties in his stories (elves, dwarves, goblins, little people, kings), but in a way unique to himself, which imbues these traditional fantasy types with an archetypal power, a sense of place against a vast backdrop of time and epic history. This makes the characterizations particularly difficult—the illustrator has to be especially careful to avoid what I call the "default setting" stereotypes if they are to do justice to the stories.

Hobbits are the perfect example of this. They are not children, nor are they short adults—they are hobbits, and any painting that depicts hobbits should ring a bell in the mind of the viewer, which lets them know, "Yes, that is what they would look like!" This is not an easy job. Like any good author, Tolkien leaves room for each reader to form their own image of what these characters look like, and apparently the author himself was not sure of what his characters looked like—the late Ian Ballantine related to me a conversation in which Tolkien admitted as much. Considering that Tolkien has done some of the most evocative illustrations for his stories, this is a bit daunting.

Then there are the elves, the most magical and evocative characters in all the books, which makes them the most elusive of all to visualize. In a real sense, the books are a history of the Elves, and their story is the hub around which all the epic revolves. So if the illustrator can draw hobbits and elves, they can do Tolkien. Or any fantasy, for that matter—this is the post-graduate course for the illustrator.

I would say the trick here is not to lean on your photo reference too heavily, unless you have pictures of hobbits or dwarves or orcs. Anyone can paint a picture, but the challenge of Tolkien is to do just the right picture, to go for the gold ring, as it were. Dean Cornwell used to paint his entire picture before he engaged his models, then incorporate the touches he liked from the model into the painting without losing the artistic unity he started with in the mundane restrictions of ordinary life. Poetry is the essence of Tolkien, and poetry has to be distilled from reality, not copied from it.

One of the things I was worried about before the films came out was the characterizations. There were two in particular that I thought a filmmaker could never get right: Frodo and Gollum. Well, as it turns out, they couldn't have been more perfect. To my way of thinking, Gollum should take Best Supporting Actor at the next Academy Awards. I was also delighted with Gandalf, Saruman, and Legolas, not to mention Treebeard, the Balrog, the Black Riders, and all the charming orcs. And, of course, the art direction was superb throughout the films. It was all that the most fanatical Tolkien reader could wish for, and more.

I'm inspired for the next private commissions I'm doing of Tolkien's work—I've got to work on the characterizations and settings, though!

The next step is working up my visualizations for *The Silmarillion*. If the Ring trilogy is the postgraduate course in illustration, *The Silmarillion* is the doctoral dissertation. Unlike my paintings for *The Lord of the Rings*, I think I would drop the raised border and title scroll format for these, as the scenes will be difficult enough to do justice to without making it any harder on myself than necessary. There is a sublimity to the imagery in *The Silmarillion* that makes this a real challenge. It is as if the poetic quality of *The Lord of the Rings* book was distilled into a single exalted draught.

Donato Giancola's Classical Art

The painting, simply titled "The Hobbit," is in full color and measures 38 inches by 68 inches—more than 3 feet tall and 5 feet wide! The original painting hung on panels at an art show at a World Science Fiction Convention in Philadelphia in

Donato Giancola's oil painting illustrating The Hobbit, *for the cover of the graphic novel edition.*

2001, where Colleen Doran stared at it in admiration, suppressing an urge to grab passersby and shout, "Look at *this!*" Reproduced as the cover to a graphic novel adaptation of *The Hobbit*, the painting, with type overlaid, is remarkable; but to see it full scale, the way the artist intended, is to experience firsthand the visual impact of original art.

When Colleen returned from the convention and we went to the local Barnes & Noble superstore, she pulled the graphic album off the shelf and handed it to me. She didn't need to say anything. I drank in the art, albeit in smaller form than she had seen it, and I realized that this man had just raised the art bar in the field so high that only he could clear it. Instead of drawing his inspiration from those who had gone before him in the field, Donato went back even further, to classical illustrators such as Rembrandt and Carravagio and Michelangelo; Donato's draftsmanship was superb, his painting skills astonishing in their fidelity, his compositions arresting, and his color sense—especially his use of chiaroscuro—remarkable.

Donato Giancola's oil painting illustrating The Lord of the Rings *for the Science Fiction Book Club edition.*

Knowing nothing about the man, I knew one thing: Here was an artist who had read Tolkien carefully, lovingly, and set out to visually interpret Middle-earth in a way that no other artist had done. To see Middle-earth through Donato's eyes (and paintbrush) is to see an Old Master at work, with the freshness of a young man's drive and ambition, for Donato is but 36 years old.

Donato Giancola's oil painting illustrating the One Ring, done for a trading card game.

A superb painter and designer, Donato's rendition of the One Ring, done for a gaming card, is perfect—a gold ring, on rock, surrounded by red-hot lava. Or consider his cover for the Science Fiction Book Club edition of *The Lord of the Rings*: In the Mines of Moria, Aragorn shelters Frodo, as Gandalf looks back at them.

Like his cover to *The Hobbit*, Donato—feeling that a large canvas is appropriate for *The Lord of the Rings*—rendered a large-scale painting measuring 33 x 51 inches.

Months later, I was in Brooklyn, at Donato's home/studio, where he directed me to his living room. Over the couch hung *The Hobbit—The Lord of the Rings* painting resides in a private collection in Los Angeles—and I was visually struck, as was Colleen earlier, by its size, its power, and its visual impact. I could then easily imagine how his painting for *The Lord of the Rings* would look because of its large size. Words fail me.

As Donato showed me painting after painting, and as he discussed his enthusiasm for Tolkien's work and how he imagined Middle-earth, my first thought was, "Why hasn't this guy done a Tolkien calendar?" My second thought was, "Why hasn't this guy published a Tolkien art book? Or an art book with the scope of *The Art of Michael Whelan*?"

Donato Giancola's oil painting illustrating a scene from The Lord of the Rings: The Return of the King, *"Faramir at Osgiliath."*

Most of Donato's work illustrating Middle-earth can be found on gaming cards, which is not likely to be seen by most Tolkien fans. Even the cover to the Science Fiction Book Club edition is not easy to find, because only those in the United States who are members of the club can buy it. Happily, the cover to *The Hobbit*, with interior art by David Wenzel, is available in bookstores everywhere.

An Interview With Donato Giancola

George Beahm: Can you give me a brief professional biography and what you're currently working on?

Donato Giancola: I have always drawn. I moved to New York City from my native Vermont after graduating from Syracuse University in 1992 with a BFA in painting to immerse myself in New York's rich and varied art world. Within months after the move, my first commissions arrived, illustrating classic science fiction novels such as *The Time Machine*, by H.G. Wells and *Journey to the Center of the Earth*, by Jules Verne. Since then, I have produced hundreds of commissioned illustrations for book covers, game cards, editorials, and advertising from such clients as

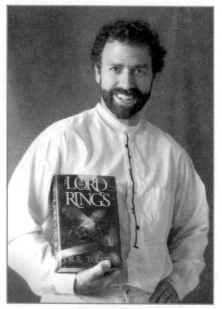

Donato Giancola holds a copy of The Lord of the Rings *with his wrap-around cover art for the Science Fiction Book Club edition.*

LucasArts, Milton-Bradley, Sony, Hasbro, Random House, Tor, Ballantine, HarperCollins, The Franklin Mint, Wizards of the Coast, and DC Comics.

My illustrations have won numerous awards, including nominations for five Artist Hugo Awards; Seven Chesley Awards, from the Association of Science Fiction and Fantasy Artists; Gold and Silver Awards from Spectrum: The Best in Contemporary Fantastical Art; and numerous awards from New York's Society of Illustrators. In addition, my work has been exhibited in dozens of shows at the Society of Illustrators and various galleries around the country.

I love to travel as a guest lecturer to various colleges, institutions, game tournaments, and science fiction conventions around the globe, where I interact with fans, perform painting demonstrations, lecture on technique, and display original artworks.

My studio, home, wife, and two daughters are in Brooklyn, New York.

GB: When did you first read Tolkien's *The Lord of the Rings*, and what was your initial response?

DG: Reading Tolkien's works for the first time was an introduction into the worlds of an incredible fantasy—the first novels I read for pleasure. As you can imagine, they left an impression so deep on my psyche that they are forever a standard to which other novels are compared. I remember being handed *The Hobbit* from my brother Michael on a Saturday afternoon, and finishing it the following day. I was hooked. Soon afterward, I purchased the three novels comprising *The Lord of the Rings*, with paperback covers by Darrell Sweet. I still have those copies in the studio today. The most enjoyable aspect of reading those novels was the incredibly rich history of the cultures Tolkien provided for his readers. A never-ending dance began as I read *The Fellowship* and referred back to the appendices at the end of *Return of the King*. Who was Beren? How old was Moria? When was the First Age? It took forever to read each chapter as I looked up names, places, and events in those notes; each offered a trip to another time and a story as complex as the tale I was engrossed within. I needed to read those books only once to be forever knowledgeable about their histories. With this compulsive behavior of referencing, you could imagine I was thrilled to discover *The Lost Tales*, *Unfinished Tales*, and *The Silmarillion* at my local library. I spent many afternoons there, immersed in the world of Middle-earth.

GB: What makes Tolkien such a challenge to illustrate?

DG: Creating a painting from the worlds of Middle-earth means you will be placed under the most intense scrutiny when it comes to details and accuracy. The admirers of Tolkien know no mercy when it comes to deviations and inaccuracies, myself included! I know those books inside and out, but still found myself making a few mistakes. I now run my sketches past my friends as a double check to catch any errors. Luckily Tolkien provided artists with a large loophole for illustrating his novels—very little physical descriptions of either characters or places. His descriptions are generally emotional and, for that reason, resonate with the reader more than the offerings of other authors. This is what I love regarding the works, a strong emotional foundation upon which to build a very broad range of physical interpretations.

GB: If given the commission to illustrate *The Lord of the Rings* with covers and interior illustrations, how would you approach the task of selecting what to illustrate and how many paintings or drawings would you feel is necessary to adequately illustrate the three books?

DG: I have always sought great challenges in my art. To this end, when looking for inspiration to illustrate novels and stories, I have always attempted to render those moments which are ill described or fleeting in nature, yet capture the essence of the characters and narrative. Simple domestic scenes are difficult to compose to appear compelling, yet a successful painting in this manner can carry much more power than a heroic battle scene. Consider your reader and viewer. They most likely have never experienced the intensity of conflict nor the range of extremes most heroes travel through. It is upon a common ground of emotion with which I attempt to build my narratives. And it is with these simple scenes that J.R.R. Tolkien makes us feel the humanity of his characters, the depths of utter darkness in Moria, Merry and Pippin smoking pipe weed after the destruction of Isengard, Frodo and Sam cooking a brace of rabbits in the shadow of Mordor.

As for the quantity of illustrations necessary to illustrate the three books, I return back to my childhood. I was happy to have only the three cover images from which to inform my imagination of *The Lord of the Rings*. I think I would have been even pleased with none. The power of Tolkien is that he does not need an artist to interpret his works for them to come to life. Yet when the artist successfully steps beyond mimicry, something more is added than mere words can describe. The two art forms resonate and create an emotional response greater than the parts. This cannot always be achieved, by any artist, but when it occurs, it is magical. I cannot say what number would be correct for the illustrations, only that they should feel properly placed in the context of the books.

GB: How did you come to illustrate *The Lord of the Rings* for Book of the Month Club and the gaming cards?

DG: My first commission for the Middle-earth Collectible Card Game from Iron Crown Enterprises (ICE) taught me a valuable lesson. I was an avid gamer back in high school and college and began collecting the ICE modules from Middle-earth, both for using them in games and for the wonderful art on the covers and in the interiors. Being a huge Tolkien fan and an aspiring artist, I sent ICE my portfolio during my senior year at Syracuse University. I never heard back from them. Bummer. It wasn't until four years later that I received a call from their art director. They were looking for new artists for their upcoming card game—MECCG: The Wizards—and was wondering if I could send them down a new portfolio. I had improved since college, and I now had a couple dozen professional book covers to show them. They were blown away by my current work. An open offer was placed before me, how many cards would I like to take on: One? Five? 30? I settled on 15 and had a wonderful time working on a subject I loved dearly. Needless to say, they kept coming back with more commissions. The lesson? Be generous to everyone and treat all clients with courtesy because you never know from where your next job may come.

GB: Beyond *LotR*, what would you have liked to illustrate from J.R.R. Tolkien's other works?

DG: Back to my childhood love of J.R.R. Tolkien's writings, I would find immense pleasure in tackling illustrations from any of the works related to Middle-earth, from *The Lost Tales* to *The Silmarillion*.

GB: What is your reaction to the Peter Jackson film trilogy?

DG: As I had mentioned before, regarding art forms which complement the written word, I have found that the movies belong within this category. Although different from the novels and paying uncompromising homage to them, they are a separate art form and add another level of interpretation and enjoyment to the story. The realizations of Gollum and his roller-coaster ride of emotions played out upon a grand screen cannot be compared to the experience while one sits in the comfort of one's own home reading the novels. They are a welcome addition to the wealth of art which has interpreted *The Lord of the Rings* through the decades. I enjoy them thoroughly!

GB: Are there any final comments you'd care to make?

DG: The goal of a passionate artist is to try and make the masterpiece each and every time, yet be wise enough to know you will fall short.

Michael Whelan: The Master

In 1980, Ballantine Books published "The J.R.R. Tolkien Calendar" and advertised it as "The Great Illustrators Edition." Because critical assessments of artists and their relative standings are subject to intense debate, and because no two people would agree as to who the best illustrators are—my list, surely, is quite different than yours—it's the call of the publisher to make the final cuts and the final call.

That said, there is *no* debate that one contributor to this calendar is the gold standard in fantasy illustration—Michael Whelan. The winner of more awards in the field than any other artist of our time, Michael is an artist's artist, a painter's painter. He is a 14-time Hugo Award winner (voted on by the membership of the World Science Fiction Convention), a three-time (maximum limit) Howard Award winner (World Fantasy Convention), and voted "Best Professional Artist" by the readership of *Locus* (the newszine of the fantasy and science fiction world) 21 years in a row, to cite some of his awards.

Not to put too fine a point on it, but what Michael does well, he does *so* well that he's in a league of his own. Let me explain. The process by which Michael determines what he's going to paint and how he's going to paint it is anything but accidental. After reading a manuscript carefully and making notes, Michael seeks to distill the novel's essence into a single iconic image. To arrive at that image, he renders several detailed sketches until he's reasonably satisfied. He then submits a selection of these to the art director, who makes the final call. It's not necessarily the one Michael would have picked, but then, he's not the client. He's the hired hand, and he's being paid to produce what the client wants.

The finished cover painting, usually rendered in acrylic, will then adorn the cover of a leading fantasy or science fiction novel, and, by doing so, will significantly enhance its eye-appeal at the bookstore, which will help separate it from the other books on the shelf.

In the end, it's about professionalism; it's about getting paid to do a job, on time, and doing it to the best of your ability; and it's about giving value to the client and to the book reader, who wants representational art he can understand—not abstract art that is reflective of the artist's private vision.

Artist Michael Whelan inscribes a copy of The Art of Michael Whelan *to Tim Kirk.*

That Michael more than fulfills the publisher's requirements by also creating a beautiful work of art in the process is a bonus. Illustration and art, Michael has proven, are not mutually exclusive.

Rather than simply illustrate a novel, he likes to add his personal touches. Symbolism, an integral part of his personal work, can be seen in his commercial illustration, as well, lending a depth that is often lacking in the work of his contemporaries.

As for what makes him an artist's artist, it is simply this: He is the master of his craft. It's that simple. He is the best at what he does because he has no areas of deficiency. Imagination? First rate. Draftsmanship? Second to none. Composition? Perfect. Technique? Matchless. Ability to draw convincing people out of his imagination? He stands alone.

Given all those things, you'd think that he'd be satisfied with himself and his artistic ability, wouldn't you?

Surprisingly to most people, he is not satisfied because he's always looking to improve, to stretch, and outdo himself. In fact, once he gets a painting back and it hangs on the wall, he mostly notices its flaws, whereas we are more likely to notice its qualities. But then, we don't have to wonder how we would have done it better, given more time.

These are "flaws," mind you, that ordinary fans can't see, as they coo in delight and admiration when seeing his originals hang on panels at an art show at a convention. Furthermore, these are "flaws" that his fellow pros can't see, as they, too, succumb to the illustrative magic of Michael Whelan's art. They scratch their heads and wonder how he does it, and then go back to their drawing boards and try to learn from his techniques.

Michael, I think, has the right mindset for an artist: He's honest enough to recognize that he's in the first rank, but modest enough to continually seek self-improvement. The case in point is the sole Tolkien painting he's done, for the aforementioned calendar. (The painting is reproduced in his second art book, as well. Both, unfortunately, are out of print.)

The painting is filled with symbolism. Illustrating what has to be *the* pivotal scene of the entire novel—Samwise holding up an exhausted Frodo, who is missing one finger, as the eagles come to rescue them, with the world literally crumbling apart around them—Michael has distilled it with a singular image. It is, to my mind, flawless. I cannot *begin* to imagine how, in terms of a work of art, it could be improved.

Michael, however, can only think of how it *can* be improved, and proceeds to illuminate me. It's a discussion that an artist would be better equipped to understand, but the gist of it is that if he were to redo the painting today, it would look different. Better, though? Hard to say. But there's one thing for sure: I'd love to see Michael go back to Middle-earth and give us more of his incomparable visions.

Currently working on illustrations for Stephen King's last Dark Tower novel—a fitting assignment in which both artist and author come full circle, because they worked together on the first Dark Tower novel in 1982—Michael keeps up a blistering pace, producing covers for fantasy and science fiction novels, producing private paintings to explore his inner visions, and looking for new challenges, new heights to scale.

In a recent interview with him, though the subject was, of course, Tolkien, the conversation wandered a bit afield, and we talked about Stephen King. I remarked that, for an artist, it's high praise when the author says that the artist has drawn the definitive rendition, as King has said of Michael's Roland the Gunslinger. Michael agreed and added that he had sent a digital image to King, to get some early feedback. King responded positively, saying that Michael's rendition of Oy, one of the characters in the book, was dead-on. "He's exactly as I had imagined him," King said.

Despite King's reassurances, Michael repeated, several times, his concern that the fans be happy with the work. As a King reader and a Whelan fan myself, I appreciate his concern, but in this instance he need not worry. If he can please the author—Stephen King, who is the harshest critic of art done for his books—he can please anyone...and he will.

Higher praise than that an artist cannot get. And *that* is the *art* of Michael Whelan.

An Interview With Michael Whelan

George Beahm: Bring us up to date on your current project. I know you've been working exclusively on finishing the art for Stephen King's seventh, and final, Dark Tower novel. It's been a real trek for him, with the fifth book due out in November, as The Path of the Beam leads Roland's *ka-tet* to a border town, Calla Bryn Sturges. What's it been like for you?

Michael Whelan: It's been quite a journey. I've never worked so long on a single project. It's been quite a challenge because it's a hell of a book, but I'm giving it everything I've got. I hope people will be happy with what I'm doing.

I'm aiming to please myself on these. I have pretty specific ideas of how Oy the Bumbler should look and other characters, and I'm doing everything I can to stay as true to that as I can.

I sent King a digital photograph of one of the paintings that has the whole ka-tet in it, and he said that I nailed Oy, so I feel good about that. Oy's in three of the paintings.

I think I'll have 12 paintings altogether. I haven't even done the cover yet. I've put that off because I've got so many good ideas it's hard to settle on one.

GB: Regarding the painting you did from *The Lord of the Rings*: Was this done for a special project, or was it done just for the 1980 Tolkien calendar?

MW: It was done just for the calendar.

GB: What is it about Tolkien's fiction that makes his work so distinctive and memorable from an illustrative point of view?

MW: What captivates me is the beauty of the language. As you're reading *The Lord of the Rings*, he does such a fantastic job of creating pictures in your mind that I don't know how anyone could fail to be influenced strongly by that and not have a desire to illustrate them.

I love the writing so much that I've listened, time and time again, to the books on tape read by Rob Inglis for Recorded Books. I listen to them with the same appreciation that I would an actual piece of music.

GB: How did the calendar assignment come about? And what can you say about the art itself?

MW: There isn't a whole lot to say about the art—I just tried to visualize the scene and bring it to life; there isn't a whole lot of interpretation available there.

The way the calendars were being done at the time, Lester del Rey would assign a particular image to a particular artist and literally underscore the part of the text he wanted to see as a painting and say, "Paint this." That's pretty much how it was given to me.

GB: It was directional art?

MW: Yes. It's like being given a screenplay and being told, "Make this look real."

Everyone's got their own ideas of how Frodo and Sam would look, and, unfortunately, in the painting they're small, so I don't really get a chance to paint them as characters. I did what I could with the time that was available to me.

GB: There's a great deal of symbolism in your work, which indicates to me that you've really thought through this process of what you're going to illustrate and how you're going to illustrate it, as opposed to simply transposing a photograph into a painting.

MW: Because it takes me so long to get a painting done, I give it a lot of thought before I get started on it. I don't want to invest a big block of time in something that is going to be frivolous or accidental—there's always a lot of thought in my paintings. Probably too much thought, actually, but that's the way I am and the way I work. It's part of what makes my work mine, I guess.

GB: What's next on the drawing board?

MW: I've got several book covers slated for DAW Books, but they are long-term projects. I won't be doing them until next year.

I really want to concentrate on my gallery work for the second half of the year, if I can manage to keep myself free.

GB: Let's play "what if." What if you were to have the opportunity to illustrate *The Lord of the Rings*? Would you do it?

MW: Certainly I'd be interested. It's the one goal in my career as an illustrator I haven't been able to achieve yet. The essential question for me is how much time I'm going to be given to get it done.

I was offered the book covers for *The Hobbit* and *The Lord of the Rings* trilogy in the United States, but they wanted all the work done in less than two months time. I won't say who offered it to me, but these are people who know how far I get booked up in advance. Aside from the fact that I am booked up with other companies for 18 months beyond when I was talking to these people, even if I had nothing else scheduled, I wouldn't be willing to risk rushing through the artwork— I'd have to do it fast and it'd be a slapdash job on books so near and dear to my heart.

Unless I was given the time to put my all into it, I wouldn't do it. That'd be the overriding issue in my mind—more important to me than anything else.

GB: Whose Tolkien art do you like?

MW: I like Tim Kirk, John Howe, and Alan Lee, but Tim's was the first that really grabbed me. I said, "Finally, someone has done them right."

GB: What did you think of the Jackson movie trilogy?

MW: When I saw the movies, I found out I was more of a Tolkien purist than I realized. I enjoyed them immensely and am very grateful for all the things that Peter Jackson got right, and that's no small achievement. On the other hand, I was dismayed to see that Jackson felt he had to change story elements and add in material. But on the whole, I liked the movies very much. I just wish that because he had gotten so close to getting it just right that he had gone the extra distance and made them perfect.

I thought all the characters were very well cast and, generally, I had a very positive feeling about the movies; in fact, Gollum couldn't have been better.

GB: As you know, two Tolkien artists—Alan Lee and John Howe—were conceptual designers handpicked by Jackson. What did you think of their work for the movie trilogy?

MW: There's no doubt that they nailed it. It couldn't have been better, in my opinion. I think they did an amazing job.

Michael Kaluta: Flights of the Fantastic

In *Realms of Tolkien* (HarperPrism), to which Kaluta contributed, his brief biography in the back states that he had done the art for the 1992 Tolkien calendar. Armed with that misinformation, fans will look in vain for it, because in 1992 the Centenary Calendar was published with Ted Nasmith's art. Kaluta's appeared in the *1994* Tolkien calendar.

A dream assignment for Kaluta, the paintings took five months to create. The result was a new visual interpretation that has a classic "storybook" feel to it: Gandalf and his horse-drawn cart laden with fireworks in boxes marked with runes, as excited hobbit children follow in his wake; Éowyn standing in front of the gates of Meduseld, framed between massive, ornate doors, as flying birds form a symbolic circle; a scene of the Entmoot, as the Ents gather to deliberate—in due time—what to do with the information Merry and Pippin provide; and much more.

Though the calendar is long out of print and commands collector's prices on the secondary market, interested fans can see one of the pieces, "Legolas Draws the Bow of Galadriel," printed in *Realms of Tolkien*; and if you don't have that book, all the pieces are reprinted on Kaluta's Website (*www.kaluta.com*).

From his 1994 Tolkien Calendar, an illustration by Michael Kaluta, titled "Éowyn before the Gates of Meduseld."

Michael Kaluta's illustration titled "Legolas Draws the Bow of Galadriel," from his "1994 Tolkien Calendar."

Considered to be one of the leading artists in the comic book field—indeed, his interpretation of The Shadow is classic, leading to early design work on the movie—Kaluta's strong sense of design and ability to conceptualize is apparent most clearly in the 40 illustrations he rendered for *Metropolis*, by Thea von Harbou.

Supplementing his considerable body of work in the comic industry—covers, interiors, and special projects—Kaluta has done a considerable amount of work for trading card companies and the television and film industry, as well.

Kaluta's major book collections include *Wings of Twilight: The Art of Michael Kaluta* (NBM Publishing) and *Echoes: The Drawings of M.W. Kaluta* (Vanguard Productions).

An Interview With Michael Kaluta

George Beahm: Give me your biographical sketch and a sense of what you are currently working on.

Michael Kaluta: I began my comic career at Charlton Comics in New York City and soon moved on to do various stories and covers for DC and Marvel Comics. In 1973, I was picked to draw the first DC comic revival of *The Shadow*, the character I would later go on to visually define. I have worked on *Batman*, *The Spawn of Frankenstein*, *Metropolis*, *Starstruck*, *Vampirella*, *Books of Magic*, *Aquaman*, and most of DC's 70s horror line. Beyond the comic industry, I have done work for magazines, calendars, movies, television, album covers, trading cards, and more.

My most recent work has been done for collectible cards manufactured by the Wizards of the Coast, AEG, and Sabertooth Games. My newest comic-related work, from DC Comics, was a Batman story in *Gotham Knights* #32. In addition, two art books have recently been published: *Echoes, the drawings of Mw Kaluta* and *Wings of Twilight*, a full color book of my paintings and illustrations.

Forthcoming are more illustration and comic book work, including an issue for the DC Comics "SOLO" line, and a number of private art commissions of Tolkien-inspired art.

GB: When did you first read Tolkien's *The Lord of the Rings* and what was your initial response?

MK: I first saw the books in hardback in a bookstore I haunted for my science fiction fixes, and, although intrigued, the books, at six bucks each, were priced beyond my means.

I first read the books when Ace put out the 75¢ unofficial versions, and I fell in love with them, though it took three attempts before I could read past" The Council of Elrond." Back then it was a stumbling block, but now it's the place I can't wait to get to, because every reading brings out more information!

GB: What, in your opinion, makes Tolkien unique among fantasy writers?

MK: His grasp of the entire picture and how everything in the world is interrelated, his ability to suggest depth of story with an aside, and his never being afraid to have his characters have human faults.

GB: What makes Tolkien such a challenge to illustrate?

MK: When one reads the words, the pictures appear in the mind. When one goes to study those phrases for illustrative detail, it isn't there.

Ian Ballantine once asked Tolkien if he knew what his characters looked like. Tolkien's replied, "I'd know them if I met them." That's good enough for me, because I have the same sense. Try as I do to "see" them in my drawings, I know I've never got as far in delineating Tolkien's characters as I wish I were able to.

GB: Given the commission to illustrate *The Lord of the Rings*, with covers and interior illustrations, how would you approach the task of selecting what to illustrate and how many paintings/drawings would you feel is necessary to adequately illustrate the three books?

MK: When doing the 1994 Calendar, I made certain to have one illustration for each 1/12th of the books. I had about nine drawings done from an attempt to interest the publishers years before. I used the one volume edition and physically marked out the places where those drawings occurred in the text. Then I filled in between those places, finding areas where I needed to have art.

Were I to illustrate the books, and had leave to do it as I wanted, I'm afraid I'd have to draw forever, adding chapter headings, spot illustrations, tag drawings, and so on, so that when one flipped the pages, one knew the book was full of art! That would be a bit inconsiderate to the reader....

I want to illustrate Tolkien because of the imagery and wonderment he made me feel with his inspiring prose. Does the book really *need* illustrations? Beyond maps, no!

GB: How did you come to illustrate Tolkien?

MK: In 1978, Ian Summer contacted Steve Hickman and me to snag the 1979/1980 Tolkien Calendar. Steve and I generated well over 16 illustrations in pencil that were submitted to the Ballantines but eventually rejected. However, as we saw from the calendars that *did* come out just post-Hildebrandt, Ian went to conventions, snagged any and all Tolkien-inspired art he could find, and published them as that year's calendar.

Had Steve and I presented him with 12 finished paintings, I have no doubt we'd have had the 1980 Calendar.

202 ⟵ The Essential J.R.R. Tolkien Sourcebook
About 14 years later, Allen & Unwin's Jane Johnston, who had kept the photocopies on file that I had sent her years ago, called to ask if I wanted the 1994 Calendar. I agreed and drew 11 illustrations.

GB: Beyond *The Lord of the Rings*, what would you have liked to illustrate from J.R.R. Tolkien's other works?

MK: Certainly any of the poems!

GB: What is your reaction to the Jackson films?

MK: My main reaction was relief! Knowing the film industry, I know the result could have been *such* a tragedy.

I can watch Jackson's movie trilogy. My hat's off to a job well done!

Tolkien History

J.R.R. Tolkien spent almost his entire adult life in England, most of it—more than 50 years—in Oxford.

Ironically, the geography of Tolkien's life doesn't begin in England. It begins in Bloemfontein, South Africa, where he spent the first three years of his life. The firstborn son of Arthur Reuel Tolkien and Mabel Tolkien, John Ronald Reuel Tolkien was christened at Bloemfontein Cathedral on January 21, 1892, and lived in the Bank House, a furnished residence provided by Arthur Tolkien's employer, the Bank of Africa, for which he was a manager. Two years later, they had a second son, Hilary Arthur Reuel Tolkien. Tragedy struck in 1896; Mabel Tolkien and her two sons were visiting family in England and informed by telegram that her husband had died. He was buried in a cemetery on the grounds of the Anglican cathedral near the market square, not far from where they had lived.

The Tolkiens never returned to South Africa.

Note: To avoid confusion because of surnames, John Ronald Reuel Tolkien is referred herein as, simply, Ronald. Also, for this timeline, I have consulted multiple sources, in print and on the Internet, which are listed at the end of the chapter. For the general reader wanting more information, the most useful resource is Humphrey Carpenter's biography, *J.R.R. Tolkien: A Biography*, with its two chronologies—personal and publications. For a much more detailed Tolkien timeline, consult Scull and Hammond's definitive reference book, *The J.R.R. Tolkien Companion and Guide*.

A modern industrial city ringed by rural communities, Ronald's early years were spent in and around Birmingham, owing to geographic displacement because of educational and residential considerations.

When Mabel Tolkien returned from South Africa, in February 1896, after the unexpected death of her husband, she moved in temporarily with her parents at **Ashefield Road**. Later that year, Mabel moved her family to **5 Gracewell**, a cottage in Sarehole, a rural community on the southern side of Birmingham.

Sarehole Mill was a favorite haunt of Ronald and his brother Hilary, where the older Miller earned the nickname of "The Black Ogre." ("The White Ogre" was a nickname reserved for a farmer who "once chased Ronald for picking mushrooms," according to Tolkien biographer Humphrey Carpenter.)

The Sarehole Mill is located at Colebank Road, Hall Green, Birmingham, B13 0DB. It is the only remaining mill in the area—once populous with dozens of them—and is now a museum exhibiting a way of life that ceased to exist years ago.

Years later, as an adult, Ronald remarked fondly about the four years he had spent in this rural environment, which he unabashedly loved and celebrated in his fiction.

Moseley's Bog, now a nature's reserve, is believed to be the inspiration for the Dead Marshes through which Sam Gamgee and Frodo Baggins crossed on their journey to Mordor.

King Edward's was the school attended by Tolkien's father. Mabel Tolkien enrolled Ronald in this school in 1900. Because of the commuting distance—four miles—between Mabel Tolkien's home and King Edward's, which Ronald had to walk because they could not afford public transportation, she moved the family to an urban suburb of **Moseley**, where she rented a house within easy walking distance.

After the house they were living in was demolished to make way for a public structure, she moved temporary to **King's Heath**, a terrace row. In 1902, she moved again to **26 Oliver Road in Edgbaston**, so her boys would be close to school. They were enrolled in **St. Phillip's Grammar School**.

In 1903, concerned about the quality of education at St. Phillip's as compared to the education Ronald had been receiving at King Edward's, she reenrolled him at King Edward's, after having secured a Foundation Scholarship.

Not long after, Mabel was stricken with diabetes and unable to take care of herself and her boys. She was hospitalized, and her boys moved in temporarily with one of their aunts in **Hove**. Mabel Tolkien partially regainsed her health—enough to set up house again—and, in June 1904, she took up residence in a rural community, **Rednal**, which reminded them of Sarehole. Ronald was then commuting by train to King Edward's.

Unfortunately, the partial recovery proved deceptive: Mabel Tolkien, at age 34, died of complications resulting from diabetes, and the boys were orphaned. Because of Mabel Tolkien's conversion from the Anglican faith to the Catholic faith, and the uproar it caused within her family, the guardian she appointed in her will, Father Francis Morgan, elected one of their aunts, Beatrice Suffield, of **Stirling Road in Edgbaston**, to care for them. However, though she provided for their physical needs, she was not otherwise involved in their lives.

Father Francis Morgan later moved the boys to **37 Duchess Road**, the home of Mrs. Faulkner. It is there that Ronald, then 16, met his future wife, Edith Bratt, who was three years his senior.

Much to the concern about the growing love affair between Ronald and Edith, Father Francis Morgan decided a physical separation was best. He moved the boys to a nearby residence and sent Edith Bratt to neighboring **Chentenham**. Wanting to move up and leave St. Edward's behind, Ronald failed to win the scholarship to **Exeter** that he had strived for, but refocused for a second attempt.

In 1910, Ronald won the elusive scholarship. Heeding his guardian's wishes—the custom at the time—he willingly postponed his love relationship for the time, but found camaraderie among male friends (which ultimately became a lifelong association). He attended Exeter and graduated in June 1915 with a degree in English Language and Literature.

In 1916, he was commissioned as a Second Lieutenant in the Lancashire Fusiliers and, instead of seeking a command posting, his natural aptitude for words and languages proved useful as he secured the post of Battalion Signal Officer. He married Edith Bratt in **Warwick**, moved to **Great Haywood**, then left for the front in the war against France—World War I. Fighting in the trenches and seeing his best friends die, Tolkien was understandably marked by the war, which is at the core of *The Lord of the Rings*—the war for the One Ring.

In November 1917, the Tolkiens had their first son, John. In 1918, after the war ended, Ronald returned to civilian life permanently and hoped to put the past behind him. He moved the family to **50 St. John's Street** in Oxford, close to his office on **Broad Street** (then the Old Ashmolean Museum, now the Museum of the History of Science), where he worked as an assistant lexicographer on *The Oxford English Dictionary*.

In 1919, the Tolkiens moved to **1 Alfred Street** (now known as Pusey Street), where they rented a small house. Michael, their second son, was born. They attended the nearby **St. Aloysius** church.

In 1920, Tolkien interviewed for a post as Reader in English Language at the **University of Leeds**, and got the post. The Tolkiens moved, taking up temporary quarters, then moved to a leased house at **11 St. Mark's Terrace**.

In 1924, Ronald became a professor at Leeds, and the Tolkiens bought their first home, at **2 Darnley Road**, West Park.

In 1925, he was elected Rawlinson and Bosworth Professor of Anglo-Saxon at Oxford. The Tolkiens had a third son, Christopher, who would later become his father's literary executor and, significantly, edit *The Silmarillion, Unfinished Tales*, and the 12 volumes of *The History of Middle-earth*. The family then moved to northern Oxford, where Tolkien bought a house at **22 Northmoor Road**. In 1929, daughter Priscilla was born, and in 1930, the Tolkiens moved to **20 Northmoor Road**, where they would live for 21 years. The family attended **St. Aloysius Catholic Church** for mass, approximately a mile into town.

Tolkien and his fellow Inklings, including C.S. Lewis and Charles Williams, met at the **Eagle and Child Pub on St. Giles**, where he read installments of *The Hobbit*, and later, *The Lord of the Rings*. (The pub has a plaque that commemorates their meetings.)

In 1939, Tolkien gave a lecture, "On Fairy Stories," at **St. Andrews University**.

In 1945, he was elected Merton Professor of English Language and Literature at **Oxford**. He held that position until 1959.

In 1947, the Tolkien family—less two children, who by then had grown up and moved out—moved to **3 Manor Road**, a Merton College house they rented. Just as the house on Northmoor Road had been too large, this house proved to be too small. In 1950, they moved to **99 Holywell Street**. It proved unsuitable because of the incessant traffic noise. Another move, in 1953, brought the Tolkiens to **76 Sandfield Road** in Headington, a suburb of Oxford.

In 1962, the Inklings moved across the street from Eagle and Child (known locally as "The Bird and Baby") to **The Lamb and Flag**.

In 1968, the Tolkiens—overwhelmed by the lack of privacy due to the endless intrusion of fans—reluctantly decided to move from Oxford to Bournemouth, a seaside town on the south coast. They movd to **19 Lakeside Road** in Poole, adjacent to Bournemouth.

Edith Tolkien died in November 1971, and Ronald headed back to Oxford—his last move. He moved into a flat at **21 Merton Street**, provided by Merton College, which honored him as a resident honorary Fellow.

In September 1973, John Ronald Reuel Tolkien died at the age of 81, while visiting friends in Bournemouth. He was buried alongside his wife at **Wolvercote Cemetery** in Oxford.

Three other places are worth paying a visit, depending on your interests:

In 1992, in **University Parks**, two trees were planted in his honor, with a nearby commemorative bench. (Also worth visiting is the **Botanic Gardens** in Oxford, and its *Pinus nigra* tree, which Tolkien deemed his favorite.)

Insofar as library collections go, two places stand out:

In England, the **Bodeleian Library** at Oxford is the repository for *The Silmarillion* and other manuscripts. Christopher Tolkien has deposited personal and professional papers by his father, as well, which makes it a treasure trove for researchers.

In the United States, **Marquette University** has, in its Special Collection, original manuscripts by Tolkien, purchased from him in 1956 for £1,500 (then less than $5,000). The manuscripts included *The Hobbit* and all its revisions (1,586 pages), *The Lord of the Rings* and all its revisions (9,250 pages), *Farmer Giles of Ham*, *Mr. Bliss*, and a vast amount of other Tolkieniana, including copies of his other works (printed, not in manuscript), secondary material (books about him), periodical literature, and private collections donated to the Special Collections from Tolkien collectors. Intended as a resource for Tolkien scholars and researchers, Marquette University is the single best repository of Tolkien material in the United States.

For detailed information on Marquette University's Tolkien holdings, go to its Website at *www.marquette.edu/library/collections/archives/Mss/JRRT/JRRT.html.*

New Zealand: Home of Middle-earth

No doubt about it, the folks at the New Zealand Tourism Bureau have brass. Those cheeky monkeys have come up with the new ad slogan "New Zealand: Home of Middle-earth."

Tolkien fans, especially in England, will likely, and understandably, take umbrage at that assertion, because there's a world of difference between England, the ancestral home of J.R.R. Tolkien, and New Zealand, which is the home of film director Peter Jackson, who chose his own country to film *The Lord of the Rings* in its entirety.

From New Zealand's Website (*www.newzealand.com/homeofmiddleearth/*):

> Here's your opportunity to take a closer look at the country behind *The Lord of the Rings* film trilogy. New Zealand's diverse and sometimes extreme landscapes made it the one place in the world that could bring Tolkien's epic masterpiece to life. Discover the amazing real-life locations behind the films, and learn about the unique experiences of the cast and crew.

The Website features actor Karl Urban ("Éomer") who takes the viewer on a tour of New Zealand's film-inspired sites, supplemented by "Explore Middle-earth," a feature that presents individual movies that show the country's connection to the Tolkien film, where 90 locations were used to help bring *The Lord of the Rings* to life.

Guidebook

For those of you who plan on actually making the trip to New Zealand, as well as for armchair travelers who enjoy reading guidebooks to get a vicarious traveling experience, avoid the usual bumper crop of books about New Zealand from the established travel book publishers. Instead, buy *The Lord of the Rings Location Guidebook* (HarperCollins Publishers), written by Ian Brodie, a native of New Zealand.

With a foreword by Peter Jackson, contributions from cast and crew, and an article on location selection by illustrator Alan Lee, this guidebook offers unprecedented insight into the process of turning New Zealand into the embodiment of Tolkien's intricate world. Author Ian Brodie has skillfully woven together local history, movie lore, Maori mythology, and Elvish legend to provide the definitive guide for the practical traveler. And because every good hobbit knows the importance of a comfortable bed and good food, accommodation and dining tips are included.

In addition to detailed maps and easy-to-follow directions, GPS references are provided to accurately pinpoint major locations. Information regarding Websites and tour companies is also provided to help those looking for specialist *The Lord of the Rings* activities and tours.

Come to Middle-earth...in New Zealand?

"It was Peter Jackson's visionary decision to shoot as much of the film as possible on location in his native New Zealand. Not using just any locations, but those that were the most visually arresting and, often, the most remote and inaccessible."

—Brian Sibley, *The Lord of the Rings: The Making of the Movie Trilogy*

This definitive guide is lavishly illustrated with photographs of the locations and movie stills provided by New Line Cinema. The book is available at *nzfpm.marketeer.co.nz/index.pasp*. (On the site's menu at the left, click "Lord of the Rings Location Guidebook," under "Store").

At first thought, the idea that *The Lord of the Rings* was filmed in New Zealand makes one wonder: What in the world was director Peter Jackson thinking?

Jackson was looking for a majestic landscape, pristine in its beauty and suggestive of a European environment, with all its varied topography, before industrialization forever marred the landscape. Clearly, England was not a suitable location for filming *The Lord of the Rings*. Indeed, Europe itself was out of the question, because much of it has been "civilized."

Literally in his own backyard, Jackson found what he had been looking for: the ideal place to film Tolkien's book, with all its varied geography, that suggested an Earth at some point in its distant past, with a pre-industrial "feel."

A country with a combined land mass roughly equivalent to England, New Zealand's tourism department got for free what money couldn't buy: an unsolicited, extended advertisement for its country prominently featured in Jackson's movie trilogy.

The predictable result was an influx of tourists who did not go to see New Zealand, per se, but to see firsthand the locations where Jackson's film crews set up to shoot what is unarguably the most expensive movie in cinematic history—the three movie installments of *The Lord of the Rings*.

Exactly just what kind of impact has the movie had on tourism? For starters, in 2002 alone, tourism added up to 2 million people, more than half of New Zealand's entire population!

A place where the U.S. dollar can go far (a New Zealand dollar is worth approximately half of the U.S. dollar, at current exchange rates) and where English is spoken, New Zealand is a great place to get away from it all—the perfect travel destination, if you don't mind an 18-hour plane flight (from Los Angeles).

For Tolkien fans, the best way to see New Zealand is through an established tour group, for several reasons. First, the group will have secured permission with local landowners to allow passage. Second, the group will know exactly where the locations are and the best way to get there. And, third, by offering tour packages, the cost can be kept within reason, because the alternative is a private tour, which is more expensive than what most people would want to pay.

New Zealand is comprised of two main islands—the North Island and the South Island—with a very small island (Steward Island) at its southernmost tip.

Following is a sampling of some of the places you'll want to visit when touring "Middle-earth."

The North Island

→ The party tree that opens *The Fellowship of the Ring*: Hobbiton is near the town of Hamilton, in Matama. Its rolling green hills made it the ideal place to construct the Shire.

→ Mordor is located in the Volcanic Plateau. It includes the spectacular Mt. Ruapehu, in Tongariro National Park, which forms the slopes of Mount Doom.

→ The field for the Last Great Alliance of Elves and Men is located south of the Rangipo Desert.

→ One of the rivers of the Anduin can be found at the twisty Rangitikei River.

→ Wellington is not only the capital of New Zealand but the home of Peter Jackson and Weta Workshop, the special effects company responsible for bringing the movies to life. Outside the city itself, one can find several key places in Middle-earth, including Helm's Deep, the Bree gate, the Weathertop Hillside, and the Outer Shire.

The South Island

- ❧ In Dimrill Dale, several scenes were shot on location.

- ❧ In Nelson, visit the "World of Wearable Art" gallery, where local craftsmen celebrate the diversity of art that can be worn, including armor-maker Stuart Johnson, whose work can be seen in the movie trilogy.

- ❧ In the Canbury high country, visit Edoras, the capital of Rohan. Also, near the town of Twizel, at a sheep station (Ben Ohau), the Battle of the Pelennor Fields was fought.

- ❧ Extensive shooting took place in the Southern Alps.

- ❧ The aptly named Paradise is also another site where extensive shooting took place.

- ❧ Queenstown was a site for shooting locations.

- ❧ On the South Island, in Fiordland, near Lake Manapouri, in the remote Norwest Lake area, one can find the Misty Mountains.

- ❧ On the South Island, southeast of Poolburn, one can find the Plains of Rohan.

- ❧ On the South Island, the area around Queenstown was the site for Rivendell and Lothlórien, as well as the battle at Amon Hen.

- ❧ On the South Island, near its southernmost point, one can find Fiorland, site of shooting locations.

Tours

For fans who want a cybertour of Middle-earth, go to *www.newzealand.com/homeofmiddleearth*, where detailed information is provided on various locations, with drop-down menus and sidebars. (**Note:** This requires the Flash plug-in.)

For fans who want a tour package, the company of choice is Red Carpet Tours (*www.redcarpet-tours.com*), which has planned out a 13-day itinerary that covers all the high points. From its Website (with my notes):

Day 1: Arrive in Auckland, New Zealand.

Day 2: To Rotorua, via Hobbiton (private land owned by a farmer; Red Carpet Tours worked out an agreement to allow them to bring sightseers).

Day 3: To Ohakune, via the Mt. Ruapehu sites of Emyn Muil, Mordor, and Gollum's fishing pool.

Day 4: To Wellington, via the River Anduin, Rivendell, and Helm's Deep.

Day 5:   Fly to Christchurch, the "Garden City."

Day 6:   To Twizel, via Edoras, Mt. Cook, and the Pelennor Fields.

Day 7:   To Alexandra, via the Great Chase location and Rohan.

Day 8:   To Te Anau, via Fangorn Forest.

Day 9:   Explore the Te Anau area or take a day trip to Milford Sound.

Day 10:   To Queenstown, via the Ford of Bruinen, the path of the Rohan refugees and the place where Aragorn goes over the cliff.

Day 11:   A visit to Amon Hen and optional jet-boating through Lothlórien country.

Day 12:   Optional activities, such as rafting past the Pillars of Argonath.

Day 13:   Tour ends.

For Tolkien fans who want the ultimate experience, for December 2003, one day is added to the itinerary, so fans can enjoy the world premiere of *The Return of the King* in Wellington.

Sources Consulted for the Tolkien History

Carpenter, Humphrey. *J.R.R. Tolkien: A Biography*. New York: Houghton Mifflin, 2000.

"JRR Tolkien's Oxford." July 2003. <*www.chem.ox.ac.uk/oxfordtour/tolkientour/index.html*>.

"Tolkien Timeline." July 2003. <*www.jrrtolkien.org.uk/tolkien_timeline.htm*>.

"The Tolkien Timeline." July 2003. <*gollum.usask.ca/tolkien*>.

"24 Hour Museum" July 2003. <*www.24hourmuseum.org.uk*>.

Chapter 13

Tolkien Websites:
The Road Goes
Ever On

If you were to type in "Tolkien Website" with the Google.com search engine and read every single reference, you'd be busy for a long, long time, because more than 93,000 will be displayed. Granted, there's a lot of repetition, with multiple references to sites with lots of pages, but the fact remains that searching the Internet for Tolkien sites is no easy matter!

In the listing that follows, I've included what I feel is the tip of the iceberg, so to speak. I think these sites are good places to start, and as with all things on the Internet, sites with links will take you down another road—an analogy that recalls the Tolkien poem, "The Road Goes Ever On."

Organizations

The Tolkien Society, *www.tolkiensociety.org.* Founded in 1969, this nonprofit organization was established to "further interest in the life and works of J.R.R. Tolkien," according to its Website. Based in the United Kingdom, this society has several gatherings, the largest being the Oxonmoot, in September, and publishes periodicals of interest, notably *Amon Hen* (a bi-monthly newszine) and *Mallorn* (a collection of critical essays). The Society will be holding a major conference in 2005 to celebrate the 50th anniversary of the publication of *The Lord of the Rings: The Fellowship of the Ring*. Most useful to new readers is a mail-order store with an excellent selection.

The Mythopoeic Society, *www.mythsoc.org.* The U.S. counterpart to the Tolkien Society, the Mythopoeic Society is (from the Website):

...a non-profit international literary and educational organization for the study, discussion, and enjoyment of fantasy and mythic literature, especially the works of J.R.R. Tolkien, C.S. Lewis, and Charles Williams. Members of the Mythopoeic Society include scholars, writers, and readers of mythic and fantasy literature. The Society sponsors an annual Mythopoeic Conference (Mythcon), Discussion and Special Interest Groups, the Mythopoeic Awards, and three periodical publications.

This society publishes *Mythprint* (monthly), *Mythlore* (quarterly), *The Mythic Circle*, and issues its own books. Unlike The Tolkien Society, it does not carry general merchandise, though it does offer such items through its Amazon.com associate program.

Travel

24 Hour Museum, *www.24hourmuseum.org.uk*. As the Website states, the 24 Hour Museum is a "Gateway to over 2,500 UK museums, galleries and heritage attractions." Type "Tolkien" in the search engine and two "trails" discussing scenery with photos are available for exploration: *"Fellowship of the Ring"* and *"The Two Towers."* Expect a third trail, *"The Return of the King,"* to be available once the final Peter Jackson film is released.

Educational

National Geographic, *www.nationalgeographic.com/ngbeyond*. To promote its feature about Tolkien (*Beyond the Movie: The Lord of the Rings*), this site provides information about Tolkien's life and influences on *The Lord of the Rings*; cultural and linguistic conservation, Tolkien's love of languages, and reflections of "real" languages in Tolkien's tongues; creating a mythological identity for England, and the myths that inspired *The Lord of the Rings*; and a forum, "Do individuals today, no matter how epic their quests, really have any power?"

Tolkien's Oxford, *users.ox.ac.uk/~tolksoc/TolkiensOxford*. An informal pictorial guide of key places in Oxford, England, associated with J.R.R. Tolkien.

The Scholar's Guide to Oxford, *www.oxford-info.com*. The best site for information about Oxford, with recommendations on lodging, a guide to the university and to the city itself, a restaurant and pub guide, information on a walking tour, and other resources.

The BBC, *www.bbc.co.uk*. The British Broadcast System is the best source for general-interest news about Tolkien and current events. Typing "Tolkien" in the BBCi (BBC Internet) or BBC yields news about him that does not generally get reported in the United States, such as a story about a new CD with Tolkien reading from *The Fellowship of the Ring*, discovered in the archives of the British Library, and Professor Michael Drout's discovery of Tolkien's translation of *Beowulf*. (Tolkien news will usually get posted on the Tolkien Society Website, with the benefit of it being put in context.)

Marion E. Wade Center (Wheaton College), *www.wheaton.edu/learnres/wade*. According to the Website, Wheaton College houses

> ...a major research collection of the books and papers of seven British authors: Owen Barfield, G.K. Chesterton, C.S. Lewis, George MacDonald, Dorothy L. Sayers, J.R.R. Tolkien, and Charles Williams. These writers are well known for their impact on contemporary literature and Christian thought. Together they produced over four hundred books including novels, drama, poetry, fantasy, children's books, and Christian treatises. Overall, the Wade Center has more than 11,000 volumes including first editions and critical works. Other holdings on the seven authors include letters, manuscripts, audio and videotapes, artwork, dissertations, periodicals, photographs, and related materials. Any of these resources may be studied in the quiet surroundings of the Kilby Reading Room.

It also has a museum that holds, among other literary curiosities, a desk owned by J.R.R. Tolkien.

Marquette University Special Collections: J.R.R. Tolkien, *www.mu.edu/library/collections/archives/tolkien.html*. A stellar collection of Tolkien material is on deposit at Marquette University. At its nucleus are original manuscripts of *The Hobbit*, *The Lord of the Rings*, and *Farmer Giles of Ham* purchased for $5,000 from J.R.R. Tolkien in 1956 due to the vision of William B. Ready, who recognized their historic importance.

The university has supplemented the original manuscripts with a large collection of secondary material—notably books and periodicals—and, through its bequests program, it is continually adding to its impressive collection.

An excellent resource for students, scholars, and researchers.

Original manuscripts have become increasingly rare, because today's author is likely to use a computer and not save early drafts. But in the precomputer days, manuscripts were typewritten several times in order to achieve a final copy, and sometimes typed only after several drafts were composed by hand—the method by which *The Magic Ring* (the original working title of *The Lord of the Rings*) was written.

The collection of Tolkien material, currently inaccessible until Marquette's new library is constructed and all holdings safety transferred, is a treasure trove for Tolkien fans who want to see his masterwork, in his own hand.

For the just plain curious, the display of actual manuscript pages—some of them, anyway—will be enough. For serious students, scholars, researchers, writers, and academicians, access to the holdings is a significant resource.

Understandably, the original manuscripts are not physically available, nor is that desirable, because excessively handled paper will inevitably show signs of irreversible wear and tear—damage that cannot be repaired. For this reason, Marquette University, like all universities, archives manuscripts on microfilm, which serves the students well and preserves the physical manuscript, which, over time, will become increasingly fragile, because the acid-based paper will slowly deteriorate.

William Ready, Marquette University, and Tolkien

The late William Ready posseses two distinctions in the Tolkien universe: He is the author of *The Tolkien Relation* (Warner Books, 1968), which Tolkien himself called "insulting and offensive" (according to Carpenter's biography), and he is also the visionary who, back in 1956, contacted Tolkien with the hope of adding original manuscripts to the permanent collection of his employer, Marquette University. He had been tasked as a newly appointed library director to aggressively expand its holdings, and he set out to do just that, in a field that he loved—fantasy literature.

Ready recognized Tolkien's genius and contacted Tolkien himself, who was agreeable to selling his manuscripts, but only through an intermediary. A London bookseller, the late Bertram Rota, served as that intermediary and, after £1,250 was received, literally thousands of pages of original manuscripts were packed up and shipped off to Marquette University.

To say that Marquette University had gotten a bargain would be an understatement. With more than 11,000 pages of original manuscripts to three major Tolkien works (*The Hobbit*, *The Lord of the Rings*, and *Farmer Giles of Ham*), the university had bought two literary "silmarilli"—jewels of incomparable beauty and incalculable worth. (The third jewel, the manuscript of *The Silmarillion* was later deposited at the Bodeleian Library at Oxford.)

Though general estimates as to the holdings conservatively runs into the millions, what, one asks, might those pages be worth?

To be honest, they are priceless, one-of-a-kind, and irreplaceable, which is why they are kept in a temperature and humidity controlled vault, the leaves carefully inserted in acid-free folders that are stored in acid-free boxes—state-of-the-art conservation methods designed to prolong the life of papers that would otherwise undergo a slow decay.

It should be noted that the Tolkien estate retains copyright on these materials, so photocopies can only be made if written permission is secured from the estate. Likewise, this material can only be published if permission is secured.

A reading room is set up to peruse the holdings. So exactly what, you ask, does Marquette University have in its considerable holdings? On its Website, the university provides a detailed listing. However, the general summary provided on the site is sufficient to give one an idea of the scope of the holdings. The following is reprinted as it appears on *www.marquette.edu/library/collections/archives/Mss/ JRRT/mss-jrrt-sc.html*:

Series 1, *The Hobbit*, ca. 1930–1937, contains a holograph version of the novel, typescripts with corrections by Tolkien, a printer's typescript with corrections by JRRT, and three sets of page proofs with the author's corrections. Also included are a watercolor rendering by Tolkien of the dust jacket used by Allen and Unwin, printed maps with corrections by Tolkien, and a dust jacket from the German edition of *The Hobbit*. The records are arranged by type of manuscript and by chapter thereunder, corresponding to the final published version.

Series 2, *Farmer Giles of Ham*, ca. 1933–1938, 1948–1949, contains a holograph version, three typescripts with corrections by Tolkien, and two sets of galley sheets with corrections by Tolkien. It is arranged by type of manuscript.

Series 3, *The Lord of the Rings*, ca. 1937–1955, includes holograph renderings, typescripts with corrections by Tolkien, a typescript for the printer with corrections by JRRT, and galley sheets with corrections by the author. There are two sets of galley sheets for Books I and II, and three sets for Books II and IV. Also included are an advance proof copy of *The Return of the King*, printed maps, dust jackets from the original Houghton Mifflin edition, several drafts for an unpublished "Epilogue," a number of unpublished sketches, and manuscript fragments for *The Silmarillion*. The records are arranged by book and by type of manuscript and chapter thereunder, corresponding to the final published version. Additional manuscripts presented by Christopher Tolkien between 1987–1998 are arranged separately.

Series 4, *Mr. Bliss*, ca. 1935, is a children's story by Tolkien. The manuscript is in Tolkien's calligraphic hand, illustrated throughout with ink and colored pencil drawings by the author. It is a 50-page booklet, in finished form. A photocopy is included, along with a transcription and a set of 51 color slides, as well as galley sheets and an advance proof copy of the facsimile edition published in 1982. The condition of the *Mr. Bliss* manuscript precludes frequent handling. The Archives reserves the right to offer patrons the set of slides for viewing rather than the original document.

Series 5, Printed Literature and Other Secondary Material Relating to Tolkien, 1938–, consists of secondary material on Tolkien and/or his works. Conference announcements, press clippings, book reviews, magazine and journal articles, books, posters, phonograph records, audiotapes, videotapes and DVDs, and ephemera are included. The series is arranged by type of material and chronologically thereunder. All books by and about J.R.R. Tolkien are cataloged in MARQCAT, Marquette University Libraries electronic catalog.

Series 6, Periodical Literature on Tolkien and Related Fantasy Writers, 1965–, contains fanzines and journals by groups of Tolkien enthusiasts. It is arranged by title of publication and/or organization and chronologically thereunder.

Series 7, Other Tolkien Writings, 1911–1976, the bulk of which were contributed by John Rateliff, contains photocopies of 30 poems by Tolkien, published from 1911 to 1974, and copies of letters and extracts of letters by Tolkien, as well as scholarly articles and obituaries. The series is arranged by type of material and thereunder chronologically.

Series 8, Screen Treatment, Scripts, and Screenplays 1957–1978, consists of a screen treatment by Morton Grady Zimmerman, written in 1957 for an animated version of *The Lord of the Rings,* with annotations by J.R.R. Tolkien; production notes and correspondence concerning the project; original donated by Morton Grady Zimmerman. Also the original script and production materials for a play cycle for "From The Lord of the Rings by J.R.R. Tolkien," written by Marian L. Kleinau and performed in 1967 at South Illinois University, donated by Richard E. Blackwelder. Also a photocopy of a screenplay of *The Lord of the Rings* by John Boorman and Rospo Pallenberg, prepared in 1970 for United Artists but never produced; and photocopies of three drafts of the screenplay by Chris Conkling and Peter S. Beagle, 1976–1978, of the animated version of "The Lord of the Rings," directed by Ralph Bakshi, donated by David N. Villalpando.

In addition, the library has acquired a considerable collection of secondary holdings, including books by and about Tolkien (approximately 300 volumes), other literature, and Tolkieniana (quoted from *www.marquette.edu/library/collections/archives/tolkien.html#secondary*)—"sketches and paintings, calendars, games and puzzles, and teaching materials, in addition to audio recordings or readings and radio adaptations and video recordings of movie adaptations and commemorative documentaries."

Marquette is, of course, interested in bequests and gifts, and interested parties should contact the university's archivist directly, at:

Matt Blessing, Department Head/University Archivist
Marquette University Libraries
1415 W. Wisconsin Avenue
P.O. Box 3141
Milwaukee, WI 53201-3141
Phone: (414) 288-7256
Fax: (414) 288-3123
E-mail: Matt.Blessing@marquette.edu

Access the university Website at *www.marquette.edu/library/collections/archives/tolkien*.

J.R.R. Tolkien's Oxford, *www.chem.ox.ac.uk/oxfordtour/tolkientour/index.html*. Using a timeline and Apple's Quicktime, this site offers a unique look at the educational, professional, and personal places in Oxford associated with Tolkien. What makes this site unusual is that the plug-in software allows the viewer to literally rotate the view a full 360 degrees. Thus, starting with a frontal view of, say, a Tolkien residence, you can "swing" the camera around to see what it looks like down and across the street as well—a fascinating perspective obviously not available in book form.

Languages

Resources for Tolkienian Linguistics: An Annotated Guide, *www.elvish.org/resources.html*. A good starting point for those interested in studying Tolkien's invented languages, with information on primary works, secondary works, recommended reading, publications, and library holdings.

Ardalambion: Of the Tongues of Arda, the Invented World of J.R.R. Tolkien, *www.uib.no/People/hnohf/*. For serious linguists who wish to know everything there is to know about Tolkien's many languages. (**Note:** Some of the pages are difficult to read, with black text on electric blue or parrot-green backgrounds.)

General Reference

The Encyclopedia of Arda, *www.glyphweb.com/arda/default.htm*. An online encyclopedia with thousands of entries on the people, places, and things in Tolkien's world. (An offline version is also available for the Windows computer platform only.)

Bibliography

A Chronological Bibliography of the Writings of J.R.R. Tolkien (Compiled by Ake Bertenstam), *www.forodrim.org/arda/tbchron.html.* Beginning in 1910, with an annotation for a "Debating Society [Report]," this list literally covers Tolkien's published writings. It has 162 separate entries, concluding with entries on *Beowulf and the Critics* (ed. Michael D.C. Trout) and *The History of The Hobbit* (ed. John Rateliff).

Personal Websites

Wayne G. Hammond and Christina Scull, *www.bcn.net/~whammond.* An editing team with numerous credits (Tolkien's *Roverandom*, the 50th anniversary edition of *Farmer Giles of Ham*, and *J.R.R. Tolkien: Artist and Illustrator*), their forthcoming project, *J.R.R. Tolkien: A Companion and Guide*, from Houghton Mifflin, will offer a concordance to persons, places, events, and issues to his life and a detailed chronology, as well.

They also publish *The Tolkien Collector*, which is, according to their Website (*www.bcn.net/~whammond/collect*):

> ...an occasional magazine for collectors of J.R.R. Tolkien. Each issue, usually 32 pages, includes news about new and forthcoming books by and about Tolkien, translations of Tolkien's works, recordings, videos, and other Tolkieniana, and Tolkien items offered for sale in booksellers' and auction catalogues and on the Internet; and feature articles on aspects of collecting Tolkien and Tolkien bibliography.

Booksellers

AbeBooks, *www.abebooks.com.* A network of member booksellers worldwide list their used books on this site with a database searchable by title, author, keyword, or publisher. This is *the* place to look for the truly rare or exotic edition of any Tolkien book.

Amazon, *www.amazon.com.* This is the U.S. site. The U.K. site is at *www.amazon.co.uk*
Note: When buying from the U.K. site, I *highly* recommend paying extra for airmail shipment and insuring the order for full replacement value.

Blackwell's, *bookshop.blackwell.com/bobus/scripts/welcome.jsp.* The premiere U.K. bookseller's U.S. site. Carries all the in-print Tolkien books and, of course, virtually anything else in print from U.K. publishers. Offers a searchable database and an out-of-print search. Free shipping to the United States.

Barnes and Noble, *www.bn.com*. The online Website of the biggest book chain in the United States.

Daeron's Books, *www.daerons.co.uk*. Independent bookstore in the United Kingdom. It carries a wide inventory of new and used books by and about Tolkien. Bills itself as "Possibly the largest Tolkien bookdealer in the world!"

Thornton's Bookshop, *www.thorntonsbooks.co.uk*. Independent bookstore in the United Kingdom. New and used Tolkien books. Its inventory is searchable by seller via the *www.abebooks.com* database.

The Tolkien Society, *www.tolkiensociety.org*. Specializes in in-print material published in the United Kingdom. (Does not carry out-of-print material.)

UK Bookworld, *www.ukbookworld.com*. Searchable database of independent booksellers in the United Kingdom. Especially useful to find out-of-print books.

Movie-Related

Official Movie Site, *www.lordoftherings.net*. The official movie Website is *the* place to go for the most authoritative information on the Peter Jackson film adaptations. Features extensive text and photos and trailers from the films, plus links for its Web shop and fan club.

Official Movie Fan Club, *www.lotrfanclub.com*. Designed to support the films, the fan club is run by Decipher and, for an annual membership fee, offers a professionally produced magazine published bi-monthly, access to a special "members only" online community, and discounts on movie-related memorabilia, some of which is not available elsewhere.

Unofficial Fan Club, *www.theonering.net*. Though it is a general-interest fan club devoted to Tolkien, its current emphasis—because of their overwhelming media presence—is on the films. Abbreviated T.O.R.N., this site is a labor of love with an emphasis on the word "fan."

Cold Spring Press published a collection of nonfiction pieces from the Website, *The People's Guide to J.R.R. Tolkien* (May 2003, 416 pages, $16.95). Informal and very fannish, as opposed to a collection of academic papers, *The People's Guide* is a catchall collection of individual perspectives by die-hard Tolkien fans.

Weta Workshop, *www.wetadigital.com/workshop/collectibles/*. Informative site explaining the history of the collectibles program developed for *The Lord of the Rings*, profile of creators, interviews with creators, and links to other Websites.

Individual Actor Websites

The list of official Websites is growing, but the list of unofficial Websites constantly changes (most often because the real world intrudes and a site goes temporarily down or is permanently closed).

A good site to check, with updated links on both official and unofficial sites of the actors from the movie trilogy, can be found at *www.unotime-eleni.net/ chemicalheart/fansites.html.*

Official

> ✦ **Ian McKellen** (Gandalf): *www.mckellen.com.*

> ✦ **Sean Austin** (Samwise Gamgee): *www.seanaustin.com.*

> ✦ **Billy Boyd** (Peregrin "Pippin" Took): *www.billyboyd.com.*

> ✦ **John Rhys-Davies** (Gimli Gloin): *www.johnrhys-davies.com.*

> ✦ **Andy Serkis** (Gollum): *www.serkis.com.*

Unofficial

> ✦ **Sean Bean** (Boromir): *www.compleatseanbean.com.*

> ✦ **Cate Blanchett** (Lady Galadriel): *groups.msn.com/ TheUltimateCateBlanchettWebsite.*

> ✦ **Orlando Bloom** (Legolas Greenleaf): *www.theorlandobloomfiles.com/.*

> ✦ **Peter Jackson** (movie director): *tbhl.theonering.net/index.shtml,* home of the Official Peter Jackson Fan Club.

> ✦ **Viggo Mortensen** (Aragorn): *www.frostyland.com/Viggo/viggo.index.shtml oberongirl.com/viggo/. www.geocities.com/nzmermaid2003/LinksViggo.htm.*

> ✦ **Hugo Weaving** (Elrond Half-Elven): *www.nuli.net/me.html.*

> ✦ **Dominic Monaghan** (Meriadoc "Merry" Brandybuck): *unofficialdom.fateback.com/home.html.*

> ✦ **Liv Tyler** (Arwen Undomiel): *www.lovelylivtyler.com/.*

> ✦ **Brad Dourif** (Gríma Wormtongue): *www.dourif.net.*

General Merchandising
(Licensed Through Tolkien Enterprises)

Danbury Mint, *www.danburymint.co.uk/lor/index.html.* A British company that manufactures sculptures, plates, and replicas.

Mithril, *www.mithril.ie.* Based in Ireland, this company manufactures an extensive line of Tolkien-related miniatures from *The Hobbit* and *The Lord of the Rings.*

Movie Merchandising
(Licensed Through New Line Cinema)

Advanced Graphics. (No Website.) Life-sized standups of characters from the films: Gandalf, Gimli, Legolas, Aragorn, the four hobbits, Frodo, and Saruman.

Antioch, *www.antioch.com*. Bookmarkers.

Artbox, *www.artboxent.com*. Trading cards called "3-D Action Flipz."

Cedco Publishing, *www.cedco.com*. Products for the student market, principally student planners, calendars, and journals.

Decipher, *www.decipher.com*. Trading card games and role-playing games. Runs the official movie tie-in fan club (see *www.lotrfanclub.com*).

Games Workshop, *www.games-workshop.com*. Miniature gaming based on *The Lord of the Rings*. Uses a rule book, miniature figurines, and dice to play simulated battles—you supply the strategy.

Noble Collection, *www.noblecollection.com*. Sells direct to the public via Website and mail-order catalog, though some of these products are sold on the official movie Website's shop. The most extensive line of jewelry from the movie, including rings, brooches, pendants, earrings, necklaces, bracelets, headdresses, and chokers; a selection of swords (like United Cutlery); and collectibles, such as sculptures, a holographic image chamber, and a chess set.

Playalong Toys, *www.playalongtoys.com*. Miniature toys (figures and playsets) designed for children, as opposed to gaming product.

Serious CD Cardz, *www.serioususa.com*. CD-ROM cards (80 megabytes) with movie-specific content for each of the three films—the movie trailer, character biographies, movie stills, behind-the-scenes stills, e-mailable postcards, screensavers, wallpaper, and music from the soundtrack.

Sideshow, *www.sideshowcollectibles.com*. An outstanding line of limited edition products—intricately painted polystone sculptures and figurines, medallions, and lithographs. For investment value and for overall quality, these products are genuine collectibles and worth your investment of time.

Topps, *www.topps.com*. Trading cards.

Toybiz, *www.marvel.com/toybiz/lotr*. A line of quality toys and figurines from the movie—action figures (Sauron, Treebeard, a Nazgûl on horse, Arwen), and horse and rider sets. Excellent packaging.

Upper Deck, *www.upperdeckstore.com*. Half-foot "bobble-head" dolls based on the characters in the film. Mathoms, all.

United Cutlery, *www.unitedcutlery.com*. Manufactures replicas from the film, including a line of swords, knives, full-scale helmets, staffs, Gimli's axe, bows, shields, spears, pikes, crowns, and tiaras. A first-rate line of high-quality product issued in limited runs. Click on "retail links" to find a source, because United Cutlery does not sell directly to the public.

Wrebbit, *www.wrebbit.com*. Puzzles based on the movie—two-dimensional and three-dimensional (Golden Hall, Endoras; and Orthanc Tower, Isengard).

Mail-Order Stores

The Tolkien Shop, *www.tolkienshop.com*. Independent store specializing in Tolkien. If there is a single source for anything and everything about Tolkien in any form, this is that store. Prices are in Euro dollars. Proprietor Rene van Rossenberg also carries an impressive line of other fantasy material. A great place to find the rare, the unusual, and the collectible!

Tolkientown.com, *www.TolkienTown.com*. An excellent single-source store for all things Tolkien.

Music

Tolkien Music, *www.tolkien-music.com*. Lists and provides links to nearly 900 CDs of music inspired by Tolkien and his work. As expected, most are from unknowns who self-publish their work and share it online or issue small run CDs.

Tolkien Ensemble, *www.tolkienensemble.dk*. A professional group of musicians who are in the process of musically interpreting all of the poems and songs in *The Lord of the Rings*. To date, two CDs (with 24 songs) have been issued.

Publishers

HarperCollins UK, *www.tolkien.co.uk*. Excellent source of information from Tolkien's primary publisher. Biographical information, interviews, competitions, interactive quizzes, art portfolios, information about all the books in print, downloadable screensavers and wallpaper for the computer—it's all here. Drink deep. *Hoom, hoom!*

Houghton Mifflin (U.S.), *www.houghtonmifflinbooks.com/features/lordoftheringstrilogy*. Detailed information on the frontlist, backlist, movie tie-in books, etc., organized by section. More for booksellers than fans—unlike the U.K. publishing counterpart—the site is well-organized and easy to navigate.

Random House: Ballantine Books (U.S.), *www.randomhouse.com/delrey/*. Ballantine is the paperback publisher for Tolkien titles in the United States. The site provides a basic listing, nothing more.

Chapter 14

The Essential J.R.R. Tolkien: My Personal Picks

There are literally thousands of editions of Tolkien books, books about Tolkien, related memorabilia, and movie-related material. If I were to pick the items I think are especially attractive to a Tolkien fan, they would include the following:

The Hobbit

Though it's not necessary to have read this book before reading *The Lord of the Rings*, it makes sense to do so because of chronology. *The Hobbit* precedes the events of *The Lord of The Rings* and, thus, sets the stage for what is to follow—the great War of the Ring. In *The Hobbit*, we are introduced to the denizens of Middle-earth—hobbits (especially one in particular, Bilbo Baggins), Gollum, Gandalf the Wizard, Gwaihir the Windlord (an eagle), Thorin Oakenshield and company, and the great and terrible dragon, Smaug.

Two editions stand out: *The Annotated Hobbit* (Houghton Mifflin), annotated by Douglas A. Anderson; and *The Hobbit* (HarperCollins UK, deluxe edition).

The Annotated Hobbit (398 numbered pages, $28) is a work of scholarship. starting with the preferred text (restored and corrected), this revised and expanded edition is fully annotated by Tolkien expert Douglas A. Anderson, who explicates "the sources, characters, places, and things" (as the dust jacket copy notes), so the reader can appreciate the historical references—necessary for a book written by a linguist and scholar. Visually, this edition offers 150 illustrations—including Tolkien's own work in various forms, from drafts to finished paintings—that show how this book has fired the imagination of artists worldwide. Bracketing the book,

Tolkien and Correspondence

"He liked visitors, but he liked to know them before they arrived, and he preferred to ask them himself."

—J.R.R. Tolkien, *The Hobbit*: Chapter 1, "An Unexpected Party"

An author's time is his own to spend, but even when the author, the publisher, and the readers are in full agreement—as was the case with Tolkien and *The Silmarillion*—he found himself needlessly distracted, most often by correspondence.

While it is understandable that a writer would get fan mail, it also stands to reason that he must, in the end, strike a balance. The work, after all, is the reason why fans write in the first place. Should those precious hours available for writing be spent producing more work or answering individual letters?

For professional writers, the answer is clear: The work is the priority and everything else a distant second. For this reason, writers such as Arthur C. Clarke and Stephen King use preprinted form postcards to respond to mail. On his Website, King put it simply. He couldn't do both, so wouldn't most fans prefer he spend time creating new work?

As biographer Humphrey Carpenter explained, in Tolkien's case, after he had retired from Oxford in 1959, the usual matters of publishing—revising and updating earlier works, completing shorter works—commanded his attention. But *The Silmarillion*, the book fans were most anxious to read, remained unfinished. Unfortunately, it would remain thus, because Tolkien found himself too easily distracted by the minutia of being an author.

Personal correspondence, for instance, was his joy...and bane. Wrote Carpenter, "A lot of his time was also spent simply in answering letters. Readers wrote to him by the score, prais-ing, criticizing, and asking for more information about elements in the stories. Tolkien took every letter seriously...."

Too seriously, as it turned out. According to Carpenter, Tolkien would sometimes write draft after draft of a letter that sometimes would never be sent. The correspondent on the other end might think that Tolkien couldn't be bothered to respond, but, in fact, Tolkien was a perfectionist, especially in literary matters, and wouldn't send out a reply unless it *exactly* expressed what he wanted to say—*close* was not good enough, and, for that reason, some letters, even after multiple drafts, remained unfinished and never sent.

Carpenter also pointed out that Tolkien, who lived in a house crammed with books and papers, found it all too easy to misplace the correspondence that so commanded his attention, with the result that he spent "hours turning out the garage or his study-bedroom until he had found it." Days, we are told, were thus spent—precious time wasted, time that could have been spent more productively.

Back then, there was no such thing as cellular phones, e-mail, and voicemail. Back then, long distance phone calls were expensive, and transatlantic air fares exorbitant.

The world is a much smaller place now and celebrities are under siege not only from the media but from well-intentioned but aggressive fans who feel a best-selling author is a public commodity.

an extensive illustrated introduction that tells of the history of the book and its evolution, and extensive appendices that include "The Quest of Erebor," by Tolkien, which tells of how Gandalf came to arrange the adventure told in this book; a discussion of regular runes and moon-runes that play an important part in this book; and a necessarily abbreviated bibliography, with useful notes.

For those who prefer a traditionally illustrated edition, Houghton Mifflin's gift edition, a large format (8 x 10.25 inches) hardback, with art by Alan Lee, is a good choice, designed to complement Lee's illustrated one volume edition of *The Lord of the Rings* and Nasmith's illustrated *The Silmarillion* (both also Houghton Mifflin).

The Hobbit U.K. deluxe edition is out of print but worth searching for, because it matches the deluxe volumes of *The Lord of the Rings* and *The Silmarillion*, as well, all from HarperCollins UK. Originally published in 2001, quarter-bound in leather, the book measures 7.75 x 9.75 inches, and is limited to 2,500 copies, protected by a matching slipcase. Printed on India paper (that is, Bible paper) stock, the book is a fine example of bookmaking and, surely, the most elegant edition ever published.

The Lord of the Rings

The cornerstone of any Tolkien collection, the challenge here is in picking, from the many available, which editions are the best value and the most collectible.

The best non-illustrated edition is the one-volume "Leatherette Collector's Edition" (Houghton Mifflin, $75). Bound in red leatherette with a matching slipcase, the book itself is printed in two color inks (red and black) and measures 7.75 x 9.75 inches. The paper stock is an off white—perfect for reading, providing the best contrast—and a map is folded inside a free endpaper. A beautiful edition at an affordable price, the Collector's Edition is the preferred edition for fans who want the book as the author intended, in one volume, and without illustrations.

The best illustrated edition is the three-volume, slipcased edition (Houghton Mifflin, $80) with 50 watercolors by Alan Lee. Oversized (8 x 10.25 inches) and printed on semi-matte paper, this edition allows the positioning of the art as close as possible to the referenced text page. (Two other editions using the Lee art, both from Houghton Mifflin, are in print—a three-volume, slipcased edition for $65, printed on book stock and inserted color plates, and the one-volume, $70 edition, printed, alas, on thin paper that shows bleed-through and makes the text on subsequent pages is visible.)

The best U.K. edition is the deluxe volume, from HarperCollins UK, printed on India paper. Quarter-bound in black leather with a matching slipcase, this is the matching volume to *The Hobbit* and *The Silmarillion* (both also HarperCollins UK).

The Silmarillion

The U.S. edition of choice is the gift edition, illustrated by Ted Nasmith, published in a large format (Houghton Mifflin, $35, 7 x 10 inches).

The U.K. edition of choice is the Deluxe Edition, quarter-bound in leather, with black cloth, and a matching slipcase (HarperCollins UK).

The History of Middle-Earth

The 12 individual volumes are available from Houghton Mifflin in trade hardback—the best editions available in the United States.

The preferred editions, in this case, are the U.K. deluxe editions, all from HarperCollins UK, which collect all 12 in three volumes, printed on fine paper and slipcased.

The alternative choice is the U.K. trade edition, also from HarperCollins, which is available in three hardbacks with a matching slipcase.

Recorded Books

For those of us who love books on tape, or CD, Recorded Books offers the best line of fiction and nonfiction imaginable. For purposes of this discussion, however, let's talk Tolkien.

Available on audiocassette and CD, unabridged recordings of *The Hobbit* and *The Lord of the Rings* are available for purchase or rental. Read by Rob Inglis and recorded with fidelity—the sound quality is extraordinary—any Tolkien fan would love to add these to his collection.

The artist Michael Whelan has practically worn out his audiocassette copies of *The Lord of the Rings*, and (as he put it in an interview previously in this book) considers these readings to be music to his ears.

The One Ring

Movie interest and tie-in licensing has produced a cascade of rings, from cheap to expensive, in various metals. As with all things of great beauty, simplicity is best. Although not authorized, my rings of choice are the ones crafted by the New Zealand firm, Jens Hansen Gold & Silversmith. This company made the One Rings seen in the movies, but did not seek a licensing agreement. The rings, therefore, do not have the Elvish inscription on the bands. Despite that omission, the rings are simple in design and elegant, available in various precious metals. Each ring comes in an elegantly packaged wooden presentation box.

Swords

Two lines of swords are available—from the Noble Collection and from United Cutlery—but my preference is for the latter line, because they specialize in blades and have the most extensive, and ambitious, line.

Choosing one sword from the United Cutlery selection is admittedly difficult because there are so many splendid designs from which to choose, but for its beauty, elegance, and craftsmanship, the line of Elven weapons is most impressive. Hadhafang, the Sword of Arwen, is especially eye-catching. Measuring approximately 38 inches, its blade constructed of tempered steel, with a wood grip and solid metal pommel, it is mounted on an ornate display stand.

Books About Tolkien

There are two indispensable books, both by Humphrey Carpenter: *The Letters of J.R.R. Tolkien* (Houghton Mifflin), which gives his worldview captured in personal and business correspondence, and *J.R.R. Tolkien: A Biography* (Houghton Mifflin), which is definitive and authoritative.

Sculpture

The line manufactured by Sideshow/Weta is first class. Issued in limited runs, constructed of polystone, hand-painted for maximum detail, and likenesses approved by the actors in the movie, this affordably priced line of busts and figures offers something for everyone.

There are so many to choose from, all excellent, but the standout value is "The Galadhrim Archer" ($125), which stands 17.25 inches tall. A run of only 2,000 pieces, this statue of an Elven warrior is a magnificent work of art.

Final Word

The Importance of Story

In 2005, Tolkien devotees worldwide will celebrate the silver anniversary publication of *The Lord of the Rings*—a party worth celebrating. The book has stood the test of time, more than fulfilling the author's original intent (upon which he elaborated in a foreword to the second edition of *The Lord of the Rings*): to write "a really long story that would hold the attention of readers, amuse them, delight them, and at times maybe excite them or deeply move them." As his own worst critic, he found "many defects," but the author acknowledged one flaw noted by others: "the book is too short."

Given that *The Lord of the Rings* is 1,137 pages in Houghton Mifflin's single-volume movie tie-in edition, a question arises: How can a book of that length be considered "too short"?

The short answer is that it's the essential difference between the film trilogy's theatrical release versions and the DVD extended edition. Fans want more detail, more information. In fact, they'll take all they can get.

Not limited to the book itself, of which there are more than 100 million copies in print, the story has enjoyed unparalleled success in multiple forms, from audio adaptations to the hugely successful film adaptations that have rejuvenated an enduring entertainment franchise—the World of Tolkien.

At a time when Hollywood favors risk avoidance by releasing sequels and tailoring its movies for predetermined audiences, and when book publishers look backward instead of forward, preferring proven retreads to new visions, it's worth noting that in today's commercial mentality, *The Lord of the Rings* might never have gotten past the first reader. A long work of fantasy by an unknown author who abhorred celebrity and never shilled the book to the media or attended book signings, Tolkien's book has prospered by virtue of word of mouth.

The story, in short, sells itself. No hype, no huge marketing campaign, no meet-and-greet with the media. Just an old-fashioned epic fantasy, plainly told, by a traditional storyteller who was motivated not by money but by love of story, love of language, and a love for history.

No one, suggests Tom Shipley in *J.R.R. Tolkien: Author of the Century*, could have written *The Lord of the Rings* except Tolkien himself. And for that reason, we will never see another book—or an author—quite like *The Lord of the Rings* again.

Of Beren and Lúthien

On a simple headstone at a gravesite in the Oxford suburb of Wolvercotte, the words "Lúthien" and "Beren" are engraved. The words strike a dissonant chord: In sharp contrast to the English names on the headstone, these are otherworldly names, recognizable only to Tolkien fans who appreciate their significance.

The gravestone reads:

EDITH MARY TOLKIEN

LÚTHIEN

1889–1971

JOHN RONALD

REUEL TOLKIEN

BEREN

1892–1973

In "Quenta Silmarillion" (in *The Silmarillion*), chapter XIX tells "Of Beren and Luthein." Tolkien writes, "Among the tales of sorrow and of ruin that come down to us from the darkness of those days there are yet some in which amid weeping there is joy and under the shadow of death light that endures."

It is the tale of Beren and Lúthien, a mortal man who loves an immortal elf-maiden, who becomes mortal to love him "that thus whatever grief might lie in wait, the fates of Beren and Lúthien might be joined, and their paths lead together beyond the confines of the world."

In a letter to his son Christopher, J.R.R. Tolkien explained why he chose "Lúthien" for her tombstone. "She was (and knew she was) my Lúthien. I will say no more now."

Two years after Lúthien was buried, so, too, was Beren.

Long before *The Lord of the Rings* went into film production, Tolkien fans have quietly gathered for years at an annual conference in Oxford, England, sponsored by the Tolkien Society to celebrate the work. It is a time to celebrate the importance of story, to celebrate a man whose literary life work was inspired not by money but the love of a well-told story.

As Tolkien fans line up to see the *The Return of the King* in the theater in December 2003, as they raid the bookstores for the new editions of his works and the movie tie-in editions, and as they buy advanced tickets for the traveling exhibit of movie memorabilia that is drawing record crowds, one can't help but think that Tolkien himself might be pleased. Neither he, nor any biographer, could ever have guessed that, from a tiny literary seed—a note scribbled about a hobbit on the back of an examination paper—would spring *The Hobbit*, *The Lord of the Rings*, *The Silmarillion*, and *The History of Middle-earth*. From seed to branch, from leaf to tree, and from forest to an imagined world called Middle-earth, the fruits of Tolkien's imagination bore literary Silmarilli—narrative jewels of incomparable beauty that, as they have for nearly half a century, reaffirm the importance of stories and, in their telling, instill in us a sense of wonder.

Appendix A

Glass Onion Graphics

www.glassonion.com (redirects you to www.michaelwhelan.com)
www.michaelwhelan.com

The front of The Glass Onion Gallery in Connecticut, the official gallery for artist Michael Whelan.

Most fantasy artists only see their artwork hung for public display in the art show at conventions—not the best presentation, because lighting is usually dim and the pegboard mounting system leaves a lot to be desired.

I can only think of one fantasy artist who has a museum devoted exclusively to his work—Frank Frazetta, the Grand Master of fantasy illustration—but it is not open year-round.

Michael Whelan is fortunate that he does have a gallery open year-round, where his posters, prints, lithographs, and original art are on permanent display, with most of it for sale.

Located in a strip mall in Brookfield, approximately one hour north of New York City, Glass Onion Graphics—named after the Beatles' song, "Glass Onion"—is owned and operated by Audrey Price, who is quick to point out that she's probably the world's biggest Whelan fan. And, incidentally, she's his wife.

Whereas Michael prefers to concentrate on producing work, Audrey concentrates on publishing, marketing, and selling it. Of course, in the store, what catches the eye most readily are the eye-poppingly gorgeous works of original art, which range from small color compositions to finished acrylic paintings, already framed, and ready to hang on the wall.

Interested in an original? Here's a sampling of some of the prices:

➼ A 9 x 12-inch tonal "sketch" (actually, it's more detailed than what most artists term a sketch) for *Goldwing*, the cover art to Whelan's 2003 wall calendar (published by Ronnie Sellers Productions). In its matching 14 x 17-inch frame, this work of art is $2,800. The art shows a dragon taking off from a cliff, etched against a setting sun.

➼ A 16 x 25-inch acrylic painting, in color, for *Amazons 2*, which shows two amazons—pirates in battle, balanced precariously on what looks to be a wooden bridge, possibly an extension from their ship—as they fight men. (You can tell this is a book cover because the top third is blank—space needed to drop in the title of the book and so on.) The price is $8,500.

➼ Titled "Lord Protector," an acrylic painting on watercolor measuring 20 x 32 inches, this striking image shows a man standing on an outcropping of rock, with a dragon—wings stretched out—in the background in full glory. The colors are gorgeous: orange, yellow, and red, suggesting fire (an appropriate symbol, as dragons do breathe fire). The original is $9,200.

➼ The crème de la crème, the piece de resistance: "Elric Demonslayer," an acrylic painting on panel, measuring 16 x 24 inches. It was originally rendered as the frontispiece of *The Vanishing Tower* by Michael Moorcock; published by Archival Press, this beautiful small press book has numerous plates by Whelan and, as a book, shows just how beautiful a book can be. This painting was subsequently used as the cover to *The World's Best Fantasy* (St. Martin's Press), where a larger world could see it. The image is available both as a poster and a signed print by Whelan—both inexpensive alternatives to owning the original, which is $38,000.

For anyone who loves fantasy art and is interested in seeing the work of a contemporary master, a trip to the gallery itself is well worth your time. But if time and circumstances do not allow a personal visit, check out its Web store, which often has seasonal sales on select items—mostly numbered and signed prints, framed and ready to hang on the wall.

As a longtime art lover who can't resist any gallery with an exhibit of fantasy-oriented art, I'm happy to see Michael Whelan well served by this gallery that offers a varied selection of product at reasonable prices to fit anyone's budget, and also shows off his work to best effect.

Glass Onion Graphics
PO Box 88
Brookfield, CT 06804
Phone: (877) 798-6063
E-mail: glassonion@michaelwhelan.com

Appendix B

The Lord of the Rings
Motion Picture Trilogy:
The Exhibition

www.sciencemuseum.org.uk

Opening to record crowds, an exhibition of movie memorabilia from Peter Jackson's *The Lord of the Rings* film trilogy is currently being shown at the Science Museum in London, until January 11, 2004. The exhibition's next venue will be the Boston Museum of Science (August–October 2004) and then the Powerhouse Museum in Sydney, Australia (2005), after which it will return home to New Zealand.

Developed and presented by the Museum of New Zealand Te Papa Tongarewa, in partnership with New Line Cinema, the exhibit includes not only art and artifacts but interactive exhibits as well, including 700 props and 15 stations to show documentaries about the making of the film.

According to the Website of the Science Museum in London, this touring exhibition spotlights costumes, jewelry, armor, weapons, make-up, special effects, models, digital effects, video interviews, and interactive and immersive experiences. The following descriptions are quoted from the site (*www.sciencemuseum.org.uk/ exhibitions/lordoftherings/overview.asp*):

Costumes

As well as enjoying an exciting range of props, jewelry, and weapons used in *The Lord of the Rings*, you'll also see a range of exquisitely made costumes from the films. They are designed by Oscar-nominated Kiwi designer, Ngila Dickson. Some of the favourite costumes featured in the exhibition include Arwen's riding costume, Galadriel's stunning dress, and Gandalf's robes.

Jewelry

The One Ring forms the central part of the entire *The Lord of the Rings* motion picture trilogy. As well as the One Ring, this exhibition will feature other beautifully crafted jewelry from the films, including Elven brooches,

Ringwraith crowns and rings, the Evenstar—the jewel that Arwen gives to Aragorn, and Galadriel's and Gandalf's Rings of Power.

Armour and weapons

With so many battle scenes, *The Lord of the Rings* trilogy used a lot of armour and many weapons—most of which were made by professionals skilled in medieval crafts, such as making chain-mail. An "armour corridor" in this exhibition features 12 complete sets of armour including King Théoden's from *The Two Towers*. Weapons belonging to Arwen, Gandalf, Frodo, and Aragorn are also featured.

Make-up and special effects

The Lord of the Rings films use a vast range of make-up and special effects. In this exhibition you will learn how some of the amazing special effects in *The Lord of the Rings* were achieved, and you can see how make-up was used to such great effect. A display on prosthetics includes Hobbit feet, Orc teeth, Lurtz's facial prosthetic, and the contact lenses used to give the Orcs their unique look.

Models

To create the epic world of Middle-earth, many magnificent miniature sets and maquettes had to be constructed. These intricate models, created in painstaking detail, took incredible skill, creativity, and patience to create. Models featured in this exhibition include Frodo's vision of the ruined Hobbiton Mill, The Tower of Orthanc, and Sauron's tower, Barad-dûr.

Digital effects

The Lord of the Rings films have become well-known for their brilliant use of digital effects. Effects explained in this exhibition include motion capture and motion control—the combining of "real" and "digital" action—and CGI (computer-generated-image technology).

Video interviews

During and after the filming of *The Lord of the Rings* trilogy, interviews were recorded with many of the cast and crew. These fascinating behind-the-scenes conversations reveal more secrets about the making of the films. Also featured are recent interviews with Oscar-winning special effects wizard Richard Taylor, artist Alan Lee, and producer Barrie Osbourne.

Interactive and immersive experiences

This exhibition includes both immersive and interactive experiences. Visitors will walk in and be surrounded by a "ring of fire" as they see one of the most important objects in the entire trilogy—the One Ring. Interactive exhibits include a "scaling" demonstration. By sitting on a cart and seeing how they are "scaled," visitors can understand the scaling technology used in the films that enabled human actors to play both large and small creatures.

Appendix C

Tall Towers, Brave Kings, Wise Wizards, and Precious Rings: A Celebration of Fantasy Art

www.storyopolis.com

www.FlightsofImagination.com

Since 1938, hundreds of professional illustrators have tried their hand at visually depicting Middle-earth, but there have been too few exhibits of those works of original art.

Storyopolis, a Los Angeles gallery and bookstore, will be exhibiting original art by American artists who have illustrated Tolkien. Though the list of artists has not yet been finalized, the tentative list includes Tim Kirk, Donato Giancola, Steve Hickman, Colleen Doran, and David Wenzel.

Kirk has illustrated the "1975 Tolkien Calendar" (U.S.), Donato Giancola has illustrated the cover to *The Hobbit* (graphic novel) and *The Lord of the Rings* (for the Science Fiction Book Club), and dozens of gaming cards set in Middle-earth. Steve Hickman has published two paintings in *Realms of Tolkien*, and David Wenzel illustrated *The Hobbit*. (For more information on these and other Tolkien artists, see Chapter 11.)

In addition to original art on display, there may be licensed movie tie-in products on exhibit from Sideshow/Weta, United Cutlery, and the Noble Collection.

The dates of the exhibit are tentative; at this time, the exhibit is set to run from December 13, 2003 through January 2004.

For the first weekend of the exhibit, several of the artists will be on hand to meet the public and sign autographs. Confirmed artists in attendance include Tim Kirk, Donato Giancola, Colleen Doran, and Stephen Hickman.

The exhibit will be sponsored in conjunction with Flights of Imagination, a company specializing in marketing, selling, and promoting the work of fantasy artists.

Presentation is everything. I was able to see *The Lord of the Rings: The Fellowship of the Ring* in Los Angeles, at a theater that had several "director's halls." The only such places in the United States, these halls show first-run movies in the best possible way: The viewing experience is unparalleled, with an extra-large screen, a 70mm print, the best sound system ever engineered for film presentation, extra-wide leather seats, and large aisles.

And so it is with original art. Most Tolkien art has been produced for commercial usage—book covers, interior illustrations, game board box designs, calendars, and so on. Disregarding the matters of reproduction, size, and overprinting of text, the printed version is a poor cousin to the original art.

To see, for instance, a 5-foot-wide painting of *The Hobbit* by Donato Giancola—the scale preferred by the Old Masters, who preferred big canvases—is to view it the way the artist had intended it to be seen. To see a delicate pencil drawing by Colleen Doran, with its exquisite line work—a drawing that takes hours, sometimes days to render—is to realize the jewel-like precision and attention to detail that informs her work. Or to see the 2 x 3-foot painting, by Tim Kirk, of Orcs marching off to war is to see a vista unfold—a large-scale, detailed, carefully painted work of art.

This, then, is why galleries exist: to not only introduce artists to the world at large, but to present their work in the best possible light, which is the goal of Storyopolis for the Tolkien exhibit.

Because I think an artist should have the last word on this subject, I asked Colleen Doran why exhibits such as this serve the public, and she responded:

> They'll get to see some interpretations of the Tolkien work that they probably have not had much access to, like the Tim Kirk work that has not been in print since 1975 or the Hickman work that has not been in print for years.
>
> Some of the work that's going to be in the show is unpublished, including private commissions, so people are going to see art that's never before been seen by the general public.
>
> Of course, it's always cool to see the originals, because some people think art is all done by machines. It freaks me out when I go to shows like San Diego and people ask the same questions time and again about my art: Yeah, I *really* drew this with my hands; a machine didn't do it, and a team of people didn't do it. This is an individual handcrafted effort that did not exist before.

Appendix D

Flights of Imagination

www.FlightsofImagination.com

Flights of Imagination specializes in fantasy art and illustration. Representing fantasy artists exclusively, the company sells original art and prints by leading fantasy artists, arranges exhibits of original art, and packages books and other specialized projects, with the goal of reaching well beyond the fan markets to reach mainstream audiences.

In the fall of 2003, the Website will feature in-depth interviews, profiles, photos, and Quicktime movies about Storyopolis and the artists who will be exhibiting at that gallery for the Tolkien-inspired exhibit, which will run from December 2003 to January 2004.

In addition, this Website will feature additional information and links for Tolkien fans who want more information on the man and his work.

In time, the gallery will have a permanent online exhibit, a gallery of fantasy artwork, and provide numerous links to fantasy-related galleries, artists, exhibits, and conventions.

The company can be reached at:

Flights of Imagination
P.O. Box 3602
Williamsburg, VA 23187

Appendix E

Ted Nasmith,
His Tolkien Art,
and the Chalk Farm Gallery

*When I interpret Tolkien, I fell genuinely at home with it
and derive great satisfaction from exploring all potential
aspects of Middle-earth. With each new illustration, I feel
a little bit more of it is captured: characters, locales,
atmosphere, and drama.*

—Ted Nasmith, from his official Website,
www.tednasmith.com

Santa Fe, New Mexico, is a town of only 60,000 people, but it supports an astonishing 600 art galleries, including the Chalk Farm Gallery, owned and operated by Sunaha Gibson. What makes her gallery unique is its inventory; more specifically, the Tolkien art by Ted Nasmith, which is, in terms of imagination, worlds apart from the Native American and Western-themed art that predominates at the other galleries in town.

Gibson says:

> At first, people were shocked and didn't know what to make of it. But as time passed, I was constantly told by everyone who comes in here that this is their favorite gallery in town. I think I'm needed here because people get tired of the straightforward western landscapes and want something with more imagination.

It's hard to argue with Gibson's perception, because Nasmith's Tolkien art has been warmly received at her gallery, first in her native England six years ago, and now in New Mexico, where she transplanted it in 2000.

The difference, she says, is that selling Tolkien art is harder here than in Europe, where Tolkien's presence throws a very long shadow across the literary landscape. As Gibson explains:

> The Tolkien following in Europe is far greater than it is here in America. People there literally know the book inside and out. Just by hearing the title of the art piece, they know the scene and will reserve the painting after knowing its size and price.

The prices, by the way, range from a hobbit-sized $90 for a 2-x-2-inch painting to a kingly $6,900 for a major work of art, such as "Boromir's Last Stand." Fortunately, an affordable alternative exists—limited editions prints, with a price range of $125 to $275, issued in editions of 275 to 475 copies. (The prints of Rivendell and Minas Tirith are close to sell-out.)

Nasmith, 41 years old, has an advantage that most of his peers do not: He had shown his early Tolkien art to J.R.R. Tolkien and gotten an enthusiastic response, so Naismith's art is officially sanctioned. It is why the Tolkien Estate sought him out to illustrate *The Silmarillion*, posthumously published and edited by Christopher Tolkien.

Up until recently, the available prints have been printed via offset lithography, but the new printing technologies offer better fidelity and offer the cost advantage of smaller runs, unlike lithos requiring runs of 500 to 1,000. For these reasons, Nasmith favors the Giclée printing process and will be using it exclusively, according to Gibson.

The exclusive agent for selling Nasmith's Tolkien originals, Chalk Farm Gallery maintains a wide inventory of original art and prints on a year-round basis, rotating the stock to ensure "fresh" exposure. Once a year, however, all the Nasmith work is gathered and hung for a Nasmith-themed show, with an emphasis on the newer originals and prints.

For 2003, two new pieces have been published—a landscape of the menacing "Fangorn Forest" ($195, signed and numbered edition of 100 prints, 11 x 15 inches) and "Fire at Weathertop" ($275, signed and numbered edition of 100 prints, 14.75 x 26 inches), a dramatic rendering of the Fellowship.

The forthcoming show is scheduled to run from December 5, 2003, through January 31, 2004. Although Nasmith maintains a busy schedule, Gibson says she's confident that he'll make an appearance for the exhibit's opening weekend, which traditionally is a Tolkien celebration. In the past, for instance, local schoolchildren submitted Tolkien-inspired art for a contest sponsored by the gallery, fans dressed up in costume, and Ted—wielding a guitar instead of a paintbrush—belted out Tolkien songs he's composed. Not your usual gallery weekend!

Current prints available include:

- → "The Glittering Caves of Algarond" ($165).
- → "Lúthien in the Garden" ($165).
- → "Minas Tirith at Dawn" ($245).
- → "Riders at the Ford" ($165).
- → "Rivendell" ($265).
- → "Shores of Valinor" ($165).

For more information about the gallery and Nasmith's art, visit Chalk Farm Gallery in Santa Fe, or visit its Website at *www.chalkfarmgallery.com*.

For more information, contact Suhana Gibson at the gallery:

Chalk Farm Gallery
Attn: Susan Gibson
330 Old Santa Fe Trail
Santa Fe, NM 87501
Phone (505) 983-7125
Fax (505) 983-7128

Appendix F

Tolkien, Licensing, and Copyrights...and Wrongs

*Please understand the consequences of what you're doing
with my property when you make unfair use of my stories
and images: you can literally destroy my life's work by doing
that, so consider carefully if you want to do that to me. I've
never harmed you in any way, so please don't do that to me.
You are literally in a position to take something from me
that took decades to create. Why would you do that? Please
don't.*

—Colleen Doran, on the theft of her copyrighted
work by overzealous fans

**Disclaimer: The material provided herein is for informational
purposes only and is no substitute for advice provided by an
attorney specializing in intellectual property rights.**

Like every other literary creator, Tolkien's works are protected by copyrights
and trademarks, and the rights to reproduce, distribute, perform, or display the
copyrighted works are owned by the Tolkien Estate, unless they have been sold or
transferred.

What's changed since Tolkien's time is the advent of the Internet and technologies that allow creative work in any form—audio, visual, textual—to be digi-
tized, stored, copied, and published to a worldwide audience, without a system of
checks and balances. Clearly, the right to publish implies a right to publish respon-
sibly, but a quick sampling of the thousands of Websites devoted to Tolkien (or,
indeed, other writers and artists) shows a fundamental lack of knowledge regarding copyright and the fair use clause by Webmasters, which gives one pause: Is this
indifference, ignorance, or a little of both?

Licensing

The eye-opening success of Jackson's movie trilogy has overshadowed everything that has gone before in the Tolkien universe. The first two movies have grossed nearly $2 billion worldwide, creating an awareness of Tolkien that dwarfs what Tolkien's own publishers could not accomplish in a half century of book publishing. The movie tie-in merchandising alone—from the ludicrous "bobbing head" dolls to elegant reproductions of the One Ring—is in itself a major industry, with no signs of abatement.

Predictably, the surging interest in Tolkien in the mainstream has been reflected, in part, by Webmasters who have discovered the joy of exploring Middle-earth online, with an inexhaustive supply of material—visual, textual, and audio.

Unfortunately, far too many of these Websites, including semi-official fan sites with hundreds of pages, interpret the fair use clause far too liberally. They feel they have the right to publish anything and everything at will, when, in fact, the fair use clause gives limited rights for specific purposes. It is not, nor was it ever intended to be, the mechanism by which people could publish with impunity.

The general guidelines for fair use—best interpreted by lawyers specializing in intellectual property—recognize that for purposes of "criticism, comment, news reporting, teaching, scholarship, and research," copyrighted works may be reproduced without permission, tempered by the following considerations (from *www.copyright.gov/fls/fl102.html*):

1. The purpose and character of the use, including whether such use is of commercial nature or is for nonprofit educational purposes.

2. The nature of the copyrighted work.

3. Amount of substantiality of the portion used in relation to the copyrighted work as a whole.

4. The effect of the use upon the potential market for or value of the copyrighted work.

The bottom line is item 4—the effect of the use on the potential market—because copyright means, literally, the right to copy, which is a right reserved for the copyright holder.

Unfortunately, the Tolkien Estate—often portrayed as the villain in any such discussions—is legally forced to protect its copyrights or risk losing them forever. If the Estate neglects to enforce the copyrights, the courts may decide that the Estate has, by default, abandoned them, at which point the previously protected copyrighted material may potentially fall into the public domain. If this happens, anyone, anywhere, at any time, could do anything they want with it—a nightmarish scenario that no creator wants to see.

Goosed by the movie trilogy, thousands of related Websites have literally sprung up overnight, many with little or no recognition of the limitations of fair use. Consequently, the Tolkien Estate's retained law firm has had to write cease-and-desist letters to Webmasters who, whether by intent or default, have exceeded the bounds of fair use.

So, you ask, what, specifically, can you do—and not do? And how do you protect yourself from the prospect of an expensive and needless lawsuit?

Copyrights and Wrongs

➤ You can write a book about Tolkien. Whether it's a parody, a biography, a companion-style book collecting original or reprinted articles and art about him, a volume of literary criticism, a collection of essays, or a book collating news, you can usually expect to publish without fear of reprisal from the Tolkien Estate. But you cannot publish a "prequel" or "sequel" to Tolkiens works or stories about Tolkien's imaginative universe and creations.

Case in point: In 2002, a copyright infringement lawsuit was filed by the Tolkien Estate against Michael W. Perry and his small press, because of the impending publication of a book tentatively titled *The Lord of the Rings Diary: A Chronology of J.R.R. Tolkien's Best-selling Epic*. The lawsuit asked for $750,000 in damages.

After several rewrites, the Tolkien Estate dropped the suit, saying it does not approve or endorse the book, but it did withdraw its objection to publication.

Ironically, Mr. Perry—who apparently has rearranged the events from Tolkien's book and put them in order, with added commentary and discussion—impeded progress toward the resolution of the lawsuit by wanting the Estate's lawyers to sign a nondisclosure agreement because of his concerns that his "format" would be stolen!

In the book publishing industry, the prevailing opinion is that the Tolkien Estate has been very tolerant of books written about Tolkien and his works, because Tolkien himself was an academician. But clearly, where necessary, the Estate draws the line as to when there's the possibility of infringement, and takes legal action as necessary.

➤ You can write a book about Tolkien's poetry, but you cannot reproduce even a single line of poetry without permission from the Tolkien Estate. Given its brevity, even one line of poetry exceeds fair use.

➤ You can write about Tolkien's unpublished letters, but you cannot publish their contents, even if you own them. Ownership of the original artifact is one thing, but the content is protected by copyright and cannot be published without permission of the Tolkien Estate.

➤ You can write, in book form or online, about Tolkien's artwork, and reproduce some as examples, but you cannot abuse this right and publish an entire gallery of artwork, in book form or online. The rights to the art are owned by either the publisher or the artist, either of whom retain the right to publish the work on their respective Websites.

The wholesale abuse by Webmasters of Tolkien artwork has reached epidemic proportions, with some publishing virtual galleries with hundreds of images, some by professional artists who drew those for books, calendar, or other licensed Tolkien-related products. In one particularly egregious instance, a Website had posted nearly 11,000 images!

➤ You cannot reproduce whole maps that appear in Tolkien's books without permission. (For purposes of criticism or scholarship, a small portion of a map could be reproduced, within the fair use clause.)

➤ You cannot publish extended sound files of audio recordings or dramatizations online, except brief portions as samples.

➤ You cannot publish an entire article from a newspaper, a magazine, or other printed source, because it will materially damage sales of the original source publication. Many newspapers maintain archives that can be accessed for a fee, but why pay a fee for an article when, for instance, a Tolkien Website has reprinted the text in question in full? Or why buy a current issue of a magazine, when all you want is the article about Tolkien, which an online Tolkien Webzine has reprinted in full?

➤ Once fixed in form—that is, once it is written down, drawn, or recorded—a work is under copyright protection. Registration, though desirable, is not a prerequisite for copyright protection. Therefore, a Webmaster who reproduces work without any copyright notice from other sources—whether downloaded or scanned—is clearly violating someone's copyright, even if he doesn't know its source.

One common excuse when reprinting art is that the Webmaster states he's gotten it from another source on the Internet, where it was uncredited and had no copyright notice, and therefore, he's reprinting it sans credit as well. The fact remains, though, that it was created by an artist who retained the copyright and, in every case, someone scanned it and posted it online, and everyone else who follows has simply copied it and perpetuated the infringement on a wholesale basis.

➤ Regarding fan fiction published on the Internet, especially "slash" fiction, with its erotic and pornographic themes, the definitive legal ruling has yet to be made, because no court case has been filed—yet. Some authors (notably, Anne Rice) staunchly demand that no fan fiction be written based on their characters—create your own, they say. Other authors simply look the other way.

This may well be the next area of major litigation regarding online publication. These are not only derivative works but also violate the spirit of the original work, as well.

Cause and Effect

Here's where we get to the heart of the issue. Consider the following:

→ On your favorite Tolkien Website, you see a scanned article, with photos, from the current issue of a popular magazine. You read it or download it, print it out, and, in doing so, have no need to buy it from the original source.

Fair use: The Website has selected excerpts from the article in question, with a summary or discussion, and perhaps one or two small images reproduced. By doing so, he doesn't remove the incentive to buy the original publication.

→ In an online virtual gallery, you see artwork by your favorite Tolkien artist. Scanned at high resolution, it is large enough to produce a color print for yourself. That being the case, why would you buy the printed postcard, the poster, the print, or the book in which the art originally appeared? Often, virtual galleries are comprised of images scanned from printed books or calendars—good enough, in many cases, to reproduce prints of astonishing fidelity.

Fair use: The Website displays a few small images, at low resolution, for purposes of news, discussion, or criticism.

→ You see a Website with hundreds of images from the Tolkien movie trilogy—video captures or publicity photos from press kits. What, then, is your incentive to buy the posters, the posterbooks, or any other printed product that draws from the same source?

Fair use: Artist/writer Colleen Doran's commonsense policy toward online usage is straightforward: She allows the use of up to three color images and five black-and-white images (as 72 dpi JPEG files, to limit resolution) and requires that her copyright and trademark information be posted prominently. This theoretically protects her art from wholesale abuse, in which an unlimited number of her images are reproduced online at high resolution with no stated copyright or trademark notice.

Other artists have more draconian policies. In terms of virtual galleries "honoring" him, Michael Whelan is the most ripped-off fantasy artist of our time. His policy, as stated on his Website (*www.michaelwhelan.com*), makes his position crystal-clear:

> We receive numerous requests from fans every day asking to use Michael's images on their Web pages. Unfortunately, Michael does not authorize free use of his images on either commercial or non-commercial Websites. If you send a simple request as such, you will receive a form letter response politely declining your request.

It is a difficult situation for any artist to say no to fans, particularly when it is a fan base as large and devoted as Michael's has been over the past three decades. The decision was not made lightly, and Michael does appreciate everyone's respect for his copyrights and ownership of his work.

In short, if your use of someone else's copyrighted material infringes on his ability to profit from his own work, you have crossed the line between fair use and infringement.

Every artist with a Website usually posts information regarding copyright of his images and his policy on Web reproduction of his work on other sites. If you want to exercise your right to construct a Website using other people's works, you have an obligation to seek out the creator and find out his policy, or ask permission if there's a question as to reproduction rights.

Common Fan Defenses: Copyright Misconceptions

The "Time" Defense

I've had this stuff up on my Website for five years, and it's never been a problem. So why's it a problem now?

Because the length of time is immaterial—whether one day, one year, or five years—the material you've published exceeds fair use, and you don't have the right to publish it without permission. (This, by the way, is not a hypothetical case. The Tolkien Estate discovered a fan had published Tolkien's maps on his site, which had been up for five years.)

The "Not For Profit" Defense

I'm not making any money on this, so why is the Tolkien Estate threatening me?

Whether you realize it or not, you may be profiting from your Website, by accepting money for banners, by accepting donations to help underwrite your expenses in running the site, by publishing through a host that gives you a discounted (or free) rate in exchange for pop-up advertising, and—in extreme cases—by asking for subscriptions of fees to defray your expenses. Obviously, the defense that you're "not making much money at all" is also an indefensible position.

Bottom line: If your usage of the copyrighted work exceeds fair use, you should expect to get a sternly worded letter from the Tolkien Estate.

The "News" Defense

I'm publishing a newszine online, so why can't I reproduce images?

You can, but it doesn't mean you can publish the equivalent of a printed book online, with hundreds of images. Doesn't a print publisher licensed to do so reserve that right? And doesn't your use of those hundreds of high-quality JPEGs, often posted with no commentary or criticism, violate that right?

For Your Own Self-Protection

As any judge will tell you in court, ignorance of the law is no excuse. Therefore, the best protection is self-protection. Make an effort to understand what you can and cannot do, which should minimize the likelihood of receiving a nastygram from a lawyer asserting copyright infringement.

Here's a primer on how to protect yourself:

1. Read up on copyright law. Rather than relying on a vague or misinformed notion of what you think copyright law is, read up on the basics and know what the law says. Written in plain English and comprehensible to the average reader, copyright law is largely common sense: Your right to use my copyrighted works ends where infringement begins.

    Go to *www.loc.gov/copyright* and check out all the related links on the basics of copyright, the fair use clause, and so on, so you have a basic, working knowledge of the subject.

    I'm willing to bet that most Webmasters have never bothered to even check out this Website, though I think every Webmaster should link to it, because anyone who publishes online must have a working knowledge of copyrights...and wrongs.

2. Buy and read *The Copyright Handbook: How to Protect & Use Written Works*, Stephen Fishman's excellent text on the subject, published by Nolo Press ($39.99, trade paperback, with CD-ROM). Nolo Press publishes, in my opinion, the best line of law-related books on the market.

3. If there's still a question about copyrights, consult an attorney—not just your garden-variety general practitioner, but an attorney who specializes in intellectual property law.

4. When publishing copyrighted material, always put the proper copyright or trademark notice on the work, to acknowledge the original copyright holder.

In the end, if there's any question as to whether or not you can use the copyrighted materials—if you aren't confident that your usage is within fair use—then contact the copyright holder, who will either grant you permission or not, or ask you to make appropriate changes.

These four steps should keep you from receiving correspondence from the Tolkien Estate's solicitors, Manches & Co. (an international law firm based in London).

The Warning Letter

The communiqué from Manches & Co. will be polite but firm. It will usually cite the infringement(s) and give the recipient 48 hours to take down all the infringed material—or face litigation.

Remember, as I've said before, the key legal point is that if the Estate fails to defend its copyrights, it risks losing them forever.

Licensing Entities

New Tolkien fans are understandably confused when they see One Ring replicas and sword reproductions manufactured by different licensees. Traditionally, one licensee has the exclusive right to manufacture a specific line of products, otherwise, confusion will ensue. In Tolkien's case, replicas of the One Ring are available through Paul Badali Jewelry (licensed by Saul Zaentz's Tolkien Enterprises) and through The Noble Collection (licensed through Tolkien Enterprises to New Line Cinema). Similarly, sword replicas are available from both United Cutlery and The Noble Collection.

Tolkien Enterprises

Because of the general confusion regarding licensing rights, Tolkien Enterprises recently updated its Website (*www.tolkien-ent.com*) to reflect the distinctions, so potential licensees could contact the appropriate entity:

➤ For rights to "produce merchandise or services based on the artwork in the New Line Cinema film trilogy," contact New Line Cinema's Director of Licensing.

➤ For rights to "produce printed published matter based on non-film artwork," contact the Permissions Department at HarperCollins UK, who in turn will consult the Tolkien estate.

➤ Other questions about licensing should simply be directed to Tolkien Enterprises for clarification.

As explained on the Website (*www.tolkien-ent.com*), Tolkien Enterprises is a division of Saul Zaentz, which owns:

> ...certain worldwide exclusive rights to the titles of *The Hobbit* and *The Lord of the Rings*, the names of characters, persons, places, scenes, things and events appearing or described in *The Hobbit* and *The Lord of the Rings*, and certain short phrases, short sayings, and the like...licenses these titles, names, and short phrases for use as trademarks and service marks in connection with various lines of merchandise.

Saul Zaentz's worldwide licensing program has encompassed a wide range of products, including:

> ...dramatizations, musicals, puppet performances,...board games, puzzles, computer games, chess sets, collectible card games, role-playing games, t-shirts, costumes, masks, buttons, belt buckles, daggers and swords, dolls, puppets, pewter figurines, porcelain figurines, action figures, metal miniature figures, coloring books, music, linens, collector plates, clocks, bulletin boards, mirrors, posters, calendars, note-cards, stationary, decals and bumper stickers.

In other words, these are rights the Tolkien Estate does not own, nor has any say in, and obviously does not materially benefit from in any way.

The licensing properties by Tolkien not owned by Saul Zaentz include *The Silmarillion*, the volumes of *The History of Middle-earth*, his other fiction (such as "Leaf by Niggle," *Farmer Giles of Ham*, and *The Father Christmas Letters*), and any unpublished works.

Admittedly, by obtaining the rights to *The Hobbit* and, especially, *The Lord of the Rings*, Saul Zaentz had obtained the crown jewels.

The Tolkien Estate

Any rights not held or represented by the previously listed entities are retained by the Tolkien Estate, which is represented by a London-based law firm, Manches & Co.

The Estate is administered by J.R.R. Tolkien's son Christopher, who is understandably protective of his father's literary and artistic estate.

The youngest of the four children, Christopher Tolkien, at 77, has established the Tolkien Trust, to ensure the estate's interests are protected after he and the two remaining surviving children pass on.

In time, Tolkien's creations will fall out of copyright protection, and the feeding frenzy will begin. Any and all things Middle-earth will be published, manufactured, and sold, with no compensation to the Tolkien Trust. In other words, the well-guarded family literary jewels will simply be up for grabs, and it won't be a pretty sight.

For now, and the foreseeable future, however, the Estate does have a say in what is done with Tolkien's works, so we will not see e-books (too easy to steal online, despite encryption efforts) and we will see familiar names illustrating *The Silmarillion* and other cherished works, because the Estate works hand-in-hand with HarperCollins UK and personally approves the illustrators for the British and American texts.

As for the movie trilogy, the Estate was offered a chance to be involved, but passed, citing that they'd want either total control—or none. Given those two choices, New Line Cinema was forced to choose "none." Therefore, the movie trilogy has neither the approval nor endorsement of the Estate. Obviously, because rights were licensed by Zaentz to New Line Cinema, the Estate can claim no legal objection to the movie trilogy.

The Estate *does* have a say, apparently, in a by-product of the movie trilogy—a traveling exhibition of movie-related memorabilia, currently on exhibit in England, where it is enjoying record crowds. For whatever reasons, the Estate has limited its run to the duration of the theatrical showing of *The Return of the King*, which impedes film director Peter Jackson's desire to establish, in Wellington, a permanent exhibit of the art and artifacts from his movie trilogy.

On this note, I believe I can speak for most Tolkien fans when I say that I would prefer to see the movie memorabilia in a permanent museum, instead of experiencing it in an online virtual gallery, on a DVD-ROM, or in book form.

In all of these discussions about *The Lord of the Rings*—the product of one man's imagination—we must remember that it was published in 1954 and 1955 and has stood the test of time. It has inspired and influenced generations of fantasy writers, entertained millions worldwide, and is likely to remain as an inimitable classic, as long as people hunger for epic tales, to be produced in forms yet unimagined, through technologies still yet to be invented, to be enjoyed by generations yet to come.

Addresses

Tolkien Enterprises
Attn: Director of Licensing
2600 Tenth Street
Berkeley, CA 94710
Fax: (510) 486-2015
E-mail: tolkien@fantasyjazz.com

New Line Cinema
Attn: Director of Licensing
888 Seventh Avenue
New York, NY 10106
Fax: (212) 956-1941

HarperCollins Publishers
Attn: Permissions Department
77-85 Fulham Palace Road
Hammersmith
London W6 8JB
United Kingdom

The Tolkien Estate, represented by: Manches & Co.
Attn: Cathleen Blackburn
3 Worcester Street
OXFORD
United Kingdom
OX1 2PZ

About the Author
and Illustrator

George Beahm wrote his first book in high school, and saw it published after graduation from college. A lifelong fantasy and science fiction fan, Beahm's books included art indices on Vaughn Bode, Tim Kirk, and Richard Corben.

A self-published author, a regional publisher, and author of several books for Andrews and McMeel, St. Martin's Press, Running Press, and Brassey's, Beahm is currently at work on new nonfiction and fiction book projects.

He occasionally updates his personal Website, *www.GeorgeBeahm.com.*

Colleen Doran won her first award for drawing at the age of five in a contest sponsored by the Walt Disney Company and was a professional illustrator by the age of 15. She now has hundreds of credits as a cartoonist on books such as *Amazing Spiderman, Sandman, Wonder Woman, Captain America,* and dozens of others. She created, writes, and illustrates the critically acclaimed graphic novel series *A Distant Soil* for Image Comics—a project she began working on

at the age of 12. Colleen also has a new graphic novel in wide release with Warren Ellis called *Orbiter*, a science fiction tale with an optimistic view of the manned space program published in 2003 by the Vertigo division of DC Comics.

In 2004, she will be publishing *Seasons of Spring*, an original graphic novel from Image Comics. Her current work also includes cocreating the series *Reign of the Zodiac* with writer Keith Giffen for DC Comics. The tale of the 12 warring royal houses of the zodiac required that Doran design hundreds of costumes and complex sets, as well as continue to draw the new monthly series. Doran has also illustrated the work of Clive Barker, Anne Rice, and Neil Gaiman. She is a member of the National Cartoonists Society, the Association of Science Fiction and Fantasy Artists, and the American Society of Portrait Artists, and is a guest of honor at Ring*Con, a licensed Tolkien convention in Germany. She has exhibited her work at galleries in Milan, Venice, Portugal, Spain, and New York, and is creating new art for a gallery exhibition at Stroyopolis in Los Angeles.

She maintains two Websites, *www.ColleenDoran.com* and *www.ADistantSoil.com*.